What people are saying about …

Two Crosses and Two Testaments

"One intriguing era in France's history, one unforgettable cast of characters, and one of the best writers in the CBA today all add up to one incredible read! In *Two Crosses*, Elizabeth Musser has achieved another literary triumph."

Ann Tatlock, award-winning author
of *Promises to Keep*

"Elizabeth Musser reminds me of Francine Rivers. The characters are real, the drama is gripping, and the Spirit rises up from the grass roots of the story. You'll love *Two Crosses*."

Creston Mapes, best-selling
author of *Nobody*

"In a novel rich in historical detail, Elizabeth Musser spins an intriguing story of the lives and loves of young people caught up in the Algerian revolution to win independence from France in 1954–1962. It was a costly conflict, and we are invited to see it through the eyes of those living on both sides of the Mediterranean. Christian convictions and patriotic loyalties are put to the test, as

God works His plans for individuals and nations. I enjoyed this book and look forward to reading the rest of the trilogy."

Ruth Stewart, AWM missionary for forty years to Algeria and France

"In this delightful story, the sounds, scents, and scenery of France and Algeria come alive. *Two Crosses* untangles the complicated history of Algeria's war for independence from France. You feel as though you know the characters. The surprising twists in the story never stop. As the book comes to an end, you are ready to immediately pick up *Two Testaments*."

Margaret Haines, former missionary with over thirty years of missionary experience among the Algerians and French in North Africa during the end of the war

Two Testaments

OTHER BOOKS BY ELIZABETH MUSSER

The Swan House
The Dwelling Place
Searching for Eternity
Words Unspoken
The Sweetest Thing

THE SECRETS OF THE CROSS TRILOGY

Two Crosses
Two Testaments
Two Destinies [coming September 2012]

ELIZABETH MUSSER

Two Testaments

—— A NOVEL ——

SECRETS OF
THE CROSS
TRILOGY
2

TWO TESTAMENTS
Published by David C Cook
4050 Lee Vance View
Colorado Springs, CO 80918 U.S.A.

David C Cook Distribution Canada
55 Woodslee Avenue, Paris, Ontario, Canada N3L 3E5

David C Cook U.K., Kingsway Communications
Eastbourne, East Sussex BN23 6NT, England

The graphic circle C logo is a registered trademark of David C Cook.

This story is a work of fiction. Characters and events are the product of the author's
imagination. Any resemblance to any person, living or dead, is coincidental.

LCCN 2012930189
ISBN 978-0-7814-0499-0
eISBN 978-0-7814-0840-0

The Team: Don Pape, LB Norton, Amy Konyndyk, Jack Campbell, Karen Athen
Cover Design: Nick Lee
Cover Photos: Shutterstock

Printed in the United States of America
Second Edition 2012

1 2 3 4 5 6 7 8 9 10

032312

This book is dedicated to my husband, Paul Alan Musser.
If I spend the rest of my life writing stories about people who keep
loving each other in the midst of life's challenges, I will never be
able to create a story as beautiful as the one I have lived and am
living with you. You are my favorite example of this Scripture verse
in my life: "Now to Him who is able to do exceeding abundantly
beyond all we ask or expect …" Two are better than one, and
my life is filled up to overflowing because of you. Je t'aime.

Acknowledgments

This new edition: Once again I want to thank Don Pape and the staff at David C Cook for making this dream a reality—getting *Two Crosses* and *Two Testaments* back in print. I am blessed indeed to get to revisit these novels and remember how I was inspired by the people and places in the Midi of France and in that beautiful country across the ocean, Algeria. And I am equally blessed to get to improve the book with the help of my dear editor and friend, LB Norton. We've both learned a lot in the past fifteen years, and it is one of God's precious hugs to have gotten to work together again on this project. *Merci*, LB!

The first edition: I think I was born with a love for God and a love for writing. Through no merit of my own, they became the central passions of my life. But often the Lord had to pull me gently away from my stubborn ideas of how to put these "passions" into practice and redirect me into a "much better way," His way. I offer to Him all my praise and thanksgiving for allowing me to serve Him through missions and through writing. The words in this book are mine, but the timing of so many details and ideas are His. I blame Him for none of the faults, but I thank Him for anything in this book that touches a heart and brings a soul closer to the One who is indeed the God of the impossible.

I especially thank the Lord for all the people He has put in my life throughout the years:

To my mother, Barbara Goldsmith; you are a great "publicity agent." As with all you do in life, your enthusiasm and fervor for my books have made a big difference. You never cease to amaze me. Many thanks.

To my father, Jere Goldsmith; my brothers, Glenn and Jere; my sister-in-law, Mary; and my grandmom, Allene, thank you for your advice, your encouragement, your support of my work, and coming to the book signings. What would I do without family?

To Jill Briscoe, who believed in me many years ago and published my first article, thank you for your continuing advice. You are an inspiration and role model to me.

To Maurice Delacoux, Lili Botella, Eliane Martinez, Josy Rivière, Ian Campbell, Muriel Butcher, Marc Roche, Annette Manzano, Mme Hernandez, and many others here in France who took the time to help me understand what life was like in Algeria during the war, I am deeply indebted to you.

To Maryvonne and Bernard Millerand, who have been my real-life *boulangers* and have given me advice about bread and Senegal, *Merci beaucoup*.

To my friends in the Protestant Church of La Pompignane in Montpellier, France; this place feels like home because of you. Your stories, your fresh faith, and the changes God has wrought in your lives have inspired me to write of others whose lives have been changed. Thank you for being so very real. We have been through a lot together, and you still love me.

To Laura McDaniel, Kim Huhman, and Margaret DeBorde, the "Atlanta fan club" and my dear friends from so far back, you read my first poems when I was a child and you have encouraged me along throughout my life. Thank you for your prayers, your letters, your insights, and for all the times you made me laugh. You are priceless to me.

To Dave Horton, my friend and editor, you have once again walked with me through this exhilarating process of producing a book. *Merci pour tout.*

To LoraBeth Norton, Greg Clouse, and the other folks at Chariot Victor, thank you for all your hard work.

To Trudy Owens, my dear friend, teammate, and patient proof-reader; you are a godly woman who listens to the Lord. He always seems to give you just the right words to encourage me.

To Cathy Carmeni, my talented "pre-editor"; your insights have been invaluable, your friendship enriching, your faith a joy to watch as it blossoms.

To Christine Montgomery and Cathy Carmeni, my prayer partners; you have watched the dream become a reality during those blessed Monday-afternoon prayer sessions. *Je vous embrasse très fort.*

To my teammates, Howard and Trudy Owens and Odette Beauregard, who have been cheerleaders, babysitters, soul mates, and family away from home, *Je vous embrasse avec tout mon coeur.*

To all our prayer partners around the world, who have prayed me through some very difficult months of illness; God has used you mightily in my life. Thank you.

To Andrew and Christopher, my sons; what would I do without you? Thank you for loving me just as I am, for helping me so much, and for never running out of snuggles and kisses for Mommy.

To Paul, my husband and partner in everything, what more can I say? You are very patient, very giving, and very wise, and I love you very much.

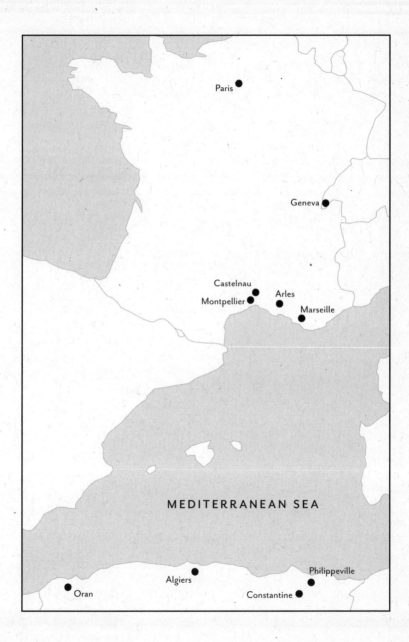

Paris

Geneva

Castelnau
Arles
Montpellier
Marseille

MEDITERRANEAN SEA

Philippeville
Algiers
Oran
Constantine

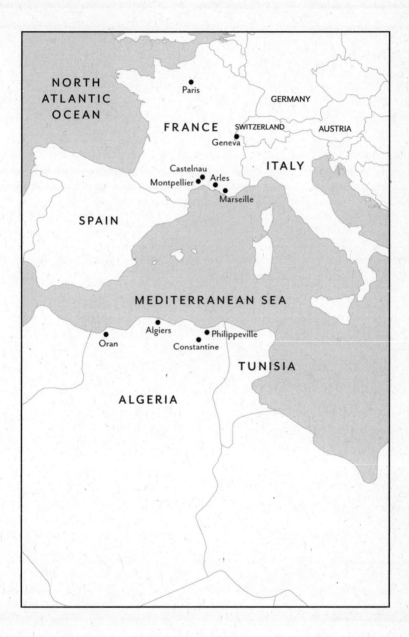

NORTH
ATLANTIC
OCEAN

GERMANY

FRANCE

Paris

SWITZERLAND

AUSTRIA

Geneva

ITALY

Castelnau

Montpellier   Arles

Marseille

SPAIN

MEDITERRANEAN SEA

Algiers   Philippeville

Oran   Constantine

TUNISIA

ALGERIA

Glossary

Algerian War for Independence from France—conflict that took place in Algeria from 1954–1962.

Casbah—the old part of Algiers, named for the Turkish-built sixteenth-century fortress that dominated the quarter. It was also the headquarters for the FLN.

centre aéré—a recreational child-care center.

FLN—Front de Libération Nationale (National Liberation Front), socialist political party in Algeria. It was organized on November 1, 1954, from a merger of small political groups that sought independence for Algeria from France.

harki—an Algerian soldier who remained loyal to the French army and therefore fought against his fellow Algerians.

OAS—Organisation de l'Armée Secrète (Organization of the Secret Army), a French far-right nationalist militant and underground organization during the Algerian War whose goal was to prevent Algeria's independence.

pied-noir—a European living in Algeria.

1

March 1962
Castelnau, France

Poppies were springing up in the fields beyond Castelnau like bright-red drops of blood staining the countryside. Seeing the flowers, Gabriella Madison took a deep breath. Lifeblood and hope eternal.

She closed her eyes and felt a stinging sensation inside her chest. Poppies reminded her of David. And poppies reminded David of her. But now he was in Algeria, perhaps already in the company of Ophélie's mother, Anne-Marie. How Gabriella wished he were standing here beside her instead.

Ophélie's voice interrupted her thoughts. "Bribri, do you think it will be today that Papa and Mama get back?"

Gabriella shook her head, her red hair glistening like sun on the river. "Not today, Ophélie. But very soon."

Were they even now laughing together, reliving old times, catching up on seven lost years? Was David explaining what had been happening here in lazy Castelnau? Had he even mentioned her name to Anne-Marie?

They had been walking, Gabriella and a whole troop of children, toward the edge of Castelnau, where the village fanned out into farmland and vineyards. The children trailed behind their young *maîtresse* in pairs, holding hands and chattering excitedly. Gabriella glanced back to see Sister Rosaline, red faced and out of breath, waving from the end of the line.

"All here," the nun called out happily in her singsong French. "All forty-three."

Gabriella waved back, smiling at the children. "Do you want to go a little farther? We're almost to the park."

A chorus of *Oui, Maîtresse* sang back to her, so they proceeded down a narrow dirt road into a grassy sanctuary enclosed by tall cypress trees. At the far end of the field were several seesaws, some monkey bars, and an old swing set.

This walk outside the orphanage had become a daily ritual after lunch, weather permitting. Mother Griolet had hesitated at first. What if people began to question? After all, the population of the orphanage had doubled in a few short months. But Gabriella and Sister Rosaline had insisted. The new arrivals were loud, afraid, and restless. Together the children acted like pent-up animals, and they needed to be uncaged in a space larger than the courtyard inside St. Joseph.

In truth, Gabriella worried for Mother Griolet. With David away and all the new children here, the old nun's predictable schedule had come tumbling down.

"It's always this way at first," she had reassured Gabriella. "During the Second World War we scrambled for a while, but we eventually settled into a routine."

But Gabriella was not convinced. Over fifteen years had passed since that war, and Mother Griolet was no longer young. Still spry, yes, but she was suddenly looking quite old beneath her habit. Her face looked more wrinkled, and her green eyes had lost some of their sparkle.

Forty-three orphans and forty-two American college women would be plenty for an energetic young woman to handle. Perhaps too much for a woman of seventy-two.

Presently Ophélie left her friends to join Gabriella.

"Bribri," the child began, fiddling with Gabriella's long red curls, "what will it be like when Mama, Papa, and you are all here together?" She scrunched up her nose, her brown eyes shining and sincere.

Gabriella cleared her throat and stroked Ophélie's hair. "It will be a wonderful reunion, Ophélie. An answer to prayer."

"And who do you think Papa will choose? You or Mama? And who will I live with?"

Gabriella bent down beside the little girl. She hoped her voice sounded light and carefree. "Dear Ophélie. Your papa will not choose your mama or me. He will choose *you*! He will pick you up and swing you around, and the whole orphanage will ring with your laughter. Don't you worry now. Don't worry."

Take your own advice, Gabriella thought as she sent Ophélie off with a soft pat on the back. Two days ago David Hoffmann had kissed her—really kissed her—and then he had left on a humanitarian mission to a country gone mad. She did not want to dwell on it, for the possibilities were too frightening. Better to think of the children.

A fight broke out between two boys, and Gabriella dashed over, yelling, "*Eh! Ça suffit!*" She pulled the children apart, scolded them playfully, and began chasing several of the smallest boys, tagging one and calling, "You're it!" A few minutes into the game she stumbled, out of breath, to the side of the field, crushing a red poppy beneath her feet.

Marseille, France

David Hoffmann stood at the bassin de la Joliette in Marseille. Amid the huge ferries, *paquebots*, and steamships, he spied a comparatively small black-and-white sailboat. The *Capitaine* was empty now, except for a grisly old Frenchman at the helm.

The wharf was awash in families debarking with trunks and suitcases. Adults and children alike looked confused, sad, hopeless. David shook his head. One little orphanage in the south of France sheltering a handful of *pied-noir* and *harki* children was a drop in the bucket. These people were French citizens, but where would they go? Did France want them? David knew the answer was no.

He slipped onto the *Capitaine* and greeted the rough sailor with a handshake.

"*Bonjour*," Jacques replied. "You sure you want to go back there now? It's a bad situation and is only going to get worse."

"Yes, I'm sure. I have to go."

Jacques looked at the ground. "I can't go back, M. Hoffmann. There's nowhere for me to dock. The ferries are taking up all the room. Thousands of pied-noirs are running away faster than the mistral gusts down the Rhône. If you're sure you have to go back, I advise you to take a ferry. It'll be a lot safer, and I guarantee you there'll be room—nobody's going *back* to Algeria."

David frowned, contemplating the sailor's words, then shrugged. "I understand, Jacques. Thank you for all your help. There are many children in Castelnau who are grateful to you."

The two men shook hands.

"*Bonne chance*, M. Hoffmann. You be careful now. Raving crazy, that country is. Raving crazy."

David stood on the deck of a huge empty ferry, his tall frame silhouetted against the night sky. The wind whipped across the sea. His hair blew back, his eyes squinted against the wind, and his jacket billowed and filled with air. He gripped the railing with his good hand, his other shoulder and arm bandaged and tucked inside his leather jacket.

The whitecaps rose up to touch the sky, and a thousand stars blinked back, as if flirting with the water. The sea air smelled fresh and strong. He wished briefly that Gabriella were snuggled beside him, then pushed the thought away.

He had twenty-four hours alone before he would step into a world of chaos, and he wanted to spend this one night well. The scene before him reminded him of a night on the beach one month ago. The night of his surrender, he called it in his mind. His surrender to the God of Gabriella.

There was no doubt that something inside of him had changed. In that moment he had actually felt forgiven, and too many coincidences had happened lately to deny intellectually that God seemed to be up to something in his life. He was twenty-five years old, yet he was somehow new. A new man. A new conscience. A Presence was with him. He had a suspicious feeling he would never be able to get rid of this God now even if he wanted to.

Algiers, Algeria

It was midafternoon at the Place du Gouvernement in downtown Algiers. The great Cathedral of Saint Philippe formed an imposing barrier between the steep, narrow roads of the Casbah and this tree-filled square that teemed with people shopping, sipping mint tea at a *café*, and milling about in carefree jubilation. There was a feeling of peace and security among the population of Algiers. The cease-fire to end Algeria's seven-year war for independence from France had gone into effect two days before.

The noise from the square was merry, loud, jovial. This was the Algiers Hussein remembered and loved. Seven years of war had stolen his boyhood away. At fourteen, he had seen more violence than many a soldier. He secretly longed for peace. Beyond the war, beyond the hatred.

Now was the time to breathe openly, to relax, to hope. No pied-noirs had ventured out into the sunshine today, Hussein mused with grim satisfaction. Ali had predicted they would leave *en masse* before official independence was declared on July 2. Algeria would be rid of the filthy French and their colonial ways.

Yet Hussein still wished he could find the woman, Anne-Marie, to placate Ali's fury. Ali Boudani was a man obsessed with revenge.

He was at one moment delirious with joy, the next moment brooding with contempt. Algeria was independent, but Ali's personal mission was not over.

Hussein glanced up at the sky, hearing a noise that sounded like a plane overhead, or maybe a missile being launched. Then his body tensed. He stood transfixed in the shadow of a building as, above him, one, then two bright flashes exploded with a terrible boom in the center of the Place du Gouvernement. Debris from the street, chairs from cafés, and bodies seemed to dance on the tips of the bright flames before his eyes. For a brief moment the deafening roar of the explosions silenced the screams coming from everywhere in the square.

Clutching one another, panic on their faces, people clambered toward the shadows of the buildings, some fleeing in the direction of the cathedral. Dead and maimed lay in the center of the square; a shrill cry of agony pierced through the din of confused voices. Everyone stopped; no one dared move. Would more bombs follow?

Then almost at once, the masses surged forward to help the wounded. Arab FLN terrorists worked alongside the French police for perhaps the first time in Algiers' bloody history. Hussein watched it all. An old woman, bloodied and disfigured, collapsed against the stones of a building. Three men lay dead. The peaceful leafy square of five minutes earlier resembled a battleground. Hussein turned on his heels and fled.

It was a lie! There was no peace for Algeria! Up the layers of tangled, dilapidated buildings of the Casbah Hussein ran, until he stumbled into the one-room office where Ali sat.

Already the Casbah was ringing with cries of indignation and fury.

"Ali! The Place du Gouvernement! Explosion!" Hussein choked on his words and took in gulps of air, his lungs burning.

Ali rose and stepped into the street as young men poured forth from their whitewashed stalls.

Other members of the FLN were already holding men back, some of them forcefully.

"Not yet! Don't run to your deaths. This is what the OAS is waiting for. Hold your ground. It's their last effort to win back Algeria."

Ali grabbed Hussein by the shoulders. "It's not over yet. You aren't afraid of bloodshed, my boy?"

Hussein gazed at him and shook his head, knowing all the while that the fear in his eyes betrayed him.

"Go then, and tell me what you see. Go to Bab el-Oued and wait. Take it all in. We must be ready."

Hussein turned and escaped through a narrow alleyway. Tears ran down his cheeks. Oh, for peace. For even a moment of peace. Then he could play as he had when he was seven and war had been only a handful of toy soldiers on the floor of his room.

A ricochet of bullets sounded in the street below the building where Anne-Marie Duchemin was staying with fellow pied-noir Marcus Cirou. She watched Moustafa hurry a young man into their building, and she quickly limped to the mirror that hung on the flaking wall. She felt a pang of despair as her reflection stared back at her. Her black hair drooped loosely upon her shoulders. She cringed at the way her protruding cheekbones accentuated her deep-set and dull eyes. Her skin looked pale and almost yellowish. She turned away.

A thick gray sweater hung impossibly over her thin frame, but she felt completely naked. David Hoffmann was about to walk back into her life, and she was not ready. Her heart belonged to Moustafa. With him, she was not afraid to be sick and disheveled. She read devotion in his eyes. But David! Her lover when they were but adolescents. She had not seen him in so long.

Suddenly she felt afraid. He was risking his life and wasting his time to help her. Why? Would he be angry to see what she had become? A pitiful, withered flower …

The door swung wide, and David stood in the opening and paused. Anne-Marie swallowed hard and met his eyes. His six-foot-one-inch frame had filled out so that he looked every bit the grown man he was. His black eyes were softer than she remembered, and the tenderness she saw in them scared her even more. His coarse black hair was swept back away from his face, but one wisp tickled his forehead. A black leather jacket hung loosely over his shoulders. As he leaned down to set a suitcase on the floor, she noticed his bandaged arm. He straightened up, not moving forward, as if waiting for her invitation.

His mouth whispered *Anne-Marie* without making a sound.

Oh, you are a beautiful man, she thought, fighting to stand her ground, willing herself against running into his arms, forcing herself to forget that last embrace seven years ago when he had kissed her good-bye even as the tiny seed of Ophélie was forming in her womb.

David cleared his throat. "Anne-Marie." He said it almost reverently, and then he moved toward her, slowly, taking long strides. He reached out and touched her frail hand, then brushed her face. "My dear Anne-Marie."

She heard the sorrow, the groan of pain in his voice, the hurt for her suffering. She bit her lip and closed her eyes, but she could not keep the tears from flowing. She rested her head against his chest and let his strong arm enclose her as she sobbed like a terrified child who had been rescued at last.

Somewhere inside she watched the years of horror and death, killing and running for life, the years that had followed her happiest moments with David. If only ... if only ... The questions of a lifetime swam before her in liquid reality until they ran down her cheeks. Her feeble energy was spent. And though she had not uttered a word, she had the feeling that David Hoffmann understood perfectly everything she felt.

David was not prepared for the emotions that surfaced in him as he held Anne-Marie in his arms. He had been playing happily in his little university world while this woman lived in hell. He hadn't known. He had cared, and yet ... Even the smuggling operation in France, with all its dangers, could not compare with what he saw in Anne-Marie: true human suffering. The weight of guilt pulled on his shoulders and bound him more tightly than the sling in which his arm rested. A sick, painful anger welled up in his soul as he held her, this woman who was no more than a dried twig fallen from a branch.

God, forgive me, he prayed as she sobbed into his shirt. *I had no idea.* She looked more like an aging grandmother or a malnourished child than a twenty-four-year-old woman. She didn't want pity, David was sure, but pity overwhelmed him anyway. A fleeting thought crossed his mind. If only ... if only she had left with him for America. Ophélie would have been born there. They would have made it, somehow. If only ...

And then the angry *why*? Why? Why did life twist and turn and torture?

He stepped back from Anne-Marie and let his good arm fall to his side. A searing pain shot through his shoulder, and he grimaced.

"What happened?" Anne-Marie whispered. She touched his bandaged arm.

"It's nothing."

Silence engulfed them.

Anne-Marie wiped her eyes with the sleeve of her sweater. "I'm sorry."

"Perhaps we could sit down for a minute?"

"Yes, of course." Anne-Marie shot him a weak smile. "I'm sorry. I'm afraid I ... I'm so glad to see you, David. Thank you for coming. It's the worst time."

He gently took her arm and led her out of the room. "Moustafa is waiting for us in the kitchen."

"Yes, yes. You must be tired after your trip. Let me fix you some mint tea."

The small kitchen was dark. Moustafa Dramchini stood with his back toward them, already preparing the tea. He turned and greeted them with sullen eyes. David helped Anne-Marie to her seat as

Moustafa set a tray on the table. He rested his hand on Anne-Marie's back and eyed David suspiciously.

"When do you plan to leave?"

"It's your call, Moustafa. As soon as you can arrange it."

Anne-Marie looked up. "Tell me of Ophélie. How is she?"

David relaxed and smiled. "She's fine. She's a beautiful, happy child who misses her mother very much." He reached into his pocket. "She sent this for you." He held out a drawing of a rainbow with the words *I love you, Mama* written in the cursive of a six-year-old.

Anne-Marie's eyes filled with tears. She ran her fingers lovingly over the picture and then pressed it to her breast. She closed her eyes and let the tears trickle down her cheeks. "Ophélie."

The men watched her in silence. Finally she spoke, her voice catching. "I've clung to the hope for all these months. I've forced myself to believe, to be strong. But to know for sure that she is safe. To dream of holding her in my arms again soon. Now I can cry, and I don't know if it's joy or fear or sorrow. Now I can believe that we're going to be okay."

David put his hand inside his leather coat and felt for a gold chain, which he handed to Anne-Marie. "Ophélie sent this as well. She wanted me to have it, to keep me safe. She said it has kept her safe, and now it will bring you back safely to her also."

Anne-Marie held the chain with the small Huguenot cross on it as if it were a priceless jewel. "My father's cross. I'd forgotten how beautiful it was. Thank you." She traced its outline with her finger and then slipped it around her neck. "Ophélie never realized the real significance of it?"

David smiled. "I don't know if I would say that. She has learned an awful lot about the cross and what it stands for in the time she has been at the orphanage. But she never understood why it was so important for us." He closed his eyes, picturing his daughter. "She's a secretive child. Do you know she kept your letter hidden and learned to read so she could know what you were telling her?"

Anne-Marie shook her head. "How did you find it?"

"I didn't. It was Mother Griolet, the nun in charge of the orphanage. I had no idea."

He explained how he had found Ophélie, a terrified and wounded child, in Paris and of his decision to bring her to the orphanage. "I had no idea what to do with a small child. But I knew Gabby would."

"Gabby?"

David's face reddened against his will. "Gabriella Madison. She's a young woman on the exchange program who helps out with the orphanage."

"The woman with the red hair," Moustafa volunteered.

"That's the one," David answered. He didn't want to talk about Gabriella now. There would be time later to tell Anne-Marie and time to understand what he was reading in the angry eyes of Moustafa.

Darkness blanketed the streets of Algiers as Moustafa slipped outside. "I'll be back shortly." His soft brown eyes, filled with distrust, met David's.

"Good." David nodded. "Then we'll discuss the plans for leaving."

"Yes, then."

David watched him go into the street. He was eager to get Anne-Marie to the port and out of the war-ridden city. They would cross the Mediterranean, and then life would resume. Anne-Marie would be with Ophélie. Her health would improve. And he would be back with Gabriella....

The sound of a chair being dragged across the floor startled him, and he turned from the window. Anne-Marie stood by the kitchen table, a thick robe now pulled around her thin frame.

"I didn't mean to surprise you. Would you like some more tea?"

He pulled out a chair, and they both sat down. "No, I'm fine."

The silence was heavy. A hundred questions raced through his mind. Where to begin?

Anne-Marie played with the ties on her robe, twisting them in her hands. Her head was bent, and for a brief moment he remembered her as a radiant, rebellious adolescent. His heart ached.

"Are you feeling strong enough to leave?" he asked, breaking the quiet.

She did not look up but still wrapped the ties around her hands. "I'm sorry I never answered your letters," she said. "How could I answer? How could I write you and keep silent about what was happening to me?"

David reached over and took her hand. "What did your parents say when they found out you were pregnant?"

Anne-Marie looked up. "They did all the right things. They got angry. Papa ranted for a while. Then they apologized. They listened. We talked. We cried a lot. They asked me to let you know, but I couldn't. I couldn't put that on you." Her eyes wore the saddest of expressions. "I knew you would come back—just to hurt your father. You'd come back for all the wrong reasons."

David stiffened and set his jaw. She was right. Perhaps he would have come back to Algeria out of rebellion and not love. Intellectually he had loved her. Physically he had loved her. But emotionally? He could not say.

"I cared deeply about you, Anne-Marie."

"I know that."

He winced inwardly at the stabbing guilt he felt.

"Mama was a saint about it. I broke their hearts, and they forgave me. And oh, how they loved Ophélie. Captain Duchemin, the staunch, strong military man! I wish you could have seen him cooing at his granddaughter." She smiled at the memory. "He rocked her to bed every night and sang her the most beautiful songs. We were a happy, odd family for a while. Until Ali Boudani ripped everything apart." She stared at him, and her face grew hard and determined. "You know the rest."

"Perhaps not everything," he whispered. "Tell me about Moustafa."

Anne-Marie looked angry. Then she smiled. "Dear Moustafa. My childhood friend, the one who helped me escape to France, then betrayed me to Ali." Her voice was barely audible. "The one who loves me."

"And do you love him?"

She closed her eyes and withdrew her hand from his. He was sorry that he had asked her so soon.

Softly she answered, "I love him, David. I love him, and every time he leaves this filthy apartment, I'm terrified I'll lose him. I am so afraid that he will be found in some back alley with his throat slit, like the other harkis. Like his father. These Arabs have remained loyal to France and fought alongside the French soldiers. But they aren't French, and they're seen as traitors by their own people. What hope is there for the harki families?"

She stood and held on to the back of the chair. "I love him, and I wish I didn't. What future is there for us? An ostracized Arab and a pied-noir. And he'll stay for his people. He won't come to France, I know. I'm so afraid that in a few days he will walk out of my life forever. And it hurts so much. It hurts like … it hurts the way …"

She stopped, but David knew the end of the sentence. *It hurts the way it hurt when you walked out of my life seven years ago.*

2

David woke abruptly, his body drenched with sweat. He pulled the sheets off and struggled to remember where he was. Algiers ... Anne-Marie.

He swallowed hard and propped himself up on the mattress with his good arm. He remembered listening to the locusts chirping in the summer nights long ago. Then he would lie awake for a long time, thinking of Anne-Marie and their clandestine encounters where their passion was spent.

He closed his eyes to the memory. They had been teenagers. Rebellious kids. His first experience of love. He had not known what had happened to her when he returned to the States, and yet he felt responsible now, housed in the same apartment. It was not lust that made him want her again. Perhaps it was pity. Or the desire to protect. For a moment he considered slipping into her room, holding her in his arms, kissing away the pain.

Moustafa lay a few feet from him, asleep. The young Arab loved her fiercely, David could see. His eyes burned with it. But Anne-Marie was right. No pied-noir would marry a harki. It would mean ostracism from both societies.

Why was life so complicated? he wondered angrily. Why was there an angelic redhead waiting for him on the other side of the Mediterranean with the taste of his kisses on her lips? Yet he was not afraid for Gabriella. She had the spunk and the faith to pull her through a long line of disappointments. Yes, the faith.

He groaned to himself. Anne-Marie did not need him. She had lived through hell, and though scarred, she would come out fighting.

But Ophélie. Surely he owed it to his daughter to give her an intact family. He rolled over and closed his eyes, listening again to the heavy, encumbering silence. Maybe if he listened long enough, this strange new God would tell him something.

By the time he finally drifted back to sleep, the first light of dawn was peeking over the horizon.

He awoke to Moustafa shaking him and saying, "Listen! Do you hear it?"

David squinted and blinked, his eyes adjusting to the morning light. The sound of gunfire peppered the air. "What is it?"

"The OAS. You know, the secret group made up of dissenters from the French army. They've taken over the neighborhood during the night. It could get very bloody."

"Right here in Bab el-Oued?" David was incredulous. "How do you know?"

Moustafa met his eyes with his own somber gaze. "I know."

David quickly dressed himself. "Should we tell Anne-Marie?"

"She's already up."

David nodded, brushing his fingers through his hair. "What do you think we should do?"

"There's nothing to do but wait."

Anne-Marie entered the room, a thick, oversized bathrobe pulled around her. Moustafa took her hand.

"The OAS has set up a military fortress in Bab el-Oued. They think they can oppose the French army." He cursed. "Trouble is coming to our doorstep. Mark my words."

❖

Hussein slipped down the alleyways of the Casbah into the streets of Bab el-Oued in the early morning. Hiding behind an old building on rue Christophe Colomb, he peered down the street to where a group of pied-noir teenagers had surrounded two army corps trucks. The youths held submachine guns, pointing them arrogantly at the soldiers. For a moment it seemed the soldiers would easily relinquish their arms. Then one of them made a move, and a pied-noir opened fire, spraying the two trucks with bullets. The driver of the first truck slumped forward until his forehead touched the shattered windshield.

Hussein's eyes grew wide as he watched two other soldiers, wounded, fall from the truck. The youths grabbed the guns of the dead soldiers and fled down the street. Hussein retreated into the shadows of the building, his heart thumping wildly. More blood! And this time the blood was spilled between Europeans. The pied-noirs—French citizens themselves—were firing on the French army. The army would no doubt fire back. This was news for Ali.

Hussein felt like a small boy watching a war movie as he witnessed the battle of Bab el-Oued. Now fidgeting in the *boulangerie* on the neighborhood's main shopping street, he watched several tanks rumbling down the street, spewing a steady stream of bullets from their turrets. From atop a roof a man fired a bazooka, missing the tanks but smashing into an approaching ambulance.

Hussein glanced up as the whirring sound of a helicopter was drowned out by the sound of the grenades it dropped, exploding on the roof where the sniper had been.

War. War between the Europeans.

Sporadic shelling continued throughout the afternoon. Hussein dodged in and out of the small streets of the neighborhood, adrenalin pumping through his small frame, his eyes glazed, impersonal, as he observed another day of murder. He was nothing but a reporter, doing his job. He repeated it time and again in his mind. A reporter for Ali.

By late afternoon he could tell the French army was winning. Four T-6 training planes zipped through the sky, launching rockets and diving toward several snipers who were still visible on rooftops. The OAS would not hold Bab el-Oued.

No pied-noirs were venturing out of their apartments. Hussein had not seen Anne-Marie Duchemin or Moustafa Dramchini. But he had seen plenty else. It would have to be enough for now.

David stared from the balcony as tanks rumbled through the street, sending vibrations like a herd of wild elephants on the march. Their guns shifted in a circular pattern, pointing toward the apartment buildings.

"Are you crazy!" Moustafa scolded, pulling David back into the bedroom. "The army has made its stand clear. They want order, and if anyone opposes, they'll fire, at Arab, pied-noir, or American." The last word he pronounced as if it were a spoon of thick, foul-tasting medicine.

Darkness had fallen, and the whole *quartier* of Bab el-Oued appeared to be in a state of shock. Marcus Cirou had rushed into the apartment and was now furiously smoking and pacing in the den, sliding his fingers through his slick gray hair. He announced the verdict to his three houseguests.

"There must be over a hundred dead or wounded among us," he said. "The army has blockaded the neighborhood. No one can get in. No ambulances, no doctors. The wounded are being hidden in homes. Bloody, catastrophic mess." Sweat beaded on his forehead as he blew smoke into the air, his eyes fiery with anger and fear.

Without warning, the entrance door to the apartment splintered open and two *gendarmes* forced their way inside, brandishing pistols and shouting for everyone to lift their hands. While one of the French police, young and gloomy, held his pistol on the four people in the kitchen, the other, older and heavyset, tramped his way through the apartment. He threw open closets, smashed in the television, yanked clothes off their hangers, then came back to the kitchen, livid with rage.

"Are you traitors too? Filthy OAS! Murdering your own countrymen. Do you want to know how we feel about that?" He jerked Marcus by the collar, the pistol butt thrust under his chin.

Anne-Marie clutched Moustafa's arm, terrified. The officer noticed, looked confused for a moment, then snickered. "What are you anyway? Crazy swine! The OAS, hiding Arabs in Bab el-Oued!

Let's have a look at you there." He moved forward, grabbing Anne-Marie and shoving her to stand alone beside the second officer. His breath reeked of liquor.

She trembled before them.

"Did you hear me?" he screamed. "Undress! What other secrets are you hiding, woman!" Forcefully the heavy officer yanked at her sweater, laughing cruelly as the collar ripped, exposing her bare shoulder.

"Please!" Moustafa stepped forward, looking the officer in the eye. "You're right. These good people have taken me in. My father fought with you. Lieutenant Dramchini, a harki. Perhaps you knew him. He was murdered by the FLN, and now I'm hiding. These people are not traitors. I'm the traitor. The traitor to my people for you. Surely you won't deal with us in the same manner as the FLN."

The officer's lip twitched uncomfortably. He released Anne-Marie, who fell toward David. He caught her and held her tight as Moustafa continued.

"We're trying to escape to leave this madness. Please, don't harm her."

The officer gave a disgusted grunt and shook his head. "You'll never get out of this hellhole, harki boy. Passage is for pied-noirs first. And after tonight, I guarantee you there'll be a whole mass of them fleeing like scared rabbits."

They spun on their heels and walked out of the apartment, leaving the door standing wide open.

The next day it rained, a gray, drizzly cold rain that stayed in the bones and caused one to shiver unconsciously. Seated at the table in Marcus Cirou's dingy, mold-covered kitchen, Moustafa watched the gloomy weather. The entrance door had been forced shut and bandaged, but the wounds were deep in Bab el-Oued. Sipping mint tea, Moustafa brooded while David stared out the single kitchen window onto the street below.

"Quarantined? Is that what Marcus called it?" David asked.

"Yes, for a week. All telephone communications are cut off. The roads are barricaded. The women can leave the house one hour a day to shop for groceries. The French army wants Bab el-Oued to think long and hard before it stages another insurrection." Moustafa slammed his fist on the table and cursed. "A week! I want Anne-Marie out of here *now*! But as it is, our best chance is for the thirtieth."

"So we must wait." David pronounced the words resignedly.

Moustafa looked up quickly. "I don't like it any more than you do, M. Hoffmann."

"Call me David, please."

"David then. What does it change?"

"It makes things less formal."

"Less formal. Ha! And what do you want? To be my *pote*? I don't need a friend like you, David Hoffmann. If I could get Anne-Marie out of here safely myself, believe me, I would never have asked you." He looked away.

Moustafa could not remember when he had first started loving Anne-Marie. Was it when they were schoolchildren, playing outside on her father's farm? For three generations the Dramchinis had worked for the Duchemins on the plot of land outside Algiers.

They had been employees and also neighbors. Moustafa had grown up beside the Duchemins' only daughter, and their friendship had been natural.

She was the mischievous one, always taking risks, pulling her Arab friend along. She had never seen the difference, never understood the wall that stood between her culture and his. He had first loved her for that. Her wild, beautiful naïveté.

She had not guessed for the longest time, not until her fourteenth year, when somehow it was no longer appropriate to hold hands and drag each other along through the orange groves just for fun. Their last run through the groves had ended with a kiss that Moustafa had planted squarely on Anne-Marie's lips.

She had pushed him back, surprised. "Now why in the world did you do that?"

He shrugged, turning his eyes down, hidden beneath the unkempt black curls that tumbled to his shoulders. Why indeed. He had known then, at twelve, that Anne-Marie would never understand. He had sworn, though, that he would love her and protect her as far as it was in his power for the rest of his life. A boyhood dream …

He realized suddenly that he was smiling and remembered David's intrusive presence. The tall American's back was turned to him. Moustafa felt the smile leave his face. What right had this cocky American teenager had to take away Anne-Marie? Steal her heart and leave her with a child. David Hoffmann was the kind of man who got his way. The kind that women looked at twice, giggling and blushing. He had money and wits and a long list of other qualities that were sure to charm. He was the kind of man Moustafa hated. A man with no loyalties. Why be loyal when he could be free and taste the honey from many a hive?

And he was an American. A free man from a superpower. What had brought him back to this tangled mass of cultures? Was it after all a desire to possess Anne-Marie again?

"I'm glad you said what you did last night, Moustafa. You saved Anne-Marie further humiliation," David commented, his back still turned.

Moustafa winced at the sound of the other man's voice—calm, controlled, condescending. "For how long?" he seethed. "There is no telling who will crash through the door tomorrow to level us all."

"Do you support the OAS?" David asked, turning slowly.

Moustafa laughed. "I support my people, plain and simple. And Anne-Marie." He rose and walked over to where David stood, and both stared out the window. Moustafa watched the rain on the window sliding into little puddles on the frame. "I don't disapprove totally of the OAS, you must understand. You know what the pied-noirs say?" He didn't wait for a reply. "They say the OAS is like the Resistance during the other war. How can they sit idly by while their people are massacred arbitrarily? The FLN started this war seven years ago—a handful of terrorists who wanted Algeria to be free. Terrorism has always been the FLN's way. It's not war. It's not combat. It's cold-blooded murder, instilling fear. Anyone and everyone is in danger.

"But now, when the OAS strike back, they are considered mur-derers. The FLN is pardoned of its years of barbaric acts, and the OAS are the assassins. Who can make any sense of it? A son finds his father slaughtered. An Arab maid is given a choice—either she cuts the throats of the pied-noir children she has helped raise, or the FLN will cut her children's throats. What do you do in a country gone mad? Where you could just as easily be blown up at a sidewalk café in the middle of the afternoon as shot to death in your apartment in the middle of the night. It is past understanding."

David, his forehead against the window, seemed lost in thought. In barely a whisper he asked, "And what will happen to your people once independence is declared in July?"

Moustafa's answer was matter-of-fact. "It will be a genocide. A complete genocide of harkis. And the world will never blink an eye."

Moustafa watched a play of emotions cross David Hoffmann's face. It looked like a pained anger, as if something from deep within him were welling up and threatening to spill over. Perhaps there was depth to this man after all.

David turned abruptly from the window. "Do you still have family here in Algeria? Who is still alive for you, Moustafa?"

"My mother, two sisters. And my older brother who is in the French army. A real harki. They are all here. I ran away once to France because I was afraid. I won't do it again. I'll stay with them and die. You must take Anne-Marie on the thirtieth. Give her daughter back to her. Then she will forget me. Then one day she can love again."

Moustafa walked out of the kitchen, feeling once again like a traitor. He had betrayed his country; he had left his family. And soon his loyalty to Anne-Marie would be but a stained memory of an unfulfilled dream.

David could not sleep. In his mind he saw the curly black hair of Moustafa shaking back and forth; Moustafa appeared as a man resigned to a fate of certain death. David reached toward the suitcase that lay at his feet and brought out the Bible Gabriella had given him. He let the large book fall open to where a folded paper had been tucked between its pages. David unfolded it and stared at the picture in the moonlight.

Six different-colored ponies, drawn in the uncertain hand of Ophélie, were running toward the sun. He closed his eyes and remembered Ophélie's explanation. *I'm the pink one. I'm leading us to Jesus. He's in the sky, in the sun. And the red pony is Gabriella, because she has such long, pretty red hair. And then after her comes Mother Griolet. She's the gray pony there, see? And you are the black one. You're catching up with us and running to the sun. And the beautiful white pony with the black mane and tail is Mama. She is far behind, but she's coming with the brown pony. That's Moustafa.*

How he wished she was right. But the word *genocide* throbbed like a migraine in his mind. And he wondered if the brown pony would make it after all.

3

The War Monument stood impressive and silent in the middle of downtown Algiers, a testimony to the bravery of Algerians, pied-noirs, French, and Arabs from another war. Rémi Cebrian, thirtysomething, compact and thick with pure muscle, reread the tract he had received earlier in the week urging pied-noirs to assemble at the monument on rue Michelet at one o'clock on March 26. The tract called for a peaceful protest march on the quarantined district of Bab el-Oued in the west part of Algiers.

It was past one when Rémi arrived at the Place, where hundreds of high-spirited young people already waited in happy expectation. More and more pied-noirs appeared, many laden with baskets of cheese and fruits and other provisions to take to their cut-off counterparts in Bab el-Oued. A few teenagers began singing "La Marseillaise," and soon hundreds of voices joined them. Children held their mothers' hands. Dogs wagged their tails, straining on their leashes. The mood was bright.

Rémi was not sure why he had come. To see. To take part. To support his fellow pied-noirs as they desperately tried to preserve their place in an Algeria that was fast becoming hostile to them. He thought of his wife, Eliane, and their three children, back at the farm on the outskirts of Algiers. He was marching today with a prayer in his heart that they could stay in their country, on their farm, in their house.

As the crowd grew in size, it surged forward, pushed by those in the back. People waved flags, swung their baskets of provisions, and laughed. But Rémi noticed the blockades of soldiers who stood rigid and tense, placed there to make sure another insurrection never got off the ground.

Soon the crowd of over two thousand fanned out onto the central street of rue d'Isly. Rémi, who was walking on the side of the pack near the front, caught his breath. Before them stood a dozen Algerian *tirailleurs*, young harki riflemen from the French army, looking angry and tense beside the young French lieutenant commanding them.

Afterward, no one could be sure what happened first. Rémi recalled that one of the tirailleurs nearest him was shaking violently, obviously terrified by the approaching mob. Suddenly a series of shots burst dryly through the jubilation. At once the tirailleurs panicked and began firing point-blank into the crowd. A woman screamed, hit in the face. The pied-noirs ran in all directions, stampeding like a herd of wild buffalo. Rémi grabbed a small child who was wailing hysterically and dragged him onto the sidewalk, ducking as bullets sped and shattered above them. A shop door opened and an elderly man shouted, motioning for Rémi and the child to come inside.

His face plastered against the shop window, Rémi watched masses of terrified people running, screaming. Blood was everywhere. Men were yelling, *"Arrêt au feu! Arrêt au feu!* Stop shooting!" For a few seconds the shooting ceased, then started up again. An old woman collapsed on the sidewalk, blood seeping from her neck. Rémi dashed outside, seized the woman under the arms, and dragged her into the store. Others had the same reflex, as makeshift stretchers were carried into the streets during the brief periods when the rifle fire calmed before suddenly bursting forth again.

"*Seigneur*," Rémi said between sobs. "Another massacre."

The firing lasted no more than ten minutes, but the carnage was sickening. Blood formed puddles in the street as if the skies had dumped red rain. Bodies lay strewn and twisted, eyes open with complete stupefaction and agony written on dead faces. Rémi stumbled into the street and reached the bleeding form of a teenage youth, who coughed up blood, then died in his arms. Sirens screamed from far away. Slowly, dazed, Rémi removed the stained French flag from the dead boy's hand. Then he fled, tripping over an abandoned basket, knocking neatly wrapped parcels of cheese into the street.

He fell onto the sidewalk, his bloody hands leaving an imprint on the pavement, and vomited.

Hussein could feel the pent-up tension in the Casbah that night. He passed between the adults, listening, watching, wondering what new plans were being made. It seemed to him that the pied-noirs needed no further encouragement from the FLN to leave Algeria—the French army was providing the impetus.

"Hussein," Ali hissed, clasping the boy's arm so tightly that he almost cried out. Ali pulled him into an adjoining room, no larger than a closet, and shut the door behind them.

Hussein watched as his leader's eyes shone bright and red in the dark room. He knew Ali was exhausted, that the red tint came from fatigue, and yet, looking into those eyes, Hussein recoiled within himself. The eyes looked mad, as if they belonged to a rabid dog.

"I have a plan," Ali stated simply. "And you will accomplish it for me."

His self-assured, harsh tone made Hussein tremble inside. The boy blinked hard, twice, determined not to show his fear. He nodded, wishing that Ali would not regard him so intently.

"You're going to France. To Montpellier. You're going to that filthy orphanage, posing as a helpless harki's son, a victim of the war. They will take you in, and then you can finish the work for me." He smiled, his lips parting to reveal yellow teeth as twisted as the mind of their master. "I will have my place in the new Algeria. I am needed here. But you—" He caught the boy by the collar, pulling him up to within inches of his face. "You will finish the work for me in Montpellier. Do you understand?"

Hussein swallowed hard. He knew he should simply agree, but the question tumbled out, unchecked. "But how? How will I get there?"

Ali shoved him hard against the cement-brick wall. His breath reeked of cigarettes. "You will go to the docks tomorrow, and you will wait with all the pied-noirs every day until you find that Duchemin woman, and when you do, you will snivel and cry until her heart breaks for you. You'll go to France with her, to that orphanage, and you'll be the devil incarnate for them." He laughed wickedly as Hussein's eyes grew wide. "I'll have everything ready for you tomorrow night," he whispered. "Everything you need."

Hussein felt a tightening in his stomach. It was impossible, what Ali was asking. Crazy! There was no guarantee that Anne-Marie

Duchemin was leaving Algeria. But it didn't matter, he realized. Ali had decided, and he had no choice but to kiss his mother quickly, as if he were simply leaving for the afternoon as he so often did. Then he would disappear, on a ferry to France with a suitcase full of weapons.

He felt his childhood slipping away. So it was not to be. He was not to know the peace of a free Algeria. His was another role. A hired assassin for Ali. Many other boys his age prided themselves on the number of pied-noirs they had killed. Now he would join them. He had no choice.

The news of the disastrous results on March 26 crushed the already dampened spirits of the pied-noirs in the quarantined district of Bab el-Oued. The casualty report that swept through the neighborhood listed eighty demonstrators dead and at least two hundred wounded. It seemed to many pied-noirs that not only had President de Gaulle betrayed them, but now the French army itself was no longer neutral. They too would kill pied-noirs, citizens of their own country. The gruesome events of the last week had proved it true.

Like everyone else, David was anxious for the quarantine to be lifted. Two more days and he would take Anne-Marie to the port and escape to France. Escape was the right word, he thought. Escape by the skin of their teeth. He had almost forgotten how much he feared war. Danger, adventure, these he could handle. But war, with its terrorism, torture, and hundreds of innocent victims, left a sickening taste in his mouth. This was the war he had known and lived as a boy. Hiding, fear, then betrayal and imprisonment and death. He had to get out soon. Before he panicked.

How could Gabby claim that her God made sense of the senseless! Why, why, why? Why this struggle and war? From within the deepest part of him, David was angry. Before, he had known that life was tragic and that survival meant dependence on himself alone. And he had survived. But now, by some cruel irony, he believed in Someone bigger and beyond, and he was caught in that belief.

Before, he would have known how to simply get Anne-Marie out of Algeria. Quickly, methodically, feelings aside. But now a heaviness engulfed him, as if he must somehow ask permission from this God to do it his way. Or did this God have another way?

L'Eternel combattra pour vous et vous gardez le silence.

It was a round the children sang at the orphanage, a verse taken straight from the Bible. He knew the context. Moses had led the Israelites out of Egypt. Now the Egyptian army was at their backs, the Red Sea before them. And what did Moses say? "The Lord will fight for you while you keep silent!"

Oh, how maddening was this God. He was always asking the strangest things of His people. Why was David remembering that verse now? He laughed wryly. Maybe it was prophetic. The FLN was behind them and the Mediterranean was in front. Was this crazy God going to open up this sea too?

It was a matter of trust, Gabby had said. Trust. But trust seemed so stagnant. Did trust have feet and a brain? Did trust act? Was trust always silent?

David did not know, and his head ached from trying to figure it out. He closed his eyes and formed a silent prayer in his mind. *In two days, God. In two days we will leave. Come with us, please. Come with us.*

A hollow gnawing inside of Eliane Cebrian reminded her what the day held as she awakened to a gray dawn. Today she was loading her three precious children into their car with two small suitcases and heading for Algiers. And sometime very soon she would kiss Rémi good-bye for who knew how long and sail to France.

Just the thought made her eyes sting with tears. She stared out the window, her hand against the cool pane, and saw in the distance the orange groves and farther out the olive trees soon to be laden with fruit. Her stomach turned, and she rested her head against the window.

She was only thirty-one, a gregarious young woman with three small children. She loved for her house to be filled with people, with the smell of roasting fowl and brewing tea. She delighted in bustling through the farmhouse, serving her guests, changing the baby, laughing with Madira, the maid.

Gazing again out the window, she saw her husband deep in conversation with the farmhands, Abdul and Amar. She buried her head in her hands and cried. All she had ever known, all she had ever wanted for her family was this little farmhouse on the outskirts of Algiers.

She closed her eyes and remembered yesterday. Madira had clung to her, the young woman's face streaked with tears. "But, madame, you must not leave! What will become of us? We need you! Algeria needs you."

It had been the echo throughout the village as she had bade farewell to the shopkeepers. "Don't go. Perhaps there will finally be peace. Don't go."

But Rémi was insistent. He had been there three days ago when the peaceful march had turned into a bloodbath. She would never forget the expression on his face when he returned home late that afternoon—a mixture of disgust, fatigue, and terror. He was covered in blood, and at first Eliane thought he had been hurt. But Rémi's wounds were not physical.

That day his dream to stay in Algeria had died. "You must leave," he'd said flatly. "As soon as possible."

It was not the first time either of them had witnessed the treacheries of this war, but Rémi decided it would be the last, at least for his wife and children. He wanted his family out, safe in France, and he promised to come soon after.

Eliane heard the soft padding of little feet entering her room.

Four-year-old Rachel looked up with her cherubic blue eyes. "Is it time to get up, Mama?"

Eliane wiped her eyes, knelt down, and pulled the child to her breast. "Yes, you may get up. But don't wake baby José … Shh." Before Rachel could turn to leave, six-year-old Samuel appeared.

"It's today, *n'est-ce pas*, Mama? It's today we leave?" His dark-brown eyes were sober for once, and Eliane read the worry in them.

"Yes, dear, Papa will take us to the boat today."

He wrinkled his brow and peered at her from behind his long brown bangs. "But, Mama, I never got to tell El Amin good-bye."

"I know, *mon chéri*, and I am so sorry. But I'm afraid there is no time. We'll be leaving after lunch."

The baby began wailing in the next room, and Eliane hurried to get him. Holding José, and with the other two children huddled around her, she felt tears forming again in her eyes. "Come now, it's time for breakfast," she called as she bustled to the kitchen.

As she busied herself with the children, Eliane tried to imagine the streets of France. A French citizen she might be, but all she had ever known was Algeria. And now her country was chasing her away. But what did she have to look forward to in France? What would they do? Where would they live? Would anyone help them?

Rémi always looked ahead. The men at the church called him a visionary. Not that he had actual visions, but he saw and knew things. "The whole pied-noir population is going to leave in a big hurry," he had predicted last January. "If we wait till the end, there will be no help left in France. You go on, Eliane. It is best."

"Dear God," Eliane prayed, "please help us. You have promised. Don't leave us now."

She whistled a happy melody and played with the children as she scurried about packing last little treasures in the two suitcases. But her heart was heavy. She was packing up her life to leave, but would there be orange groves and palm trees and bright bougainvillea in France? What would life be like on the other side of the wide sea?

The children were playing in the dirt behind the house. Eliane had scolded them once and then decided to let them play one last time. She placed three neatly folded shirts in the trunk that was already overflowing with clothes. She smiled to herself, knowing that some-how Rémi would get it closed.

This was the trunk she was packing for the future. She could not hope to manage it now, along with the children, but Rémi promised he would send it later, when she got settled. In this trunk she would store the rest of her treasures. The photo albums, the silver baby cups, the framed photographs, the children's books, a few favorite pieces of china, the family Bible that traced the Cebrian heritage back to the early Huguenots. Someday these treasures would decorate her home in France, she assured herself. Or perhaps, and this was her fervent prayer, someday they would return to the farm here in Algeria. Once the madness calmed. Surely then they could return.

She knew that Rémi secretly hoped for this too. He had decided to stay behind and protect the farm from the Arabs' looting. His rifles were placed under each window, and he had already used them more than once. She shuddered. Too many horrible memories of Arab against European and random murders, year after bloody year.

A thick envelope sat on the bed that was now bare except for a pair of worn floral sheets. A heavy sigh escaped Eliane's lips. What was she to do with the testament of Captain Maxime Duchemin? She had been declared the executor of the will, but the Duchemins' only child, the sole beneficiary, had disappeared. Four years had passed since the captain and his wife had died in the massacre.

To think they had been neighbors. And now they too were dead, their farmhouse empty, abandoned. Eliane remembered the Duchemins' beautiful little daughter traipsing through the orange groves with her Arab friends. So long ago. Later the girl had given birth when she was barely more than a child herself. And now she too was most likely dead. There had been no word from her since her parents' death.

Eliane closed her eyes to shut out the possibilities. Better think practically now. The best, Rémi had assured her, was to pack the testament in the trunk with their valuables. Perhaps one day the Lord would see fit to reveal to them what should be done. Rémi had said it reverently, full of faith. Eliane laughed to herself. Dear Rémi. He believed the Lord would come down and touch him on the shoulder if he needed. And sometimes it seemed as if the Lord did just that.

Time dragged on slowly, filling her with dread. Better that it be over quickly, Eliane thought, than endure this prolonged torture.

She heard Samuel laugh loudly and looked out the window to see his best friend, El Amin, racing across the field to greet him. Eliane's heart stung again, and she could not stop the tears. El Amin, Madira's son, had grown up beside Samuel. They had shared everything during their short lives. She remembered Madira's words last year as the two young mothers had watched their boys playing soldiers.

"They do not know that they are playing the truth. Friends betraying each other. Friends killing each other. They play with plastic guns, but other friends hold hard metal in their hands and fire at each other." Her eyes had been deep and sad.

"Why must life be so unjust, Mme Eliane, why? Where in the politics is there room for Algerians and pied-noirs who are friends?" Madira had shaken her head as the sound of little boys fighting and laughing echoed in the background.

Now El Amin held out his hand to Samuel, and Eliane saw her son's bewildered expression. He shook his head and replaced the treasure, unseen to Eliane, back in his friend's hand. But El Amin was smiling, the bright, confident smile of a six-year-old, sure of his gift. Something for Samuel to keep to remember El Amin. Samuel would have other friends in France, surely, Eliane reassured herself as she wiped her eyes. But he was old enough to understand what leaving meant. And his little heart hurt.

From across the field, another figure approached, waving, with a basket on her head. Madira! Eliane left the window and, picking up José, rushed out into the yard.

"I forgot to give you the oranges! Such sweet oranges for the trip. For the children." She set the basket down, and the women embraced. They both knew the oranges were a pretext to say one last good-bye.

Eliane swallowed, but still her throat felt full, as if an orange itself were stuffed in the back and she was slowly choking.

Madira read the suffering. "It will be over soon," she said ambiguously.

"I will never forget you," Eliane whispered, her voice catching. It was pointless to promise letters. Her friend could not read. And a visit? Would she ever return to Algeria?

"El Amin," Madira called to her son. The boys looked up suddenly, their eyes narrowed as if daring their mothers to pronounce the judgment. The end of a boyhood friendship.

Madira nodded, and El Amin came obediently to her. The sun was hot, and a quick wind stirred the sand so that the children shielded their eyes.

"Good-bye, Madira," Eliane said. "God be with you."

Madira smiled. El Amin waved to Samuel. The woman and child turned and walked across the field, past the orange groves and the olive trees. Samuel ran into the house as Eliane cradled the baby in her arms and watched them disappear in the horizon.

4

Anne-Marie stood looking out the bedroom window. The streets were silent even though the quarantine had been lifted that morning. There was nothing to see but black sky. A hard knot sat in her stomach and felt like it was growing like a cancer. She blinked back tears.

She heard Moustafa enter the room, but as he came gently beside her, she could not look in his eyes. She buried her head in his shirt, feeling suddenly sick. *I don't want to go.* She only mouthed the words.

It had been almost simple for all these months. There had been nothing safe around them, so they had built their safety in each other. And she had let herself love him. But now this choice. Reunion with Ophélie meant separation from Moustafa.

He was a good man, her loyal friend. Even in betraying her those months ago, he had tried to protect her. To act her enemy so he could be with her. She loved him for his fierce devotion.

She had known he loved her all those years ago, though at first she had dismissed it as a silly infatuation. He was just a twelve-year-old boy. Her best friend. But he had never once faltered. Every time she had needed him, he was there. Year after year, despite all the times she had run, rebellious and afraid, into the arms of another.

And then the love had simply appeared at the doorstep of her heart one day months ago in that prison-like room in the Casbah, and she had said, "Of course." So simple. There had really been only one other whom she had ever loved, and now, ironically, that man was taking her away from Moustafa again.

"Moustafa, come with me to France. Please," she said, looking up at him.

He brushed his hand through her hair, his eyes still full of devotion. Then he tightened his embrace, lifting her off the ground as if she were a doll. He breathed heavily, burying his face in the nape of her neck. She felt his hot tears.

Two months ago they had said good-bye, but fate had brought her back to him. How many times had he saved her?

"I want to be with you always, Moustafa. Please. Please come build a life with me in France."

He set her down, cupping her face in his hands. "Do you mean it, my *habibti*?"

She nodded and felt a smile cross her lips. "I mean it."

He smiled too, and the gentle gesture made her ache all the more. He kissed her forehead, leaving his lips there, lost in thought, then took her hands in his and stepped back. She wished she were wearing something stunning. A low-cut cocktail dress that hugged her in all the right places. She wanted to be beautiful for him tonight.

"I cannot come with you now." He brought her close to him again before she could protest. "But I will come. If you really want me, with all that will mean, I will come. First I must help my family escape. You know what independence will mean for the harkis. But somehow I will get my family away. And if you want me, Anne-Marie, I'll come. You are all I have ever wanted."

He brought his lips to hers, and when he kissed her, she felt stunning indeed.

The rumors had grown so that no one was sure what was fact and what was fiction. Whole families were being murdered on the way to the ferries. The time to leave was in the middle of the night. And carefully. David had been in Algiers for only a week, but he had seen enough to believe anything. He sat beside Marcus Cirou in the front seat of the old Renault 4 with its ripped upholstery. Marcus leaned forward in intense concentration, never taking his eyes from the road.

In the backseat Anne-Marie sat rigid, her hands in her lap, physically distancing herself from Moustafa, whose arm hung limply over her shoulder. David watched them in the rearview mirror as the car crept through the alleys of Bab el-Oued toward the sea.

He wasn't prepared for what they saw at the port. An army of people was spread across the docks like frightened nomads. Women with small children asleep in their laps, men pacing nervously, smoking cigarettes and blowing blue puffs into the cool night air. An exodus. Like the Israelites with Moses. The pied-noirs were running from Algeria, and only the sea stood in their way.

He climbed out as Moustafa helped Anne-Marie from the car. With a simple nod of his head, Marcus was off. Anne-Marie clutched Moustafa's arm and let out a low moan. "Look at all the people. We'll never get out of here."

There was a faint edge of panic in her voice. David was determined to stifle it. "I've heard it may be a day's wait, perhaps two. But our turn will come. Don't worry." She limped between the two men onto the nearest docks. At their feet people lay sleeping, oblivious.

"It's still a few hours till dawn. Try to sleep, Anne-Marie. There's nothing to fear." David shuffled around several families huddled together and found a space near the edge of the dock. He sat down awkwardly. Moustafa joined him, offering his hand to Anne-Marie. She did not speak but, as if in a trance, took his hand and seated herself beside him, staring ahead at the smooth black sea. After a moment she rested her head against the small suitcase she had been carrying, pulling her legs up beneath her. She closed her eyes. Moustafa pulled off his coat and covered her with it.

Dawn was just breaking over the city of Algiers when Hussein arrived at the docks, still rubbing the sleep from his eyes. A scowl was on his face, which he hoped covered his fear and that other painful sensation somewhere inside. He had left the house even before his mother awoke as he had done on the three previous mornings. She never questioned him but waited anxiously each day. One day he would not come back, and after a while she would turn mournful eyes toward the other Arab women who wept for their lost sons, and they would understand.

The docks were humming with activity. Hundreds of pied-noirs crowded together, clutching children and small suitcases. From the distance it looked to Hussein like victims from some natural disaster, waiting at a shelter for help. He saw their rescuer, looming out at sea, slowly approaching the docks. A paquebot, one of those huge ferries that could carry hundreds of people. It was a pitiful scene. Ali would gloat, but Hussein took no pleasure in it. He simply felt drained, weak, and afraid.

He stuck out in this crowd with his soft brown skin, and he could not ignore the cold, harsh stares as he squeezed in and out of the mob, looking for Anne-Marie. Ali's instructions were clear. He was to find her, show her a drawing of the Huguenot cross, and plead for help. The story was made up in his mind, and he kept repeating it until it seemed more true of his life than what he had actually lived.

By four in the afternoon the crowds had thinned. Two ferries had already left the port, and there was hope for a third before dusk.

"You see, we'll be on the boat by tonight," David said in an almost triumphant manner.

Moustafa touched Anne-Marie's face with the back of his hand. She felt the stiffness in his fingers as she placed her hand over his. She tried to smile, but it caught on her lips. She was hungry, and her legs were beginning to throb.

She had tried to push away thoughts of the last time she stood on these docks. Then they had been deserted, except for the handful of children with her ... and one of Ali's snipers. The throbbing in her legs reminded her of the bullet wounds, the fall into the icy water ... and Moustafa, appearing out of nowhere. Moustafa her savior. Moustafa her lover. In only an hour, maybe two, she would touch his lips with her fingers to seal in the memory, and then she would whisper good-bye.

"I think I'll walk about a little," she said. She brought her thin jacket closer together, fastening a button. The wind had picked up, and the whitecaps on the sea were blowing along rapidly as if in a hurry to catch something.

Mingling among the people, she listened to snatches of conversation and watched the dull, tired faces. A young woman was struggling to nurse a baby, calling out to two children who chased each other. Something in the woman's face looked familiar. Anne-Marie found herself staring. A young boy dashed past, stepping on her toe.

"Samuel! *Mais alors!* Calm down!" the young mother called. She looked up at Anne-Marie. "*Je suis desolée.* Sorry."

"It's nothing." She leaned down to where the woman sat. "Eliane?" she whispered. "Is it you? Eliane Cebrian?"

The woman removed the baby from her breast, startled. She looked quizzically into Anne-Marie's eyes. "Yes, but do I know—" Then she gave a short gasp, and her face lit up in a broad smile. "Anne-Marie! Anne-Marie Duchemin! I would have never recognized you. You're so ... so changed." Her voice betrayed concern. "How are you?"

Before Anne-Marie could answer, Eliane chuckled, but it was a bitter laugh. "How indeed, if you're here with the rest of us, *n'est-ce pas?*" She shook her head. "Anyway, sit down. Are you alone? Is your daughter ..."

"My daughter is in France. I'm going to meet her."

"Oh, well, what a relief. How wonderful. We should make the next ferry, from the looks of it. How good to have a chance to catch up after so long."

"Yes, that will be good." Anne-Marie stood. "I'll be back, then. I've only to retrieve my bag. A friend is watching it for me."

Eliane laughed again, and it was the musical, carefree laugh that Anne-Marie remembered from years ago at her neighbors' farmhouse. "Take your time. I'm not going anywhere, as you can see!"

When Anne-Marie reappeared from another part of the crowded dock, she looked to David suddenly years younger. Her gait was stronger and her eyes held a flicker of surprise.

"Moustafa! David! You'll never believe it. I've run into my neighbor, the woman who lived next door to us while I was growing up—Eliane Cebrian. Remember her, Moustafa? I haven't seen her in years." She was almost breathless with excitement. "She's over there with her children. Isn't it wonderful? We'll be on the same boat. Come with me, Moustafa. She'll be so happy to see you again."

"You go along, my *habibti*. I'll come shortly," Moustafa said softly. "I want to get you a few things to eat. From the looks of it, they won't be serving couscous on board."

"No, you're right. Not couscous. And I'm starving. But where will you find anything?"

"I've been watching the crowds. There must be a little *épicerie* and a few cafés not far away. Now where will I find you?"

She pointed to the adjoining dock. "You see, near the front. She has a baby in her arms. No, not there—further away. See? A little boy is running beside her."

"Yes, I see. Who would believe it! Eliane Cebrian. Good. Then I'll be back in a little while."

David watched the young couple, feeling awkward. It was as if he were not there with them.

Anne-Marie glanced toward him. "Do you want to come with me, David?"

"No, you go ahead. I'll go with Moustafa. It looks as though we won't be waiting long." He pointed to the sea, where another paquebot floated into view in the distance. "Save me a spot if I'm late."

He was sorry the moment he spoke, because the carefree expression left her face at once. "I'm kidding," he said. "Go on. Find your friend. We'll be back soon."

He left with Moustafa, following a handful of men who were heading toward shops in the distance. Across the wide boulevard that emptied onto the port, they walked behind the chic stores into a small street running perpendicular to the boulevard. He could see a boulangerie sign near the end of the street.

David was not thinking of anything but a good *baguette* filled with ham and cheese when three youths appeared from nowhere—Arab boys. They were laughing, but there was anger in their eyes. The tallest, wiry and thin, spoke with disgust in his voice. "Well, if it isn't another hungry pied-noir going to stock up on bread before the long trip to France. And he's here with a harki boy. Everybody knows what happens to harki boys, don't they?"

He motioned to his friend, shorter, sullen, no older than seventeen, who stepped forward and drew a switchblade. "Aren't we in luck today, *les gars*? Two for the price of one. Doesn't look like you'll be taking that ferry ride after all."

David felt more anger than fear. They were merely boys, threatening with knives. He was ready to fight; his shoulder ached, but at least his arm was free of the sling. But before he had a chance to react, Moustafa pulled out a revolver and pointed it at the boys. "Leave us!" he yelled. "You think you own Algeria and everyone in it. You think murder is a game. Get out."

The three boys scrambled away, one of them turning to curse him: "You're done for, harki boy. You'll never leave this country alive." They fled down the alley.

David placed a hand on Moustafa, who was trembling violently. "Let's get out of here. I shouldn't have let you come down to the docks. It's too dangerous. Did you know those guys?"

"No. But they know us. They know every last stinking traitor and their families. That kid was right. We'll never get out of here."

"Good thing you had that gun. I didn't know—"

"I never leave the apartment without it." He chuckled without humor. "A gift from the last person who tried to kill me. One of Ali's men."

They bought several sandwiches and a bottle of water, but David had lost his appetite. The harkis would be massacred, just like the Jews. There was no escape for them. Didn't anyone care?

His mind was whirling now, wondering. If Anne-Marie had a friend on the boat now, a companion to help her make the trip, maybe ... could he not finish his mission?

But what was his mission? At first it had been Operation Hugo, the mission to help Anne-Marie rescue those children threatened by Ali Boudani. That he had accomplished, yes, but his mission was also simply to help Anne-Marie—the mother of his child. This would be his final help to her. First she would have Ophélie, and then she would have Moustafa. She would have her impossible love.

He was unsure, almost angry at himself for thinking of it. Gabriella would not understand, and neither would Ophélie. Mother Griolet needed him. But the mission....

"Where will you go, Moustafa?" he asked softly.

"I'll be okay. Don't worry. Just get Anne-Marie back to France."

"I'm not going back. Not yet." He spoke with conviction.

"What?" The young Arab wrinkled his brow in disbelief. "What are you saying?"

"I'm staying with you. I'm going to make sure you get to France. I'm doing it for her."

"You're crazy, David Hoffmann. You can't. The harkis aren't your problem."

"You saved my life back there. I figure if I stick around long enough, I might be able to return the favor." He saw the distrust in Moustafa's eyes. "Please, Moustafa. It's the least I can do for you. The least I can do for her."

Moustafa narrowed his eyes. "You really mean it, don't you? You really are a crazy American." He shook his head and cursed, but David saw a glimmer of hope in Moustafa's eyes.

It was almost dusk when Hussein saw her. He blinked twice to be sure. She was sitting on a small suitcase, her straight black hair thrown back as she talked animatedly to a short, plump woman holding a sleeping baby. Yes! The fine, thin face, the small nose and dark eyes, the thick brows. Ali was right. Once she must have been beautiful. Now she looked disheveled, out of place, like the rest of the pied-noirs.

Nervously he inched toward her on the dock. She was only fifty feet away. His mouth went dry and his mind blank. Who was he? The story Ali had invented for him seemed trapped somewhere in the back of his throbbing head. He retrieved the note from his pocket.

When he reached the two women, it was the other one who noticed him first and motioned with suspicious eyes to Anne-Marie. Even before she had turned around, Hussein was on his knees beside her.

"*Mademoiselle Duchemin?* It is you, *non?*" He thought of his mother, and that brought the necessary tears to his eyes. "I've been searching for you all these weeks. Please, please, will you take me with you?" He leaned forward and whispered. "My father has been murdered, my mother too, and my cousin's father. And last week, my cousin and his mother disappeared. They will kill me too if I stay. Please. I have heard you have a safe place in France for harki children." He produced the note with its funny cross and cryptic message.

The woman called Anne-Marie stared at Hussein, her mouth open. It took a moment for her to speak. "Where did you get this?"

"From Mme el Gharbi, before she was killed. She said if I would only show it to you, you would understand."

"You knew Mme el Gharbi? You know her children?"

For a brief moment Hussein panicked. He could not remember the names of the children. "I do not know them well."

The woman with the baby was staring pitifully at him. "Whatever is he talking about, Anne-Marie?"

The young woman did not look at her friend. "It's too long to explain right now. Perhaps later." She took Hussein's hand, and the gesture startled him. He pulled back in fright. "No, don't worry. I won't hurt you. What's your name?"

"Hussein."

"I … I don't know what to say to you, Hussein. Perhaps, yes, surely there would be room for you at the orphanage."

Hussein fell on his knees again, head bowed. "I will do anything. Only don't leave me here. Please. They say you are a woman of great mercy. Prove it to me, I beg you. Prove it." He buried his head in his hands and prayed to Allah that she would say yes.

The giant paquebot huffed and steamed into port, crawling slowly to the dock. Its decks were completely empty, and it looked like a forlorn whale rising out of the sea in a children's fairy tale. David was walking briskly in front of Moustafa and reached the docks first. Moustafa caught up with him and produced a bag full of sandwiches. One glance assured David that there would be no mention of the incident with the Arab youth. But at the right moment he would tell Anne-Marie of his decision.

It was not like him to act impulsively. Something within was propelling him to do so. Something strong and final. Moustafa would get to France. He was convinced he could get Moustafa's family on another boat soon. They would all flee within the next weeks, while there was still room, before the rest of the harkis turned on their heels and ran. Anne-Marie would have that. He did not dwell on the other part: the disappointment in Gabby's eyes when only Anne-Marie descended from the train. The betrayal she might feel. Later he would have time to explain to Gabby.

A young Arab who looked no more than ten was sitting with the women. Moustafa had slowed his gait and was eyeing the boy suspiciously.

Anne-Marie stood and caught Moustafa's arm. "See, Eliane. It's as I told you. Moustafa is with me."

The woman called Eliane rose and embraced Moustafa with a kiss on each cheek. "I never expected such a reunion between old neighbors." She had chestnut eyes, cheerful, kind eyes.

Moustafa reached out for the baby. "Rémi's littlest son I suppose?"

"Yes, the other two are over there. Restless." She cleared her throat. "Rémi brought us here last night. He's back at the farm now. Anne-Marie tells me you won't leave." The woman touched his arm. "Moustafa, if you ever need help, go to Rémi."

David immediately liked this woman. She at least had some hope left in her in spite of the war. He glanced down at the boy, and Anne-Marie spoke.

"David, Moustafa. This is Hussein. He's only just found me. And look, look...." She held out a slip of paper with the Huguenot cross scribbled in the corner.

Moustafa took it quickly. "What does he want?" His voice was brusque.

"He's a harki's son. He knew Mme el Gharbi and her children. He's orphaned, like so many others, and begs to go with us. Oh, David! What do you think? Surely the orphanage will take one more?"

David suddenly felt claustrophobic. He had not expected this. His mind was still spinning with his own decision. The boy was wiping tears from his face.

"Perhaps there would be room at the orphanage. It's so overcrowded now, what would one more child matter?" He shook his head. "What do you think, Moustafa?"

Moustafa touched the boy's shoulder. "You've lost your parents?" The child nodded.

"Let him go. Yes, send him on."

David felt a release of tension and broke in quickly. "Anne-Marie, I won't be going yet. I've decided to stay behind for a week or so. Until Moustafa can get his family out."

Anne-Marie's face drained of color. "You're staying too? But, but what about—"

"Eliane will keep you company on board. If you have any trouble, she'll be there to help you." Moustafa broke in as if he had already rehearsed the lines.

As indeed he had, David thought.

"Of course. Of course, I'll be glad to do whatever I can." Eliane nodded.

"Here's the address of the orphanage and the phone number. Call them when you get into Marseille. Ask for Mother Griolet." David fished in his pocket for some bills. "And here's some money.

This will be enough for the boat and the train. We won't be long. Tell them that. Tell Ophélie that Papa won't be long." He thought of Gabriella again and wished he had time to scribble a note. "And tell Gabby ... tell Gabriella that ..."

They were all staring at him, the small group, and he turned his eyes down. "Tell her that 'ignorant armies clash by night.' She'll understand."

Passengers were rushing to the paquebot.

"Hurry now, quickly, get on," Moustafa said, but his voice cracked.

David shared his pain. He walked ahead toward Eliane and helped her gather the bags and children, motioning for the boy to follow. He left Anne-Marie alone with Moustafa to say what he hoped desperately would not be their final words.

People were pushing and shoving, children irritable and crying as the line toward the ferry formed. Tickets did not seem to be a requirement; just get on and get out. Hussein felt sick to his stomach. Sick with excitement and fear.

So Moustafa Dramchini was here too. Hussein wanted to run and tell Ali. Both of them were here. He clutched the suitcase in his hands, hoping no one would guess that there were firearms within, wrapped amid his clothes. He was going to France with Anne-Marie Duchemin. It had been rather easy after all. And surely Ali could deal with Moustafa.

The plank was lowered. It looked to Hussein like the mouth of a great fish, waiting greedily to swallow these filthy pied-noirs. That would suit everyone just fine, he supposed, if they were swallowed up at sea.

Anne-Marie, Moustafa, and David were pushing him along now. An officer stepped in his way. "Who is this?" he asked angrily.

"A harki's son, sir. Orphaned. We're taking him with us." Anne-Marie's voice was shaking.

The officer placed a hard hand on Hussein and shoved him out of the way. "No room for harkis on this boat. Can't you see we're clear full as it is?"

Hussein heard the thumping of his heart. He didn't dare to speak.

"P-please," Anne-Marie stammered. "The child's all alone."

"Did you hear me?" the officer demanded. "If you want to get on this boat, come quickly, but leave the Arabs to take care of themselves. Go on, boy. We've got no room for you."

Hussein turned to flee, but Moustafa caught him.

"Hold on, son," he said. Then he looked at Anne-Marie and said, "I'll bring him with me. Later. Go on. Don't worry."

She nodded halfheartedly, blew Moustafa a kiss, and limped up the gangplank after Eliane.

Hussein cursed his luck. But then he smiled to himself. Moustafa Dramchini had just promised to bring him along. Things could be worse.

5

Mother Griolet laid the letter down on the mahogany desk, then picked it up again. She considered tearing it into thin strips and depositing them in the wastebasket. It was the third one this week. The same polite opening followed by the same questions. The same accusation. *What is going on in Castelnau, and why is our daughter's education suffering? Is this exchange program perhaps too much for you now?* She sighed.

Caroline Harland was responsible. She had threatened to write her father about M. Hoffmann's long absences, and doubtless the word had spread among the other parents. Oh, that silly, pompous girl! Jealous of her housemate Gabriella, no doubt, for winning the affections of the handsome American *professeur.* Now three polite, firm, threatening letters sat on her desk, with more sure to come.

It was true she had been distracted lately. They all had—David, Jean-Louis, Gabriella, and the Sisters. Too many irons in the fire. It had always been her weakness. She was rarely sick and had found it easy to rise before dawn all these years. She worked and gave and seemed never to need a break.

She rested her face in the palms of her hands and felt very old. Perhaps she had been wrong to participate in the rescue of the children—but it had seemed so right. Children who were not merely victims of war, but targeted by a madman for murder. She had rescued children before, and God had blessed it.

But during the other war, she had only had the orphanage to manage. The university exchange program had come later. She frowned, reminding herself that she'd had no idea David Hoffmann was involved in the smuggling operation to save Arab children from a vengeful madman when she hired him. It was not her fault.

Just as quickly she reprimanded herself. She was slipping into self-pity, defending herself. That was not to be tolerated.

She leafed through the children's files. Adoption prospects were not bright. Young couples wanted to adopt healthy, cooing babies, not wounded children. Yet in the past she usually found homes for them. She had rarely had to send a fifteen-year-old off alone to the state's care.

But in the past she had been dealing with French children. Plain French, not pied-noir, and certainly not Arab. Perhaps some of the new children's parents were still alive. Perhaps they would flee to France too, as so many were doing, and find their children. She could only wait and pray and keep working.

She hoped David would return soon. Maybe that would solve the problem of the angry letters. He would come back for the trip to Paris and charm the girls so they would write glowing reports home to their parents. The year would finish successfully, as in the past. If only he would come back.

Poor Jean-Louis, droning along, annoying the girls because he was fat and bald and boring. It was as if those girls needed M. Hoffmann to help them dream and flirt.

"Bother it all," she muttered to herself. *"Ce n'est pas possible."* The program had thrived for years before David Hoffmann came. He was not the only thing that held it together! The girls must simply grow up.

She glanced at the letter again, then closed her eyes. *Dear God, forgive me, please. I am trying to figure this out on my own. Hélas! I can take the criticism from the parents. I can even take the idle talk from the townspeople. But for the children. For the children, please help me find a way.*

She stood with difficulty, pushing back the chair and resting with both hands on the desk. She took two deep breaths, straightened up, smoothed her black habit, and left the office.

Gabriella leaned on the desk and faced her fellow students. She could feel her face going red even before she said a word.

"Hi." It was all she could think of.

The girls giggled.

"Go on, Gabriella. Don't be nervous," Stephanie Thrasher said.

Gabriella smiled, thankful for the support from one of her fellow boarders at Mme Leclerc's.

"Well, yes. M. Vidal has kindly asked me to teach M. Hoffmann's class for the next few days. I ... I have always been fascinated by the work of Victor Hugo. His genius was in poetry, drama, and fiction, and he's been called the greatest writer since Shakespeare.

"Like Shakespeare, he was adored during his life and enjoyed the praises of many. He was a powerful man, with a huge appetite and endless energy. They say he would pop a whole orange in his mouth and eat it—without removing the peel."

The girls laughed again, and Gabriella's legs stopped shaking so much.

"He was very active politically, using his literary genius to either ridicule politicians or enhance their stature. But of course, he is best known for his novel *Les Misérables*. It was actually a collection of stories and appeared as a continuing humanitarian epic, holding the whole world in rapt attention month by month."

She picked up a hefty paperback copy of the book. "Of course, we will not tackle the work in its entirety, but rather this version that David—" She stopped, mortified, then cleared her throat.

Stephanie smiled back nervously. Caroline, on the other hand, looked delighted with Gabriella's slip and batted her eyes.

"This version that M. Hoffmann provided. He left a note indicating that we will be studying this novel for the next two weeks."

Caroline raised her hand politely.

"Yes, Caroline," Gabriella responded.

"Gabriella, do you have any idea when M. Hoffmann will be back? I thought maybe since you and he are such ... good friends, you might have an idea."

Gabriella felt her cheeks burning. "I really can't say," she mumbled.

Stephanie stood up quickly. "Hey, Gabriella, would you like some help handing out the books?"

A wave of relief came over her. "Yes, Stephanie, that would be great." She walked behind David's desk and stared at the neatly written notes that he had left for M. Vidal.

Come back, she groaned inside. *I can't do this. I need you.* Her throat tightened. Not two weeks ago he had held her, kissed her, handed her back the exam that he had crafted just for her. It seemed like forever. She thought for the hundredth time of his brief note at the bottom of the last page … *When you begin to question, read this exam again and know that I meant every word.*

Gabriella glanced up and realized that the girls were waiting. How long had they been staring at her, letting the silence speak for itself? She ran her hands through her curly mane of red hair and stared back. But for the longest moment, she could not think of anything to say.

The coffee sat untouched in the dainty demitasse cups that Monique Pons used for her daily visit with Yvette Leclerc. The steam curled between them as they talked.

"Well, I am sorry to say it, but she is asking for trouble, bringing all those other orphans here at this time," Monique declared.

"Yes, but Mother Griolet has been so good for the town. I don't see how she does it all. *Ooh là!* She's a good five years older than I, and heaven forbid that I would have to take care of all those wild orphans *and* the young women. Three American girls are enough to keep my hair graying!" Yvette finally noticed her cup of coffee and took a sip mechanically. "But you're right, of course, Monique. Castelnau does not need to be invaded by pied-noirs, even if they are only children. Goodness knows we've enough problems of our own."

"And it isn't just pied-noir children, mind you," Monique said. "I've heard from a reliable source that there are Arabs there too. Arabs! They can stay in their soon-to-be-independent country. There are enough of them swarming around France already." She shook her head forcefully, and the loose skin under her chin jiggled back and forth.

"But, Monique, these aren't just any Arabs. They're the orphaned children of the harkis. They did fight for us, you know."

"Humph! It's all the same to me. Let them patch things up between themselves, the Arabs. We don't need them in France. Stealing our jobs, producing a brood of kids that drains the government! It's a mistake, and I don't mind if she hears it from me."

"Oh, don't you worry. Mother Griolet has already heard it from half the town, I'm sure."

Monique picked up her china cup and regarded it intently. "Tepid coffee! Useless!" She bustled to the sink, where she washed the coffee down the drain. She poured herself another cup and sat back down at the table, satisfied.

The sky was clear, and from the deck of the ferry Anne-Marie counted the stars, laid out brilliantly without the lights of a city to obscure them. It looked as if a gleeful painter had taken his brush filled with creamy paint and flicked it time and again across the black canvas of sky.

Every part of her body ached, but especially her legs. She wondered if they would support her when she finally forced herself to rise in the morning. For the moment six-year-old Samuel Cebrian lay curled in her lap asleep. Once he had cried out, talking to some unseen person in his dream and then laughing loudly so that those seated around her had frowned and stared.

Eliane sat beside her, propped up against her two suitcases. Her daughter, Rachel, leaned on one shoulder while Eliane held the baby to her breast. Everyone slept.

The ferry was crammed with pied-noirs. There was no comfort and certainly no couscous. Anne-Marie smiled wryly, thinking of Moustafa's comment. She was thankful for the sandwiches she had been able to share with the Cebrians earlier in the evening.

She shivered involuntarily and wished she could fall asleep. The night was chilly, and her coat was wrapped around Samuel. She placed her hand on the boy's hair, stroking it gently, and for a moment she imagined it was Ophélie in her lap. Just for tonight she let herself think of Ophélie, not with fear and apprehension but with a hope that seemed sure. A hope that tomorrow she would hold her daughter in her arms. Seven cruel months of separation. If she thought long enough about Ophélie, she knew the other ache, the painful longing for Moustafa, might disappear.

She was somehow peaceful, thinking of David there with him. Alone, each one of these men wielded a power that amazed her. Together they would surely be indestructible. She would not believe that she might never see them again.

The small distant spots of white, so silent and steady, made her envious. They were always in their place. Even when light made them invisible to her eyes, they were there. Did they have decisions to make? Did they choose between two places in the universe and blink good-bye to neighboring stars, drifting off to another corner of the sky? She thought they did not.

But man was made to choose. It was the constant breath of life, the daily struggle: always a choice, even in not choosing. This pitiful lost flock of humanity drifting on the sea was being flung out like the stars to fill another spot of earth. But no one was guiding, no one pointed the way. Their destiny was as random as the galaxies.

When light finally did paint the skies with streaks of orange and yellow, Anne-Marie opened her eyes, squinting to enjoy the changing picture before her. Somewhere in the night she must have fallen asleep.

"You aren't too cold?" It was Eliane whispering beside her. "Look at you, Anne-Marie! You're icy to touch! Take back your coat. Samuel will be fine."

Obediently Anne-Marie lifted the light wool coat from the boy's shoulders and wrapped it around herself. She rested her arms on the boy's back, hoping he would not awaken.

Rachel slept still, but baby José stared wide-eyed at Anne-Marie, a smile forming on his lips. Then he screwed up his face, and his skin wrinkled like that of an old man. She could see the wail of hunger coming, but before he uttered a sound, Eliane put him to her breast.

"It won't do to have you wake the whole ship, wee one. *Mais non!* We need all the friends we can get right now." She flashed a smile at Anne-Marie. "Do you know where you'll be going then, once we land?"

"I have a number to call when we get to Marseille. Ophélie is staying at an orphanage near Montpellier. I'll just go there, I suppose. And you?"

"I haven't the slightest idea! Well, hardly. Rémi said I should stay in a hotel in Marseille until I can get a place of our own."

"And when will Rémi come?" Anne-Marie asked cautiously. She was not used to exchanging information so freely.

Eliane's face clouded. "I don't know. He wants to try and save the farm from the looters. To see what the situation is like after independence on July 2."

"You hope to return then, to Algeria?" Anne-Marie wondered if her voice betrayed her surprise.

"Hope, yes, but of course no one knows." Eliane cleared her throat. "May I ask you a question, Anne-Marie?"

"Yes, I suppose," she answered softly. There was something in the cheerful, kind voice of Eliane that pleased Anne-Marie.

"I couldn't help but overhear the conversation with the young boy and what he said about you providing a safe place in France. And the slip of paper with the cross. That was the Huguenot cross, n'est-ce pas?"

"Yes, but it has no spiritual significance. It was only … only a sign for us, you see. A way to communicate."

"And the tall young man. He's quite handsome. I've seen him before, haven't I? Years ago at your father's house. He was a good friend to you then?"

Anne-Marie felt the color rise in her cheeks. "Yes, a friend …"

"I'm prying. It's a bad habit. Forgive me."

"No, no. It isn't that." Anne-Marie looked into the soft, round face of Eliane, and suddenly she wanted so badly to tell this kind young woman what life had been like for her these past years. "If I tell you my story, will you keep it for yourself?" she whispered.

Eliane smiled and patted her arm lightly, as if Anne-Marie were another of her children. "I won't breathe a word, Anne-Marie." Her eyes filled with compassion. "Whom should I tell anyway? I know no one in France. Your secrets are safe with me."

For hours the two women talked. They spoke of the past, of the farms that had been in their families for years. Of the wealthy land-owner who rented them the land. Of their Arab friends. Anne-Marie felt suddenly free as she explained to Eliane what she had never been able to explain before, not even to Moustafa or David. The baby, the pain, the impossibility of telling David.

She spoke of Ali's brutality and how she had become his pawn, collecting valuable information for him. She let each detail tumble forth, afraid that if she stopped talking she would never again have the courage to tell it all. And each time she looked into Eliane's eyes she saw compassion and at times tears.

"So you see, I'm a soiled woman. And yet Moustafa loves me still. We know it cannot work, but it is all I hope for. Moustafa and Ophélie."

"And this man David? You have no feelings anymore for the father of your child?"

"Yes, I do. But they are feelings that torment me, feelings of the past. And he loves another woman. He's not right for me, Eliane. I cannot explain it, but I know."

Eliane looked away, waving to Samuel and Rachel, who were grasping the railings, laughing as the seawater sprayed their faces. "Be careful, you two. *Attention, eh?*"

José slept peacefully, bundled in a coat on Eliane's lap. It seemed to Anne-Marie that she was weighing her words, choosing them carefully in her mind before she pronounced them out loud.

"Anne-Marie," she said finally, "there are things that you brought on yourself. But there are many other things that happened to you, terrible things. You must not carry the guilt. Don't stay a victim all of your life. It will do you no good." Suddenly she took Anne-Marie's hand, clasping it tightly in her own. "You have a chance to start over. It will be better now. I'm sure of it."

She spoke with such assurance that Anne-Marie felt she could almost believe it.

"Aren't you afraid, Eliane? Doesn't the unknown make you afraid?"

"Oh, yes, yes." She laughed, and her bobbed hair swung around her head. "I look at all of us on this wretched boat, and the rest of the pied-noirs, and I think, *No one wants us.* The French don't see us as one of them. And somehow I think they blame us for this awful war."

Eliane stared in front of her, but Anne-Marie was sure she was seeing something else besides the sea.

"I am afraid at times," she continued, "but then, I have my faith. You know. Like your father." She seemed embarrassed to say it. "I know you didn't agree with him, but it is that faith I trust in now."

"You liked my father, didn't you?"

"Your father was a wonderful man. There was such a tenderness beneath that rough military exterior."

"He gave me this," Anne-Marie said softly, pulling out the Huguenot cross from under her blouse. "We decided to make it our password for saving the children. But it was so much more to him. It was a symbol of what he believed."

"You have your father's courage, Anne-Marie. You've helped save lives. I hope one day you will share this faith." She looked at Anne-Marie quietly, penetratingly. Then she changed the subject. "There's something I've wanted to tell you ever since you found me. Your father left you a will. I was the executor, but you have never seen it because we didn't know how to find you. Rémi will send other trunks as soon as I get settled, and in one of those trunks I have stored your father's will. I'll bring it to you then, just as soon as I find it."

"His will? I never even thought of it. I couldn't even come to the funeral—everything happened so fast." She blinked back tears. "Yes, that would be nice, to have his will. A memento. Although I'm sure there is nothing left now."

Eliane nodded sadly. "You're right. Nothing at his farm, nothing in the banks in Algiers. I'm afraid we have lost it all. Not just you. All of us. We've lost our heritage."

A sadness had crept into her voice, but she brushed it aside.

"But we can start over. In just a few hours, you'll see. This is a chance to begin again. God will see us through."

Anne-Marie admired the young mother with the sunny disposition, but she knew that no God of Eliane or of her father would stoop down to help her. It was okay. She had grown used to being alone.

6

The Washington papers ran big headlines on the first of April 1962. Women and men alike still idolized John Glenn for his three orbits around the earth in February. The Americans might beat the Russians in the space race after all.

Troops were headed to Vietnam, but rumor had it that the war would soon be over. A little more American support, a few more troops shipped over, and the whole thing would be done with.

But on the home front, here in America, the situation looked sticky indeed. Whites and blacks were not getting along, and the South was protesting any rise toward equality. Crazy "freedom riders," intent on having the same rights as whites, were actually pushing their way onto buses. And the white lawmakers didn't respond graciously. Racial tension could be tasted in the air.

Roger Hoffmann slammed down the phone angrily in his office on Capitol Hill. Another belligerent reporter seeking information that Roger could not give. Would not give.

His steely six-foot-four frame towered over his desk. He was a handsome man for his fifty-four years, and he knew it. The flecks of silver in his black hair gave him a distinguished look, and he carried himself with cold, calculated confidence. His rare smile broke through like a sunbeam in a cloudy sky, at just the right moment, when a deal needed to be closed or a woman's favors won. No one needed to be told to respect Roger Hoffmann.

He sat down and spread his long, thin hands across the cherry finish of his desktop and sighed. From behind a tray of neatly stacked papers he drew out a picture of a young man dressed in black gown and mortarboard. The man in the photograph had the same lanky yet powerful build, the long, handsome face, the closely cropped black hair, the fine aristocratic nose, the thick black eyebrows and lashes. Only the eyes were different. They were Annette's eyes. Her beautiful black, brooding eyes.

He placed the picture back out of sight behind the file tray. Annette Levy Hoffmann, his lovely Jewish French bride, had been swept out of his life twenty years ago by the rifle of a cocky, bloodthirsty SS guard. That same gun had murdered little Greta, their three-year-old daughter. He could still see her cherubic face and ringlets of black hair and blue eyes. His blue eyes.

He could not bear to remember. For fifteen years he had lived with his son in a pained silence, never looking into those eyes that betrayed his mother's heritage. It wasn't that he didn't love his son. It was just the unbearable memories David's presence brought back.

Five and a half years had gone by since he had last really looked at his son. At the train station on a sultry September afternoon he shook David's hand and wished him well as he headed north to Princeton, Roger's own alma mater. Roger had been proud to send him there, proud of his son's achievements, proud of his own financial status that made an Ivy League school possible.

He had visited only twice, once for David's induction into an honor society and then for graduation. There had been no letters between them, no friendly comparing of notes about the good ol' days. The wall had been built brick by brick over fifteen years, and the geographical distance between them now only strengthened the stony silence.

Roger massaged his brow. Top of his class from Princeton, and now the kid had disappeared somewhere in Europe. What had the reporter said? The Algerian War. What the heck was David up to now? Roger remembered distastefully his son's affair with the daughter of a captain in the French army. But that was years ago. Why would he go back now, especially with the mess that country was in?

From under the neat stack of official government papers, Roger pulled out a newspaper clipping he had received anonymously two days ago. A remarkable story of a young man falling 160 feet to his death from the top of some ancient Roman aqueduct in the south of France. And another man, a David Hoffmann, falling as well—not to his death, but into the swollen waters of a normally placid river. A miraculous survival. No picture accompanied the article, but Roger was sure it was his son.

Roger folded the clipping and tucked it into a drawer. He did not have time to contemplate David's audacious acrobatics. Not today. Washington was waiting for him.

Gabriella stood on quay number 2 at the train station in Montpellier, holding tightly to Ophélie's hand. Her palms felt sweaty, and she hoped the child could not tell how nervous she was. In five minutes the train from Marseille was due to arrive, carrying Anne-Marie Duchemin and David Hoffmann.

Perhaps they would step off the train hand in hand, faces beaming with reunited love. Perhaps David would not dare to look her in the eye, embarrassed for her to read the truth she would find there. Perhaps ...

The sound of train wheels screeching pulled her back from her thoughts. Heart pounding, she watched the train slowly grind to a halt. Then she looked down at Ophélie. The child's eyes were shining.

"Oh, Bribri! I can't believe it. Mama is here! Mama and Papa!"

The doors to the train opened, and people began pouring out onto the quay. Gabriella's eyes searched up and down for Anne-Marie and David. Suddenly Ophélie let out a squeal, dropped Gabriella's hand, and dashed toward the end of the train. "Mama!" she cried. "Mama!"

Tears formed in Gabriella's eyes as Ophélie practically tackled her mother on the steps of the train. At once Gabriella admonished herself for her jealous thoughts. Anne-Marie Duchemin buried her face in her child's hair and wept.

She was but a wisp of a woman, thin, malnourished, limping badly. Suddenly Gabriella remembered what David had told her. *Moustafa fears she will die.* Indeed, Anne-Marie looked as if she had been battling death for a long time. A wave of pity swept over Gabriella as she watched the feeble young woman caress the cheek of her little girl.

But where was David?

After several minutes Ophélie took her mother's hand and led her toward Gabriella. "Bribri, I want you to meet Mama," she announced proudly.

Anne-Marie's strong grip startled Gabriella. Behind the tears, Gabriella saw deep gratitude.

"How can I thank you enough, *mademoiselle*, for all you have done for my daughter? Someday I hope I can return to you the blessing that you have given me." She gently kissed Gabriella on each cheek.

"You have a wonderful daughter," Gabriella said, clearing her throat with difficulty. "It has been a pleasure to get to know her."

The woman looked as if she might collapse right on the quay. "We must get your mother to the bus, Ophélie. She needs to sit down." Gabriella put an arm around Anne-Marie's waist to support her, then dared to ask. "David ... did David come back with you?"

Anne-Marie shook her head. "He got me to the boat and made sure I would have a place. But then, quite suddenly, he decided to stay behind with Moustafa—to stay and help until it is all over."

Gabriella did not want to hear any more. This was worse than she had imagined. She was not losing David to another woman, but to a country and a cause she could not understand. If he loved her as he claimed he did, why didn't he come back? She needed him here! He had classes to teach, and goodness knows there was an abundance of work with the orphans. Mother Griolet was completely overwhelmed.

The threesome stopped at a bench for Anne-Marie to sit down and rest. "He asked me to give you a message, *Gabrièle*," Anne-Marie said, pronouncing her name in French. "He said a strange phrase, but he was sure you would understand. Let me only remember...." She closed her eyes. "*Ah, oui, ça y est.* 'Ignorant armies clash by night.' That's what he said." She smiled almost apologetically.

At first the phrase made no sense at all to Gabriella. Anne-Marie had spoken in French. Then it dawned on Gabriella, as she translated it into English. "But that's from 'Dover Beach'!" she said aloud.

"Oh, I don't know it. Is it a poem?" Anne-Marie asked politely.

"Yes, a poem. By Matthew Arnold," Gabriella replied absently. "The last line." Her voice fell. She didn't want this message from David. She thought of the last lines of this pessimistic poem that she loved and feared.

And we are here as on a darkling plain
Swept with confused alarms of struggle and flight,
Where ignorant armies clash by night.

"Dover Beach" was beautiful in its tragic tone. The doubt and darkness between the speaker and his woman. But couldn't David have sent her a line of hope?

Ophélie and Anne-Marie were chattering excitedly together. They did not see her pain, and she was glad. She forced David's message out of her mind and regarded Anne-Marie with pity. She wore a white blouse and a black skirt that fell to her ankles. A black shawl covered her thin shoulders, and a light wool coat hung over one arm. She looked like a refugee. Gabriella supposed that indeed she was. A French citizen and yet a stranger in this land. A pied-noir.

Ophélie snuggled in her mother's lap, talking happily. "And you will meet Anne-Sophie and Christophe. And see my doll and the panties with the lace on them. And Mother Griolet has set up a bed for you ..."

"The bus is coming now," Gabriella interrupted softly. She helped Anne-Marie to her feet. Together they walked the short distance to the bus stop. With great effort, Anne-Marie stepped onto the bus as Gabriella and Ophélie steadied her. Mother and daughter found a seat together. Gabriella seated herself behind them, the words of the poem echoing in her mind.

The moment Anne-Marie stepped into the halls of St. Joseph, she felt safe. It seemed to her tired eyes the most idyllic plot of earth imaginable.

The nuns stood quickly, beaming, when Gabriella led her into the chapel.

A small elderly woman greeted her. "Welcome, *Mademoiselle Duchemin*. I'm Mother Griolet. We are delighted to have you among us." The nun kissed her tenderly on each cheek and then bent down toward Ophélie. "*Ma chérie*, would you like to introduce your mama to your friends?"

The scene moved in slow motion before Anne-Marie as her daughter led her by the hand to each child. Anne-Marie's eyes clouded with tears as she recognized the faces of the children she had helped to flee from Algeria. Several reached out to her and hugged her tightly.

Eventually she felt dizzy from standing and seated herself in a pew.

"My, how rude we've been!" the elderly nun exclaimed, coming beside her. "Ophélie, run ahead with Sister Rosaline and get a plate of food ready for your mother."

Anne-Marie watched her child scurry off proudly and felt a lump in her throat. Ophélie was healthy, beautiful, happy. It was more than she could have hoped. And now they were together.

"Can I bring you anything here?" Mother Griolet asked. Although her pure-green eyes sparkled, she looked tired to Anne-Marie. Tired like herself.

"No, *merci*. I'll just rest a moment longer, and then I'll be fine."

"Good. Then Gabriella will show you to your room. We're a bit tight on space. I hope you won't mind sharing with Sister Isabelle."

"No, of course not. Your hospitality is overwhelming."

"Well, I hope it will do," Mother Griolet said with a chuckle. "And M. Hoffmann has not come back, you say? That is too bad. Do you think he will be long?"

"I hope not, *Mère*. I'm sorry. He stayed to help a friend of mine. I hope they will both be coming soon."

"We will pray that God sees fit to bring them to us soon." The nun turned to the children. "Come along, *les enfants*. Dinner will be ready soon. *Allez-y!*"

The red-haired woman waited beside Anne-Marie while the children filed out of the chapel behind Mother Griolet. A timid Sister Isabelle followed in the rear, glancing shyly in her direction.

Everyone seemed kind. Sorry for her and kind. She stood up, ignoring the pain in her legs, forcing them forward. She tripped, and Gabriella caught her.

"Hold on to me if you need to," she said.

Anne-Marie obliged. She was a beautiful, angel-like woman, this Gabriella. It was no wonder David loved her, with her creamy skin and flaming hair and delicate face, the bright-blue eyes and fine, thin eyebrows, the long auburn lashes. She was sorry that David had not stepped off the train into this woman's waiting arms. He deserved a woman like Gabriella.

"Thank you so much for all you have done for us, for Ophélie and me," she repeated again as they walked through the building that Gabriella called the parsonage and out into the courtyard.

The red-haired young woman only smiled, a red flush creeping onto her face.

Jeanette Griolet pulled herself from her bed in the early-morning light. She shuffled her toes into a pair of worn gray slippers and gathered a blue cotton robe around her. Eyes closed, she breathed in slowly, concentrating, and winced.

"Jesus," she whispered as she felt for the bed and with great difficulty lay back down on top of the rumpled sheets. "Jesus," she cried as a pain stabbed at her. Involuntarily she clutched at her heart.

She thought of the orphans overflowing into every corner of the buildings. Who knew what to do with them? Who knew the right people to contact so that some would be adopted? Some stodgy old man from "higher up" would come and assume the leadership of this ancient orphanage when she was buried. Oh, the havoc it would cause.

She sat up straight in bed and said out loud, "No!" The action itself startled her. She felt as if she were wrestling, like Jacob, with God Himself. Her respiration came in long, encumbered breaths as she willed herself to stay right here on earth.

No, Jesus. Don't take me yet.

She lay back down, propping herself up on one feeble arm, afraid that if she stretched out completely, her soul would rise out of her body.

I have disobeyed You, Lord. You've been telling me for years now to pass on the baton, and I was too stubborn to listen. But You have my attention now, Holy God. Grant me only time enough to train these women.

She listened to her own heavy, labored breathing, but it seemed a stranger's. Surely this could not be her time to die? Sister Rosaline and Sister Isabelle would stay on. They did not have perhaps the capacity to teach and to work out the administrative details, but the food and the dormitories—those practical matters they handled like a dream. And dear Gabriella. Perhaps she would stay.

Will You not call her to stay here, God? In the world's eyes, it is perhaps a waste of brains and talent. But for the children ...

She felt herself slipping into sleep but forced herself to sit up.

And this young woman, Anne-Marie. She has only just arrived, but I can tell she has suffered. She understands the children. And she has nowhere else to go. Perhaps it is she You will choose.

Another sharp pain shot through her chest, and Mother Griolet cried out, green eyes shining. "Not yet, Lord!"

Don't punish the children because of a stubborn old woman's selfishness. Give me time ... a little time....

The strength to fight left her, and Mother Griolet slumped back on her bed. From somewhere far away she thought she heard a heavy thumping sound. It echoed in her ears, but she couldn't move.

7

The Monday-morning paper lay across the bed with its bold headline: EVIAN AGREEMENT OVERWHELMINGLY APPROVED. The day before, in a referendum opened only to French citizens living in France, voters had agreed to an independent Algeria.

Eliane put her head in her hands and cried.

The children were finally asleep, but she had no idea for how long. Since their arrival in France, bad dreams woke Samuel every night, and baby José slept fitfully, wailing from swollen gums and a stuffy nose. It was all natural, she reminded herself.

But she missed Rémi terribly. She missed curling up behind him in bed and feeling the warmth of his rough legs against her smooth skin. She missed laughing with him after the children slept peacefully and he would come to her, his strong arms encircling her waist.

"It's not so thin anymore," she would tease him. "I may never get my figure back, you know."

Then she would catch Rémi's eyes, all full of love as he held her and kissed her hair. "Don't change one bit," he would whisper. "Don't change a bit."

But here she was with other abandoned pied-noirs in a cheap hotel with sagging beds and torn wallpaper. Some of the fortunate ones had family to go to and money to spend, but most of them had just one small suitcase. It seemed as though the French regarded them all as spoiled rich children fallen on hard times and resented them for appearing on their doorstep.

Even at the church, le Temple Protestant, she had felt the cold stares. Harsh eyes, unsmiling faces peering down at her and her children as if they were curiosities in a peddler's shop. "Not here too, Lord," she had moaned.

Now she fiddled with the little paper that held the address of the orphanage.

"Please, call me. Let me know how you are," Anne-Marie had begged as they parted on the docks of Marseille six days earlier. "Thank you for all your help. You're as kind as I remember."

Eliane wiped her eyes and thought that it had been just the opposite. Anne-Marie had helped her. She had held the children in her arms on the ferry ride and watched them once they landed, while Eliane had inquired about a hotel.

Eliane tiptoed downstairs to the lobby, running her fingers over the French francs. Just to hear a friendly voice. That would be enough.

The news of Mother Griolet's heart attack shocked Castelnau. For a few days the gossip turned from the pied-noir and harki children at St. Joseph to the terrible shame it would be to lose Mother Griolet.

Jean-Louis Vidal contemplated the town's fickleness as he sipped a *pastis* in the *café-bar* on his way home, following the afternoon classes. He had seen Jeanette in the hospital that morning, so frail and still.

Jeanette, don't leave me yet. He shut his bloodshot eyes and remembered her as she had been so many years ago. Petite and feisty, determined, charismatic. His brother had loved her during the first war, and Jean-Louis knew why. A woman of faith and action. A rare woman indeed.

When the war claimed his brother's life, Jean-Louis, twelve years younger, was not quite an adolescent. Later, he had not dared declare his love for this nun who was so many years his senior. He did not possess the charm and easy speech of his brother. He had been sure that Jeanette Griolet would not turn in her nun's garb for him. But she had always cared for him as if they were united by the same pain that came from loss.

He placed a *casquette* on his balding head and stood up, leaving the pastis unfinished on the café table. He chuckled to himself. If her infirmity could turn him from so much drink, Jeanette would most assuredly lift her hands and sing "God be praised."

The breeze tickled his face as he shuffled out onto the cobblestones and retraced his steps to St. Joseph. The side door to the chapel was ajar, but the hollow church was empty. He took off his casquette and silently, cautiously, walked to the front of the chapel and knelt before the simple stone altar. Above, a ray of light seeped through the sole small stained-glass window, and he moved to the left, leaving the colored spot of sun unhindered on the stones beside him.

He crossed himself, head bent, and spoke in a voice that cracked with emotion. "She is a fine woman, *Seigneur*. All these years I have loved her, and I have asked nothing of You but to be near her. But now I ask that You spare her until … until I can tell her the truth. A little time, *mon Dieu*. Only a little time."

He rose shakily, eyes still turned down. The spot of light was a kaleidoscope of pale color splashed onto the old, worn stones. He watched it for a long time, until a cloud outside obscured the sun and the patch of color was gone.

Anne-Marie sat down on the lower bunk that belonged to Ophélie and ran her hand over the clean sheets. She touched the small chest of drawers at the foot of the bed and smiled, remembering Ophélie's delight as she showed off her new home. "These clothes are all mine, Mama! Mine!"

Anne-Marie smoothed the skirt she wore. It was a light wool black-and-white herringbone that Sister Rosaline had fished out of the clothes closet in the basement. When Anne-Marie had pulled it around her waist and fastened it, she had blushed at Sister Rosaline's enthusiastic *ooh là*.

"It fits you like a glove," the nun said. "You look like a model." She scurried back to the closet, returning with a white blouse and a matching herringbone jacket. "It's all from the same wealthy lady. Look at you, *Mademoiselle Duchemin*. You look like you've just stepped out of one of those fancy designer shops in Paris."

It was true that the clothes became her. It was like a small miracle. Even the black leather pumps that Sister Rosaline's sharp eye had uncovered fit comfortably with a little cotton stuffed in each toe. She was clothed like a princess, and she hadn't paid a *centime*. This place seemed made for miracles, as Ophélie said.

Just then her daughter raced into the dormitory, red faced, with dirt stains on both knees. "Oh, Mama!" she said, laughing and throwing her arms around Anne-Marie with such force that they both collapsed backward on the bed.

"Can you believe we are here together, *ma chérie*? Who would believe it? It's a fairy tale, *n'est-ce pas*?" She held Ophélie in her arms and drank in the smell of the afternoon on her clothes. "We're in the palace of a kind, aging queen—"

Ophélie interrupted her mother. "Yes, and we must pray, Mama, that Mother Griolet gets well soon."

"Yes, of course, sweetheart. That's true."

Even that sad news could not destroy the lyric peacefulness of the orphanage. It was a dream, and Anne-Marie was determined to do whatever she could to make the dream last, for Ophélie, for herself.

❀

Gabriella slipped silently into the hospital room where Mother Griolet lay asleep in a starched white bed. The nun's face looked pale and flat, the translucent glow gone. The skin sagged, pulling her closed mouth down into a frown.

Gabriella looked away, then sat down stiffly in a chair to wait. She needed Mother Griolet to open her eyes and listen. She had questions to ask, doubts to discuss with her elderly confidante. At once Gabriella felt a blush forming on her cheeks. It was shameful, she chided herself, to come to a hospital expecting to receive. For once Mother Griolet deserved to be the one cared for.

The nun's eyes flickered and opened. She looked around with a bewildered expression on her face until her eyes found Gabriella.

"My child," she whispered, clearing her throat. "How kind of you to come see me." She stretched out her hand from under the sheets, and Gabriella clasped it.

"How do you feel?"

Mother Griolet gave a feeble chuckle. "My child, don't look like that! It will frighten me. Do they all think I'm going to die? *Mais alors!* I have a bit of work to complete before I can meet my Maker."

She spoke in a light, kidding voice, but Gabriella saw that each breath came with effort.

"Shh. You rest. Of course we don't think you will die. But you did scare us! We're just waiting for you to hurry on home."

"Gladly. It's terrible to be confined to a bed like this." A faint sparkle had come into her green eyes. "And you, Gabriella, what makes you sad today?"

"Me? Nothing. Except, of course, it is disconcerting to see you here. But I'm sure you'll be better soon." She patted Mother Griolet's hand.

"And everything is running smoothly at the orphanage?"

"Yes, everyone is pitching in. Sister Rosaline and Anne-Marie mopped the dormitories this afternoon, and I changed the sheets. The children's lessons are coming along fine. It's all fine."

"Except that something is not quite right with you."

Gabriella reddened. "Why do you say that, Mother Griolet?"

"Your eyes, Gabriella. They aren't shining."

Gabriella twirled a strand of her hair between her fingers. Then she whispered, "It's Anne-Marie."

"Ah ... I see. She is not fitting in well? *C'est ça?*"

"No ... I mean, yes. She fits in fine. You won't believe how much better she looks in just these few days. Stronger, healthier. And she is so happy just to be here, in the orphanage. With Ophélie." Gabriella bit her lip. "The problem is, I don't feel one bit happy. I mean, look at her. She's lived through hell ten times over, she has no family, no work. What will become of her? And she has no faith. Yet she is happy. How can it be?"

As usual, Gabriella could not keep from speaking her heart. "And I'm jealous. Jealous of a woman who is half-starved, terrorized, alone with a child. I have a wonderful family. I have lots of possibilities for the future. I even have a young man who ... who cares for me, I think. And I have the Lord. All this, and I don't feel joy. I feel fear. Yet she is happy and thankful, and I ..." She covered her face with her hands. "Why am I spilling all this out to you when you're ... you're so ..."

"I did ask, after all," the nun said.

Gabriella wiped her eyes with her sleeve. "What a mess I am. Making the patient counsel the visitor."

"Gabriella, goodness!" Although weak, Mother Griolet's voice was stern. "Who in the world are you trying to be, anyway?"

"What do you mean?"

"I mean, who are you trying to be? Are you carrying Anne-Marie's problems for her? Do you think you are responsible for her pain?"

"No, of course not."

"And yet because she is happy and you are anxious, you have somehow failed?"

"Yes, well, I mean as a Christian. My example. What will she think?"

"She will probably think that you are a human being. That things bother you. She will probably be quite relieved to find that you aren't perfect." Mother Griolet turned her head on the pillow and met Gabriella's eyes. "For goodness' sake, Gabriella, just be her friend. You don't need to feel guilty that your life has been easier than another's. That is God's business."

Gabriella started to speak, but the old nun continued.

"Gabriella, God is ... how do you say it? Chiseling. He is chiseling away some of the imperfections. Sometimes it hurts. Be honest with Him. You'll see. It will all be fine." She closed her eyes again.

Gabriella stood up, leaned over, and gently kissed Mother Griolet on each cheek. "*Merci.* I'm so thankful for you. I pray night and day that you will be back soon."

"Go on now," Mother Griolet murmured, "and tell them that this stubborn old woman will be back sooner than they think. Sooner than they wish, perhaps. *Mais oui!*"

The meal had gone really well after all. Gabriella had not looked forward to an evening at Mme Leclerc's with Anne-Marie and Ophélie, but she couldn't turn down her landlady's offer without being rude. Fortunately there had been no awkward pauses or teasing remarks about M. Hoffmann from Caroline.

Anne-Marie had smiled politely and answered Mme Leclerc's questions. She had sat poised and still, reflective, her dark eyes filling up like little puddles of rain when she spoke of her thankfulness at being reunited with Ophélie.

She was only two or three years older than the other girls, yet it seemed to Gabriella that she surpassed them in knowledge and wisdom by many more. And dressed in the smart outfit that Sister Rosaline had rescued from the clothes closet, Anne-Marie was beginning to look stunning and sophisticated. Caroline and Stephanie seemed oblivious to this as they joked and teased with Ophélie, and the little girl relished their attention and chattered along with them.

"May I see your room?" Anne-Marie asked Gabriella softly.

"Why ... yes," Gabriella stammered, caught off guard. "Yes, of course."

Leaving the table, she led Anne-Marie down the hall into her bedroom.

"Oh!" Anne-Marie exclaimed. "It's perfect. Cozy, simple." She leaned against the window. "You have a view of the town. And your very own olive tree to brush the window."

She sat on the bed lightly, bringing her feet under her so that she resembled a fine, shining black cat, regal and sure, yet unassuming.

"And are you ever homesick, Gabriella?" she asked.

Gabriella pulled herself onto the bed beside Anne-Marie, and somewhere a board creaked and groaned. The young women caught each other's eyes and burst into laughter.

"I hope it will hold us," Gabriella said. "After all, we are both quite hefty women."

This sent them, for some reason, into hysterical laughter as they looked at their almost-emaciated shapes.

Gabriella realized, to her astonishment, that this woman, who was the last person she had wanted to get to know, was somehow becoming her friend. It was as if, for that one brief interlude of laughter, the Lord had pulled back the curtain and revealed a future scene. Sisters. Soul sisters. Mother Griolet must have been praying very hard indeed from that hospital bed.

8

The last two weeks had crawled by for Hussein. He was staying with Moustafa Dramchini and the tall man, the American called David. He was proud at how smoothly it had flowed, how easily they had believed his story and accepted him into the apartment in Bab el-Oued. The men had waited till dark to return to their home that first night after the ferry left. They were afraid of the FLN, Hussein thought with satisfaction.

The men did not talk freely in front of him, but Hussein had eyes and a good brain. He noted every detail for Ali. After two weeks, he decided he had enough information to risk his life and climb back through the winding labyrinth of the Casbah. Still, his heart raced. What if Ali slit his throat before he had a chance to explain? The fear made him hesitate and turn instead toward his mother's apartment. He walked into the kitchen where she worked and wished at once that he had not come.

She turned and saw him, and her face went pale. For a few seconds she did not move. Then she engulfed him, moaning, "My son," while he suffocated against her large bosom. She cried and rocked him, and he never said a word.

When she finally let him speak, all he could say was, "Mama, I have been working. I must go again, and I don't know when I will see you. Pray for me, Mama. Allah will protect me. He has, you see. Don't worry. Only pray."

He left her standing with her back to the sink, wadding her apron between tightly clutched fists, tears running down her face like water from a spigot. Her cry of *My son* followed him out the door.

It was almost time for curfew when Hussein, watching from his hiding place, saw Ali return to his apartment. His stride was quick and angry, and again Hussein hesitated. Finally he pulled his shoulders up, took a deep breath, and knocked on the half-open door.

"Who is it?" Ali asked.

"It is I," Hussein replied, stepping into the dim light of the room.

"Hussein!" His name was pronounced almost with warmth. Then Ali's tone grew angry. "Why are you here? You are supposed to be in France!"

"I am going ve-very soon," the boy stuttered. He blinked hard, squared his shoulders, and looked Ali in the eye. "But I have been busy here. I have found out where Moustafa lives, with an American who has been helping him in France. M. Hoffmann. David Hoffmann. He is here too."

At the mention of the two names, Ali's face broke into a smile.

Hussein hurried on. "Anne-Marie Duchemin has escaped to France. The guard would not let me on the ferry. But Moustafa promised to get me there soon. They believe I am a harki's son. I have done nothing to lose their trust. You can find them. As soon as I am safely away to France, you can go and take care of them. It will be easy. And I will … will finish the work in France."

Ali rubbed his chin, then lit a cigarette and offered one to Hussein, who accepted, steadying his shaking hand while Ali bent close to him with the fire of the match. Ali took a long draw before speaking.

"This is good, Hussein. Not as I planned, but good. Perhaps better." He twirled around and slapped Hussein hard across the face, so that the cigarette flew out of his mouth, landing on the dirt floor. Ali crushed it with his foot.

Hussein stared at the floor as blood oozed from his lip and dripped down. He moved his foot forward, so that the blood landed on his shoe. His whole body was trembling. He did not want to see the knife. *Let it be over quickly, Allah. Quickly.*

"That is only to remind you who is in charge." Ali laughed, and Hussein looked up in surprise and saw the mad gleam in his eyes. "You have done good work, boy. Tell me more."

Hussein spoke quickly. "Moustafa is trying to convince his mother and sisters to come with him to France, and this David is staying to help him. It was not planned at first. David came to bring Anne-Marie back, because she was so ... so ill. But she met a woman at the port, an old neighbor, and they left together. They would have taken me, I tell you, but for the guard.

"And now the two men wait and plan. They're afraid, I can tell. And M. Cirou—that is where they stay, in his apartment. He works for the OAS. They plan to send me on the ferry first, because I am small and easy to conceal. Later they will come, with Moustafa's family. You'll have time to do whatever you want. I'm not sure when I will leave ... it may still be a few weeks. I try not to be too eager. I listen and do what I am asked."

Ali nodded, and there was a cruel satisfaction in his eyes. "Stay with these men. Keep their confidence. And when you are getting ready to leave, come see me. I will finish the work here, as you say." He dropped his cigarette on the ground, and as he crushed it, he pointed to Hussein's shoe. "Be sure to wipe off the blood before you go back there." He tossed him a dirty bandanna. "Take care of yourself, boy," he said, slapping him hard on the back. "I'm a very busy man these days. Don't bother me again until it is time."

Hussein stepped into the alleyway and fled down the street. *Pray for me, Mama*, he cried in his head. *Pray for me.*

One small spot of blood remained on the floor, and Ali wiped it clean with a piece of tissue. The surprise of seeing Hussein with his interesting news brought another quick smile to his face. He ran his tongue over his teeth, crooked and stained from tobacco, and thought through the plan.

On the warped wooden desk piled high with documents, he found a file labeled *US Aid*. From it he pulled out a list of material supplied by the United States to the FLN during the years of the war.

It had not been free aid, humanitarian though it might have seemed. Oh no. The US wasn't stupid. They were bargaining for oil when Algeria was finally independent. Oil! And he had instructions from the top of the FLN to continue clandestine negotiations. He laughed. It was perfect! Ironic and perfect. He read the names of the men he could call on in the States. Five names. He took a pencil and circled the third one. M. Roger Hoffmann, former ambassador to Algeria, residing now in Washington, DC.

"Come for a visit, M. Roger Hoffmann. See what surprises await you. Then your son's punishment will be complete. And after he has

known, as I have, the agony of losing a father, I will be finished with
him, too."

David grew more and more impatient. Didn't Moustafa want to be
out of here? The waits were growing longer by the day as more and
more pied-noirs, convinced of their fate, packed their belongings
and headed to the port.

"You aren't going to leave, are you?" David asked him point-
blank, as they sat in the kitchen sipping mint tea and watching the
paint flaking from the ceiling.

"I'm glad you stayed, David," Moustafa answered cautiously. "But
I don't expect you to understand. My people have no one. You saw the
French officer at the port, the one who turned the boy away. He does
not care that we fought alongside him to keep Algeria French. It's our
problem how we will survive in this country when the army leaves.
They have enough problems of their own." His eyes grew dark and
somber. "I tell you, one day France will regret our pain."

"And do all the officers feel the same way?"

"No, not all. Many treat us like brothers. They weep, they try to
help. But this is a political war, and we are only a tiny minority. You
cannot understand."

"But I want to understand. Then I'll know how to help."

Moustafa cursed, staring at David with bitterness that seemed
to seep out of his soul. "Perhaps if your skin were black, you would
understand. But you are a wealthy white American. Your life has not

been touched by political squabbles. It's not your fault. It's just what makes it impossible for you to know."

David stood. "I'm an American, a rich American," he said, hovering above Moustafa, feeling the power the Arab accorded him. Then he sat back down at the table and said, "I am also a Jew."

Moustafa gathered the coffee cups, rose, and went to the sink. With his back turned to David, he muttered, "So?"

"So ..." David repeated, "so I understand. Did Anne-Marie never tell you my story, Moustafa? You do not know that I survived the camps as a boy? The only child in my camp to survive? That I watched my mother and sister die? Don't judge me too quickly, Moustafa Dramchini."

Neither spoke for a moment.

"Do you have a cigarette?" David asked.

"I didn't know you smoked."

"I don't. Not usually at least."

Moustafa pulled one from the drawer in the kitchen cabinet and offered it to David, who took a match from a box by the stove.

"I don't know why I'm here," David said. "It's more complicated than simply wanting to get you back to Anne-Marie." He inhaled deeply, then let the smoke escape in a long curl from his lips. "When I saw what shape she was in, it reminded me of my mother in the death camp. I was furious with myself that I had not realized the full extent of her pain."

"How could you know? She didn't want you to know."

"I was playing at war. She was living it. You are living it." He watched the smoke float before him like a hazy memory. "I lived through a war a long time ago, and I am only now beginning to accept it. I shut it out because I was helpless to do anything else. The pain of doing nothing would have destroyed me."

Moustafa watched him with a sort of fascinated gaze. He didn't try to interrupt.

"Now, strange as it sounds, I'm learning to accept the past. To forgive." He laughed loudly. "What a crazy word! It was Gabby's idea. Gabriella—my friend."

Moustafa nodded.

"To forgive and to trust again. To trust not only myself, but others." He flicked the butt of the cigarette into the cheap white ash-tray Moustafa had placed on the table. "I stayed here because I want Anne-Marie to be happy with you. I want to make that one thing right. And I stayed to prove to myself that I could fight, not out of hatred or revenge, but out of love. Do you understand, Moustafa? Does that make sense to you?"

"Perhaps I judged too quickly," Moustafa replied. "But this forgiveness, this love. I don't know what you mean. It is something bigger than what you feel for a woman, *n'est-ce pas?*"

"Yes, bigger. It's a love as big as God Himself. That is why I stayed, and it scares the— It scares me. Because maybe I don't have the guts to do what it wants me to do."

"You're a strange man, David Hoffmann. Someday, I may call you my friend."

David crushed out the cigarette and nodded. "So be it then," he said. He reached his hand over to Moustafa, who clasped it. "So be it."

It hurt to think of Gabriella. Just saying her name out loud to Moustafa had brought back the feeling he got when he was with her. That heady excitement, that quickening wit from being with a woman who could read him. A woman who loved him. A woman whom he loved.

David picked up a pen. "How safe is it to send mail from here?" he asked.

Moustafa was sprawled on a mattress a few feet away. "Safe enough if you go through my friends. You want to send a letter to your girl?"

"You guessed it."

"Write her then. Tomorrow I'll take it to my friend. I have a letter of my own to send." Moustafa held up a piece of paper and laughed a bit sheepishly. "Great minds think alike."

"You got that right." David rolled back over on his mattress and began to write.

> *Dear Gabby,*
>
> *My girl! How I miss you! How confused I feel in this mad country. Did you understand why I stayed? Did you see I had to? I'm redeeming the time of my past. I'm buying it back so that I can have a future. So that we can have a future, free from bitterness.*
>
> *I put a heavy load on you, and I hope, I pray that you are managing without me. You should teach Victor Hugo; it would help Jean-Louis. You were born to teach, my Gabby.*

He chewed on the end of his pen, reflecting; then quickly he wrote about the events of the past weeks. He mentioned Anne-Marie only briefly. He did not want to spoil the letter for Gabby by trying to explain emotions that could not be explained.

This is a hellhole. Murders have become almost mundane. It's hard to believe a good God could allow such brutality. It makes me wonder, question. It makes me angry. But somehow, too, I see this God of yours (of ours!) in the working out of each day. I can't explain it. But then, you have already understood, n'est-ce pas?

The poppies must be all over the place by now. Pick one for me, my beautiful redhead. I am seeing you in my dreams.

Please give Ophélie a big hug for me. Tell her that I love her, that I miss her very much.

Keep praying for our safety. And always remember I love you.

David

Why had he stayed? Everything that mattered in his life was on the other side of the sea. He wondered if he could slip out of the apartment and get on a ferry for France tonight.

Then he looked at Ophélie's picture of the ponies hanging on the wall in front of him. If he left, in his heart he knew that the last pony would never catch up with the others. He glanced over at Moustafa, who was still writing, and realized how much he cared about the man.

Moustafa was not a handsome man. He often looked a little disheveled with his curly, unkempt hair. But he was sturdy, loyal, observant.

A door creaked. Hussein slipped into the apartment, mumbling "*Bonsoir*" as he passed the bedroom. David glanced at his watch.

The boy had been out late for the first time since they had met him. Where he dared go after curfew, David could not guess. If he was to get out of Algeria alive, this harki kid had better be careful.

David felt no loyalty to the child. Not yet. But perhaps it would come and surprise him, as it had tonight with Moustafa. This was war, and the strangest things happened in war.

9

Mother Griolet worked in slow motion these days. Just putting on her nun's habit was exhausting. Her old heart was slowing down.

She stood in the middle of her office and looked around at the crowded walls. Children's faces smiled back at her from worn photographs in simple frames. Most of the orphans had been placed in families. Many had grown up, married, and now had children of their own.

One picture caught her attention: M. and Mme Cohen with their three children. The parents had been taken to a concentration camp, the children found hiding in a false door behind a huge armoire. They were brought to the orphanage and hidden for months until one day their parents, emaciated but free, stumbled upon St. Joseph to claim them. With thankful hearts, they had started over again.

Now M. Cohen was a wealthy merchant in Geneva. He wrote Mother Griolet often. *Come visit us. The Swiss mountains will do you good.*

She fingered several worn volumes on the shelves that were stacked sometimes two deep. Here and there, another photograph or trinket sat in front of the books. She reached for a foot-high replica of an old woman with a bundle of branches on her back. Mother Griolet lifted the clay *santon*, its floral dress and cloak made from real Provençal material, off the shelf. She recalled the frightened Jewish children who had come to the orphanage in the night, left on her doorstep with nothing but the santon in their possession. The older child, a girl of eight or nine, had whispered, "It is a gift from our parents for keeping us. Please take it. It is very important."

The parents never returned, and the clay figurine had come to symbolize to Mother Griolet the whole of her mission in life. Giving. Giving what you have for the Master to do with as He wishes. The children had given their only possession. In turn, Mother Griolet had given all she could—protection. The children had survived, grown, prospered.

She set the santon on her mahogany desk, beside another letter from an irate parent threatening to discontinue his support of the Franco-American exchange program. How quickly rumors spread! The stooped clay woman seemed to peruse the letter, but her serene expression did not alter.

Mother Griolet pulled another letter from a stack of papers, this one from her superiors in the church demanding that she immediately do something to reduce the overcrowding at St. Joseph. She exhaled. *Lack of appropriate space for the proper development of the orphaned children*, they said, but Mother Griolet read between the lines. The townsfolk of Castelnau did not want these pied-noir and harki orphans. They had protested to the higher authorities.

"I protest too, to a different Higher Authority," Mother Griolet said aloud. "Don't let them take the children away, *mon Dieu*. Always You have provided in the past. Just what we needed. I am too old and weak to fight, but You are the One who changes hearts. Change the hearts of those dear souls in Castelnau. Change their hearts."

She replaced the santon on the shelf and sank into the thick black-cushioned chair, suddenly feeling very old.

A light tapping on the door brought Mother Griolet out of her sleep. She sat up, flustered with herself for having nodded off. "Come in," she said.

Anne-Marie Duchemin walked into the office, looking remarkably changed since the last time Mother Griolet had seen her. "Excuse me for interrupting you, Mother Griolet," she began. Her voice was barely a whisper, soft and velvet. "I can come back if this is not a good time."

"No, no, my child. Come in and have a seat. This is a fine time."

The young woman stumbled through a request to help with the orphans, her face relaxing as Mother Griolet assured her that she could find work for her and that she and Ophélie could stay at St. Joseph for as long as they wished.

"Thank you, Mother Griolet," Anne-Marie said. She rose to leave, then added, "And I was wondering, if I may ask. Have you had … any more news from Algeria?"

Mother Griolet reached out and patted Anne-Marie's hand. "No, dear. Nothing yet. You'll be one of the first to know if I do."

The young woman paused, letting a hundred different emotions wash across her face. She sat back down.

"Will you pray to your god for Moustafa? He's a good man. He is responsible for the fact that so many orphans left Algeria. Will you pray that he is safe?"

Mother Griolet watched lines of worry form on Anne-Marie's brow.

"I do not know how to pray, but Ophélie says that your prayers are beautiful. And they work. You prayed for me, and I am here. Please," she said, closing her hands around Mother Griolet's. "Pray for Moustafa … and for David." Anne-Marie turned away. "I don't deserve your prayers, Mother Griolet. I am not good enough for your god. But these men, they are good. They deserve another chance at life."

Mother Griolet gently pulled her old, rough hands out from under Anne-Marie's and reached to touch her face. "Do not be so quick to judge yourself, Anne-Marie. You have perhaps some misconceptions about this God." She stood up and went to the bookshelves. Pushing musty volumes aside, she brought out a small leather-bound Bible. "Take it, child. It is old and well used. I have many, you see. Read what our Lord says in the gospel of John, at the beginning of chapter 8. Read it and see that perhaps He is quite different from what you expected."

Mother Griolet could feel God's strength coming back. It was there whenever a lonely sheep needed to know of His love, and this lovely, broken woman certainly did.

Anne-Marie reluctantly took the small Bible and smiled almost apologetically. "*Merci, Mère Griolet.* Ophélie will show me. The gospel of John, you said? Chapter 8. *Merci.*"

As she left the room, Mother Griolet glanced again at the old santon, winked, and whispered, "The power, old woman. He is not done with me yet."

Gabriella and Anne-Marie walked leisurely along the cobblestones, heading to the outskirts of the village.

"Close your eyes and smell," Gabriella said. "The hyacinths so sweet, the cypress, the wild thyme, and rosemary. And then with those luscious smells in your mind, open your eyes and see the fields. The crooked vines with their sprouting green leaves, and the tall, splendid plane trees whose knobby limbs are beginning to sprout too. And the poppies. Everywhere the poppies.

"Oh, excuse me." She felt her face redden as if Anne-Marie might guess the secret of the poppies. She had been so caught up in her own descriptions that she had forgotten who was with her.

"Whatever for, Gabriella? I love experiencing all of this with you. You're a teacher even out of the classroom."

"That's just a diplomatic way of saying that I talk too much!"

"*Mais non!* I think it's wonderful that you feel things so deeply." Anne-Marie frowned. "For the longest time I have tried not to feel anything at all. It was too painful. But here, life seems to have flavor again." She turned to face Gabriella and took her hands. "Thank you so much for loving my daughter. She told me all about the incident in Paris and David rescuing her ... and you being here to care for her. And the crosses." She turned and stared toward the open fields and breathed in deeply. "It's such a beautiful story."

"A tapestry," Gabriella said.

"What do you mean?"

Gabriella shrugged. "Just a phrase Mother Griolet uses. She says God weaves lives together to make a beautiful tapestry. We can't see the finished work, but He does. And I think she might be right."

They began to walk again.

"That's a lovely philosophy, but hard to believe," Anne-Marie commented. "My life is not a tapestry. It's a long, tangled piece of yarn, hopelessly knotted and unfit for use."

"That's an awful thing to say," Gabriella blurted.

"I suppose it is. Maybe it's hard for someone like you to under-stand. It's just that my life has been so ... different from yours." She smiled. "You're so good. So kind and thoughtful. I'm glad David loves you. He deserves you."

She did not seem to notice how bright Gabriella's cheeks grew as she continued. "I've done so many awful things. The only good I think that has come from my life is Ophélie. It's a miracle that from something—" Her face grew red. "That fate could bring me such a wonderful child."

"But you see, Anne-Marie," Gabriella said softly, "that's what Mother Griolet means by a tapestry. She says God specializes in bringing triumph out of tragedy." She was silent for a moment. "That's what has happened to me."

"Really?"

Gabriella told Anne-Marie how her mother had been raped when Gabriella was a little girl and given birth to Ericka, the little sister who died before her sixth birthday. "I only found out a few months ago. Sometimes it still makes me so angry. But then Ophélie came into my life, and it was as if God said, 'You see, life continues.' Ophélie is helping me heal."

"Helping you heal? What a strange thing to say."

"Heal my heart. My memories. That's what I mean." Gabriella suddenly knew she must confess. "I was afraid that when you came back, you would steal away Ophélie ... and David ... from me."

She blushed. "You see, I'm not so kind after all. I was so jealous of you."

"Of me?" Anne-Marie asked, incredulous. "Oh, Gabriella. I'm happy my daughter loves you. I would never steal that love away. Someday, when you have children, you'll know that assurance that your child will always love you. You wonder why, but it is so. Even after the most awful things. I'm happy she has other adults to love her too, like you and Mother Griolet ... and David." She met Gabriella's eyes. "David loves you, Gabriella. Don't be afraid of me. I hope he comes back and marries you and you have lots of children."

Gabriella chuckled. "You're the kindhearted one around here, Anne-Marie. But I can't think of marriage and children right now. Too much is uncertain. And I have enough children on my hands at the moment."

"I don't see how you do it all. You have your own classes plus the one you've been teaching for David. And then the children.... You're so busy."

They had reached the edge of a hill and stood observing the vineyards below.

"Oh, I love everything I do. It's just when I get tired and start feeling sorry for myself that things go wrong."

"Does that happen a lot?" Anne-Marie asked.

"Often enough to keep me humble. When you see all the garbage inside you, the pride and self-pity, you can't get a very big head."

Anne-Marie sat down on a large rock and folded her arms around her knees. "I'm sure your garbage is nothing compared to mine. What are a few well-justified selfish thoughts compared to a ... a girl who has slept with cruel, filthy men? Who has condemned whole families to be murdered? I wish my sins were as small as yours."

"But you've survived!" Gabriella exclaimed. "You're different now. You're strong. I'm just innocent and naive."

"Well, I hope you're not ashamed of that!"

"No, of course not." Gabriella brushed back her hair. "Anyway, in God's eyes, sin is sin. I mean, any sin is big enough to keep us away from Him—a bad thought or a murder. And yet no sin is so big that He won't forgive it. That's the remarkable thing about God."

Anne-Marie wrinkled her brow. "That's not what I've always heard. Anyway, confession seems so pointless. All the people I've ever known just confessed to the priest so they'd feel okay long enough to go out and do the same sins again."

Gabriella patted her hand. "Well, see what God has to say about it. Sometime read the story in John 8."

Anne-Marie narrowed her eyes. "Have you been talking to Mother Griolet about me?"

"No! I mean ... what do you mean?"

"That's just what she said to me this afternoon, before I came to see you. She gave me a Bible and told me to read John 8. Now that is strange." She seemed lost in thought.

"Tapestry, Anne-Marie. Tapestry. Read it then. You'll see." Gabriella watched the young woman huddled on the rock and knew she had found a friend. She reached over and hugged her tightly. "That's what Americans do," she said quickly, feeling Anne-Marie stiffen to her touch. "That's how we welcome a friend."

Anne-Marie glanced up and softly touched Gabriella's face. "Tapestry," she whispered with a smile.

Yvette placed ten francs on the counter as the baker, Pierre Cabrol, handed her three baguettes. "I hear Mother Griolet is having problems with her superiors. Such a pity for that good woman, but really, it just won't do to have all those other children at St. Joseph."

Pierre's wife, Denise, had come out from the back of the shop.

"They're so loud," Yvette continued. "Lucie Lachat lives right next to the church, and she says the noise is deafening at all hours of the day and night. *Ooh là là!*"

Denise nodded. "It's as you say, Yvette. The Sisters take those children on a walk in the afternoons, with your little redheaded boarder, I might add. And what a racket. It's all the little Arabs. *Mal élevés* they are. No manners at all."

Pierre cleared his throat. "You women! Leave the poor woman alone. *Mais alors!* She almost died two weeks ago of a heart attack. Why don't you go over and help her with the wild little Algerians if they bother you so much? It's a fine thing she's doing. A child is a child. And an orphan, an orphan."

Yvette shrugged and bid him good day. *Now what has gotten into Pierre?* she wondered as she left the shop. *Everyone knows what those Arab children will do to the reputation of Castelnau.*

Sister Rosaline looked around the refectory table at Sister Isabelle, Gabriella, and Anne-Marie. "It has to be a secret until we arrange all the details. Then we'll let her know, and she won't be able to argue a bit."

"Right," Gabriella said. "Now let's go over what each of us is doing. Anne-Marie, could you teach the children in the mornings, with Sister Isabelle's help?"

Anne-Marie bit her lip. "Yes, I think so. If Mother Griolet will leave her lesson plans. And if that's okay with Sister Isabelle." She looked questioningly at the nun.

"Oh, yes. I'm sure we'll manage just fine. But that will leave you alone in the mornings until eleven thirty to prepare for lunch, Sister Rosaline. That won't be too much on you?"

"*Mais non. Ne t'en fais pas!* We've been preparing the same meals for all these years—I think I could do it with my eyes closed. I may be well padded, but I can work fast!" She laughed, patting her thick sides. "And you, Gabriella, will teach in the afternoons. You're sure you don't mind missing out on M. Vidal's history class for two weeks?"

"Well, it will be one of the hardest things I've ever had to give up."

All four women burst into laughter.

"*Quel dommage! Ah, oui.* Such a shame," Sister Rosaline said, her eyes dancing. "Well then, it's all set. As soon as Mother Griolet goes to the girls' dorm for devotions, I'll slip into her office and make the call."

"Perfect!" Gabriella grinned.

"Oh, it's just so exciting!" said Sister Isabelle as she stood up. "I've got to get back to the boys' dorm and make sure they're getting into pajamas." She scurried out of the dining hall.

"And I'm late for dinner at Mme Leclerc's," said Gabriella. "See you tomorrow, everyone. It's a great idea, Sister Rosaline. A great idea."

Anne-Marie curled up on her cot, trying to get comfortable as she leafed through Mother Griolet's worn Bible.

"What are you reading?" Sister Isabelle inquired timidly, peering at Anne-Marie from her bed in the tiny room they shared.

"I'm not sure. I haven't found it yet. Something in the gospel of John. I've never read the Bible before." She laughed at Sister Isabelle's shocked expression. "No, I wouldn't be a very good candidate for a nun, I'm afraid."

Sister Isabelle blushed, and she cleared her throat uncomfortably. "Well, don't worry about that. I mean, everybody has to start somewhere. At least that's what Mother Griolet says."

"Do you like being a nun?" Anne-Marie asked bluntly.

"Me? Well, yes. Yes, I do."

"And you really believe that God hears your prayers? And answers them?"

"Oh, yes. And Mother Griolet says—"

"I don't want to know what Mother Griolet says," Anne-Marie interrupted. "Forgive me, Sister. I don't mean that the way it sounds. I just want to know what you think."

Sister Isabelle's cheeks were crimson. "I'm … I'm not very eloquent, you see. But I know I believe. I have seen God's miraculous provision so many times."

"Like when? Tell me about them."

"Oh, I don't know …" She thought for a moment. "Like when the SS came here, when we were hiding Jewish children during World War II. We prayed and prayed that God would blind their eyes. And in the end, the SS guards couldn't find the children.

"And another time, when a soldier was questioning Mother Griolet, God gave her the words to answer his trick question correctly. And he went away.

"And surely Ophélie has told you what happened most recently? That awful madman came and tore the place apart looking for her and the Arab children. But when he got to the closet where they were hidden, well, he said, 'Never mind!' A miracle! All kinds of things like that happen, so that you really can't say it is coincidence. You know it's because you've prayed.

"And little things too—like having enough clothes for the children. At just the right time a warm coat will be donated, or socks or a sweater. And the food. Out of the blue one time, during the war when we had no food left—well, a carton of *pâtes* and flour appeared. At just the right time. Oh dear, I am talking so." She blushed. "I guess I can be long-winded after all when I get going."

"I don't mind," Anne-Marie said. "I like hearing it."

"I'm afraid you'll hear a lot more if you stay at St. Joseph," Sister Isabelle said with a chuckle. She reached over and turned off her bedside lamp. "You read. I'm going to sleep. Good night, Anne-Marie. I'm glad you're here."

"Me too," Anne-Marie whispered.

She found the eighth chapter of John. It was a story of a woman caught in adultery, and the religious leaders wanted to stone her to death. But when they brought her before Jesus to be sentenced, He said the strangest thing: *He that is without sin among you, let him first cast a stone at her.* One by one the religious leaders left until it was just this Jesus with the woman.

Anne-Marie could hardly read the words. Her eyes were blurred with tears. She felt as if Jesus were in the room now with her, asking that question. "Woman, where are thine accusers?"

She closed the Bible and flicked off her lamp. Then she lay down, staring into the darkness. *Neither do I condemn you; go and sin no more.* What a strange, wonderful thing for Jesus to say. Anne-Marie turned over, pulled her covers around her, and gradually relaxed. With the words still in her head, she fell asleep.

10

Moustafa sat beside his mother, gently shaking her shoulders as she wept. "Mother. Mother, please listen." He cursed under his breath. Every encounter with his mother in the past month had ended the same way: she wailing, he waving his arms in exasperation and leaving the apartment.

He never explained his long months of absence, and she never asked. Neither did he speak of Anne-Marie, but sometimes he thought she had guessed the truth years ago.

"Mother, can't you see we must leave? The OAS are murdering people daily. All the pied-noirs will be at the ferries by the middle of June. Let's go now, now before May is upon us. While there is still room."

"Your brother is fighting in the army. He won't leave until they disband at independence. And I won't leave until we can all go together."

"But, Mother, think of Rachida and Saiyda. Your daughters deserve a chance. Please! I'll stay for Hacène, but please go to the boats. There is help in France. You go first and find a place for us. Please, Mother."

She looked up at her son. The skin beneath her eyes was dark and sagging. "You ask to break a mother's heart. Isn't it enough that I have seen my husband slain? Now you ask me to abandon my sons to the same fate. I would rather die with you!"

Moustafa ran his hands through his curly hair. "I won't argue anymore tonight. You keep the list of the orphaned harkis. When

I find out if I have permission, I'll send for them. These children will need a chaperone, Mother. Wouldn't you go then? To care for them?"

"Perhaps, my son. Perhaps I would take my daughters and flee with the children to France … where I would wait every day with my prayers rising to Allah until you and Hacène join us there … in this other country that does not want us. Exiled to a life without meaning."

"It will be better than that, Mother. I promise." He grabbed her hands. "It will be better than that, because nothing could be worse than this."

❧

Eliane Cebrian waited until baby José was fast asleep to open the letter from Rémi. On the phone two weeks ago he had been distracted. "Yes, perhaps it would be better for you in Montpellier. Let me think it all out. I'll write and tell you what to do."

She worried that a letter from Algiers wouldn't get to her, but Rémi had laughed and said he could get letters out easily enough. He told her to go to a boulangerie down the street from the porte de la Joliette in Marseille and ask for a *pain de campagne*. Sometimes Rémi said the strangest things, but ten years with this man had taught her not to question.

And now … sure enough. Samuel and Rachel were wiping their soup bowls with the delicious wheat bread that had moments earlier held this letter. Amazing! A letter hidden in a loaf of bread. She let her eyes dart quickly down the page, looking for a hopeful phrase, willing that there be no bad news.

> *Dear Eliane,*
> *I miss you, my little oranger!*

She smiled at the term of endearment. An orange tree. Rémi had always said that she was as fertile and fragrant as an oranger that grew in their groves.

> *I have considered what you said. Yes, go to Montpellier. Let Anne-Marie find a reasonable hotel for you. To have a friend would be invaluable for you, my dear.*
>
> *I cannot say when I will be coming, but things don't look promising. Seventy-three murders of Algerians by the OAS this week. And two pied-noir farmers a little farther out have received the warning from the FLN. One week to get out of Algeria. It is their choice: la valise ou le cercueil. If it comes to that for me, of course I will leave; I will choose a suitcase over a coffin.*
>
> *What a surprise that you met the Duchemin girl. How good of God to give you to one another for that long crossing. I have not seen Moustafa, but have news from him. Don't worry. We'll take care of each other. Amazing to find our old neighbors after so long, n'est-ce pas?*

*I will send one of the trunks along as soon as you
have an address. All your heirlooms, my sweet. Then
even an old hotel room will begin looking like home.*

*Oh, Eliane, give the children such hugs! Tell them
Papa misses them so much. I pray every day that you
are all safe.*

*If you have news to send, take it to the boulanger.
Say it is for me. He will understand.*

*Don't forget, Eliane. Isaiah 42. He is leading even
if we cannot see right now. Don't forget. And never
forget l'autre chose.*

Je t'aime,

Rémi

She placed the letter on her lap and smiled. *L'autre chose.* Their
little code. When Rémi raised his eyebrows and looked at her and
whispered *l'autre chose*, it meant … well, it meant that tonight they
would share more than just a bed.

She felt a quickening pulse at the thought. She hoped it would
be soon. How she missed that man! But he had agreed for her to
go to Montpellier. That was a bright spot in the day. She would call
Anne-Marie tonight.

Sister Rosaline walked through the basement of the parsonage
and out into the dark streets of Castelnau. All the heavy wooden

shutters on the houses were still closed as she walked briskly through the village to where one light shone from the boulangerie.

Lately she had almost doubled her order, with the arrival of the new children. She slipped into the shop and pressed a small bell that sat on the counter.

The graying baker came out of his shop, covered in flour, a sheepish look on his face. "*Bonjour*, Sister Rosaline," he greeted her. "Today I have a little *cadeau* for two of your friends."

"What kind of present? And for whom?" she asked, narrowing her eyes.

He laughed as he brought out a large paper sack full of warm baguettes and placed them on the counter. "Your regular order, Sister Rosaline. Plus this *pain de seigle* for Mlle Madison and a *pain complet* for Mlle Duchemin." His eyes were merry, as if he had just played a trick and was trying to hide it.

Sister Rosaline nodded. "I understand." She was just a simple link in the chain. But as she picked up the bag, she could not help saying, "Just like old times, *n'est-ce pas?* Just like old times."

She was back at the orphanage in five minutes, and everyone still slept. Except for perhaps Mother Griolet. She was an early riser too. Or at least she used to be.

Sister Rosaline unlocked the door to the refectory, flipped on the light switch, and began placing bread in the long straw containers on the tables. Yes, Mother Griolet was tired, she mused with a smile on her face. But today she would announce the news to the old nun. Today she would tell her that she was expected for a two-week vacation in the Swiss Alps in the very near future.

She tucked the pain de seigle and the pain complet under her arm and stashed them in a kitchen cabinet. So there was news for the two young women too. Good for them. News all the way around today.

No sound of children's voices echoed out into the hallway as Anne-Marie stepped into the building from the courtyard. The girls' dormitory sat empty and quiet. She stretched out on Ophélie's bed and withdrew a letter from her skirt pocket. The crusty, oblong loaf of pain complet had held a priceless treasure, and she unfolded the wispy sheets of paper, smiling to herself as she remembered Gabriella's delight at having received a letter from David baked inside another loaf of bread. News from their men!

> *Anne-Marie,*
>
> *I am sending this the way we have sent messages to that lonely orphanage for so long. Are you safe? Are you happy to be with your daughter? Are you stronger? And your legs? I think of you constantly and hope that you and Ophélie are well, laughing together. I miss you, my habibti.*
>
> *There is no laughter here. The madness only increases. The FLN continue to terrorize the pied-noirs. The OAS have killed nearly a hundred Algerians just this week. All innocent victims.*
>
> *I am glad David stayed. He is careful and smart. Mother refuses to leave until Hacène comes, but I hope*

*to send her as a chaperone to other harki children going
to the orphanage. For that she will leave with Rachida
and Saiyda. The boy you met at the docks, Hussein, is
staying with us. We hope to send him along soon. I am
in contact with Rémi Cebrian, and he has several ideas.*

*Write to me, Anne-Marie, through the boulanger.
I will get your letter. I dream every night of being back
with you. A new life in France. This I imagine. I am
not good with words, but you know my heart. Give my
love to Ophélie.*

A bientôt, j'éspère,

Moustafa

She closed her eyes and tried to imagine what it would be like to
have Moustafa here with her. She could not see it. The thought sent
a chill up her spine as if in warning. She should not expect too much
happiness. She did not deserve it. A tarnished woman.

Hath no man condemned thee? Those words spoken by the enig-
matic Christ. But was He to be trusted? How could she be sure? If she
were not condemned, perhaps she could dare hope for a future—for
Ophélie, for herself, even for Moustafa.

Everyone at this orphanage said the same thing. *Trust.* Well, of
course they would. They were religious. But even David believed
something now. That puzzled her. What would make a sworn atheist
believe? She wished she could ask him the questions of her heart.

"Neither do I condemn thee," she whispered and left the dormitory, holding the letter tightly in her hands.

11

Roger Hoffmann walked along the Potomac, admiring the blossoms on the cherry trees that were reflected in the Tidal Basin, looking like snow on the twisted branches. The Washington Monument stretched before him like an elongated finger pointing to the heavens. Daffodils tossed their yellow heads in the mild breeze at the foot of the Lincoln Memorial, as if to entice the president to come down from his pedestal to play.

He'd better enjoy the scenery now, Roger reminded himself, because in three short weeks he'd be leaving for another part of the world whose landscape would provide a sharp contrast. Of the five Americans whose dossiers had been presented to the FLN, he had been chosen.

He had balked at the idea of going to Algeria now, before the country was officially declared independent on July 2, but the word from the FLN was adamant. Important negotiations about oil needing immediate attention. Russians have expressed similar interests. The message was clear: first come, first served.

He felt a gnawing apprehension, which perhaps was not even directly related to the war. It was that blasted journalist asking questions about his son. And the newspaper clipping from mid-March. Somewhere in the recesses of his conscience, he wondered what David was doing in the south of France.

Might as well look him up while I'm over there. He scoffed at the idea. He had no clue where David was. *Get the work done and get out if you know what's good for you.*

In the meantime, Roger had plenty to keep him busy. Details to handle. Conferences to attend. Counsel to be sought from a few men in the know. And a plane to be caught in the middle of a warm afternoon to take him to a country whose gaping wounds had surely swallowed up any hint of springtime renewal.

The train pulled into the quay in the Geneva station. Mother Griolet listened to the loud whistle and the incomprehensible announcement that came over the intercom.

So, she thought. *I'm here*. A forced rest. The other women's scheming had worked out perfectly, and she was glad for it. She had felt excitement, anticipation this morning when Jean-Louis drove her to the train station. But after five hours on the train, she had no energy to move from her seat.

A good thing this was the end of the line, she decided, or she might just stay put and take off to some unknown destination without the strength to protest.

A tall, silver-haired man in a dark-blue business suit stepped into her compartment. "There you are, Mother Griolet! How wonderful to see you again." He bent down and kissed her cheeks. "You look just the same." He held her arm as she stood shakily. "But I imagine you're exhausted after the trip. I'll have someone fetch your bags."

"*Merci*, Joseph. I'm delighted to be here. How kind of you to come to get me." She straightened up with difficulty, holding tightly to Joseph Cohen's arm.

"Emeline has everything ready for you. Tonight we will stay at our home in Geneva, and tomorrow we'll have a short drive to our chalet near Montreux. The perfect spot to rest. Just the lake and the mountains to charm you. Two weeks of complete rest—that's what the Sisters ordered, and we intend to see that you get it!"

Mother Griolet felt as though a burden had been lifted from her shoulders and any dark clouds had dispersed. She let her eyes drink in the scenery. France's beauty was wild, almost untamed, but Switzerland looked as if someone had mowed the mountains so that every blade of grass was in place.

They followed the shoreline of Lake Geneva all along the drive, and the contrast of the placid deep-blue lake with the tall caps of the mountains reminded Mother Griolet of a psalm. *O Lord, our Lord, how majestic is Thy name in all the earth!* Majestic was the word to describe the picture that moved outside her window.

Joseph parked the car by a chalet that sat perched on the mountain like an ornate triangle high above the lake. The narrow dirt driveway continued down at a steep angle where the lower part of the chalet was built into the sloping mountainside. Mother Griolet took Emeline's arm, and they walked in the front door.

Beyond the entrance hall unfolded a spacious sitting room with a stone fireplace and a picture window that encompassed the entire side of the chalet. A sliding glass door led to the balcony with its finely sculptured wooden railings. Four oblong planters blossomed with bright-pink and red geraniums that cascaded down from the railing.

Emeline slid open the glass door, and Mother Griolet cried out in spite of herself, "A taste of paradise! It's more than I could have hoped for." She took her friend's hand, squeezing it as they stared into the radiant sun.

"Yes," whispered Emeline with a catch in her throat. "Much more than we ever imagined. Jehovah Jireh—the God who provides. Who would have thought that after the hell of the camps we would ever live to see these exquisite mountains?" She cleared her throat. "Let me get your bags. I'll be right back."

Elegant at forty-five, Emeline Cohen carried her tall frame with grace and poise. A woman of standing, the French would say. Her blond hair was swept back in a soft chignon. Such a contrast from the skeletal woman who had appeared at the orphanage in 1945. "My children," she had said pitifully. "I am looking for my children."

It was a dark memory, yet it shimmered with hope, because the three Cohen children had survived. Mother Griolet could still hear their squeals of delight as they ran into the arms of their mother and father. Jehovah Jireh.

"I've given you the room just off the den here," Emeline called out as she crossed the spacious room. "That way you won't have any steps to manage. I hope you'll find it comfortable."

Mother Griolet left the balcony, following Emeline through the den into an immaculate bedroom. "Oh, Emeline. *C'est trop beau.*"

"*Mais non!* Nothing is too good for you."

The furniture was all light pine, crafted in simple Swiss symmetry. A fluffy white down comforter covered the bed, and a porcelain vase filled with wildflowers sat on the bedside table. The large window opened to the same view of the lake and mountains as that from the den.

"We're so glad that you're here," Emeline said. "You must be tired. Why don't you lie down for a few minutes while I get lunch ready?"

Mother Griolet did not argue. Instead, she unlaced and removed her black shoes, pulled back the comforter, took off her wimple and veil, and lay down on the bed. She had one flickering thought—*The whole earth is full of Thy glory*—before she drifted off to sleep.

The evening air turned chilly as the sun left the mountain in shadows. It touched the lake, making it glisten with a few waning rays, and disappeared. Joseph had lit a crackling fire in the fireplace and was sitting down in a comfortable chair, puffing on his pipe.

Emeline brought out plates. "It's a bit late in the year for *raclette*," she apologized, "but I remember how much you like it."

"It is my favorite—you spoil me."

"You deserve to be spoiled a little," Joseph teased.

They talked freely, laughing often. The Cohens knew how to appreciate life, Mother Griolet observed silently. They had narrowly escaped having theirs cut short, and now, with generosity and warmth, they welcomed beauty and laughter into their chalet.

Later in their conversation, Joseph's voice grew more serious. "And how are things in Castelnau?"

"Just a few matters of concern."

"Tell us, Mother Griolet," Joseph said, as they placed squares of cheese into little cupolas that were set under a grill to melt.

She sighed. "I'm afraid the town is turning against me—not that I care for myself. But for the children. People are so narrow-minded and fickle!"

Joseph nodded. "Did you expect them to be different?"

"Of course not. You know it was like this before. They lauded me for helping in the Resistance, then they turned up their noses at the Jewish children."

Emeline nodded solemnly. "At our children and so many others. But *you* didn't! You have never turned up your nose at anyone. And look how Jehovah has taken care of you! And there are others who help you, *n'est-ce pas?*"

"*Oui, bien sûr.* I'm not alone," the old nun replied. "God has given me a group of compatriots." She laughed at her choice of words. "Compatriots from different countries! Senegal, America, Algeria, France. And I suppose you've heard about the pied-noir and Arab children?"

"Only a quick *résumé* from dear Sister Rosaline," Joseph said with a chuckle. "It didn't surprise us a bit. You're still rescuing—" His voice caught.

Quickly, before haunting memories could destroy the evening, Mother Griolet explained the smuggling operation from its inception until the present situation, with the overcrowded dormitories and the complaining townspeople.

"I suppose I could understand if these children were just Arabs. But they're harki children. Their fathers died for France. Ah well, prejudice is prejudice. But of course you understand all about that."

Emeline nodded. "Jews, Arabs, pied-noirs. All unwanted."

"So the people have complained, and I'm afraid the church may cut off its funding. And the parents who support the exchange program are equally irate. I let one of our best teachers—the most handsome and eligible—go to Algeria to help in a terrible situation, and one of the young American ladies is mad or jealous. Unfortunately her father has quite a lot of influence with those businessmen who support the program.

"Dear Jean-Louis is taking up the slack, but … well, you know Jean-Louis. He doesn't exactly fit the part."

The Cohens nodded sympathetically. "So you're lacking funds all the way around," Joseph summarized.

"Well, not yet. I can finish out the school year, but if the parents cut their support and spread rumors of incompetence, we'll have to close down the exchange program. And you know I've been on shaky ground with my superiors for years. If I retire and there is no one to take over, I'm sure they will shut the orphanage down too."

"So you're thinking about retirement?"

Mother Griolet chuckled as she poured the bubbling cheese over a potato. "I should have considered it years ago. Not quitting, but training someone else. I got my theology confused—thought I would be immortal on this side of heaven.

"Actually there are a few young people who could take over, if they were properly trained. One is the daughter of Protestant missionaries in Senegal, another is a single-mother pied-noir with no religion whatsoever, and the third is this intellectual young American who is off in Algeria. Each has the energy and the heart for such a job, but I'm afraid the church wouldn't approve of any one of them."

"If the orphanage had proper funding, could it be privately run? Or could it be taken on by the state?"

"I don't know. I've never considered it. Perhaps."

Joseph wiped his mouth with a napkin. "Let me think about these things. Give me a little time to investigate."

Mother Griolet smiled at the couple, her eyes grateful. "Thank you, thank you both. And, Joseph, I have another little matter of interest to discuss with you. It's about my will."

"Mother Griolet, you're not planning on leaving us yet!" Emeline scolded.

Mother Griolet laughed. "I hope not. Nevertheless, things must be in order, and I have a few changes that need to be made. I thought you might have a lawyer friend who could look at it."

Joseph squeezed her hand. "I have a dear *ami* who would like nothing better than to spend an afternoon looking out on the lake with a charming lady."

Mother Griolet laughed, her eyes twinkling. "Well, then, I can see why the Lord sent me here. You will help me solve all my problems. But I've burdened you enough for one night." She rose from the table, feeling very old.

"Anything we can do to help," Emeline said emphatically, and Joseph nodded his approval.

"*Merci. Mille fois merci.* You're so good to me."

Snuggled beneath the warm comforter, Mother Griolet watched the luminous white moon so stark against the pitch-black sky. By its incandescent light the snow-capped tips of distant mountains were barely visible, looking somehow surreal. *Give me only a little while longer, Lord*, she prayed. *Only a little while. I am coming soon.*

The new terror in the month of May spread from the bowels of Bab el-Oued into all of Algiers. Teenage pied-noirs, aligned with the OAS but now uncontrolled, exploded into complete madness. The death count in the first week climbed toward two hundred. Seven Arab women were shot in the back of the head as they walked from their homes to the pied-noir residences where they had worked for years. A thirteen-year-old youth interrupted a young couple in the road, pulled a trigger, and shot the man in the face.

A booby-trapped truck blew up at the docks while hundreds of Arab men waited in line to be hired for the day. Over sixty perished. A priest watched twenty Algerians murdered within the church, while he stood by helpless. Postmen, store owners, street vendors, housewives. Random and terrifying, pied-noirs and Algerians alike watched and wondered when the horror would end.

Rémi Cebrian thanked the Lord every day that his wife and children were safe in France. Perhaps not happy, but safe. And by now Eliane would be in Montpellier, near Anne-Marie. How ironic that their lives were entwined again with their old neighbors. The Duchemin girl in France, the Dramchini boy here in Algiers.

Rémi brought a tray of steaming mint tea into the main room of the farmhouse. The two young men who sat before him looked intent on their business.

Rémi listened as Moustafa and the American, David Hoffmann, explained how their rescue operation had worked in the past. They told him of the orphanage in Castelnau and their conviction that more war orphans could be saved using the same means.

"It won't be easy to get the harki kids onto the ferries," Rémi commented.

"Yes, we have already realized that," the lanky American said wryly. "Is there no other way?"

Rémi thought for a moment. His eyes fell on the two trunks in the corner of the room. "I have an idea," he said softly. "Just an idea, so bear with me. I have these wooden trunks to send to Eliane. Perhaps we could smuggle a child in one of these."

David frowned, and Rémi forestalled his argument. "No, look. If we cut holes in the insides, enough for a little air. Once the trunk is on the ferry, the child could get out—at night while everyone slept. No one would throw him into the water once he was already on board."

"And how do you propose to get a trunk on the ferry?" Moustafa said skeptically. "The people are fleeing with tiny suitcases."

"We'll think of a way. There has to be a way." Rémi had already opened one of the wooden trunks and begun taking out the contents. "Yes, a child could fit in here. Have a look. How old did you say this boy is that is staying with you?"

"Around ten, I think," David said.

"Would he fit?" Rémi asked.

David pursed his lips. "Possibly. Uncomfortably, but it is possible."

"Good! I'll start working on it tomorrow!" Rémi patted Moustafa on the back. "Give me two weeks. That gives you time to warn your people at the orphanage and me time to inform Eliane." He grinned. "And time to make some contacts about getting a trunk onto an overcrowded ferry."

In the adjoining bedroom at Marcus Cirou's apartment, Hussein could hear David and Moustafa talking in hushed tones. Planning his escape. He frowned, suddenly claustrophobic at the thought of being stuffed into a trunk and smuggled onto a boat. But he had no choice.

"Should we tell the boy yet?" Moustafa was asking.

"Better wait until a little closer to the date," responded David. "I'm glad we can at least get that poor kid out. And to think that here in Algiers, it's kids only a little older who are doing the killing now. Senseless!"

Hussein frowned again. David was wrong. The youths were his very own age. Fourteen. It was only that he looked much younger. He felt a slight twinge of guilt to think that these benefactors were sending him to do exactly what many of the Arab and pied-noir boys were involved in here. Murder.

But pity was not allowed. He tried to think of something that would stir up his hatred for the pied-noirs, so that he would not consider the kindness of these two men. He thought of the dead Algerians he had seen yesterday at the café. That worked. With plans to appease Ali's desire for vengeance floating in his head, Hussein fell asleep.

It was long past midnight, but neither man could sleep. They stared at each other from their mattresses.

Moustafa's voice cut through the silence. "Are you ever afraid?"

"Sometimes," David whispered. He paused, considering his answer, then said, "What are you afraid of?"

Moustafa shifted on his mattress, throwing off the sheet. "Of having been loyal to the wrong thing. To something that has no meaning."

He watched as David seemed to struggle with the idea.

"I can understand that," David said finally. "For the longest time I wasn't loyal to anyone but myself. I worked out a neat little philosophy that protected me from being hurt."

The idea intrigued Moustafa. "And does it work? Does it keep you from fearing yourself?"

David chuckled. "I don't think I'm a very good person to ask that question of right now. I'm in the process of changing philosophies. But I haven't figured the new one out yet."

Moustafa pressed him. "What kind of philosophy is it?" He wanted to pick the brain of this American intellectual, to know what someone so far removed in culture from this hellish war thought in his soul.

"Nothing that would interest you. Christianity."

Moustafa sighed, disappointed. "Ah, yes. Catholicism."

"No. Not Catholicism. Not Protestantism. Not Orthodoxy. At least not for right now, Just the Christ. I'm trying to figure

Him out from the Bible, without a myriad of religious traditions attached."

"That's good. Go to the source." This was what Moustafa wanted to hear about. Another man's searching. "I read the Koran."

"And do you find it helpful? Spiritually? And practically?"

"Yes, at times I have. But now …" He did not want to state his opinion. He wanted to hear David's.

"What?"

"I wonder if truth exists. My religion says that if you die a martyr in a jihad, this is the only sure way you will get to heaven. And some claim that according to the holy book, a husband is allowed to beat his wife if she isn't submissive. The hope it offers is through violence."

David laughed, holding up his thick Bible. "This book tells of violence too. It seems full of contradictions. Jesus says He comes to bring peace. And then in another place He claims it is not peace, but a sword. Strange." He set the book down. "But I can't get around it now, for all my questions. I think I'm stuck."

"Stuck?"

"Yes, stuck with this Christ. I've come to understand that Christianity is all about relationship with a higher power. Being known by God and knowing Him. Without the need of all the religious traditions or the intermediary of a priest or prophet."

"And how does that make you 'stuck'?"

"Perhaps I did a foolish thing. In a moment of weakness, I gave in to this God. I bared my soul to Him and gave Him my life. And even if I want to take it back, I have the feeling I can't. Oh, I can turn away from Him, but He's sealed me for eternity. It says something like that in the New Testament. Sealed for life by His Spirit. I don't own my life anymore."

Moustafa was fascinated. "That's a terrible shame. Unless, of course, you find purpose in this religion … this relationship."

"Yes. It's a religion of forgiveness and trust. And freedom. Kind of paradoxical. You choose this God, and He forgives you. Frees you to live without guilt. But binds you to live in obedience. And this obedience is freeing. Very strange."

"And does it work?" That was the question burning in his soul. Did anything work?

"I'm new at it, Moustafa. At first I felt a sort of freedom—emotional freedom. And I even found it stimulating intellectually. But now … now I am only angry that a God who claims to be in control of all life could watch this around us and do nothing." He cleared his throat. "So give me a little while. You see, I'm only just starting to figure it out. I have the feeling it will take me a long, long time."

"My religion is simpler. You pray five times a day. You fast. You follow the laws. But there is no freedom. What I want is an oasis. An oasis here." Moustafa pointed to his heart. "Have you ever seen one? A real oasis?"

"No."

Moustafa closed his eyes. "It comes to you out of nowhere, like a mirage in the desert. Only it's real. In the middle of the unbearable heat, the loneliness, the dust that fills your lungs, it opens up before you, fertile and green. And you are suddenly satisfied." He ran his hands through his curly hair, measuring his words. How much could he say to this American? "That's what I am searching for. An oasis for my soul."

David rubbed his chin. In the shadows his face looked almost misshapen, long, thin, skeletal. The American seemed vulnerable and insecure. "Do you have a copy of the Koran?"

Moustafa looked at him, surprised. "Not here. But at home, yes. Mother does."

"Could you get it?"

Moustafa laughed sarcastically. "Sure. On my next futile trip to try to convince her to leave, I can get it."

"And when will that be?"

"Soon, I guess. Now that Rémi has a plan."

"Good. Get the Koran. I have this Bible. We'll compare. We'll look and see what these holy books say. Maybe I'll even find out if I've made the right choice."

Moustafa shrugged. "Maybe I will see if there is a choice to make after all." He pulled the sheet over himself and rolled onto his side. The night was still, but he was afraid. Displaced loyalty. All he wanted right now was a place on a ferry and a chance to see Anne-Marie, coming to him with the warmth of her love for him in her eyes. An oasis.

12

Gabriella's nose was pressed against the glass window of the train as she watched the scenery rush past. The whistle screamed and the wheels screeched as the train slowed and entered the Gare de Lyon. Paris! Something awesome and grand danced within her. For a moment she forgot that forty-one other young Americans were on the train with her and that she and Sister Rosaline were supposed to be in charge.

David should have been here. He had been the guide for the Paris tour last year, and every girl on the program had fallen in love with him.

Why couldn't he be here now, with her? She should have the kiss in the Tuileries gardens as flowers bloomed and fountains splashed around them. She should be held in his embrace on the banks of the Seine as they stared at the flying buttresses of Notre Dame and admired the green foliage that tumbled down toward them from walls beside the giant cathedral.

She thought of the letter she had given to Pierre two weeks ago. Surely David had received it by now. Was he thinking of Paris as he read it? Did he want to be with her? *Why aren't you here?*

The girls chattered excitedly, grabbing suitcases, laughing and causing everyone elsé on the train to stare.

"*Les filles,*" Sister Rosaline called out, exasperated. "You're acting quite rude." She rolled her eyes. "We must catch the Métro to the hotel. It is not very *compliqué* if you will only listen. There are tickets for each of you. You only need one, but keep it to use when we change stations. *Comprenez?*"

The girls nodded, only half listening. Sister Rosaline caught Gabriella's eye and shrugged. Gabriella shrugged in return, and they laughed. Forty-two American girls in Paris with equally as many daydreams in their pretty little heads. What had she gotten herself into?

The hotel was not a hotel at all, but a convent that each year housed the Americans from Castelnau for their stay in Paris. In previous years this had lasted two weeks, but due to the circumstances this year, their visit had been shortened to five days. The furnishings were sparse, mattresses on the floor of the chapel and hard bread and coffee for breakfast. But no one was looking for comfort. The convent was only a place to come to at the end of an exhilarating day, a brief pause before rushing back out into the wonder of Paris.

After the first disastrous morning when it had taken three hours to get everyone from the convent to the Eiffel Tower, Gabriella grew impatient. "Must we always stay together?" she asked Sister Rosaline. "We'll never see anything."

"You're right, Gabriella. They aren't children. They each have an itinerary and two books of Métro tickets, a map of the city, and their own money. Let's leave them alone, let them enjoy. If they need help from us, we'll hear about it."

"That is an absolutely wonderful idea." Gabriella breathed a sigh of relief. There was so much she wanted to see, and she secretly hoped no one else would tag along behind her.

As the girls stretched their necks to see the fascinating latticework of iron from their position under the Eiffel Tower, Sister Rosaline called out to them. "You're on your own now, everyone! Just remember, if you want the student discount, show your cards. And curfew is at eleven o'clock. You'll be locked out after that."

In no time at all, the girls had scattered with their friends, and Gabriella was left standing at the base of the immense tower with Sister Rosaline and Stephanie Thrasher.

"Well, what are we waiting for?" Stephanie called. "Let's go up!" She found a place in line, chattering to Gabriella as if the Eiffel Tower were nothing more than a huge Ferris wheel at a county fair.

Gabriella and Stephanie walked through the Latin Quarter on rue St-Germain-des-Prés at dusk. Paris by night. Student artists displayed their pastel prints on the sidewalks beside beggars and vendors. The quartier was littered with theaters and sidewalk cafés. They sipped *chocolats* at Les Deux Magots, and Gabriella imagined Sartre or Hemingway sitting at the same table, scribbling notes for a novel. They admired the magnificent eighteenth-century architecture, still well preserved, and they watched the city bustle by.

Then they took the Métro to the Right Bank, where they listened to a violinist playing "Pachelbel's Canon" within the recesses of the subterranean passages. Its melancholy melody echoed in their ears as they hopped onto the subway and emerged at the Place de la Concorde, where Gabriella could imagine in all its grisly detail the guillotine falling down to decapitate the king, the queen, and countless others in the late eighteenth century. By the lights of the city, they left the Place and strolled up the majestic tree-lined Champs-Élysées, one of the most famous avenues in the world.

"Oh, look, Gabriella! Godiva chocolates! Let's just have a look," Stephanie said, pulling Gabriella toward the richly adorned store. The window displayed ornately decorated boxes filled with deep, rich chocolate. "Too bad it's closed."

They walked to the end of the avenue, then took the underground passageway to the Arc de Triomphe. Stephanie and Gabriella stood in respectful silence before the tomb of the unknown soldier under the immense Arc.

"It was commissioned in 1806 by Napoleon to commemorate French victory," Gabriella told Stephanie, reading from her guidebook. "And there are twelve avenues that radiate from the Arc. It's called L'Étoile."

"The star. That makes sense."

"Can't you just imagine the uniting force of the French as the troops marched in procession after the Liberation of Paris in 1944? Wouldn't you have loved to have been here on one of the grand occasions when all of Paris turned out on the Champs-Élysées?"

"Hmm. Sure, why not?" Stephanie shrugged, nibbling a fingernail. "If you ask me, just being here tonight is pretty wonderful."

"You're right." Gabriella smiled, interlocking arms with her friend. "Of course, you're right."

Stephanie was fun and energetic. Seeing Paris with her was easy. But at every new monument Gabriella would stop and think, *You should be here beside me, David.*

She said it the next morning as she stood at the base of a flight of hundreds of steps leading to Sacré-Cœur. The impressive white Byzantine basilica loomed proud and picturesque on the green hill, surrounded by a blue sky with billowing clouds. Halfway up the steps they paused, panting, to take in the brilliant view.

Inside, the church was filled with mosaics. Gabriella lit a candle for David and prayed for his safety. On the chancel vaulting, she admired the immense mosaic of Christ, the Sacred Heart, and wondered how many of those who stopped in reverence before the glorious Christ really understood.

When they left the church, the sky had turned gray, and it was raining.

"Oh, look, Gabriella," Stephanie exclaimed, pointing to her right. "Isn't that just what you'd expect to see outside of Sacré-Cœur?"

A beautiful rainbow arched across the gray sky in yellows and blues and reds and oranges. A promise, Gabriella thought, watching the rainbow.

"You should be here now," she whispered again as they headed out into the rain.

Gabriella was determined to see the museums, even if she had to do it alone.

"Sorry, Gab, but I get bored in those places," Stephanie apologized after breakfast on their third day. "Anyway, Caroline and I are going to check out some of the shops on rue St. Honoré."

Sister Rosaline declined her offer as well, preferring to chat with another sister at the convent. Everyone else had plans, and Gabriella felt a sudden relief to be alone. Except that Paris was meant to be shared ... if not with a lover, at least with a soul mate. Someone who would run with her through the rain, entering the Jeu de Paume museum sopping wet, and stand, bedraggled but mesmerized, before the painting of Degas' ballerinas.

As it was, Gabriella stood there alone. She shivered, not so much from cold as from pleasure, as the graceful ballerinas danced off the canvas in the first room of the Impressionist museum.

In every room she found herself talking to David as if he were beside her, commenting on a certain painting as he had done while showing slides in class.

When she reached the room where Monet's poppies spread across the far wall, she stopped. *Les Coquelicots.* Without thinking, she whispered, "Exuberance that softly spread to capture fields of dreams and hearts." A line from David's poem to her, inspired by this painting.

"Why aren't you here?" she said, her soul aching with the distance.

And then she knew. She *was* sharing Paris with him. In her mind, he was here beside her. Now she must simply put it on paper. She would write him every thought and impression, every fragrant wisp of the perfume in the spring flowers, every detail of this tableau.

It was their last evening in Paris and the only one for which everyone's attendance was required. They had eaten at La Bonne Fourchette, a charming little restaurant hidden in an alcove off the rue St. Honoré. Then the whole troupe had literally danced through the streets of

Paris, singing songs from Broadway musicals, until they arrived on the Île de la Cité and came to the Sainte-Chapelle. *Exceptionellement*, Sister Rosaline told them, the Chapelle was offering a concert of Vivaldi's "Four Seasons" this night, and they had been fortunate enough to get tickets.

Once inside, there was still enough light in the sky to shine through the superb stained-glass windows in the upper chapel. "It is a jewel," Gabriella whispered.

"Yes, indeed," Sister Rosaline agreed, as the girls took their seats and strained to hear the nun's whispered commentary. "The chapel was built in the thirteenth century, supposedly to house the Crown of Thorns. The stained-glass windows are the oldest in Paris and among the finest produced in the thirteenth century."

Sitting in the beautiful chapel, her eyes feasting on the play of light through sublime windows, her ears tuned into the lyrical harmonies of one of the world's favorite composers, Gabriella absorbed the superlatives with delight. This was a night to inspire. This was a night when the heavens themselves were singing out to applaud creation. Tonight it was perfect. Tonight she was sure that wherever David was, he could hear it too.

The letter had arrived in the bread, and as David unrolled the paper, a flattened poppy fell out. He held it in his hand as he read. Gabriella wrote as she lived, words tumbling out faster than she could put them together, covering page after page of onion-skin paper. She wrote of the orphans, of Anne-Marie's appearance, of David's absence and her fears. Of her sudden bonding with Anne-Marie. She wrote of Mother Griolet's heart attack and their plan to send her to the Alps. She wrote of their scheduled trip to Paris.

She wrote as a woman sure of his love, and he was glad.

And now, she was surely in Paris with the rest of the young women in the program. He wished he could introduce Gabby to Paris himself. He laughed at the thought. He was sure that the two of them, the girl and the city, would get along quite well.

For a moment he forgot about the war that was ripping apart this little universe which had parenthetically become his home. Gabriella and Paris. Sisters in their depth, in their beauty and vitality. He would give anything to share it with her. Someday, he promised himself, he would.

Anne-Marie and Sister Isabelle had managed the orphans fine for the two weeks that Mother Griolet was in Switzerland, but with Sister Rosaline and Gabriella away, Anne-Marie felt less capable. Mother Griolet was back, looking healthier. But they had to make sure they didn't let the old nun tire herself out. As it was, Anne-Marie felt exhausted. She collapsed on her cot while Sister Isabelle watched the children in the courtyard.

"You're an answer to prayer," Sister Isabelle had declared before the American girls had left for Paris. "If you weren't here, we'd never be able to manage it. Not with Mother Griolet so weak."

Anne-Marie did not believe in answers to prayer, and today, she thought, she didn't feel like the answer to anything. The children were frazzling her nerves. Another morning with them and she might snap.

It did not help that she had received another letter from Moustafa. Not a love letter at all. Just the news of that little harki orphan, Hussein, coming to St. Joseph.

"Well, isn't that just wonderful," she had said to herself. "Just what we need."

Immediately she felt guilty. How could she be so quick to give up, when only six weeks ago she had been the one fleeing Algeria? Couldn't she still see the fear in the young boy's eyes as he pleaded with her?

She was embarrassed by how quickly she could let herself become pampered by a safe lifestyle. A few short weeks ago, St. Joseph had been to her an idyllic haven. Now she longed to escape from its confines with her daughter in search of a little peace.

She put her head in her hands and sighed. What was really bothering her, besides plain old fatigue, was the note from Moustafa. She read it again.

New orphan scheduled to arrive. Jeudi 24mai 19h30SNCF.

That was all. David Hoffmann would have written something else to Gabriella, she was certain. David …

She hit her pillow with her fist. Maybe he didn't care. Maybe all of the kind, loyal words in Moustafa's last letter were only that. Empty words. Were they true? She felt him being pulled by his people back into the heart of the war. He would never come.

Moustafa spoke French as well as he spoke Arabic, but his culture was completely different. How had she believed he could put that behind him? He was an Arab ostracized by his people. A tiny microcosm of a culture that had turned inside out.

Why did I let myself love you? I could have been free. Truly free. Now you weigh me down, Moustafa. I am weighed down by your love, and it will suffocate me.

She sobbed into her hands. Weighed down by love. By an impossible love.

"Mama," Ophélie said softly, entering her mother's bedroom. "Mama! Why are you crying? What's the matter?" She watched her mother brush the tears from her face, and then she rushed into her arms. "Oh, Mama! *Je t'aime!* My beautiful mother. Sometimes, when I wake up in the night, if I've had a bad dream, do you know what I do, Mama?"

Her mother shook her head.

"I tiptoe into your room and kiss your cheek, and then I thank Jesus that we are here together. I can always go back to sleep after that." She sat down in her mother's lap and wrapped her arms around her neck. There should not be tears in her mother's eyes. "Why are you crying?"

Mama hugged her daughter tightly. "It's nothing, my precious little one. Mama is just tired. Sometimes, when I am tired, I forget how wonderful everything else is."

Ophélie snuggled even closer. She loved the feel of her mother's fingers in her hair. "I know why you're crying, Mama. You miss Moustafa, right?"

Her mother looked down.

"It doesn't hurt my feelings, Mama. I know you miss him." She studied her mother's face, thinking hard for something to say. "When Papa came to get you in Algeria, didn't he show you the picture I drew him? The picture of the ponies?"

"I ... no, I haven't seen it. Tell me about your picture, sweetheart."

"I drew it when I was going to meet Papa for the first time. Well, not the first time, but the first time after I knew he was my papa. I wanted to take him something, and when Bribri suggested a picture, I just saw in my mind what I should draw. Ponies, different-colored ponies, all running to Jesus. There was me and Bribri and Mother Griolet and Papa, all running, and then you, you were the prettiest pony of all. And behind you, there was Moustafa. He was behind you." She knitted her brow. "But I am sure he was coming. I saw it."

Mama smiled, but it looked to Ophélie as if tears were still in her eyes. What else could she say to make Mama feel better? Ophélie took her mama's hands and held them, as Bribri had done to her when she was sad. She looked straight into her mother's face.

"Why don't we pray? When we're tired and afraid, Bribri says we must pray. She says that's when Jesus comes to our rescue. He loves to be strong for us when we are very weak." She frowned. "I think that is hard to understand, but I'm glad that He said it. Now let's pray." She closed her eyes and waited. Then she opened one eye, squinting up at her mother, who had a faraway look in her eyes. "Mama! Close your eyes," she reprimanded. "And pray."

Mama lifted Ophélie's chin and brushed her fingers across the child's face. "I don't know how to pray, *ma chérie*. I'm sorry to disappoint you, but I don't know how."

"Oh! Is that all?" Ophélie exclaimed happily. "Well, that's no problem. I'll teach you. Just like Bribri taught me. It's very easy. You just say exactly what I say. Okay?" She closed her eyes again. "Are you ready?"

"Yes, dear," her mother said softly.

"Dear God," Ophélie said. After a moment's silence, she whispered, "Mama, you're supposed to say the same thing I say."

"Yes, Ophélie … only …"

"What?"

"Nothing. I will follow you. Go ahead."

"Dear God."

"Dear God."

Ophélie folded her little hands together, and in a voice full of innocent faith she began to pray. "You see that Mama is tired and sad."

"You see that I am tired and sad."

"And You say that You are strong when we are weak."

"And You say that You are strong when we are weak."

"So please be strong for my mama now. Oh, please, Jesus. Oh, please, bring Moustafa back to Mama. And Papa too. I know You can do it. I know You can."

She had forgotten to wait for her mother to copy her words, but when she peeked again, her mother's eyes were tightly closed and tears streaked down her face.

Ophélie hurried on with her prayer. "Please, God, make Mama happy again. Thank You so much for bringing her back to me. You listened when I prayed for Mama to come back. Please listen again. Amen."

She sat with her head buried in Mama's lap as her mother stroked her head. Sometimes, Bribri had said, sometimes the best thing is just to cry. So Ophélie let her mother cry while she prayed the same prayer over and over again in her mind.

13

"Look at this," Eliane said, holding out a letter for Anne-Marie to see.

The French government was promising housing to the repatriating pied-noirs and offering loans to help them get on their feet. And meanwhile, the hotel Anne-Marie had found for Eliane and her children on the west side of Montpellier was adequate and the owner sympathetic to pied-noirs. He provided them with two little rooms with an adjoining door and breakfast and dinner served at the hotel, all for a reasonable price. Things seemed brighter.

"I'm sorry I haven't been more help to you," Anne-Marie apologized. "But we had our hands full with the orphans last week."

"*Au contraire*, you've been of great help. This is so much better than Marseille, I assure you."

Anne-Marie sat down on the bed, and the mattress sank under her weight. She laughed. "You're right. This isn't so bad. And you've got the little park across the street for the children."

"It's really fine, all things considered," Eliane agreed. "And with you and Ophélie here today, everything is perfect. Shall we go outside?"

Ophélie, Samuel, and Rachel enjoyed a game of tag in the park, while the women strolled José.

"There are Arabs everywhere in this neighborhood," Eliane said. "Most have been here since the end of World War II. They came over to France as cheap labor and live in government housing."

"Are you afraid of them? Are they hostile?"

"No, not really. We just keep to ourselves and so do they. Separate groups, living in our own little worlds. It makes me sad. I wonder if any of us will truly integrate into the French population."

"You mean as we were in Algeria before the war, a happy hodgepodge of people. Or at least we thought everyone was happy," Anne-Marie said. "It's too early to tell what will happen. For now you're here, we live closer, and Rémi will be coming soon."

Eliane looked anxious. "I don't know about that. He's wrapped up in saving children. You got a letter too, *n'est-ce pas*? They're sending the harki child. In my trunk, of all things!"

"Your trunk?"

"Didn't Moustafa say? Yes, they're smuggling him in a trunk, my trunk, filled with all our treasures. Well, I suppose the treasures won't be coming after all. Not all of them. But Rémi is sending the most important. The baby things, a few scrapbooks, and your father's will." She gave Anne-Marie a wry look. "And a young boy."

"You'll be happy to have a few things to make this place seem like home. But in a way, I've found it's almost freeing to have nothing."

"Yes," Eliane agreed. "I much prefer this life to the absurdity of what's going on in Algeria. We may not have much, but at least the children are safe." She reached over and squeezed Anne-Marie's hand. "And pretty soon our men will be here too. You'll see."

Anne-Marie shrugged, and Eliane knew she did not sound very convincing.

Lodève was a small village west of Montpellier with a rich and secret past. From the sloping hills surrounding the town, Henri Krugler liked to look down on his adopted city. The thirteenth-century Cathedral of Saint-Fulcran in the center of town still displayed its Gothic tower and some of the original fortifications. The whole region surrounding Lodève was dotted with chateaus, ancient abbeys, and remarkable geological monuments dating back, some said, to the Neolithic period.

Five years ago Henri had moved from a picturesque village in Switzerland to Lodève, not in search of archaeological ruins, but out of conviction. A direct descendant of the Huguenots, proud of his heritage and undaunted by rejection, Henri was a pastor with a dream straight from the heart of God.

A widower with grown children, Henri needed another mission in life to give him a reason to wake up in the morning. Even the lush mountains of Switzerland lost their charm when his Louise died. And so he prayed, and God answered.

The small Protestant church he presided over in Lodève was home to no more than two handfuls of old people. The youth of the city were mostly Arabs. Lately several harki families had fled to the village, with more sure to come. Henri's dream was integration. Catholics with Protestants and Arabs. And the means was a *centre aéré*, a recreational center for children. All children. A place to draw families together. After two years of French paperwork, the center was ready to open, the dream to come to fruition.

The townspeople, suspicious at first, had grown to love the passionate giant with the blazing eyes and the kind heart. He was a robust man, a man of endless energy. With his white hair and goatee, he resembled a huge mountain goat. The stooped Arab women smiled at him from behind their white scarves, and the fragile ancient *fidèles* at his church called him pastor with the assurance and comfort that should anything befall them, he would be there.

It had not been out of the blue that God's finger had led him to Lodève. Years ago his friend Captain Maxime Duchemin had recommended the village. "A stone's throw from Montpellier, a perfect place to retire. Which is what I intend to do."

Henri Krugler did not like to think of Maxime's "retirement." He shook his white head. *Retired unto the Lord.* This was true. And it sounded somehow more hopeful than *murdered by the FLN*, which was also true. And that made integrating anyone who had anything to do with the Algerian War into society in France a very delicate problem.

Hussein found Ali examining papers at his desk. "It is time for me to go. Everything is arranged," the boy stated.

"And your housemates?"

"Staying behind until Moustafa can convince his mother and sisters to leave. They hope to send other harki children along as well." He fished in his pocket. "Here is their address. Smack in the center of Bab el-Oued."

Ali spun around in his chair. "You have everything you need? The guns, the explosives? You remember what I have taught you, Hussein?"

"Yes, sir," he whispered, cowering as Ali reached out and grabbed the collar of his shirt. "I remember."

He knew his mission. Destroy the Duchemin woman and her child and anyone else in the way. He tried to make his face look hard, set with hatred. But the thought that worried him broke forth. He cleared his throat and asked in his deepest voice, "And what shall I do when I have finished this mission?"

Ali released the boy and smiled. "Do not worry. Allah will guide you." He handed Hussein a wad of French bills. "This is all you will have. But if the work is well done, then you will see how well I can reward you."

"Yes, sir."

Ali grabbed him again and pulled him close so that Hussein inhaled the taste of Ali's rancid cigarettes. "You aren't afraid, boy? There are many younger than you who have already killed half a dozen people in broad daylight in this city." He softened his voice. "What could be easier than a few timely explosions in a peaceful little orphanage? It will be simple. No one will even know to be afraid...." He burst into laughter. "Until it is all over and much too late. Go on now, my boy. Allah be with you."

Rémi felt the farmhouse growing distant and cold around him, as if it were preparing itself for his departure. He watched out the window as the farmhands, Amar and Abdul, continued harvesting the oranges. The groves spread out in every direction. Rémi had always felt a type of virility at the farm, with the fertile trees all around. Life had been good here.

But the end was blowing toward them like the fine, stinging sand from the Sahara that forced them to take shelter during a dust storm. Algiers offered no shelter. So all the pied-noirs were leaving. The engineers, the store owners, the doctors and nurses, the farmers like himself.

He recalled the scene at the airport yesterday where he had taken a neighbor who was fleeing with his family. Babies slept in boxes on the floor of the overcrowded terminal. Flies flitted on sleeping children's faces. Mothers cried. Suitcases supported the backs of the elderly.

The official limit for each traveler was two small suitcases. Rémi patted the heavy wooden trunk that sat in the den, where he worked on it day after day. The trunk was three feet high, four feet long, and two feet wide. Nobody would call it small.

Why didn't he leave now? What could he gain by staying and waiting by his window at night with a gun in his hand? In six weeks, Algeria would be independent. Then he would lose everything. Why wait for the inevitable?

Even now, many departing pied-noirs burned their belongings rather than leaving them to be looted by the Arabs. So this was how the war would end. Mass exodus, terror, flight, and a razed countryside. And every plot of land, Arab and pied-noir alike, stained by blood.

Glancing out the window again, Rémi saw David and Moustafa approaching. Relief flooded him as he opened the door and invited the men in. They declined drinks, and he read the determination in their eyes.

Rémi proudly displayed the trunk. "The boy will crouch in the center, knees tucked under him. I've made two boxes to fit on either side of him. They're filled with a few of Eliane's favorite things. When the trunk is closed, the boy can control the lock from the inside. So he will be able to free himself once it's dark and the ferry is at sea." He pointed to little barred openings at the front and back of the trunk. "And the air holes are here."

Moustafa patted Rémi on the back. "It's good work." He stepped into the trunk and carefully lowered himself into a crouched position. "Yes, the boy will fit. He'll have plenty of room. I think I might even make it for a few hours." He eyed David. "Good thing you're not an Arab. With those long legs, we'd never conceal you."

"I've written the address of the orphanage on the top and bottom of the trunk," Rémi continued. "Looks pretty convincing, *non*? An innocent trunk heading to Castelnau. But you must go to the right guard, the one my friend has paid. The others will never allow this monstrosity on the boat. Families are waiting for two or three days to get on. And you must be there at precisely nine thirty—he will be watching—and take the trunk on." Then he added, "He has no idea, of course, what is inside."

Moustafa ran his hands over the large box. "This chest will carry a treasure, like a pirate's chest. A priceless treasure."

"One life. It's worth it," David stated.

"Of course it's worth it. I only wish I could climb in there too."

Rémi nodded. The harkis were slated to be killed. If he could help a few more, well, then perhaps he could make some sense out of the end of this war. The men standing before him still had some sort of hope in them. He did not want to extinguish that.

"And once the ferry leaves the port in Algiers, no one will care. The boy can let himself out and be inconspicuous. Then in Marseille, he must simply hire a taxi driver to take him and the trunk to the train station. From there you say he will have someone to meet him in Montpellier."

"Yes," David confirmed. "He only needs to call them to give his time of arrival. They've already been told of the date."

Rémi looked skeptical. "You are sure this boy can handle it? I don't want Eliane's things lost. Or Captain Duchemin's will." He pointed to a thick envelope pressed tightly between two large photo albums.

"He's a responsible lad. Quiet and smart. He has nowhere else to go. He's afraid, and for fear, he will do whatever we ask. Don't worry," Moustafa assured him.

"Good luck to you then," Rémi concluded. "I hope you won't have any trouble at the port."

"Pray for us," David said. "We'll let you know how it turns out. If it's successful, you may have a lot of work ahead of you, Rémi."

"I wouldn't mind a bit. Keeps my mind off other things."

The three men carried the trunk from the house to Marcus Cirou's waiting car. Rémi stood motionless as he watched the car drive off, letting the dust blow into his eyes and settle on his clothes. He was not leaving yet, but time was running out. Soon it would be his turn. He brushed the sand from his eyes and whispered, "*Bon voyage.*"

It was the way they had spent every evening for the past two and a half weeks, and tonight the added advantage was that it eased the tension as they waited. With two hours before them, Moustafa and David took out the holy books and read. Because the Koran was approximately the same length as the New Testament, they had decided to read each through once, then compare their findings.

Tonight David questioned Moustafa. "So Islam includes some of the prophets of the Bible yet maintains that Mohammed is the greatest. And wherever the Koran contradicts the other inspired books—that is, the Pentateuch, the Psalms, and the Gospels—the Koran supersedes them all."

"Yes, this is what we believe."

"But what I don't see in the Koran is the provision for sin. What has Allah done for his people? How do you communicate with him? In Christianity, there is the sacrifice of the Christ—God who dies for mankind and resurrects Himself to conquer death."

"Islam is total submission to the will of Allah. The prayers five times a day show one's devotion."

"But where is the guarantee of eternal life?"

"The only guarantee is through jihad. Soldiers who die in a holy war are assured of their entrance into heaven."

"But, Moustafa," David argued, "can you accept a religion of laws and recitations? Where is the meaning?"

"There are many who find great meaning in the tenets of Islam. I, as you, have questions. I am still searching. You agree there is one true God, *non*?"

"Yes, I agree."

"But you see, for the Muslim, the Christians' belief in a trinity is polytheistic. Christians worship three gods."

"But that is not how they see it. They say He is one God with three distinct aspects."

Moustafa shrugged. "My mind is not on it tonight. We should get the boy ready."

"You are angry?"

"Not angry. Just restless to know how it will all turn out." He grimaced, then said sarcastically, "*Inshallah*."

Moustafa placed the books on either side of him. "Which holy book is right? These two books are like Algeria. The Arabs hold the Koran, the pied-noirs the Bible. There are two cultures and two religions and two languages, eternally separating us. Who dares to step over the line?"

He picked up the Koran and held it out to David. "Algeria's end was inevitable. You cannot reconcile two cultures if one people feels repressed. The Europeans have been wrong. And I, my family, we too have been wrong. We chose the wrong side."

David looked at Moustafa's face in the shadows, obscured. He could have been anyone. "You believed in *Algérie française*. You fought for that."

"We were wrong. And now we have nowhere to go. No hope for the future."

"You're thinking of Anne-Marie?"

Moustafa gave David a hopeless smile. "When am I not? When we were young, we did not see the invisible line that separated us. Then we grew up and acknowledged it. At least I did. She didn't need to fear it, for I was just a childhood friend. And then we had these months together … to awake a forbidden love. And now she waits and worries.

"If only she had no hope, then she would forget me and build her life again. Why am I such a coward as to give her hope when the whole world separates us?" He reached in his pocket and took out an envelope. "But I can't help it. I have to let her know I love her, no matter what. I'm going to put it in the trunk."

"You're right to send her a letter. I tell you, Moustafa, I'm no expert on faith, but there is something about this God of the Bible. He seems to have a penchant for love stories. For the most impossible ones." He winked at his friend. "No more worries tonight."

❖

When the men lifted the trunk from the backseat of the old Renault, Hussein felt butterflies dancing in his stomach. Fear and excitement mixed together, kneading themselves into a tight ball. Above all, he had to remain calm. He reminded himself that he didn't have to fear suffocation. The air holes were large and sufficient.

Already that afternoon he had sat in the trunk, with the top closed, for more than an hour. Then, at Moustafa's bidding, he had slipped the small key into the inward lock and freed himself. The top opened without difficulty.

But now, as they carried him, stopping and starting, bumping a railing, setting the trunk down only to pick it up again a moment later, Hussein felt queasy. Eyes were staring, he was sure, burning their questions through the little barred holes where, despite himself, he pressed his nose against them and stared back.

The crowds had grown since his last visit to the port nearly two months ago. People occupied every open space, making transporting a trunk a challenge. With a thud, the men set it down in the midst of the bedlam. A small girl came and sat on it, and her long, thin legs obscured the barred hole. Hussein shrank back, placing a thin blanket over the hole and holding it in place with his feet. He breathed deeply.

Why had they set him down in the middle of the crowd? Surely a guard would come and order the trunk removed, or worse, opened. In his lap, Hussein clutched his small oblong sports bag. Every grenade, each gun, and the explosives had been wrapped with minute attention within his underwear and shirts. Two small bombs were tucked in the pocket of a pair of pants.

David had insisted on going through his little bag of possessions. To empty his mini arsenal and conceal it in the apartment while David searched the bag, and then to rewrap each article, well, it had not been easy. He smiled to himself, pleased; he had done it. And now, if he could only sit still for another hour or two, then he could release himself from the prison. The prison that was bringing him to liberty. A twisted liberty.

Up went the trunk again, and this time David's voice came through the bars in a whisper. "Now's the time, my boy."

Hussein closed his eyes tightly, as if in not seeing, he would not be seen. He counted the seconds, listened to Moustafa talking in hushed tones and David saying gruffly, "Go on. Hurry!"

Then the trunk came to rest once more, and David was bending down beside it. "You're on the ferry. All went smoothly. I can't tell you exactly when to come out, but wait until at least an hour after the ferry pulls out of port. You'll hear the announcement. You're near the toilets on the upper deck. Hide in there if need be. Remember, call the orphanage from Marseille. Take the taxi. And don't forget the trunk.... God be with you, Hussein."

Then he was alone. Waiting. His palms were sweaty and every muscle stiff. He rested his head on his bent knees, breathing deeply, forcing himself to remain calm. Telling himself that the wet tears that seeped into his pants were nothing more than a simple reaction to adventure.

Somehow, in the heavy, closed atmosphere of the trunk, Hussein had fallen asleep. When he awoke with a start, he momentarily forgot where he was. Immediately his claustrophobic quarters reminded him, and he panicked. How long had he slept? Was it light outside? He listened but could hear only the low rumble of the ship's engine.

He winced with pain as he tried to straighten one arm that had fallen asleep and was now numb. Eventually he succeeded in removing the small key from his shirt pocket. Waiting again until the tingling sensation left his hand, he turned the key in the lock.

He pulled back the latch and slowly pushed up the lid. He breathed in a mixture of sea air and gas. He strained to hear voices. Nothing.

He lifted the lid higher, until he could stand hunched over. Quickly he stepped out of the trunk, ignoring the stiffness in his joints. He almost stepped on a child's arm and realized that most people were sleeping outside, strewn across the boards of the boat like victims from a natural disaster.

He reached back into the trunk, retrieved his sports bag, and closed the top. His first thought was to find the toilets that David had said were nearby. That done, he observed some people, looking like shadows, huddled together by the railings. Many slept with their heads resting in others' laps or on suitcases.

The night air was cold, and Hussein quickly took the blanket from the trunk, secured the lock on the outside latch, and slid down beside it. He wrapped the blanket around him, covering his face. For some reason, the scene of this mass of pied-noirs made him want to cry. He swallowed, trying to force the lump out of his throat.

Freedom, a strange, knotty freedom, lay before him. He could not stop thinking about his mother. For days he had refused to let himself dwell on their last encounter, but now, with no recourse, it was safe to think of her.

"Good-bye," he had whispered, petrified that he might tell her too much, yet desperate to see her one last time. "Pray for me, Mother. Pray that Allah's will be done."

He was small, and this endless black sky so big. But the task that lay before him seemed bigger than the universe itself. It was a task for Ali, and Ali had assured him that Allah would be there to guide. When the first wrinkles of light rose in gentle rays along the sea on the horizon, Hussein knelt and bowed his head.

"There is no God but Allah," he whispered, reciting the Shahadah, "and Mohammed is his prophet."

As the ferry docked in Marseille, the pied-noirs stood, confused, waiting to debark. They looked like a huge flock of sheep, Hussein mused. Sheep without a shepherd. Sheep who would perish in the arid Sahara if left alone. Would they fare better in France?

The wait seemed interminable. When at last the people were freed onto the docks, they wandered aimlessly, a lost, vacant expression in their eyes. Only a few were greeted by waiting friends and family at the port.

Hussein took it in as a spectator, telling himself that he was not lost. He had a job and a place to go. The thought brought a feeling of relief, if he did not think about what he had come to do. He clutched the sports bag closer to his chest.

A taxi. That was the first order of business. He squeezed through the jam of pied-noirs, pitying their predicament. He could not laugh like Ali. He had seen the blood that soaked the sidewalks in every quartier of Algiers. It was human suffering on a large scale, and Mother said that Allah wept over all human suffering. He had to be weeping now.

With his bag tucked under his arm, Hussein left the dock. Hundreds of nameless pied-noirs stood resignedly in lines behind signs marked Taxi. He cursed. Never mind the taxi; he could reach the train station by foot. The map David had given him showed the station only twelve blocks away. It would do him good to walk, to break away from the suffocating masses, to use his muscles after the confinement of the trunk. The trunk!

Hussein considered it only for a moment. What did he care about an old trunk? He would be quite happy if he never saw his wooden prison again.

The docks at the bassin de la Joliette in Marseille had finally cleared of most of the pied-noirs. The way they arrived in France was a pitiful sight to see, mused the old concierge as he shuffled through the huge ferry, picking up a stray scarf, a lost mitten, an empty carton of cigarettes. People fleeing for their lives with nothing but a suitcase in their hand and a hollow, hopeless look in their eyes.

And what the devil was France supposed to do with them? Mighty fine fix that President General de Gaulle had gotten them into now. The papers claimed the president had not expected such an exodus. Already over two hundred thousand had left Algeria, with hundreds of thousands more expected. And where would these pied-noirs end up? On the doorstep of France. As far as he was concerned, they should have stayed in Algeria. That was their home, they had insisted all throughout the war. They might have been French citizens, but everyone knew that the pied-noirs were different.

His trash sack was almost full, the fifth one from this ferry. He came near the toilets and paused for a breath, wheezing.

"Now what do we have here?" He tapped a large wooden trunk with his knuckles. "*Bon sang*, how in the world did this get on the boat? And now someone's just left it here for me to deal with. Ignore the regulations and then leave the treasure."

He tried to lift the lid. A small lock held it in place.

"And how in the heck am I gonna get this stinking box off the ferry? Break my back, hauling it around. *Punaise!*" He pulled on a handle, and the trunk slid awkwardly toward him. To his surprise, it wasn't too heavy.

Ten minutes later the old trunk sat on the dock, surrounded by overflowing bags of trash and lost clothing, waiting for someone to come and claim it.

"Am I supposed to pay the postage to get it to some little village in the Midi?" The concierge laughed. "Ha! Let it sit there till it rots."

14

The rest in Switzerland had done her good. Mother Griolet closed her eyes and saw the perfectly manicured green slopes outside the Cohens' chalet where the cows grazed, shaking their big, lazy heads at the flies, causing the thick bells around their necks to go *thunk, thunk.* She recalled the vivid colors, the crisp air, the landscape so perfect it looked as if an artist had painted it.

Two weeks there had brought back a little vigor to her steps. She'd changed her will, and M. Cohen had offered several suggestions for the orphanage. But her best idea lay within the hands of the fiery redhead who at any minute would burst into the office, full of enthusiasm and energy. She hoped that somehow God was preparing Gabriella for this encounter.

Moments later Gabriella arrived, out of breath, eyes shining. She fell into the chair and pulled her long, curly hair into a thick strand, lifting it off her shoulders. "Whew! I'm burning up. Those kids are wild at tag!" She wiped a bit of perspiration from her forehead and straightened in her chair. "Sister Rosaline said you wanted to see me. Is something wrong?"

Mother Griolet smiled serenely. "No, my child. Everything is fine. I was just remembering the scenery of Switzerland and thanking the Lord for that vacation. You girls have spoiled me."

"Oh, not a bit! Sister Rosaline says she should have forced you out years ago. I don't see how you keep going."

"Yes, well, it is precisely about this that I wanted to talk to you. About my future." The old nun leaned back in her black cushioned chair. "The Lord has brought to my attention through these last incidents that I have neglected to prepare myself and the orphanage for my eventual retirement."

Gabriella sat still, a look of concern on her face.

"I have ignored the problem for many years because I didn't want to admit that I was, shall we say, mortal. So foolish of me."

Gabriella opened her mouth to protest, but Mother Griolet hurried on. "Don't defend me, child. I have been wrong. Proud. Thinking I was indispensable, God's answer for the orphans. But He is the One with the answers."

She looked away. "I was so afraid that the church would send a strict, rigid woman to replace me, and I would have no say in the matter. It terrified me, the thought of an orphanage completely devoid of love."

"But what of Sister Rosaline and Sister Isabelle?" Gabriella asked. "They're perfectly capable!"

"Yes, they are. They are wonderful women. But they cannot teach. And this orphanage has always been a school too."

"Oh," Gabriella mumbled. "I see."

"I have been praying for these weeks, asking the Lord to show me what to do." The nun hesitated, moistening her lips. "And I have come back again and again to you."

"Me?" Gabriella laughed. "What do you mean, Mother Griolet?"

"I mean, *mon enfant*, that I want to ask you to consider becoming my apprentice, with the eventual goal of taking my place as director of the orphanage."

Gabriella's face went white. Silence invaded the room.

"I'm sorry to shock you, Gabriella. You don't have to answer right away."

"Me, the director of the orphanage? But that's impossible! I'm not even Catholic. And I'm certainly not a nun and … and excuse me for saying it, but I don't want to be one. I'd make an awful nun! And I'm only twenty-one. I haven't finished school. My parents would never approve of my leaving my studies. And as for teaching, well, I enjoy it, but I've only had two years of studies in Dakar. This is my first practical experience—"

"Hold on, dear! Slow down." Mother Griolet chuckled. "You sound like Moses in front of the burning bush. My, wasn't he full of excuses?"

She stood and came around her desk and placed her hands on Gabriella's shoulders. The young woman looked up at the old nun, her blue eyes full of questions.

"My child, don't be afraid. I would not throw this in your lap all at once. You would be my apprentice for the next year, maybe two, learning the ropes. How do you Americans say it? Ah yes, an internship. A paid internship. At the same time, you could finish your teaching degree at the Faculté des Lettres in Montpellier. Get your teaching degree and let me train you at the same time."

She could see that Gabriella was not at all convinced. "Dear child, God will provide. He has always provided in the past. Perhaps I am wrong; perhaps it is not you He has chosen. All I ask is that you consider it. Before you answer, I simply ask that you talk to the Lord about it."

Gabriella frowned. "Mother Griolet, I'm not afraid to ask, but how can I be sure that what I hear will be from Him?"

"Trust, Gabriella. God does not change. Neither does His Word. Through all the changes in our lives, He does not change. He is perfectly trustworthy."

"And what if He says yes and I say no? What if I don't want it?"

"God is perfectly capable of convincing you of His will, if you listen. He is also perfectly capable of redirecting a stubborn old nun."

In those few minutes, Gabriella's whole appearance changed. Worry lined her face, and her shoulders slumped as if a real weight had been placed on her back. "Why are there so many decisions in life? Why won't they just go away and leave me alone for a while?"

"Shh, now, my child." Mother Griolet caressed Gabriella's hair, and the young woman rested her head in the nun's skirts. "We will talk again soon about all your fears. For now, let's leave it with Him. Shall I pray for you? For us?"

Gabriella nodded, her head still bent, and Mother Griolet prayed.

She shut the door as Gabriella left the office, then stood for a moment in the middle of the small room. The faces of the orphans smiled down at her from the walls. So many, many years ago, when she had been a young woman, she had stepped into a calling that left her scared and unsure. But God had been faithful every step of the way.

Mother Griolet chuckled. Gabriella was right. She would make a poor nun. "But that is not what I am asking," she said softly. "I am only asking her to be herself. That will be quite enough for this old orphanage, I am sure."

The balding, heavyset old man who met Hussein at the train station wore a foolish grin on his face. *He would not be smiling if he knew why I'm here*, Hussein thought. He had to act polite and very, very thankful. But not too happy. He needed to show grief in his eyes too. It was a role for an actor, not a fourteen-year-old boy.

"Well, we are certainly glad to see you, Hussein," the old man said. "I'm M. Vidal. You'll find the orphanage is a bit crowded— a mixture of French children and pied-noirs and, of course, harki children like yourself."

He talked on and on in the dullest voice. Hussein hung his head sullenly, glancing up from time to time to nod or mumble an answer to a question. All the while he took careful note of every detail of information.

When they arrived at the orphanage, M. Vidal explained that the other children were in class and led Hussein across a court-yard enclosed by buildings. "Here is the boys' dorm. Your cot is there in the corner, right beside Hakim's. You'll like Hakim. An Arab, like you." The old man rubbed his chin. "How old are you, Hussein?"

"Fourteen."

"Ah, fourteen! Really? I would never have guessed from your size ..." M. Vidal grew flustered.

Everyone did that when they realized they had mistaken him for a much younger child. Hussein wished the boring old man would leave him alone.

"You must be tired. Perhaps I should let you rest?"

"Yes, that would be good. *Je suis vraiment crevé.*"

"Yes, well, that's to be expected." He rubbed his bald head. "Hmm. You can keep your things inside this dresser. I'll tell Mother Griolet that you're here."

"*Merci, monsieur,*" Hussein grumbled. "It was very kind of you to come and get me."

"*Pas de quoi.* Good luck, my boy. I'll be seeing you around."

As soon as M. Vidal left the dormitory, Hussein opened every drawer in the dresser. They were filled with clothes. He cursed, then laughed. Extra clothes meant extra hiding places for his weapons. He started to unpack his sports bag, then hesitated, wondering if the nuns around this place checked through the kids' belongings.

The room was crowded with eight bunk beds and three cots. Each bed had an old, mismatched dresser beside it. A few of the dressers were really oversized trunks. Hussein thought of the trunk left on the ferry. Maybe it would have been a good idea to bring it after all. Too bad.

He walked into the hall. A bathroom with three shower stalls and several toilets and urinals was just outside the main room. Beside the bathroom were two other rooms, their doors locked. At the end of the hall, he found the girls' bathroom and dormitory.

As he headed back into the boys' dorm, he saw an old nun approaching across the courtyard. Quickly he emptied the contents of one of his drawers into another and stuffed his sports bag into the first, sitting down on his cot as she entered the dorm.

"*Bonjour*, Hussein," she huffed, out of breath. "God be praised, you're here. I'm Mother Griolet, the director of the orphanage. I hope

you will be comfortable here. Sister Rosaline has put some things in
the drawers for you." She walked toward the dresser.

"Yes, I already saw," he answered quickly. "Thanks."

"Well, fine. Now if you find you need anything else, you just
let us know. The children are just finishing up afternoon classes.
They're eager to meet you. Would you mind coming with me
now?"

Obediently Hussein followed the old nun through the courtyard and into the basement of the building that M. Vidal had called
the parsonage. In the classroom, he stared at the children, counting
silently to himself. Over forty of them. Kids of every age. Each one
rose and introduced himself. Hussein met eyes with the Arab boy
called Hakim and almost smiled before he caught himself. He wasn't
here to make friends.

"Ophélie Duchemin," a little girl was saying. The carbon copy
of her mother. A cute kid with pigtails. Hussein felt sick to his
stomach.

When all the introductions had been made, Mother Griolet
dismissed the children for afternoon play. "The children have thirty
minutes of *récréation* before they do their chores. Dinner is at seven.
Would you like to rest for a while?"

"*Oui, merci*. I'd like to be alone."

"Go ahead then. Tomorrow I'll fill you in on our rules, chores,
and the way school works."

Hussein hung on the edge of the courtyard, watching the kids
at play. From the corner of his eye, he saw a young woman waving
at him. Leaving a group of children, she walked over to him. Anne-
Marie Duchemin.

The emaciated woman he had last seen at the port in Algiers looked healthier. "Healthy" was the polite way to put it. His friends in the Casbah would call her a *nana*. A real number. Shining black hair and dark, lustrous eyes, with thick lashes and full lips. And, he thought, moving his eyes down her body, a shape that any teenage boy could not help but notice.

"Hussein! You're here!" He stiffened as she took his shoulders and kissed him on the cheek. "I'm so glad you made it."

"Yeah, me too," he mumbled. "Thanks for all your help."

She ruffled his hair. "Welcome to St. Joseph. I think you'll like it here." She turned and called out, "*Coucou*, Ophélie! Come over here and meet Hussein."

The pretty little girl skipped across the courtyard to her mother. Hussein longed to disappear. If he didn't know them, if they were just things to be eliminated, then he could do it.

"I've already met Hussein, Mama, in class." The child beamed up at him. "Mama said she met you when she was leaving Algeria. I'm glad you're here." She touched his arm with her small hand, and suddenly her big brown eyes looked imploring.

"Did you see them? Papa and Moustafa? How are they? Please, how are they?"

Again the sick feeling overtook him, and his skin felt clammy all over. "Fine. Moustafa and David are fine," he stammered. They wanted more details; he could see it in their eyes. His head was swimming. More details about the men who had sheltered him and arranged his escape. More details about the men he had betrayed to Ali.

"I feel sick," he murmured, and he didn't have to act to make it seem real. "I need to lie down."

"Oh, of course, of course." Anne-Marie touched his head with her warm hand. "How rude of us. You must be completely worn out. Do you want me to show you to the dormitory?"

"No, thanks, I've already seen it." Hussein left, almost running, hearing Anne-Marie Duchemin assure her daughter that he would tell them about her papa and Moustafa later.

On his cot, Hussein fell facedown and wept. He hated himself for his tears. He had to be brave, like his Arab brothers. Not a coward! If only they wouldn't be kind to him here. And not ask him questions about those young men.

He knelt on the floor beside his cot. "There is no God but Allah, and Mohammed is his prophet."

He collapsed again on the cot, but his head was still spinning, his stomach cramping. He made it to the boys' bathroom, where he hung his head over the sink and vomited.

Gabriella lay on her bed, the shutters closed. The pain had begun near the nape of her neck, working upward until her whole head was throbbing. Feeling nauseated, she had declined dinner. A migraine, Mme Leclerc had assured her with several *ooh là làs* to go with the diagnosis.

Gabriella relished the silence in the darkness of her room. The clanking dishes, the silverware being set on a plate, the burst of laughter from the girls around the dinner table, every sound had been like a shrill, piercing siren meant to drive her mad. But now the meal was over, and the girls were studying quietly in their rooms.

"You're just worried," Caroline had commented matter-of-factly as she gave Gabriella two aspirins. "You're doing too much—with those orphans and teaching David's class." She raised her eyebrows when she pronounced his name. "You're just worn out, that's all. You should have some fun."

Maybe Caroline was right. Maybe she should just hop a train with the other girls and see the sights of France. Even without David, Paris had been fun.

But now responsibility was crushing her. Why, why in the world had Mother Griolet asked her to be her apprentice? Gabriella felt a rush of anger. It was as if with those few brief words the nun had stolen her youth, and a weight much too heavy had dropped with a thud on her shoulders.

Of course, agreeing to the plan would ensure that she would still be near David. Otherwise, in two short months, she was planning to fly to the States with her family for their furlough, and she might never see him again. If only he would come back from Algeria so she could know his thoughts. At any rate, taking on such a job just to be close to him was surely pitiful reasoning.

She tried to sleep, but her mind was racing. She flicked on her bedside lamp. The light made her wince with pain. She took her Bible from the nightstand and wondered where she should read to find the answers to her questions. She fumbled through the pages, but her head hurt too much to concentrate.

Mother. Mother could help her with the answers. For all these months, Gabriella had turned to Mother Griolet as a type of spiritual mentor. But now she needed advice from someone else. Someone removed from the situation.

She slipped out of bed, got a piece of stationery and a pen, then cuddled once again under the thick comforter. She started with news of the orphans and Anne-Marie. Then she cautiously mentioned David, knowing from her mother's letters that she was already worried about their relationship. Finally she mentioned the proposal by Mother Griolet.

> *Mother, I am so confused! How can I know if God wants me here in this little village? It seems confining, crazy. I'm not patient enough to deal with the children all the time. And there is so much else I want to do and see. Maybe that is selfish. If I say yes, will I regret it later? And if I say no, will I feel guilty that maybe I missed God's will?*

She answered her own question. No one had said she would have to do this for the rest of her life. Maybe she could have a contract for a few years. Until someone more suitable could be found.

Suddenly she knew what Mother would do: make a list of the pros and the cons. Her head was still throbbing as she wrote furiously in the column under *cons*. In spite of her headache, she laughed. It was easy to see that the cons would win out.

But then she thought of Moses. Surely his list of cons had been longer than hers. Yet, in the end, he had gone because he was convinced that God had called him to the task.

But he had heard the living God speak to him, she reminded herself. Seen the burning bush and his rod changed to a snake. It would be easy to know what God wanted with all those signs!

Gabriella put down her pen and prayed silently. *I don't want this, God. It's too big, too hard, too everything for me. But You're the One who is in control, and I do trust that You see beyond my feeble reasoning. Show me, Father.*

She picked up the pen again and wrote under the side of the page marked *pros*, and by the time she finished, an entire page was filled.

She thought of her mother. She had left comfort and a promising future to follow her father to the lost country of Senegal when she was barely on the brink of womanhood. Her mother's life had been hard, painful, isolated. But she knew what Rebecca Madison would say to all that. "Phooey! When you're doing what God has called you to do, there is something that goes way beyond all the trappings of the world. It's the beauty of sacrifice. I can't explain it, Gabriella. You'll have to discover it yourself."

15

A heavy fog hung over the runway as the small aircraft touched the ground in Algiers. Roger Hoffmann breathed a sigh of relief. At least he had made it into this war-ridden country without a bomb exploding within the plane's cabin. Yet, despite thirty years as a diplomat and all he had read of the gruesome details of the final showdown between the OAS and the FLN, the atmosphere inside the airport shocked him.

He was well acquainted with human misery and displaced citizens, but as he looked about at the hundreds, maybe thousands, of pied-noirs waiting for their planes, sitting on suitcases, pacing aimlessly, he thought, *These are the saddest looking people on the face of the earth*. The smells of tobacco and perspiration caught in the muggy afternoon air, suffocating him as he made his way through the crowds.

Eight years ago, when he had lived among these people, the country was in peace. Of course, the grumbling was growing louder. Rumors of a small terrorist group among the Algerians had spread. But no one had imagined it would gain such force as to become the powerful FLN of today. He had left at the right time.

Outside the airport, lines of cars were stopped in traffic, ready to deposit more pied-noirs and their few belongings. The telegram he had received in Washington just before departure instructed him to look for a red Peugeot by the northernmost exit. With suitcase and

briefcase in hand, he strode confidently through the crowds, ignoring the stares. A six-foot-four American in a pin-striped business suit
would stick out anywhere in Algeria.

Ten minutes later the Peugeot appeared. Roger half expected a
turbaned Arab to emerge from the car with a machine gun in hand,
opening fire on the restless throng of people. No one got out. As
he approached the Peugeot, the passenger-side front window was
lowered. A smartly dressed, middle-aged Arab nodded to Roger.

"*Bienvenue dans notre pays.* Welcome, M. Hoffmann," he said
politely. He nodded to the backseat. "Please get in."

"*Merci,*" Roger replied. Experience had taught him to be on his
guard. In a moment's time he had sized up the situation. Simply the
driver and the older Arab. The revolver concealed cleverly within
his suit jacket was enough insurance for the ride. He opened the car
door, placed his luggage beside him, and pulled the door closed. The
Arab turned around. His skin was the color of weak tea, his eyes dark
and hard.

"We're very glad that you arrived safely, M. Hoffmann. My
name is Ali Boudani. I am looking forward to working with you in
the next few weeks."

Five Arabs welcomed Roger Hoffmann to their headquarters in the
Casbah. The headquarters consisted of a twenty-by-thirty-foot room
concealed behind a cement wall within the recesses of a crumbling
apartment. A low round table surrounded by richly embroidered

cushions sat in the center of the room. After handshakes and official greetings, the men sat down on the thick cushions.

"I hope you enjoy couscous, M. Hoffmann," Ali Boudani commented.

"Indeed I do." He had been looking forward to such a meal. He smiled unconsciously, thinking of steaming lamb and vegetables heaped on top of the tomato-tinged wheat grain.

Two women, their heads covered with scarves, brought out an overflowing, enormous round porcelain bowl. The men ate from the "common bowl," as it was called, each dipping his spoon into the mound of couscous that sat in front of him.

They spoke loudly, in Arabic. Roger followed little of the conversation. As the bowl was taken away and a green salad brought out, Ali Boudani changed to French, addressing him. "The FLN has appreciated the aid your country has given to our refugees during the war."

"I can assure you that the American aid will continue after independence."

"Very helpful, yes. Independence is only five weeks away." Ali raised his eyebrows, and the other Arab men nodded approvingly.

A bowl full of large oranges was set on the table, and the men attacked the fruit with eager, greedy hands. Ali held one up to Roger. "See what beautiful fruit we produce in this land? We have much to offer the world."

Roger began cautiously peeling the fruit, as if with one wrong move it might explode on his plate. "I have several proposals to present to you during these few days together."

"Excellent."

"And several US executives are ready to negotiate prices on oil and gas in the southern Sahara."

"Yes, we have heard. The oil is most attractive to you Westerners." He bit into the orange, and its juice sprayed forth in a little gust. Ali laughed.

The meal ended with a rich cake for dessert. Ali wiped his face with a cloth napkin. "Tomorrow morning we'll meet again. For now, I am sure you are quite tired from your trip. Mahmud will show you to your room."

Roger did not protest. He was exhausted, his head spinning from an evening in Arabic and French. The other four Arabs rose, bowed slightly, and filed through the door that transformed into a kitchen cupboard as it swung outward.

"You understand that secrecy is of utmost importance," Ali confided, as they stood alone in the hidden room. "Many things in this country are best kept secret. Our little negotiations included."

"Of course."

"Well then," he said, pushing the door outward, "we'll meet again tomorrow. Good evening, M. Hoffmann. A pleasure to see you here." He gestured to the elderly Arab who waited by the entrance to the apartment. "Mahmud, M. Hoffmann is ready. Oh, and, M. Hoffmann. I'm sure you recognize the risk of wandering around the Casbah alone? You are a bit conspicuous."

"Don't worry." Roger spoke smoothly. "I'll stay put until one of your friends comes to get me."

"Very good. *Bonsoir.*"

Roger followed Mahmud through the whitewashed apartment and into the alleyways of the Casbah. He was sure he would not sleep. There was much too much to think about. Images of what he had seen driving from the airport flashed before him. Hollowed-out buildings, carcasses of bombed cars, shattered glass in the window fronts of neighborhood stores, filthy slogans painted on the sides of buildings, empty apartment buildings. Algiers was a skeleton of what it had been. If its people hoped to rebuild it, they would need plenty of American aid.

When Gabriella's second letter made its way across the sea and into David's hands, he devoured every word, hungry for some happy news. He thought of her standing before him, her creamy-white skin, the bright-blue eyes and long, blond lashes, and her fine, small nose. He imagined her shaking her thick red hair, sending it dancing in every direction. He imagined these things, and his heart ached.

He read her words and let himself be carried away by her enthusiasm for Paris. It moved him that she had caught every thought and detail and saved it for him. She was right. He had been there with her, and her letter gave him a window into her soul. She was struggling with her emotions, wondering what was next.

I know what is next for us, Gabby. I hope I know.

He needed to feel the hope that radiated from her words. Hope was fleeing fast in Bab el-Oued. Death was stalking the streets. He wished he could paint the blood of the lamb on the doorposts, wished that Almighty God would promise him protection, as He had the Israelites.

Last week it had been the postmen killed. Ten of them. This week the boulangers. Shot down in cold blood. No one was safe. He heard the clock ticking in his mind. A few more weeks, a month at best. And if they did not leave by July 2, the clock in the bomb would certainly stop ticking for Moustafa, and his life would simply be blown away.

David picked up his pen and started a reply. What could he promise her?

> *Gabby, dear girl! I'm afraid that I am having a hard time trusting in your God over here. Nothing makes sense. Pray that I will understand and, if it is not to be understood, that I will not persecute myself with trying to figure it out....*

He was sorry for the anger and bitterness that crept into his letter. He changed the subject to the class she was teaching for him.

It scared him to think that school was almost over for her. What was she planning next? They had never discussed it. Never had a chance to see past that blissful, fragile moment when they had acknowledged their love.

I am coming back as soon as I can, Gabby, he wrote.

He wanted to add, *And the only prayer I can pray is that you will wait for me*. But that wasn't fair. He couldn't ask her to wait when he himself had no idea what was next.

He signed the letter with a heavy heart. Too many unanswerable questions. Waiting. It had always been for him the hardest part.

❋

The whole neighborhood of Bab el-Oued had dried up like a withered vine. With the massacre of pied-noirs at the end of March, the dream of an *Algérie française* had died. Now what was left of the pied-noir population huddled inside their apartments, terrified.

It was late afternoon when the old Arab crept through the silent streets with a young Arab girl following him like a faithful puppy. It was not a safe time for an Arab to roam through Bab el-Oued, but Mahmud knew Ali too well to argue. He was paid to obey orders. Yesterday the order was to retrieve Roger Hoffmann at the airport. Today, a quick visit to make sure Hussein's information was good. The child went along to lend credibility to his task.

He found apartment number 28 on the second floor of a nondescript building that sat in the worst section of the neighborhood. He knocked quickly on the door, eyeing the child. "It's almost time for you to play your part."

A middle-aged man, pudgy with greasy gray hair, answered the door. He looked at the two visitors suspiciously. "What do you want?"

"Please, sir," the young girl pleaded. "Please let us in. I am a daughter of a harki. Please! This is my grandfather. Hussein gave us this address."

The stocky little man opened the door reluctantly, looking about the hall. "Come in. Just wait here in the entry."

Mahmud patted the child on the head approvingly. Presently a tall man, of striking resemblance to Roger Hoffmann, strode into the room. He was no more than twenty-five, almost as tall as his father, black hair and eyes, with the same angry, confident look on his handsome face.

Mahmud cleared his throat and bowed slightly. "Sir. Please forgive the imposition. We have taken a great risk in coming here. For me, I will stay and face my fate. But for the girl, Fatima. She deserves a chance like Hussein. He has told us how good you were to him. He thought perhaps—"

"Who has he told?" David demanded.

"Us. Only us."

"I told him to speak to no one. I don't believe you."

The child looked up at Mahmud, worried. The old Arab spoke softly, "Do not be angry with the boy. He has not told others. He hesitated to tell us, but you must understand. We are like family."

Fatima grabbed David's wrist and began to sob. "Please, *monsieur*! Please take me to France! They will kill me here! Please … Hussein said you were kind. He said you would help!"

Mahmud watched David Hoffmann closely and noted with satisfaction that his face softened. Fatima was a pretty child, almost ten, already skilled in the ways of her real grandfather, Ali Boudani. She would grow up to be a beautiful, dangerous woman.

"Let me think about it. How can I reach you?"

Mahmud quickly spoke. "Do not trouble yourself, *monsieur*. May we call again in a few days? Would that give you enough time to decide?"

David rubbed his chin, his eyes flashing angrily. "Two weeks. I'll expect you in the afternoon. Good-bye."

He showed them into the corridor and closed the door. Mahmud squeezed the young girl's hand and smiled. But they did not say a word until they were safely out of the neighborhood and climbing back through the alleys of the Casbah.

Ophélie saw many things that she never spoke about. Her life had taught her to observe and keep quiet. Even now, in the safety of the orphanage, even with so many who loved her, she did not always reveal what she saw.

She watched the new boy, Hussein, carefully. He was not a handsome boy. His dark hair was wiry and unkempt, his nose flat and wide. He had large, round eyes and thick lashes. Mama said he was Hakim's age, but he looked much younger. Perhaps he was ashamed of his size, Ophélie concluded. He did not seem one bit happy to be in France, even though Mama said he had begged her to take him with her.

He kept to himself and only spoke when directly asked a question. Even then he would turn his eyes down and give a one-word response. He needed a friend, Ophélie decided, and she was determined to be that friend.

She sat beside him at supper and smiled brightly. "How are you today, Hussein?" She watched his face darken.

"*Ça va,*" he mumbled.

"Are you very mad at me, or is it just because you are in France?"

He looked up at her, surprised. "Mad at you? No, it's not that."

"Don't you want to make friends?"

He nibbled a piece of bread. "I don't need anyone."

"Oh." She furrowed her brow, thinking. He was a very stubborn boy! "Would it make you very angry to tell me about my papa and Moustafa? I miss them so much, and I know you have seen them. Could you just tell me that? It doesn't mean we'll be friends. Please."

He glanced at her out of the corner of his eye and scowled. "Yeah, I guess." He wiped his plate clean with the bread, then stuffed the piece into his mouth.

Ophélie waited quietly as he chewed and swallowed.

"They're okay. David and Moustafa are okay." His voice caught, and he took a drink of water.

Ophélie smiled brightly. "Did Papa show you the cross I gave him? And the picture of the ponies? Did he say anything about them?"

"We didn't talk much."

"But did they say anything at all about when they will be coming back? Surely they said something."

Hussein lifted his eyes and stared at her with a tortured face. He looked angry and sad and afraid. "Can't you see I don't know anything? I told you we didn't talk much!" He stood up abruptly and left the dining hall.

Hussein made her afraid. But more than that, she felt sorry for him. After she put up both their trays, she walked into the courtyard and whispered a prayer: "Help me be his friend, God. He really needs a friend."

Hussein fell on his cot, breathing deeply. Why did that kid have to be so darn persistent? And cute? He needed to hate her. Hate a six-year-old who was friendly as a puppy, and her beautiful mother too.

But the only person he felt hatred toward was Ali Boudani.

Five times a day Hussein said his prayers to Allah, and every time he begged him to spare David and Moustafa.

He felt so confused. He had thought it would be easy to hate the harkis and the pied-noirs after all the horrible years of war. But what he saw when he got to know them was kindness. They were bewildered people, just like him, caught in a war that divided and killed.

His people deserved freedom from the condescending Europeans! They had rightfully gained their independence!

But at what price?

Freedom sounded grand and heroic until he attached faces, human faces that he knew, to those who must be eliminated. Ali said these people were traitors, spies, murderers. But all Hussein saw were kind young men who had sheltered him and a mother and child who wanted only to befriend him.

He had no choice. Allah, through Ali Boudani's orders, had sent him on a difficult mission. He opened the second drawer in his dresser and fingered the revolver tucked beneath his clothes. At least he need not worry that the Sisters would snoop in his belongings. Mother Griolet had assured him of privacy, and Sister Rosaline had stated matter-of-factly that anything that needed washing had to make it to the dirty-clothes bin. She did not have time to sort through the drawers.

He needed a plan. He considered using explosives in the dorms. No, first he should deal with the little girl. She would be the easiest.

To do something so incredibly hard, Hussein had to progress logically. Start with Ophélie.

With that settled in his mind, he felt reassured. Allah would be with him. *Inshallah.*

16

A dark cloud hung over St. Joseph, threatening rain. A similar cloud seemed to have perched itself above Mother Griolet's head. Her hands trembled as she skimmed through the letter. Her mouth was set in anger, and her bright-green eyes shone with rage.

"*Seigneur, ce n'est pas vrai!* It is not fair! How can we go on?"

> *Though we most heartily applaud your efforts at caring for the misplaced war children, it has come to our attention that their conduct is causing trouble in your village. Without the financial support of the townspeople, we cannot guarantee the continued functioning of St. Joseph. Several camps are being set up to keep these harki children. They will doubtlessly be happier in their own communities....*

Mother Griolet felt sick to her stomach. For years she had been considered a renegade, a troublemaker. But she had never lacked the money to run the orphanage and exchange program, and so the church had not complained. She was left alone, as long as she kept quiet and the villagers did their part.

But this wasn't fair. The rumors simply weren't true! Yes, the orphanage was overcrowded. But the children did not make noise in the middle of the night. It was glaring prejudice, and it made her sick.

Couldn't the villagers of Castelnau see what the government was doing to these people? Parking them in camps, away from society. They would never integrate. She was sure the memory of what they were doing to the harkis would one day come back to haunt the French.

The old nun buried her face in her hands. "Lord God, I'm tired and angry. Forgive me for this anger that burns in me. Please remind me that You are in control. If You want this little place to keep running, I'm sure that You will find a way to do it."

But to be honest, she couldn't see how.

The problem of the exchange program could be rectified quite simply, she was sure, if David Hoffmann came back before the school term ended. His presence at the school would reassure the girls and their parents.

But the presence of a dozen harki children was not so easily resolved.

In a sense she did not blame the townspeople. The whole country was in upheaval as masses of pied-noirs poured in daily. This region of France was especially scrambling to provide housing. People were hesitant, worried, suspicious.

She sifted through the rest of the mail, and her eyes fell on handwriting she knew well. The return address on the envelope was Senegal. Gabriella's mother, Rebecca. Four sheets of stationery fell onto her desk. Before she had read the first word, Mother Griolet felt tears brimming in her eyes.

It is difficult to be so very far away, to read of one's daughter's struggles and feel powerless to help.

*I am so thankful she has had you, Mother Griolet!
Her letters bring you back to me in full color! God
has touched many, many lives through you. You
know the joy and the pain of serving Him. Thank
you for being there for her, as you were there for me
so long ago.*

*We are hoping to be able to come in July to spend a
few weeks in Montpellier before going on to the States
for our furlough....*

The old nun smiled as she read. How like her God. He had
inspired a woman in Senegal to write this letter weeks ago, so that
on this day when she needed it so desperately, Mother Griolet would
receive a word of encouragement.

It was not coincidence. It was tapestry. Thunder grumbled outside, but the dark cloud had completely disappeared from Mother
Griolet's heart.

Anne-Marie looked in the bathroom mirror. Her exterior was soft
and smooth, but inside she churned. She had hoped, even expected,
that Hussein would bring a letter from Moustafa, but there had been
nothing. The boy was silent and reserved. She wanted to grab him
by the arms and demand that he tell her everything. Was Moustafa
well? Did he speak often of her? Had his mother consented to come
to France? Was there reason to hope?

She chided herself. The boy was alone and terrified. She expected too much from a child. Maybe she even expected too much from Moustafa. She told herself there was no reason to doubt his love. But she doubted his resolve to come to France. His loyalty, the trait she most admired in him, might keep him away from her forever.

She wished he could see her now. Even her limp was hardly noticeable. She could run into his arms, those solid, strong arms, tousle his unkempt hair, and look into the chocolate-brown puppy-dog eyes. But would she ever have the chance? Would Moustafa return?

She took out a sheet of stationery and wrote quickly, pouring out her heart on the pages. She told him of Ophélie, of the kind people, of the strange way they looked at their faith, and of her certain love for him.

A soft rap came on the door. Anne-Marie swung around, almost embarrassed to see Gabriella standing in the doorway.

"Did I interrupt something?" she inquired.

Anne-Marie blushed. "No, just my feeble attempt at a love letter. I wish I could write like you. My words seem so trite...." Her eyes filled up with tears.

"Anne-Marie!" Gabriella sat beside her, putting an arm around her shoulders. "Are you all right?"

She shook her head. "I just wish I had what you have. A faith, an assurance that somebody cares and is in control. And a man who is coming back for you." She was crying softly now. "I have nothing. Nothing but a weak dream." She held Gabriella tightly. "What is Ophélie's future with me? No family, no country, no hope." She covered her face with her hands. "I'm sorry. It is just, just that I miss him so much. I had hoped so for a word from him. I'm afraid, Gabriella."

Gabriella held her for a long time without speaking. "Did you finish your letter?" she whispered finally.

Anne-Marie sniffed and nodded.

"Let me have it then. I know just how to get it to Moustafa." She squeezed Anne-Marie's hand. "I'm sure it will be exactly what he needs to hear." She stood up and faced her, and Anne-Marie saw that Gabriella's face too was streaked with tears.

"You are *une vrai amie*. Why in the world do you care about me?"

"I care because God has knit my soul to yours. And I am crying because, even though my life is very different, I think I understand how much it hurts to love someone."

"Would you look at this, Monique!" Yvette set down a basket full of fruits and vegetables with a huff. "Did you get the same thing in the mail yesterday? A petition from Denise Cabrol."

"I got it," her friend replied sourly, "and I don't like it one bit. She's scheming, that woman. She wants to close the exchange program. That's fine and well for her—she doesn't have her income tied up in it. I'd lose a third of my monthly revenue without the exchange students. A third!"

"*Ooh là là!* Don't I know it. *Catastrophique!*" She furrowed her brow, revealing a half-dozen fat wrinkles. "But didn't you approve of the measure to rid the town of the Arab orphans?"

"Of course I did. But Arab and pied-noir orphans have nothing to do with the exchange program. Denise is overzealous. She never liked Mother Griolet in the first place." She leaned over the kitchen table and whispered, "If you ask me, she's been jealous all these years that her Pierre and Mother Griolet get along so well." She winked. "She's just been waiting for an occasion to get back at her!"

"Really! And after all the good that nun has done for us! Well, what did you do? Did you sign it or not?"

Monique stood up and retrieved a folded piece of paper from the counter. "Here's what I did. Read it for yourself."

Yvette scanned the paper.

> *I am most heartily in favor of the removal of the disruptive children from the orphanage, which has, up until the present time, run quite smoothly. I cannot, however, approve the termination of the exchange program, as I do not see that it in any way reflects upon the problems the orphanage is now experiencing, being a completely separate program.*

At the bottom Monique had signed her name.

"Well said, Monique!" Yvette cooed. "Do you mind if I copy it?"

"Go ahead. After all, it is your Mlle Caroline who started all the rumors about problems with the Franco-American program. Can't you talk any sense into her?"

Yvette shrugged. "She's jealous about your M. Hoffmann, so she claims that the classes are not up to college level. But it was a bit foolish of Mother Griolet to let M. Hoffmann go away again. What can I say?" She stopped talking, intent on copying every word of her friend's objection.

Monique prepared the coffee, chattering as she moved about the kitchen. "Did you see the morning paper, Yvette? Over two hundred thousand pied-noirs have left Algeria so far. Pouring into our country without an inkling as to what they'll do here."

Yvette scribbled a moment longer and then set down her pen. "A mess. A huge mess is all I can say. Send them to the west side of Montpellier. They'll be happy over there with the Arabs for neighbors."

Monique nodded. "Sounds like a good idea to me." Picking up her cup of coffee, she asked, "Now what did you decide to fix for the girls' supper tonight?"

"The asparagus was beautiful. I'll have that *au gratin* for the *entrée* and then a leg of lamb with macaroni." She laughed. "They're always surprised when they taste the real thing. You know those Americans. They eat everything from a box. *Quel horreur!* Macaroni and cheese from a box."

The ladies laughed and planned and, before separating, stuffed their petitions in an envelope and sealed it shut.

"What do you mean I have to call another depot? You're the tenth person I've talked to today, and every single one of you is giving me a different story!" Eliane shook her bobbed head and slammed down the phone so hard that Samuel and Rachel looked up from their game in surprise.

"Mama, what's the matter?" Rachel asked.

Eliane bit her lip, fighting back the tears. "Nothing, children. *Ça va*. Mama's just a little bit tired today, that's all."

She stood by the window and watched the rain drizzle outside. She hated this hotel room. She was tired of being cooped up with the kids all day, especially on Wednesdays when Samuel and Rachel didn't have school.

Not that school was pleasant for them. They reported with sad eyes that the other children made fun of their accent and wouldn't play with them at recess.

And now this. The harki boy had left the trunk in Marseille. Her trunk! With her belongings. When Anne-Marie called to tell her, Eliane cursed, shocking the children. All those things that she cherished—baby pictures of the children, their silver cups, the old family Bible with the family tree inside, her grandmother's set of Limoges china—all lost. Eliane felt sick just thinking of the heirlooms the trunk held. And of the stupid Arab boy who had left it there. How could he?

The porters in Marseille gave her little hope of finding it. No one could even direct her to the right warehouse where lost items from the ferries were stored. They just laughed and said it was probably pretty well picked over by now anyway. Behind the laughter, she could hear the sarcasm. *It serves her right*, she imagined them thinking. *The pathetic pied-noir, sending a trunk over at a time like this.*

If she hoped to find the trunk, she would have to go to Marseille herself. But the thought of dragging her children around on buses in that chaotic city overwhelmed her. She would just have to wait for

Rémi. His last letter had sounded very pessimistic. He had not yet received the cryptic warning—the suitcase or the coffin—but plenty of others had. With one month until independence, she doubted he would hold out much longer.

"I want to go home," she whispered to herself. "Oh, God, how I wish I could go home."

That night on the ferry, crossing the Mediterranean, she had clasped Anne-Marie's hand and assured her that she had a chance to start over. That God would see them through. Eliane had believed it then.

She groaned to herself and felt that anger lurking again, below the surface. Why should life be easy when you can make it hard? That was her new motto for France, and she disliked the bitterness that was creeping into her soul.

Even at church she felt it. The stares, the cold, formal politeness. *Quel dommage*, she had thought. *We're few enough Protestants as it is. Can't we at least get along?* But every week it was the same—an aloofness that screamed, *You're different and we don't care to get to know you.* Finally she had stopped going to le Temple Protestant altogether.

Thank goodness for Anne-Marie and Ophélie. Their weekly visits were the bright spot in an otherwise dreary and complicated existence.

She picked up the phone and dialed another warehouse in Marseille. The phone rang on and on. No one answered.

Jean-Louis gladly surrendered his position in front of the class to Gabriella and took a seat in a chair beside the desk. He personally considered *Les Fleurs du Mal* nasty, no matter how beautifully it was written, and he did not relish the thought of explaining it to these young women. As it was, he fixed his gaze on Caroline Harland's shapely legs and let himself daydream.

He realized he must have nodded off when he was awakened by a thin ripple of laughter in the classroom. He straightened up in his chair, pushed his wire-rimmed glasses back on his nose, and turned his attention to Gabriella, whose face was bright red.

She smiled weakly at Jean-Louis. "As I was saying, some of Baudelaire's poems were censured and literally had to be cut out of the collection of verses before the volume was put on sale. Soon after that event, Baudelaire died of paralysis at age forty-six."

He thought she was handling a delicate subject extremely well and resumed his contemplation of Caroline's figure—until she suddenly caught his gaze and raised her eyebrows. Jean-Louis was sure he blushed all the way to the top of his bald head.

When Gabriella asked the young women to read several poems silently, he slipped out of the room, giving her an appreciative nod. He walked down two flights of steps into the basement and stood outside the children's classroom.

Jeanette was going over multiplication tables. He did not enter the room but contented himself to stand outside and listen to the nun's firm, happy voice. Something tugged within his heart. Something much different than the quick rush of excitement that the sight of Caroline's legs brought him.

He told himself that Jeanette's voice sounded as strong as ever. He told himself that she was in fine shape. He recalled her as a young woman with sparkling, mischievous eyes and a wonderful, ringing laugh. He reached into his pocket and brought out a yellowed envelope. The ink was faded, but her name was still legible on the outside.

Jean-Louis turned the envelope over and over in his hands. Perhaps the time had not yet come. He walked back through the basement, up the stairs, and out into the gray drizzle, tucking the envelope safely back into his coat pocket.

17

Hussein was weary from fighting off sleep. The other boys had long since closed their eyes, and their peaceful breathing testified that all were asleep. He got out of bed and with shaking hands pulled on a pair of pants over his pajamas. He reached into the drawer and fumbled through the clothes until he touched the revolver. The silencer was in place. He had prepared it in the afternoon. He tucked the gun into his pants, his pajama top concealing it. Not that it mattered, he told himself. Everything was perfectly quiet.

Hussein made his way down the hall and slipped into the girls' dormitory. Ophélie was sleeping so peacefully, a smile on her lips. Her brown hair fell over the covers, and one arm hung outside the sheets. Hussein touched it lightly.

"Ophélie," he whispered. "Ophélie. Wake up. It's Hussein." He shook her lightly, and after a moment, the child's eyes fluttered open. Immediately Hussein put his hand over her mouth. "Shh. Don't make a sound. Come with me. I have the most beautiful thing to show you."

Ophélie rubbed her eyes and sat up, frowning.

Hussein smiled weakly. "I thought of you. How much you love to imagine. I wanted to …" He tried to swallow, but his throat was so dry. "To show this to you, since you've been so kind to me."

The little girl's eyes brightened as she slipped out of bed. Hussein took her hand and led her through the hallway. He pushed on the door leading out to the courtyard, but it was locked. Panic seized him.

"Oh, *zut alors*! We can't get out." His head spun.

Ophélie tugged on his sleeve. "We can get out through the bathroom window. Hakim did it once. It's too high for me to climb up, but if you help me, I can do it." She gave him a mischievous smile.

He felt his resolve slipping. "But how would we get back in?"

"Oh, that's easy. You just get Mother Griolet's chair. It's always in the garden. Hakim put it under the window and climbed back in. Come on." She grabbed his hand, leading him toward the boys' bathroom. "This is fun!"

Hussein saw that she was right. If he stood on the toilet, he could open the window and then hoist himself up. He hesitated a moment. He had been so sure that it must be done in the courtyard. Now he wished he had just shot the child in her bed while she slept.

"Okay, Ophélie, you come first. Just stand on my shoulders and see if you can open the window."

She did so easily, climbing through the opening and dropping lightly to the ground outside. Hussein followed quickly.

The sky had cleared after the afternoon showers, and the stars flickered by the hundreds. In the middle of the dark expanse sat a bright white full moon. Hussein sighed with relief. For some strange reason it mattered that he had not lied to her. Not yet.

"It's sooo pretty!" Ophélie strained her neck upward and stared at the scene. "Thank you for showing me. It's so quiet and peaceful. I hope Papa is staring at the same sky right now and remembering how much I love him."

She was whispering as if in a dream. Hussein slowly backed away from her, pulling the revolver out of his pants. He wondered how many shots he would have to fire to make sure she was dead.

He brought his other hand up to steady the first. *There is no God but Allah*, he repeated silently, desperate to regain his concentration. *This is for Ali, for Ali, for Allah.*

The little girl still stood with her back to him and head upturned, as if mesmerized. Sweat poured down Hussein's face. *Do it now!*

"Do you ever think about heaven, Hussein?" Ophélie asked, still looking at the stars.

Fire! Kill her now before she turns around and sees what you will do.

"I can't wait to go there and be with Jesus. Bribri says in heaven there is no more crying or war or bad men."

She wants to go to heaven, and I will send her there with one pull of the trigger.

Hussein aimed. He touched his finger to the trigger. Everything in him trembled, and tears ran down his face. "I can't do it," he said aloud, and a wave of relief ran through him. He dropped the gun in the grass.

"Can't do what?" Ophélie turned around to face him. "Go to heaven? Oh, Hussein. Don't worry. Jesus loves you. He'll take you to heaven when you die, if you ask Him."

She walked over to him. She was like a ghost or an angel, standing there in her white nightgown. Her fine, small features looked so fragile and delicate. A soft breeze blew through her hair. Hussein stared at her, trembling, crying.

"Whatever is the matter, Hussein? Don't you find it beautiful?" She wiped a tear from his face. "Oh, I know. It's like Bribri says. Sometimes people cry with happiness. Sometimes your feelings get all mixed up, and you can't think if you are sad or happy or both."

Suddenly Hussein laughed out loud. She was right, this little girl. His emotions were all over the place. He was terrified at what he almost had done and equally terrified that he had not done it. But mostly he was relieved and ecstatically happy that Ophélie still stood before him, alive.

"We'd better go in now," he whispered hoarsely.

"Aw ... well, okay. I'll get the chair." She ran over to a corner of the courtyard. As she did, Hussein stooped and picked up the revolver, tucking it back into his pants. He had the strangest feeling that the heavens were blinking down their approval.

"One of the children has been playing with my chair again," Mother Griolet commented good-naturedly. "Right under the bathroom window. Dear me, I hope none of the new children are trying to run away. You could hardly blame them if they did."

Gabriella picked up the wicker chair and brought it into the shade of an olive tree near the courtyard wall. "Sit down, please, Mother Griolet."

"Thank you, child." She leaned over and touched a pansy. "Poor thing. It's getting too hot for them now. They'll soon be dying out. Ah well, they've been so very helpful, haven't they? Got us through the winter cheerily, with their bright splashes of color."

Gabriella brought a chair from the dining hall into the courtyard and sat down beside Mother Griolet. "I wanted to talk to you while the children are out on their walk about ... about your offer."

"*Ah, oui, ma fille.* Of course." She spoke with difficulty, as if her mind were on something else.

"Are you still interested, Mother Griolet? I've been thinking about it a lot—praying too, of course. It scares me to death. I don't possibly see how I could do it." She turned her hands in her lap. "But I'm willing to give it a try."

Mother Griolet said nothing, staring lamely in the distance. Gabriella watched her carefully. She had expected the nun to be ecstatic, or at the least enthusiastic.

"Are you all right, Mother Griolet?" She touched the old woman's hand.

The nun looked around and smiled at Gabriella, but her eyes were filled with tears. Gabriella thought that perhaps she had not heard her. She started to speak again, but the old nun began talking.

"Forgive me, dear. A bit reflective these days. Thank you, Gabriella. Thank you for being willing to stay. You are a spunky young woman. The Lord will do many things through you, I have no doubt." She patted Gabriella's hand. "But I am not sure it will be here."

"What do you mean?" Gabriella had wrestled with this decision for two weeks. "Are you saying you don't want me after all?"

"Of course not, Gabriella. No, that isn't it." She shook her head slowly. "We've been receiving a lot of disturbing mail lately, and it seems the church and the government agree that this place should be closed down."

"What? There's not a better orphanage in all of France. And the exchange program! What about that?"

"The parents are withdrawing their support. You must under-stand that a good deal of the funding comes from a handful of wealthy Americans who have supported this program since its inception. Without their money, it can't go on."

"But why are they withdrawing support?" She answered her own question. "It's Caroline, isn't it? She wrote her dad."

"Yes."

"And all those important businessmen believed her? That's crazy!"

"Her father is very influential. I'm afraid little St. Joseph has gotten caught up in a political game of power that really has nothing to do with us."

"And the orphanage?"

"The townspeople have worked up a petition demanding that the Arab children be sent away. They are no happier about the pied-noirs, but what can they say? The church feels that the place cannot stay open without the town's support—they do provide a good bit of the financial backing. Some of the more prominent families have always been extremely generous ... until recently."

"But they can't just close it down! What will happen to the children?" Gabriella felt faint, angry.

"Some will be adopted, the rest sent to other orphanages. The harki children will doubtless go to the refugee camps that are being set up in the region."

"And you can't do anything?"

Mother Griolet laughed. "I am not a very popular person in the higher echelons. People have put up with me, but few will be sorry to see me go."

"Go! Go where?"

The nun shrugged.

"It's impossible! I won't let it happen! Surely Sister Isabelle and Sister Rosaline can do something! No! We won't give up. It's not like you to give up."

"My fiery little redhead! I appreciate your zeal. Of course I don't want to give up. But it seems God is closing the door."

"He can't be. Not when I'm ready to step through it." Gabriella stopped herself, realizing that she had been shouting. She lowered her voice. "Aren't you the one who said to trust? That God always provides? You've said it to me a hundred times. Please don't give up." She grabbed the nun's hands. "Please teach me. Teach me everything. School will be out in a week. I'll have all my time to learn. All summer to see your files, to understand how you have done it."

"I don't deserve you, Gabriella. If you wish, I'll show it all to you. But I can't promise you or David a job for next year. Our Lord can do as He pleases. He's got my attention now, and I'm not sure where He's leading."

"I'm not afraid of whatever comes. You'll be here to show me. I'm sure God will do the rest."

The talks about oil were leading nowhere, and Roger Hoffmann had a strange feeling that they never would. He could not put his finger on it, but something was amiss. For the past two days he had felt sluggish, unable to think clearly. His flight was scheduled to leave tomorrow, to his immense relief. His suitcase was packed, and official good-byes had been said. He decided to find a taxi and ride to the airport tonight to make sure nothing changed his plans.

Suddenly his hotel door was forced open and two hooded men rushed in. Before he could even speak, one of them hit him hard across the face and sent him reeling.

"What in the—?"

"This is a message from the OAS, Hoffmann. No more dealings with the FLN. You shouldn't be here. We're going to make sure you never come back."

The letter from Anne-Marie had come through his friend Luc at the épicerie just this morning, and Moustafa tore open the envelope with trembling hands. A letter from Anne-Marie. He knew that he was grinning foolishly. He couldn't help it. Today he had two reasons to celebrate. He grabbed David by the shoulders, shook him hard, and laughed. "It's a miracle! Mother has agreed to leave with my sisters! And here's a letter from Anne-Marie. Maybe your God is smiling down on me today."

David patted him on the back. "Go enjoy your letter, *mon ami.*" He raised his eyebrows. "And afterward, I want to hear all about it."

Moustafa stretched out on the mattress in the bedroom, letting his eyes soak in the reality of Anne-Marie's penmanship in her first three words: *My dear Moustafa.* The doubts that had plagued him for the past two months seemed to fade away.

I am happy and safe in this little haven. It is so perfect, and yet I am sick for missing you.

The future was suddenly bright with possibilities. Anne-Marie knew they could make their love work if only he would come to her, she said. Then she wrote about Ophélie and about Hussein arriving. Moustafa frowned at the news of the lost trunk. That meant she had not received his letter.

> *Gabriella is becoming a true friend, Moustafa. You will like her.... All the adults at the orphanage read the Bible for themselves. Even Ophélie can quote verses from the Holy Book and explain them to me. I hope I am not shocking you, but I am reading it too, just to see. These are things we will discuss when you are here.*

Moustafa shook his head in wonder that Anne-Marie was also discovering the Bible. It made a chill run down his back, as if maybe Allah, or whatever this God's name was, actually wanted them to be together. How he longed for a safe place, away from the suffering, away from the pain.

Maybe she was right. Maybe there was a life for them in France … if only he could get there!

Rémi Cebrian had another trunk at his farmhouse. But Moustafa knew one trunk could not conceal his brother and him. There was talk blowing around, his mother had whispered to him this morning, that a French officer was renting a whole ferry to take his harki troop, of which Moustafa's brother was a member, to France on July 3. If his brother could secure two places on that boat, they would be guaranteed safe passage. But one boat was only a drop in the bucket for the hundreds of thousands of harkis and their families who needed to escape. He had two and a half weeks to find a way.

A knock came on the front door, and by the sound of David's voice, Moustafa knew it was the Arab girl calling. Two weeks to the hour. He tucked Anne-Marie's letter under his mattress and came into the den. The girl and the turbaned man nodded politely.

"We've come to see if Fatima will be able to leave with you."

"I'm sorry to be unable to give you more information. We are in the process of working things out with a friend," David explained. "Could you come back in a few days? The details should be firmed up by then."

Moustafa shot him a glance. "Yes, is there a way to reach you in a hurry, in case it comes together quickly?"

"No, that is impossible. We are in hiding." The turbaned man did not try to hide his frustration. "We will come back in three days."

When they had left the apartment, Moustafa showed Anne-Marie's letter to David. "She said Hussein left the trunk in Marseille. Why in the world would he do that?"

"Maybe it was too much of a mob."

"But he knew it contained valuables."

"What are you getting at?"

Moustafa thought out loud. "I don't know. Anne-Marie says he wouldn't tell her a thing about us. Don't you find that strange? What has the kid got to hide? He's an orphan."

David's eyes narrowed. "I don't have any idea. He never was very talkative anyway. But it's a shame about the trunk."

"Yeah, a rotten shame."

They squatted in the fine sand around a bucket of ripe black olives, eating the fruit and spitting the seeds out on the ground. Rémi was shaking his head as he listened to Moustafa. "How could the boy do it? Leaving Eliane's trunk? It had her favorite heirlooms in it. I thought you trusted him."

"We did. He seemed happy to help in any way." David stood up, stretching his legs. "Look, Rémi, I don't know what to say. We miscalculated. I'm sorry."

"How could you know? It's just for Eliane. She's already been through enough, and now this. She must be heartbroken."

"Surely they wouldn't destroy the trunk. There must be a warehouse where lost items are stored." Moustafa threw a seed into the sand.

"You're right. It is all the more reason for me to leave here soon." Rémi rose. "I've been fixing up the other trunk like the first. I've put the rest of her favorite things in it, and there's plenty of room for another child. But now I wouldn't trust anyone." He laughed bitterly. "Maybe I'll hide in it myself. Maybe that's how I'll get to France."

The men talked on. A worry line crept over Rémi's face as Moustafa spoke of securing a place on a ferry for his mother and sisters so that they could leave immediately.

"Have you been to the docks lately? It is claustrophobic. Hundreds of panicked pied-noirs. The wait is days long. No room for Arabs. I am afraid your mother and sisters would be left sitting by the sea when independence comes. It is much too dangerous." He saw Moustafa's face fall. "I'm sorry."

"There has to be something we can do," David said, tossing an olive seed forcefully into the yard. In a second, his face lit up. "Of course! Why haven't we thought of him before? Jacques and the *Capitaine*!"

"We haven't thought of him," Moustafa said sourly, "because you told us he refused to make any more trips. Too dangerous."

"Yes, yes, you're right. That's what he said. But you know Jacques. He needs a lot of coaxing, a feeling of importance. One last trip. We'll fill the boat with the harki women and children and tell him he'll be a hero. Which is the absolute truth."

"And how will we convince him? It's not like we can trot on over to Marseille tomorrow."

"Your friend, Moustafa. At the épicerie. He's sending and receiving mail with the ferries. Jacques could have the letter in a matter of days." David sounded confident. "If I word it right, I'm sure Jacques won't fail us. We'll get the children ready. Tell them it will be in less than two weeks. I'll write the letter today, and you will leave with your mother and sisters."

Moustafa shook his head vehemently. "I promised Mother that I'd stay until my brother goes. She won't leave unless I do. But don't worry. I am planning a trip to Philippeville on the second of July."

"That's three hours away. What will you do there?" Rémi asked, narrowing his eyes.

"My brother and I will be on the harki ferry. Protected by the French army. I'll do anything to be on that boat." He smiled at the men, but his eyes were solemn. That same determination, that loyalty, was fixed on his face. "Will you drive us there, Rémi?"

The basket of olives was almost empty. Rémi reached down and pulled out one last small black fruit, turning it over in his fingers. "Some of the finest olives anywhere in the world. Grown right here. *Chez moi.* How I hate to leave it." He tossed the olive up in the air and caught it in his mouth. "I'll take you, Moustafa. Nothing would give me greater pleasure than to watch you ride away from this putrid place to find a future in France."

18

The sun was hot and forceful as Henri Krugler straddled the roof of the farmhouse, working on some loose tiles. He wiped his forehead to remove the perspiration. His back was burning, he could tell, and reluctantly he pulled a white T-shirt over his thick torso.

For a moment he looked toward the rolling hills surrounding Lodève. These were not the majestic mountains of Switzerland, yet the rugged, wild beauty of the Cévennes pleased him. He liked to think of his Huguenot ancestors hiding in these mountains, refusing to abdicate their faith to the cruel King Louis XIV. That same zealous, fervent blood ran in his veins. Because of the atrocities, the Huguenots had fled to many other countries, notably Switzerland. There his ancestors had prospered and multiplied, and he felt proud to have so rich a heritage.

And now he was back in the same Cévennes mountains, carrying his message of hope and reconciliation not only to the French but also to the Arabs.

The sun on his white hair and beard gave him a look of power, sitting like a huge troll on the roof of the centre aéré. The ancient farmhouse was never intended to be a children's center. But it had been left in his keeping for these five years, and it appeared that he would have it forever. His apartment a few minutes down the road was plenty adequate for his needs. So when his requests to buy other buildings for the centre aéré were turned down, Henri decided to transform the house into a center. The additions were actually minimal: another bathroom, insulation for the basement, an enlarged eating area. He had enlisted the children, French and Arab working side by side, to peel off the soiled wallpaper and apply fresh paint.

Henri knew the predictions. Soon Lodève would be flooded with Arabs, more specifically harkis. The parents' prejudice had grown and ripened over the years. He could not change that. But two afternoons a week with the children might just start something in Lodève. He was betting his life on it.

He waved down to the pedestrians who walked by and gawked up at him. "*Une belle journée, n'est-ce pas?*" he roared down to the elderly women who watched him in awe. They nodded back, their old eyes wide.

Since its opening a month ago, the centre aéré seemed on the road to success. Every afternoon after school, forty children invaded the farmhouse. On Wednesdays, when there was no school, Henri had the children for the entire day. And soon, during the summer break, he would fill this little farmhouse with children every day of the week.

The children loved the friendly giant. Lonely Arab teenagers hung around the center in their free time, offering to help with the work, content to be in Henri's presence. Henri seized these opportunities to build friendships and raise questions about the meaning of life. During the hours that the centre aéré was open, he could not talk religion. But afterward he spoke to the children, who stared at him with eager eyes, of a gentle prophet who was also a priest and a king.

So it seemed that quite naturally God was guiding Henri in the next step of his dream. A centre aéré met the needs of the children, helped the parents, and provided nonthreatening integration. The next step was to form a group for the teenagers and young adults, a group that spoke of faith but respected culture. A safe place to come and talk. An oasis.

This afternoon, in only thirty minutes, the first meeting of Oasis would take place. Henri climbed down from the roof and headed for the shower. Afterward he dressed and towel-dried his white mane so that it stood up on his head in every direction as if to demonstrate the power of an electrical current. He let himself into a newly wall-papered bedroom upstairs and sank to his knees.

"Father God," he prayed aloud in a rich, booming voice made for a pulpit. "Thank You for making the dream a reality. Thank You for this house. You provide in the strangest ways. And thank You for the children who will come today. Give them the courage to attend despite their fears and prejudices. And, dear Father, give me the words and the actions to show them that this is indeed a safe place. An oasis for their souls. Amen."

The warehouse smelled of mildew and rotting fruit. A young French soldier, weary from his journey and a few too many bottles with his departing comrades, stumbled through the large building that was packed with newly delivered boxes fresh from the ferries. Other soldiers had already picked through the good fruit and the clothes. What was left was junk. The soldier laughed to himself, recalling a saying his father had often repeated: "One man's trash is another man's treasure."

But there was no treasure here. Absentmindedly he walked through the warehouse, running his finger over suitcases with broken handles, split umbrellas, a doll with one button-eye missing, boxes of mildewed clothes. Why didn't someone throw out all this rot?

And it was all rot, everything that had to do with this stinking war. But he was home now, on friendly French soil. Four years in Algeria had made him doubt that any place was friendly. Too much blood, too many tortures, too many men behaving like raving lunatics. He might still be there if it weren't for the bullet that had grazed his head. He touched the bandage. Thanks to the bullet, he got to go home a whole two weeks early.

He spotted an old wooden chest squeezed in beside a larger container and a metal trash bin. He bent over to inspect it. Now that was a nice piece of work. A trunk. A treasure chest fit for Robinson Crusoe, he thought, chuckling to himself. He ran his fingers over the rounded top with its black metal casing. His mother could use such a chest to store their blankets and quilts during the summer months. He lifted the lid, and a broken lock fell to the floor.

He felt a tinge of disappointment. Papers and china and old dolls and a big family Bible. Pictures of children, knickknacks. It was strange, though. The contents had been picked through, lying randomly in two compartments in the interior of the trunk. But the center space was empty, with grilled-in open windows in the front and the back. It looked like, well, it looked like somebody had been in the trunk. Now that was an ingenious way to get to France. Hidden in a treasure chest. He let the lid fall back in place and noticed the address written in bold letters on the top. *Castelnau.* Never heard of it. But the postal code meant it must be near Montpellier. Too bad for whoever was looking for their treasure. They'd never find it in this old warehouse. Just a piece of junk.

He rubbed his stubby chin thoughtfully. He'd ask his mother about it. If she seemed remotely interested, well, he could find his way back to this warehouse. It wasn't so far from where he lived. Yeah, if that would make dear old Mama happy, he would take it home, clean it up, and give her a nice surprise for her birthday in July. He left the warehouse, muttering to himself, "One man's trash is another man's treasure."

Gabriella did not know how she felt as she stepped out of the parsonage after her last exam. A few more days and the program would be officially over. She heard a small voice in her head. *Now is when the adventure begins.*

She winced involuntarily. What adventure? All the nights spent wrestling and praying over the decision had been for naught if Mother Griolet was right. No more exchange program. No more orphanage. She swallowed hard.

Little Castelnau. The town had welcomed her, delighted her, instructed her patiently in the ways of the Midi. She took one of the tiny side streets that led away from the church. This was perhaps her favorite part of town, crammed with small stone houses that were joined together and hidden behind the main roads and could only be reached on foot through the narrow alleyways.

Vines were clinging to the stone walls where palm trees poked their long-leafed heads over the top. Potted geraniums and petunias decorated every ancient windowsill. An old woman sat in front of her house on a tiny cement veranda, the vines above her making a living canopy to shade her from the strong June heat. A parakeet sang to her from its cage. A few white T-shirts hung from the upstairs window.

Gabriella followed the twisting passage, climbing up and down its wide steps. Every corner held a new surprise: a jubilant daisy bush, bright white with its green shoots pointing in every direction; a low-tiled wall that gave a view into the town below; a rounded little alcove with a stone bench hidden inside. *I'll have to bring David here when he gets back*, she thought.

She sat down on the bench and took his latest letter out of her book satchel. She had already practically memorized it. They would leave by July 2, he had said. Thirteen more days. That wasn't too long to wait.

But what was she waiting for? A job in an orphanage that might be closed down, and a man who had promised her nothing. Did he even consider the possibility that she might not be here when he got back? Had the thought even entered his head?

He sounded so angry, so despairing. The biting tone that had put her off so many months ago had found its way into his letter. She understood, or at least she tried to. Trust. What a huge word for its single syllable. How did you trust when the whole world was exploding in front of you?

The sun felt so soothing on Gabriella's face. Castelnau was oceans away from the war, and yet she did not feel peaceful. She closed her eyes. She had made the hardest decision of her life. She had agreed to stay in this tiny town, to take over an orphanage. She had decided without consulting David, in faith that her God would work out the details. She thought that it would be easy after the decision had been made. No, not easy. Clear. But Gabriella could not see anything at all.

Suddenly she sat up straight. Maybe God *was* making things clear. Originally she had planned to travel around Europe with her family during the month of August and then go with them to the States, where they would spend a year's furlough. She was already enrolled in a college there. Maybe she was supposed to do just that.

Those plans seemed centuries old now. Or maybe, maybe her life in Castelnau was the dream. Was she really considering giving up travel and a year in the States for this? For an aging nun and a cocky Ivy League grad? It sounded crazy when she thought about it. Maybe God was rescuing her from wasting her life in a lost little village in France. She had tried to reason it out, and she had been wrong. The answer was no. Now she must simply get on with her life.

She reread the letter that had come this morning from her mother, saying that the whole family would arrive in less than a month and asking if she could find a place for them to stay. Gabriella groaned inwardly. She didn't even know where to look. The knot in her stomach returned.

She would ask her landlady. Mme Leclerc would have an idea.

Gabriella left the bench and walked down the steps that let her out onto the main cobbled road of the town. The fountain sprayed beside her. Across the street, a small island of velvet green grass harbored some bright pansies and two tall cedars.

"But I love this town," she whispered to herself. "I could live here for a long time and be happy."

It thrilled her to walk on the cobblestones and touch the fruit displayed in a worn cart outside the épicerie, to contemplate bunches of purple grapes that had been painted on the stone wall by the liquor store. A hair salon was next, tucked inside an ancient vaulted room. She passed Pierre's boulangerie and smiled at the graying baker. She wanted to walk past these stores every day for a long, long time. She couldn't explain it. She just knew. She belonged in Castelnau.

She had made a wide circle through town and now came back to St. Joseph.

Anne-Marie stepped out of the chapel. "There you are! I've been looking for you. *Félicitations!*"

"Congrats for what?" Gabriella asked, surprised.

"For finishing your last exam. Don't you feel relieved?"

"Oh, that." Her voice fell flat.

"You mean it doesn't matter?"

"I don't know."

Anne-Marie fell into step with Gabriella, and they walked on through the town to where the road became paved.

"I guess I should feel relieved, but I only feel confused."

"About David?" Anne-Marie asked gently.

"David and everything else. I told you Mother Griolet had asked me to stay on at the orphanage—to be trained to take her place?"

"*Oui.* I remember."

"Well, it looks like the orphanage is going to be closed."

"*Non! Ce n'est pas possible!*"

"That's what Mother Griolet thinks. Everything shut down. And I had just told her I'd stay. Doesn't make sense, does it?"

Anne-Marie shrugged. "I don't think much in life makes sense. It doesn't seem like much of a tapestry to me."

They walked past the stately homes of Castelnau, which stood proud and private behind thick walls and high, neatly trimmed hedges. Farther out on their walk, some poppies tossed their heads beside the road.

"A tapestry always appears confused and tangled if you look at the back. I have a feeling that's all I'm seeing right now." Gabriella stopped to pick a poppy. "But surely God knows what He's doing, even if I don't."

"You're struggling with your God, *n'est-ce pas*? I wonder, does that happen often? And if it does, who wins?"

Gabriella chuckled. "That's a very good question, Anne-Marie. You have a way of seeing things, you know?" She bent over and pulled a few more tenacious poppies up by their roots. "Yes, I guess I struggle with Him a lot. I don't know who is going to win this time."

She pointed to her left, where the fields and vineyards opened out below them. "Could anything be more beautiful than that? An ancient countryside with stuccoed houses and vineyards and tall cypress and little flocks of sheep and goats." She looked down at her watch. "Oh my! We've got to get back for the orphans!"

They turned around and headed back into town.

"I still have a question," Anne-Marie remarked. "Do you mean that your God is not strong enough to convince you that His way is best?"

"God doesn't work that way. How can I explain it? He gives us a choice, never forces us. And His Spirit guides us. If we listen."

"But you have tried to listen, and you are not sure. Now what do you do?"

Gabriella turned to her friend, admiring both her dark, natural beauty and her honest questions. "You wait. That is the hardest part. You just wait."

The letter from Rémi helped to soothe Eliane's frazzled nerves. He wrote that as soon as he arrived in Marseille he would try to locate the lost trunk. He said he missed her. And he explained that some other harki children would be arriving within the next two weeks.

"Great. More harkis," she grumbled. Then she felt ashamed. Poor people. Slaughtered in Algeria.

At the end of the letter Rémi gave the slightest hint that he would be coming to France soon. Was she reading it into the letter? No. It was there.

I have done all I can do here. Time is running out.

If she held on a few more weeks, then surely Rémi would be here and maybe she would stop feeling as though her life had been put on hold.

"Come on, children! Time to go. The bus will be here in five minutes."

She placed José on one hip and locked the hotel door, letting Samuel and Rachel go in front. The bus stop was just across the street.

For their first visit to Anne-Marie at the orphanage in Castelnau, she didn't want to be late. She only hoped she didn't see that harki boy. She might just give him a piece of her mind.

Today had been the last day of the exchange program. Tonight the young ladies, Mother Griolet, M. Vidal, and the Sisters were celebrating with dinner at a restaurant in Montpellier.

Anne-Marie was relieved that she and Eliane had been left to watch the children. With all the clamor of the kids, plus keeping an eye on baby José, Eliane had not had time to ask her any questions. Anne-Marie did not want her to know how afraid she was.

But once the children were settled in their dormitories for the night, including Rachel and Samuel, Eliane took Anne-Marie's arm. "We could take a little walk here in the courtyard, if you want. I'll just put José in the stroller."

Reluctantly Anne-Marie agreed. They walked slowly around the silent, empty courtyard.

"Something is wrong, isn't it?" Eliane probed.

Anne-Marie nodded. "I didn't want to mention it, but … it's the new boy. He didn't bring any news of Moustafa. I think it's strange."

"He's a selfish little tramp," Eliane said. "I'm sorry he's had a rough life, but he could at least have had the decency to bring me my trunk. After all, it did carry him to freedom. Hmph. I'm sorry about your father's will."

Anne-Marie shrugged. "I'm afraid, Eliane. Gabriella has said that the orphanage may be closed soon. I have nothing. Not one centime. What will happen to Ophélie and me if Moustafa doesn't come back?"

Eliane took her friend's hand and placed it on the buggy handle, with hers on top. "It's hard, isn't it? I'm afraid too. It feels like my life has stopped. We've gone from one hostile environment to another. Not the terror of war, but the prejudice of racism."

"You talked about a new beginning, Eliane. Do you still believe it?"

The cheerful young mother with the ready smile suddenly looked pensive. "I do believe it." She measured her words. "But it isn't going to be easy. I'm trusting God to show us. It is awfully hard to wait, though."

"You sound like Gabriella. She said that was the hardest part, the waiting. But at least you believe Someone is there to answer. I have no one to call on."

"Do you want to have Someone?"

"What do you mean?"

"If you want God to be your God, He's there, waiting. Membership is not reserved for some elite group. It's open to everyone who truly believes."

Anne-Marie felt uncomfortable. "I hope you won't take this wrong, but I'm just not convinced. It seems so easy for you, for Gabriella, for Mother Griolet and the Sisters. But you all grew up believing. I did not. Papa didn't start attending church until he was over forty."

"Yes, I remember. We were all surprised to see the well-known captain walk in the door of the Temple Protestant."

Anne-Marie got up her courage. "Tell me what he was like there, Eliane. At home he was so strict and aloof. He tried to explain his new beliefs, but I didn't understand."

"Did he act different?"

"Not really. Not at first. And then the war came, and he was gone so much. When he would come home, he had this urgency in his eyes, but I couldn't understand. I was in my rebellious years. I didn't want to hear. But now I do."

The extreme guilt that had weighed her down years ago rushed back upon Anne-Marie. "We weren't exactly on the best of terms when Mama and Papa were killed. I was living at home with them with Ophélie for a while. It was awkward. They did their best. But I was awful." She covered her face with her hands. "Finally I moved out. And then they were killed. It was terrible, Eliane. I never really knew my father. Mama and I were close, but …"

They were leaning over the end wall of the courtyard, staring out at the leafy trees and the tiled roofs of the village.

Eliane's voice was quiet, soothing, her hand gently squeezing Anne-Marie's. "Whenever your father came to a prayer meeting, he would pray for all of you. He loved you so much. Maybe he couldn't say it, but it was written on his face. He wanted you to know the peace he had found. It was so tragic, their deaths. So pointless and tragic."

"Did you read his will, Eliane? Did you at least read it?"

"Yes, as executor, I read it. He left the house, his possessions, everything to your mother, and then, of course, to you if she were not alive. But there is nothing left to claim now. The house has been looted many times. It stands empty, waiting for the Arabs to take it over. But there is a letter for you with the will. I didn't open that. I'm so sorry the trunk was lost."

Anne-Marie suddenly longed for that letter. Anything in her father's writing. To know he loved her, to know he forgave her. Something. Anything. But Eliane's trunk was gone, so it looked as though what Anne-Marie would have was nothing at all.

The girls pored over the menu at Le Ménestrel, one of the oldest restaurants in Montpellier, debating between the *saumon fumé*, the *magret de canard aux figues*, and the *foie gras aux épinards crus*. Candles flickered on each table of four, and soft strains of Handel and Bach drifted in the background. The young women talked in hushed tones, only occasionally bursting out in a ripple of laughter. It didn't matter. They were the only ones in the restaurant.

Later they enthusiastically sampled different cheeses, undaunted by the strong smells that had become so familiar to them over the past months. Stephanie chose a goat's cheese and a bleu as well as a Saint-Marcellin.

"You're brave!" whispered Gabriella, who took a wedge of Brie and a slice of Pyrénées.

"It's my last chance," Stephanie said cheerfully.

Gabriella closed her eyes briefly, soaking in the peaceful ambience, so different from the bedlam at the orphanage. She noted that the Sisters were enjoying every minute of "indulging the flesh," as Sister Isabelle called it. Even M. Vidal seemed lively and talkative tonight, sharing stories of the war with an astonished group of young women. Mother Griolet's voice sounded almost carefree as it mingled with M. Vidal's, adding a detail here and there to an adventure.

When the group finally rose and left the restaurant, it was well past eleven. For Mother Griolet's sake, Gabriella felt extremely thankful that the evening and the program had ended on a happy note. Even without David.

After breakfast the next morning, Gabriella and Mme Leclerc helped Caroline and Stephanie gather their bags and take them down the winding staircase to where a taxi waited. "Well, we're off to the train station and three weeks of travel," Caroline said happily. "You sure you won't change your mind, Gabriella? We're going to see seven countries in three weeks. It should be a real adventure. Take your mind off other things."

Gabriella hesitated. It would be so nice to escape for a few weeks. But she had already made up her mind. Mother Griolet needed her. "No, I'm going to stay."

"Waiting for David, huh?" Caroline eyed her slyly. "Well, I hope for your sake it's worth it. Good-bye. *Au revoir*, Mme Leclerc." She stepped into the taxi.

Gabriella turned and gave Stephanie a warm hug. "Have a good time on your travels. And be careful!" She was sorry to see her friend go. Stephanie looked at life so simply, taking whatever came without reading into it a deeper meaning. Gabriella gave her a kiss on each cheek. "I'm going to miss you. Thanks for everything."

"We did have some fun times, didn't we?" Stephanie laughed, then whispered, "And don't pay any attention to Caroline. She's just jealous. Promise me you'll tell me how the story ends!"

"I promise."

The taxi drove off over the cobblestones with Caroline and Stephanie waving from the backseat.

Mme Leclerc stood beside Gabriella, wiping her eyes. "It is always so *difficile* to see my girls go. *Ooh là là!* Thank goodness you're not leaving me yet. And it will be *un vrai plaisir* to meet your family. When did you say they arrive?"

"On the sixteenth."

"And I'll be leaving for a month starting on July 23. It will work out just fine."

"Thank you so much, Mme Leclerc. I don't know what I would have done with them otherwise. It's not as if they could stay at the orphanage."

"*Oh là, non!* That's for sure." Mme Leclerc rolled her eyes. "I'm delighted to have them here. And don't you worry about that Miss Caroline. I'm sure your M. Hoffmann will be coming back."

"*On verra*," whispered Gabriella. "I hope so. We'll just have to wait and see."

19

David had been right. Reluctantly Jacques came back for one more run with the *Capitaine*, agreeing to bring a last load of harki women and children to Marseille. Within the week, Moustafa had rounded up fourteen children as well as his mother and two sisters, all of whom were now ready to leave. They stood on an otherwise abandoned dock ten kilometers outside of Algiers. The sky was dark.

Jacques looked proudly at the assembled little group. "You did right to ask me, M. Hoffmann. You sure you won't be coming with me now?"

"No, Jacques. Not yet. I have to get Moustafa to Philippeville on Tuesday. The harki boat is leaving then. Once he and his brother are safe, I'll go too." He patted Jacques on the back. "Thanks for coming back, Jacques. You don't know what this means."

Jacques flashed him a timid smile, shook his hand, and bellowed to the group, "Time to go, folks. Let's get outta here!"

Mme Dramchini hugged her son to her breast. "You come soon, with your brother." Before Moustafa had a chance to answer, his mother was scurrying about, counting children, memorizing names.

Moustafa had said she would be perfect for the job, and David could see he was right. Mme Dramchini was a real mother hen. Moustafa's two teenage sisters followed her orders, gathering up luggage, wiping tears from little faces, whispering words of encouragement to frightened children.

"Did you get the message out soon enough?" Moustafa asked.

"I certainly hope so. I'm not sure what Jean-Louis will say when he sees this load of passengers." David chuckled, then suddenly grew very serious. "There's no room for them at St. Joseph. Gabby has written that the townspeople are protesting the arrival of Arab kids."

"What will they do?" Jacques asked.

"If there's no place at St. Joseph, they'll be sent to the refugee camps," Moustafa replied grimly.

Jacques cursed under his breath. "A prison in France."

David shrugged. "At least they'll live. Don't worry, Moustafa. They'll be safe. And when you get to France, your family will be waiting for you. A new beginning. You'll see."

David knew that his words did not sound convincing to Moustafa as the young Arab waved good-bye to his mother and sisters. Yes, at least these few would get away. But Hussein's friend Fatima had not shown up. David thought it quite strange. She knew the day and the time. She had been so adamant about going. But there was no sign of her. David hoped she did not lie dead in some forgotten side street.

They couldn't wait any longer. He motioned for Jacques to leave, and the *Capitaine* cast off from the docks and floated peacefully out into the Mediterranean.

For an instant, David felt the peace. He wished to high heavens he was on that boat. But everything was going to be okay. There was less than a week to wait. That was no time at all.

"Come on, Moustafa. They're safe. Let's go find Rémi and get home." David yawned. "It's past midnight."

Moustafa nodded, and he and David walked through the heavy brush without talking, listening to the crickets' incessant chirping.

Somewhere a twig cracked. The two men stopped. David put his finger to his lips. Nothing.

Moments later, out of nowhere, three men in ski masks appeared. There was only a brief scramble before one of the hooded men caught David from behind. David looked around for Moustafa. The Arab lay on the ground, unconscious.

One of the men held his hand over David's mouth, twisting his arm behind his back. "Where's your car?"

David did not reply. The man hit David hard in the stomach, and he doubled over.

"Answer me if you want to live."

"A friend let us off at the road," he gasped. "He'll be back soon." Then everything went black.

Rémi Cebrian waited in his car three kilometers from the dock, concealed in the bushes. He was the eyes of this mission, his job to watch and warn if anything looked amiss. Another car, a dark-colored Peugeot, had driven by twice, slowed to a crawl, and parked five hundred meters up the road, near the path. Rémi flicked a match and read his watch. After midnight. The rendezvous for the children had been an hour ago. Why would someone show up so late?

He touched the rifle on the seat beside him, hesitating. Slowly he stepped out of the car, shutting the door with the slightest of sounds. He jogged through the bushes, toward where the car had disappeared.

Not far away he heard a faint rustling of leaves. He stepped farther into the foliage and heard David's voice, followed by a curse and a thud. Then silence. From the hiding place he saw two masked men carry Moustafa and David over their shoulders and push them into the backseat of a car, while a third climbed into the driver's seat. The doors slammed shut, and the car screeched on its wheels as it backed around and flew through the night.

Rémi felt his muscles go weak with fear. Then with some strange strength, he ran to his car and pulled into the road. He did not turn on the headlights but drove recklessly, terrified, in pursuit of the Peugeot. The stretch of road was deserted. Within five minutes he had picked out the car, still careening madly in the distance.

It was a brief prayer he sent to the heavens: *Give me eyes to see. Give me eyes to see.*

When David came to, he was afraid to open his eyes, afraid to see Moustafa's lifeless body beside him. He was aware of a terrible throbbing in his head. His mouth was gagged with a cloth, his throat parched. Through blurred vision, he took in his surroundings. He was lying on the floor in a basement, his hands secured behind him, his feet bound tightly.

Eventually his eyes adjusted to the darkness. He heard the heavy breathing of someone who slept. He tried to turn onto his side, and a piercing pain shot through the same shoulder that had received a bullet wound in March.

Cold fear overpowered him. Were the hooded men here too, waiting for him to wake up so they could torture him? That could be the only reason for leaving him alive. His mind was foggy. He couldn't think.

Even darkness is not dark to Thee. At once the debilitating fear left. He was not alone. Trust. With the psalmist's words in his mind, David fell back asleep.

The faintest light of predawn broke through a small barred window near the ceiling of the room. Moustafa blinked his eyes, hoping to shut out the nightmare, but this was real. He was sitting in the same dingy basement where he had spent five weeks with Anne-Marie last fall. He wanted to cry out, but the sob stayed in his throat, held in place by the thick handkerchief secured in his mouth.

David Hoffmann lay stretched out uncomfortably on the floor nearby. Moustafa watched him intently. Yes, he was breathing. Relief flooded through him. Together there was hope.

He rolled over awkwardly and caught his breath. They were not alone. An older man, unshaven and wearing a white T-shirt and suit pants, slept, his head resting against the cement wall. His hands and feet were bound, as were Moustafa's and David's.

Somehow Ali had caught up with them. How? Moustafa knew the answer immediately. Fatima. The girl had not shown up for the boat. She was the only other person who knew where the meeting was to take place. And if Fatima had led Ali to them, then what about Hussein?

He swallowed hard. Now it all made sense. Hussein showing up, begging, leaving in the trunk and then abandoning it at the port.

He couldn't speak. He couldn't move. Moustafa lay flat on his stomach and felt his tears form a small wet patch on the ripping mattress. A low moan echoed in his soul.

Anne-Marie. Anne-Marie.

When David woke again, the room was bathed in gray shadows brought on by a single barred window. Moustafa lay on a mattress nearby. Their eyes met, and they read each other's thoughts: sorrow and relief. They were both alive.

Moustafa motioned with his head toward a corner of the room. A man sat with his back against the wall, still asleep. David scrutinized him carefully. His legs were tucked up against his chest, bound. *He must be very tall*, David thought. His forehead was bent forward, resting on his knees. His hair was peppered with gray.

David scrambled to sit up, and the noise caused the older man to stir. Slowly he lifted his head, blinking his eyes.

David could not cry out. Only his eyes registered his terrible surprise. Sitting across from him, ten feet away, was his father.

What was his father doing in Algeria, in the hands of whom? The FLN? Was it another level of Ali's sadistic revenge? The madman had won. His last victory would be for David to watch his father die. Then Moustafa. Was that the plan?

David felt tears in his eyes, and they surprised him. This man he had hated, this distant father, sat weak and helpless before him, gaunt and unshaven. David did not want to feel sympathy. He did not want that part of his heart exposed. But with arms and legs tied, unable to move or speak, unable to control his emotions, he sat and let the tears fall down his cheeks.

He swallowed hard. *We are going to die here together, and I've never once heard you say you care about me.* But in that pitiful gaze from his father he read something, perhaps not love, but concern. He brought his head to his knees and wiped his face on his pants. Still the tears came.

Roger Hoffmann, bound and gagged in the same manner, stared at him with an expression of deep sorrow. One tear, then another. A wet gleam in his eyes. It trickled down his cheek.

David heard Mother Griolet's words. *Your father wept.* Perhaps it was true after all. Perhaps his father had cried when he had found him at the orphanage all those years ago. The tears on his face at this moment suddenly made anything possible.

Rémi had worked frantically through the night, but light was coming too soon. Now his little band of men raced through the Casbah, looking for the building where he had seen Moustafa and David imprisoned in the night. The tiny white bits of material he had left on signposts had been the only way he could possibly retrace his steps in the labyrinth of the Casbah. He whispered a prayer of thankfulness that it had worked.

Now Abdul and Amar, his friends and farmhands, stood panting beside him. Their Arab faces would be accepted in the Casbah if dawn broke before they could free the prisoners. Rémi admired their courage, their willingness to risk their lives for him. That was the Algeria he knew and loved. Friendship, not betrayal.

Each man carried a rifle over his shoulder. After one last turn into a tiny alleyway, they reached the building where the prisoners had been enclosed. *Let them still be there*, Rémi prayed. Abdul and Amar climbed with Rémi onto a low roof beside the building. From his perch, Rémi peered into the barred window. Three men, bound and gagged, sat in the room. Abdul dropped to the ground and tried the door. It was bolted with a lock. They would have to use the small explosive to free the men, and quickly.

Rémi tossed a small stone through the window. Immediately three pairs of eyes looked toward him. Pressing his face against the bars, he whispered, "We're going to have to blow it open. Move back, and be ready."

The men nodded, relief in their eyes. But before he had taken the explosives from their bag, Abdul climbed up beside Rémi. "Someone's coming," he whispered.

Rémi felt a sinking in his heart. Four men approached in the predawn light. What should he do? Shoot them now? But that would awaken the whole neighborhood. They crouched out of sight, hearing their own hearts pounding in their ears.

The tallest man, older than the others, inserted a key in the locked door and threw it open, motioning to his men to follow him inside. Then the door closed behind them, and Rémi watched the scene through the window, dizzy with fear.

The tall man slapped David across the face, then rammed his head with the butt of his gun and laughed. "So, David Hoffmann! At last you are here." His voice was soft and seething. "It could not have worked out better for me. You are all here. Our dear Moustafa—"

He nodded to one of the men, who kicked Moustafa in the stomach.

"Easy," the tall, angry Arab muttered. "Don't kill him yet. I want them to know every last grisly detail." He turned back to David, who was crumpled on the floor, blood seeping from his head. "And your estranged father, Roger Hoffmann. Brilliant to have you all here together. You will watch him die slowly, painfully, as my father did. This will be my final revenge.

"No one has escaped. Not one. Have you not guessed? Could you not read the mind of my prodigy, Hussein? Of course not! We are too smart! He is even now accomplishing his task in Castelnau at the little orphanage." He laughed madly. "The timing! The incredible timing! Today I have word that Hussein has successfully completed his little task. He has eliminated your friends."

Moustafa stirred, crying from within the gag, but it was only a muffled sound. Rémi saw the anguish in his glare.

So this was Ali Boudani. Rémi had heard them talk of the revenge-obsessed man. Everything they had said was true.

Ali was snickering, "Not only Anne-Marie, mind you. Her daughter! Yes, her daughter was the first to go. And then the redhead. And all the children. They are all gone. Explosions in the night in both dormitories. Nothing left of that place but an old nun, and she will die soon enough as it is." He paced gleefully around the room as the three bound men turned their eyes down and wept.

The sun was rising over the stack of buildings in the Casbah. Soon people would awake. Rémi sensed that it was now, while Ali Boudani was momentarily distracted by his own sickening pride, or never. With a quick whispering, the men were ready.

Abdul and Amar dropped to the ground without a sound. They kicked open the door and fired. Several bullets sprayed forth, hitting two of Ali's henchmen, who fell to the ground, stunned and wounded. Rémi fired from the window, and his shot lodged in the back of the Arab who held Moustafa.

Enraged, Ali turned his gun toward the window and fired twice. The bullets ricocheted off the stone. He turned his gun on Moustafa and fired two more times. Moustafa screamed and fell to the ground. Amar came at Ali. From close range, Amar's bullet hit Ali in the gut. Ali cursed, clutching his stomach and dropping his gun. Abdul started cutting furiously at the prisoners' ropes.

"Hurry, run!" Rémi urged.

Ali lay dazed beside Roger Hoffmann. He reached for his gun, while the older American struggled to stand. Rémi fired another shot. Ali never reached his pistol.

Supporting the prisoners, the three rescuers half ran, half stumbled into the streets. Doors opened; people screamed.

Abdul looked at Moustafa. "Can you get us out of here?"

Moustafa was losing blood, but he managed to reply. "Yes, I know the way."

"Good," Abdul said. "I'll stay behind and divert them. No one will know I am not an inhabitant of the Casbah myself."

"Thank you, friend," Rémi said. "Be careful. God be with you."

In broad daylight the men fled through the streets of Bab el-Oued and piled into Rémi's car.

Rémi sped like a madman out of the city and to his farmhouse outside of Algiers. There, a friend of his, a pied-noir who had practiced medicine in Algiers for thirty years, came at his summons to examine the wounded men.

He quietly addressed Rémi. "I can remove the bullets from the Arab here. It will be painful, but there is too great a risk in taking him to the hospital. Do you have any alcohol?"

Rémi nodded.

"Get him drunk then. It is the only way he will stand the pain."

Two hours later Moustafa floated in and out of consciousness. Through persistence Rémi had gotten half a bottle of whiskey down his throat. The doctor was ready to begin.

David lay on the couch in the den of the Cebrians' farmhouse. The doctor had diagnosed a broken rib and advised him to have it x-rayed as soon as he got to France. He also had a nasty head wound, from the butt of Ali's gun, and his whole body ached.

He tried to make sense of the turn of events, but he could not think straight. He could only hear the crazed Ali explaining the fate of the orphanage. Surely, surely he was wrong. Hussein? With bombs?

David would not believe that they were gone. Gabriella, Anne-Marie, Ophélie. All the others. It was too grotesquely impossible to imagine.

But he feared with everything in him that it was true.

No, God would not permit it!

Every ounce of faith drained away. Bitterness engulfed him. If it were true, then all he had left was his dying father. He did not want him. It was not a fair trade.

His father slept on a mattress hauled from one of the bedrooms. Starvation and torture, the doctor had whispered. He needed medical help badly. But it would have to wait until they got to France.

David was glad he could not see the procedure the doctor was performing on Moustafa. In spite of his rage and grief, the only thing that seemed to make any sense was prayer. He closed his eyes. *God, I don't understand what is happening. I'm too afraid to learn the truth. Gabby has always said You are a good God. She says that the righteous will prosper. I have read it in Your Word. Please, bring Moustafa through.* David shut his ears to the low moans coming from the other room. *Bring him through, God. And ... and give me a word, a simple word to say to my father.*

Before he had finished his prayer, Roger Hoffmann whispered, "David?"

"Yes?"

"Are you badly hurt, son?"

"No. No, Father, I don't think so." The words were like glue in his mouth. "And you?"

"Fine." He sighed. "The plane has already left."

"Father?"

"Be sure, Annette, to show your American passport if there is any doubt. I'll be back in three days."

"Father! Father, what are you saying?"

"Detained, David. I was detained for questioning." He looked at his son, his eyes dull. "It was the SS. They found out our work. Took me to a camp. It was the torture, David. I thought I would say nothing. The torture. All my fault. For you, for Annette and Greta. All my fault." His father's voice was cracking with emotion. "I had forgotten what you say when you are tortured." His breath came in sporadic sighs. "I'm so sorry, David. It was all my fault."

Roger Hoffmann was sobbing like a baby. At first David could only stare, wide-eyed. Surely this wasn't his father, confessing in tears before him. Why had he never explained it before? Why had he not said that he too had been taken to a camp?

David felt he would vomit. He put a hand on his forehead. "You were in a camp?"

"Only for a few months. My passport worked for me. But there was no word of you and your mother and sister. By the time I traced you, it was to that orphanage in France. And you were alone."

"You hated me for surviving, didn't you? You wanted it to be Mother, not me." There was no accusation in David's voice. He might as well have been asking a question about the weather.

He heard no answer, and at first David thought his father had fainted. His breath came slowly and with effort.

"I didn't hate you, David. I hated myself. For all these years, I have hated myself. Annette. Greta! Why did I leave that day? I have asked myself that question a thousand times. And the only answer is self-hate. I contaminated you with it, David. I thought I had ruined your life, as I had my own.

"But you were strong and smart. You survived in spite of me. You didn't need me. And I couldn't bear the sight of you. Your very presence accused me."

David did not want his father to see that he was crying again. With difficulty he asked, "And now?"

"Now." He spoke resignedly. "Now the nightmare has come back to haunt us both. Another war. Another chance to betray the one I love." He did not look at David. The words floated in the stifling air.

When Moustafa awoke, he was aware of incredible pain. It was more than physical; it was psychological, invading his being. He wished he had died from the bullet wounds. Now the torture was only prolonged.

There was no reason to leave for France. Anne-Marie was dead. His thoughts spiraled down to despair, imagining his mother and sisters arriving in France with all the children. What would they find? A shelled-out orphanage? A crazy kid tossing bombs as if they were stones? Who would warn them?

Another thought came to him from the corner of his mind. *He's lying.* Ali had done it before, months ago, telling Anne-Marie that they had captured Ophélie. The thought made his heart soar with hope. Of course! A lie. Hussein would not murder. But how could he be sure?

Trust? Whom? There was no one to trust.

The Christ. He heard the words in his mind. He fought to push them away. Impossible! No God could save them from this hell.

And yet, for now, they were alive and safe. It stung him to think of it. Despair or hope. He could choose. He closed his eyes, wincing with pain, and, reciting something he remembered reading in the New Testament, Moustafa whispered, "I believe. Help Thou mine unbelief."

20

The petition from the townspeople of Castelnau was conclusive. Get the Algerian children out and now. Only Pierre Cabrol, the boulanger, and Jean-Louis had voted to keep them. Every other person had expressed, some vehemently, dissatisfaction with the overcrowded, understaffed, and integrated orphanage of St. Joseph. The situation was already grim, and now another fourteen harki children had arrived in the night with three Arab women.

Mother Griolet leafed through each petition, reading the angry notes. She could almost feel the embarrassment of her friends and neighbors as they scribbled their signatures. People she had loved and trusted and helped. People who had given their money to the Church of St. Joseph. She reread the latest letter from her superiors and gave a bitter laugh.

The choice was hers. Send the Algerian children away, or be sent away herself. There really was no choice at all. She would not send orphaned harki children to be cloistered from French society. Here, at least, they could learn to function within a small village, find some safety, integrate. With all her heart, Mother Griolet knew that the answer to the harki problem was not refugee camps.

She fingered a letter from Joseph Cohen. She wished for a moment that she were back at the chalet in Switzerland, sitting by the roaring fire with Joseph and Emeline there to advise her. As it was, they counseled her now through a letter. Joseph urged her to get in touch with his Swiss friend Henri Krugler, who now lived in Lodève, an hour's drive from Montpellier.

He would be sympathetic to her cause, Joseph said—"a giant of a man whose heart in every way matches his size." She reread Joseph's description of Henri Krugler's centre aéré in Lodève, which had recently opened to both Algerian and French children. Perhaps indeed this man could help her find homes for the children before the church dispersed them to the camps.

With great determination the old nun picked up a pen and wrote a letter to this intriguing stranger.

It was love that propelled Mother Griolet to enter the empty chapel later that afternoon. A strange kind of love. She stepped slowly onto the stones, relieved to escape the brutal heat of the sun in the cool interior. Feeling dizzy, she placed her hand on the back of the last row of wooden pews to steady herself. She closed her eyes briefly.

With labored steps she walked toward the west side of the chapel into a small alcove. She paused in front of a stone pillar, one of several that supported the roof. Then she touched the simple stone monument that rested on the pillar. She read the words through blurred vision.

Nos frères, nos fils, nos maris qui ont donné leurs vies pour notre pays. 1914–1918.

On the plaque was a list of thirty-eight names of men from Castelnau who had died during the First World War. She ran her fingers over the stone, feeling the rise and fall of the chiseled letters until her hand came to rest on the last one. Sebastien Vidal.

She let the memories come, let the emotions rise as she remembered the soft kiss on her lips and the terrible searing in her heart when he had left. The bittersweet agony of knowing he loved her and knowing he must leave. She leaned against the stone to keep her balance. "Sebastien," she whispered.

She shuffled to a wooden pew and sat down. "Dear Lord, my Savior. I have never accused You of taking Sebastien. There are things too hard to understand. I have known Your power and grace for all these years. And now this place that has been my calling is being taken away from me. But it is not mine; it is Yours. Work Your will, Divine Father, and may I accept it. You have always provided for every need, for me, for the Sisters, for the children. I trust You now."

She closed her eyes and pictured the orphans in the courtyard, laughing. She thought of Gabriella and Anne-Marie.

"Please, Holy God, give these women Your courage to face the future. I understand the pain of waiting. And show me how I can help. Surely You will not forsake Your own. We are Your people and the sheep of Your pasture."

She did not hear Anne-Marie enter the chapel, so that when the young woman sat down beside her, the nun let out a small gasp.

"I'm sorry," she said. "I didn't mean to scare you. Am I bothering you if I stay?"

"No, of course not. I was just finishing my conversation."

"Your conversation?" Anne-Marie asked, looking around the empty chapel.

"With the Lord."

"Oh." Anne-Marie lowered her eyes. "Excuse me." She rose to leave.

"My dear, don't go. The Lord and I have been talking for many years. He understands interruptions. Especially those that He ordains. Please, sit back down."

The young woman could not look the nun in the eyes. "I'm so afraid, Mother Griolet."

"Afraid?"

"Afraid of the future, if the orphanage is closed. Where will I go? You and the others, you have saved my life and that of Ophélie. I don't want to return to the life of fear and hiding. I long to start a new life with Ophélie. I had hope. But now ..."

Mother Griolet turned toward Anne-Marie, blinking back a stubborn tear. "Life takes many twists and turns. It bruises and burns and rips apart. But it also loves and heals and forgives." She took the younger woman's thin, smooth hands into her own. "Perfect love casts out all fear. And there is only one perfect love. It's in Christ. In seventy-two years, He has yet to let me down. He's in control when life is completely out of control."

She searched Anne-Marie's eyes for understanding. Perhaps there was a gleam, a hint. Mother Griolet sensed an urgency to open her heart to this brave young woman.

"It's the truest word in all of time. If you are in Christ, nothing, nothing, my child, can separate you from His love ever again. Not tribulation or distress or persecution or famine or nakedness or peril or sword."

Her words were melodic and powerful as she sang the scripture as much for herself as for Anne-Marie. The lively little nun recounted the promises of God to Anne-Marie, and as she did, God's peace flooded into her own soul once again.

Jean-Louis found Jeanette dozing at her desk. The sight of her, mouth opened, face supported by one hand that leaned precariously on the desk, embarrassed and frightened him. He had never known Jeanette to nap in the middle of the day. He fidgeted with his hands, running the yellowed envelope between them, back and forth, back and forth. Perhaps he should turn and leave. Taking a deep breath from the hallway, he rapped softly on the open office door.

There was a shuffling sound, then Jeanette cleared her throat and called, "*Oui, qui est là?*"

Jean-Louis took two steps into the office, keeping his eyes turned to the floor. His temple pulsed. "I just had a little matter to discuss with you," he mumbled.

The nun straightened up, flashed him a tired smile. "Of course, Jean-Louis. Come in and sit down."

Always a shy man, he was often embarrassed in the presence of women. But life had forced him to overcome some of the timidity. He sat stiffly on the edge of the chair, still clutching the envelope.

"Whatever is the matter, Jean-Louis? You look positively moribund!"

He removed his wire glasses and ran his fingers around his bloodshot eyes. "I have something for you." He held out the envelope. "But before you read it, I must tell you one thing. I have kept this letter all these many, many years, not out of hurt, but out of love. I have loved you, Jeanette, as much as Sebastien did, and more."

His hands were shaking violently. He could not look her in the eyes, but his voice was steady. "It has been my greatest pleasure and joy to know you, to work beside you, to watch you. We could not be man and wife. I knew that so long ago. But you have been my sister." He smiled bashfully at the pun. "A sister closer than blood. I admire your tireless work for the children, for this town, for the young American women, for me. You are a fine servant of our Lord. Don't let those letters get to you. I will do everything I can to keep St. Joseph open. I had to tell you now, so there would be no doubt. Whatever you need, I will help you."

He stopped talking abruptly, feeling the sweat on his forehead. He placed the envelope on her desk. "I could not give it to you sooner. Forgive me." With a slight bow of the head, he rose to leave.

"Jean-Louis," Mother Griolet said softly. She took his hand and squeezed it. "Thank you. You have always been here for me. You are a blessing in my life."

He squeezed her hand in return, then turned and left the office.

Jeanette rested her face in her hands and stared at the yellowed envelope. Her name was written across it in a handwriting that she recognized immediately, even after half a century. The envelope had been ripped open, then taped shut; and the tape, equally yellowed, no longer held any stick.

Her hand shook the slightest bit as she pulled out two pieces of paper, one yellowed, one white. She opened the yellowed sheet and felt a tightness in her throat. Fifty years could not make her forget the way her heart leaped when she had received a letter from Sebastien. This one was barely legible, but nonetheless his hand.

Ma chère Jeanette,

I fear I will not see you again on this earth. I cannot bear to tell you the extent of my injuries or the nightmare we face. I only want you to know that I have loved you for two years. I could not love you more. But I must release you to God. Go forth with strength, examine your heart for your service. It is worthy. More worthy than I.

I wanted to share life with you. If not me, let God lead you into your calling. Only please care for Jean-Louis. He will miss me so. And his love for you is as strong as mine.

Sebastien

The second sheet, clean and white, was scribbled by Jean-Louis and dated several weeks ago.

Forgive me, Jeanette. This letter was found on Sebastien's body. I could not give it to you all those years ago to place an extra burden on your heart. Somehow you fulfilled his wish without knowing of it. God is gracious. Merci.

Jean-Louis

It had startled her to see Sebastien's handwriting. Why now? Why after she had permitted herself that brief moment of memory in the chapel? She thought about the letter, and then she thought about Jean-Louis's note. Dear Jean-Louis. He had seen it lived out before him. There was no burden in the task. Surely he had understood what had been evident to her for years. His absolute devotion and her complete love.

To say that people at the orphanage seemed frazzled was a gross understatement. Fourteen new Arab children and three Arab women were, as the French said, the drop that makes the vase run over. The children had slept on mattresses on the floor of the dormitories. The three women had spent the night in Mother Griolet's den, but as soon as more mattresses could be found, they planned to move into one of the classrooms on the third floor of the parsonage. With almost sixty children at the orphanage, the buildings seemed to somehow shrink. Room was running out.

At least the girls from the exchange program were gone, Gabriella thought as she pushed several straggling children into the refectory. The din of silverware clanking on plates and voices shouting greeted her ears. One of the new Arabs screamed and another threw his food. Gabriella observed Sister Rosaline's displeasure. She snapped at them, then asked Hakim to see what they needed.

Sister Isabelle wrung her hands together, completely overwhelmed. Gabriella caught Anne-Marie by the arm and whispered, "This is bedlam. We've got to do something."

"I agree, but what?"

Suddenly Gabriella grabbed a soup spoon and a pot, stood on a chair, and banged on the pot with the spoon. The noise was deafening. Immediately all was silent.

"*Eh, les enfants! Taisez-vous!* Quiet down, won't you? Everyone find seats. Now."

Three of the boys who had been flipping peas across a table scrambled to find a chair. They clamped their arms between their legs, looked down, then caught their friends' gazes and giggled.

"This is not how we behave at St. Joseph. Manners are a must if we are all to get along. I think it would be appropriate for those of us who have been at St. Joseph for a while to welcome our new guests. As I call your name, come stand in three rows beside me. Anne-Sophie, Christophe, André, Ophélie, Hakim, Jérémie …"

Gabriella called all forty-three names, and one by one they came, grinning sheepishly, and stood before the newly arrived Arab children. Quietly and yet with great animation, Gabriella drew the children around her. "First we'll sing '*Pour ce repas*' in a round. Then '*Eclate de Joie*' and finally, '*Je t'aime, O Jésus.*'"

A short time later Sister Isabelle and Gabriella were sitting in chairs facing the group of orphans. As they began to sing, a chill ran through Gabriella. The voices of angels. She turned around and saw that the Arab women and children were mesmerized by the different melodies. When the song ended, silence reigned. Then a wide smile formed on the face of one of the Arab women, and she began to clap. Soon all the others joined in. By the time the impromptu program was over, order had been restored to St. Joseph.

Mother Griolet had not come to dinner. Gabriella slipped out as the orphans sat back down to be served dessert. She found the nun in her office, writing letters.

"Mother Griolet, are you all right?"

"I'm afraid that I'm being buried by all this paperwork," the nun replied, not looking up. "And perhaps I don't quite have the strength to face all the children. There are several possible adoptions I'm working on. I must finish them before, before ..." She set down the paper. Her eyes fluttered closed briefly, and she ran her hand across her forehead. "The petitions arrived today. All ninety-three of them. And the final warning from the church. We have thirty days to get the Arabs out. I'm afraid I am going to lose my post, Gabriella. I'm just trying to get as many children situated as possible before that happens."

"You mean there's no hope for St. Joseph?"

"My dear child. I am so sorry to have misled you. I asked you to make a tough decision, and now my control over it has been yanked away. Of course there is always hope. But not as I had imagined. I will not be staying around unless I agree to send the Arabs away to refugee camps. I don't intend to do that."

"It's not fair! They can't force you to go away. It's wrong!"

"It's not as I had hoped and prayed, but my superiors see it differently. My responsibility is to stand up for what I believe. But I cannot convince others that I am right."

"But the townspeople love you. The church has admired your work. How can they not see the good?"

"It's a dangerous thing to want everyone's approval, Gabriella. You must be willing to stand firm and take the risk of being misunderstood. We must find our approval at the feet of our Master." She closed her eyes again. "It's a lesson I have learned over and over. We're to expect suffering, in whatever form it comes— physical, emotional, spiritual. The Holy Book promises suffering for those who follow Christ."

She placed her unfinished letter in a stack of neatly folded papers. "Come now, Gabriella. They'll be needing us at the refectory."

Gabriella helped Mother Griolet up, then interlocked arms with her and walked slowly down the steps into the basement and through the hallway. She felt her mouth go dry. Thirty days. That was all the time they had. It was much too short.

Anne-Marie regarded the big-bosomed, gray-haired Arab woman who was now patting the heads of the children who had crossed the sea with her. She had not seen Mme Dramchini in years, nor her daughters, Saiyda and Rachida. In the confusion of the day she had not yet gotten to speak to them. Now she could have news of Moustafa. She approached them slowly.

"*Madame Dramchini, bonjour.* Do you remember me, Anne-Marie Duchemin?"

The gray-haired woman nodded and took Anne-Marie in her arms, kissing her cheeks. "*Ma fille,*" she exclaimed with a heavy accent.

Knowing that Mme Dramchini had never mastered French, Anne-Marie addressed her daughters. "*Bonjour,* Saiyda and Rachida. How very good to see you."

The young women embraced. Politely Anne-Marie answered their questions about how she had arrived with Eliane Cebrian on the ferry. Of course, they remembered Eliane. Yes, yes, Rémi had followed them to the dock. Anne-Marie's head was swimming. She did not know what Moustafa had shared with them. She did not want to seem too eager for information. As glibly as possible, she asked, "And Moustafa. How is he?"

Oh, he was very well. He and the American had taken them to the little sailboat with the funny Frenchman for a captain. Moustafa was coming with their other brother, Hacène, the day after independence on a boat just for the harkis.

They babbled on, smiling, and Anne-Marie knew then that Moustafa had never mentioned a word to them about what had happened during the months that he was missing. They did not know she loved him. Not yet.

She could not help but smile with great relief to hear of his plan to come to France. With his mother and sisters here, right here at St. Joseph, and a boat waiting to bring him. It was a miracle. Moustafa would be coming. The day after independence. Tonight was June 30. She had only three more days to wait.

Hussein spoke in Arabic with the new kids, placing himself within hearing distance of Anne-Marie and the three Arab women. It took every ounce of concentration for him to keep up a conversation with the children and still hear what the women were saying. He gathered that these Arabs were the mother and sisters of Moustafa. He heard, yes, he was sure that the younger girl said that Moustafa would be coming on a boat in a few days. A hint of a smile crossed his lips. *Allah be praised. They are alive!* He let out a long sigh.

21

The mood in Algiers on July 3 was one of joy and celebration for the Arab population. Hundreds of thousands of jubilant Algerians packed the streets, singing, waving flags, raising their arms in a cry of victory. Rows of women with white-veiled heads marched behind FLN army men. Today the heavens were raining down not mortar and bloodshed, but a bright ray of peace.

Mahmud and Fatima celebrated with their countrymen, but Ali was in no shape to join in the festivities. He was lucky to be alive, the doctor had told him somberly when he had regained consciousness yesterday. So he sent Fatima to be his eyes, to take part in the merriment and report back every detail.

Two hundred fifty miles from Algiers, in the small port city of Philippeville, a thick tension hung in the air in the open square, the Place. One after another, Arab soldiers from an Algerian auxiliary troop of the French army walked up the plank of the ferry that awaited them. French officers stood guard, brandishing arms as they welcomed their harki brothers aboard; in the faces of the Arabs they read pain, sorrow, and relief.

FLN officers milled around the square, looking disgusted as the harkis prepared for departure. When the old Renault pulled to within sight of the ferry, Moustafa squinted, searching for Hacène. How would he find his brother in the crowd?

"He'll be there. Don't worry," David reassured him.

Moustafa nodded. He fixed his thoughts on the feat before him, walking the five hundred yards to the boat. He had not walked more than a few feet since the shooting four days earlier. Two bullets had been removed: one from his shoulder, quite easily, the other with considerable pain and a good bit of blood from between two ribs. He still felt terribly weak.

"I'd better be going," he mumbled to David and Rémi. The thought of leaving Algeria left him numb. The uncertainty of what lay ahead in Montpellier made him sick with fear. He chose to imagine a different scene.

First there would be Anne-Marie running to him as he stepped onto the dock in Marseille. She would run with no effort, laughing, as she had when they were teenagers playing in the fields, hiding in the orange groves, letting the sweet scent of the fruit make them heady with their power and youth. He could almost feel her arms around him, holding him, her soft voice whispering, "Everything is fine now, Moustafa, my love. It is fine." Behind her, his mother and sisters and Ophélie would be huddled like a peck of hens, cackling with pleasure. Hacène would go toward them, and all would be well.

As he stepped from the car, he was greeted by a blazing hot sun and the overwhelming smell of gas fumes and seaweed. His head swam. He leaned on the Renault for a long minute, watching the sea glisten in the port.

"Good-bye, David. Rémi." He shook their hands.

"We'll see you soon in Montpellier," David called after him. "It will all be fine."

One foot in front of the other, Moustafa inched along toward the ferry. He shivered as he walked, despite the fierce heat. He sensed the eyes of the enemy on him. His people, these newly independent Arabs, were burning their hatred for the harkis through a hard stare like the sun on the back of his neck. His ears wouldn't stop ringing.

"Allah, or whoever you are, God. Whoever you are, have compassion on us," he said out loud, but it was as if the words were not his own, as if this whole scene were unreal.

Harki soldiers climbed up the plank, hurrying, tasting for the first time, he imagined, the hope of safety as they stepped off the soil of this country gone mad. This country that was not safe for so many of its former inhabitants.

No more than a hundred feet from the boat, Moustafa stumbled, fell, and caught himself with his hands, touching the slimy hot pavement. Then he saw Hacène.

"Moustafa, what's the matter? What happened to you?" Hacène grabbed him around the waist, dragging him forward.

"Never mind that now. I'll explain everything on the ferry."

"Yes, that will be good." His brother looked nervous, his eyes darting from side to side. "Moustafa. I … I've had a hard time getting you a right of passage. You must understand that this ferry has been hired by our top French officer. There are so many, so many who have fought in the war." Moustafa could sense the edge of panic in Hacène's voice.

Moustafa shivered again. He felt light-headed and placed one hand on his forehead. "I have to sit down," he said with a groan.

"Yes, of course." Hacène knelt down by him as Moustafa collapsed on the dock. "I'll get a stretcher and tell them you are wounded. They'll let you on," he whispered, his voice shaking. "They must."

Moustafa realized his mistake at once. He was not a part of this Algerian troop. How foolish to have believed he could simply slip on the boat unnoticed when all the others wore their military uniforms. But Hacène had seemed so sure. Moustafa turned to look out at the square that swarmed with Algerians, giddy with their new independence, now circling the ferry like a pack of hungry wolves.

God, don't leave me here to die. He pulled his body to the edge of the dock. The oil on the sea reflected a rainbow of colors two feet below. Moustafa looked up. The gangplank was almost within his touch. So close.

From the car, David strained to see what was happening on the ferry. "We have to get out of here," Rémi insisted. "This place is crawling with FLN. Moustafa is with his brother; he's safe. Safer than we are right now."

David watched as the French officers motioned to one another to pull up the plank. Had Moustafa gotten on? He could not be sure. There was a brief discussion, and then an officer of the FLN approached the ship. Hundreds of Arabs now surrounded the ferry, chanting in angry Arabic. David could barely see past them to the officers, still arguing by the plank.

"Rémi, there's trouble. Something's not right. I'm going closer to see."

"Are you crazy?" Rémi grabbed his arm. "What can you do?"

David swung around. "I promised Anne-Marie he'd get there. I'm just going a little ways. Just to see."

Rémi nodded. They left the shelter of the car, walking toward the ferry, then stopped before entering into the crowded square. Jubilant Arabs carried guns and knives, looking like cruel barbarians. Looking like everyone looked in Algeria. Crazed, half-mad.

David heard loud shouts in the distance. A chilling scream. Another. He felt a cold sweat drench his body. Now the French officers, the same ones who had moments ago welcomed the harkis aboard, were forcing them to get off the boat with guns at their backs. And the harkis were clinging to the Frenchmen, begging, screaming in anguish. They were being pushed off the ferry into the angry Arab mob, who yelled, "Traitors! Cut their throats!"

First a dozen harkis, then twenty more, then a whole tangled group of them, staggering, lurching, cursing, helplessly being fed into the violent crowd. It couldn't be happening, David thought, trembling.

Rémi gagged beside him, crying, "No, God, no."

A massacre. They were witnessing the harki massacre that Moustafa had been so sure would come. The ferry promising safety had turned into a cruel, taunting decoy. David could not bear to see more, and yet his eyes were riveted on the scene. The harkis grabbed on to railings, flooring, other men, pleading. It was useless. The Arab mob surged upon them, pulling them down and then stabbing, shooting, and finally slitting their throats.

"No!" David cried out. "No!" He started forward, but Rémi caught him from behind.

"David!" he yelled. "David, listen to me. It's hopeless. This whole stinking world has gone crazy. The French are betraying their comrades."

David stumbled backward, eyes glued to the horrific scene.

"There's nothing we can do but be murdered as well if we stay." Rémi was sobbing. "We cannot help Moustafa now. It is too late."

Too late. David's throat constricted, and the muscles in his chest tightened. Still backing toward the car, he cried, "Moustafa! Moustafa!" Then he broke into a run. "The sea!" he cried.

Rémi seemed to understand, and together the two men raced to the water's edge. Hidden by a thick-leafed plane tree, they kicked off their shoes and dived into the murky water. They swam furiously underwater toward the ferry. When they surfaced, the sound of their heavy breathing was swallowed up in the chaotic babble on shore.

"God, let us see him," David prayed. The screaming men, sobbing and groping, slid down the gangplank that was forty feet away. He watched the knife of a muscular Arab find its target in a harki's neck. Recklessly he cried, "Moustafa!" And again, "Moustafa!"

Two Algerians ran toward the edge of the dock. "Who is there?" one spat angrily. David and Rémi dived down again underwater, watching a spray of bullets above on the water's surface. Rémi shook his head slowly in the water, pulling at David's shirt, swimming back away from the dock. Thirty seconds later, lungs burning for air, they emerged.

"It's no use," Rémi gasped. He pulled himself out of the water, then caught David under the arms and dragged him out. They lay on the grassy shore for a moment, their chests rising and falling. Everything in David's body burned.

"Can you get up?" Rémi stood, offering David his hand.

They stumbled to the car, crawling inside and slamming the doors as several Arabs, detoured from their butchery, ran in pursuit. Rémi stamped on the gas, and the tires squealed. A bullet grazed the back window as they sped toward the road.

David glanced back. The whole square was engulfed in red. "Moustafa," he groaned again.

Philippeville was but a drop of red in the bucket of blood filled up on July 3, 1962. Throughout the cities in Algeria, FLN troops and their supporters stormed the houses of the harki traitors. Men, women, children were murdered, whole families, thrown down on the floors of their houses and slain.

Farther out in the fields, busy soldiers dug deep, wide graves into which the dead bodies could be rolled. The fresh dirt was pushed back over the lifeless Arabs, covered with leaves and sand, camouflaged from the world. No one could count the number. No one cared to know. Not President de Gaulle, not the Algerian socialist Ben Bella. No one.

Yet it was simple to calculate. Soon there would be no harki families left in Algeria. Some would get away, the lucky ones, Ali mused. Some had already fled. But that could be no more than ten, fifteen thousand at best. The vast majority would perish with their throats slit. France would not know, would not care. No one in the outside world would question. But inside Algeria, Ali and his comrades would exchange knowing glances. A hundred thousand murdered. One hundred fifty thousand, easily.

Ali lay in his bed draped in a sheet and gave the orders. Mass graves to be dug and bodies to fill them. The vegetation would grow over them in some areas. In others, the fine, hot sand would drift on top. And the world would not know.

It served the filthy traitors right! They had abandoned their homeland to support the French army. He only wished the punishment, the terror, and the unbearable pain would last a bit longer.

Suddenly Ali slammed his fist on his bed. Hussein! He did not doubt that the boy had made it to France, although he had not received word yet. Hussein was quite capable. What was taking the boy so long?

But there was not time to worry over Hussein; Ali must reserve every bit of his strength for the future of Algeria. The new government. He intended to be part of it! He cursed his wounds and sank down in his bed, and his thoughts returned to the skirmish in the Casbah. Perhaps David Hoffmann and his father would find a way out. But that harki boy, Moustafa. If he hadn't already died from the wounds he received in the Casbah, there was no worry. He was a harki boy. Dead meat.

Ali closed his eyes and imagined the throngs of happy youth invading the streets, celebrating freedom. The confetti, the loud horns, the dancing. Ali Boudani chose to think of the celebration. The graves would be forgotten. A just end for those who had betrayed their country. Algeria was free!

�֍

David and Rémi did not leave Philippeville. Instead they parked among the thick foliage ten minutes out from the port. Rémi had agreed to go back to the square by the port after dark to see. The thought now made David sweat. What did he hope to find? Moustafa lying among the carnage with his throat slit?

Earlier, they had driven recklessly through the town as if their mad flight might somehow bring Moustafa back. Bedraggled and shivering, they had listened to radio reports throughout the afternoon. Tears mixed with seawater. Disbelief and fury. Again and again Rémi cursed the fact that he had not brought his rifles. Why had they been so naive as to think things would go smoothly?

The radio did not speak of the massacre. Its airwaves were filled with victory announcements and news of Ben Bella's return after five years of imprisonment.

Now they drove back through the night without speaking. Perhaps Moustafa had gotten away. Perhaps they were not all dead. Little phrases of hope. Make-believe hope. They had seen the massacre with their own eyes. No one had gotten away.

Rémi saw the trucks first. Covered, camouflaged trucks leaving the port, driven by silent Arab men. He stopped the Renault by the Place, shutting off the engine and headlights. In the dark of the summer sky, Rémi and David watched the men at work, lifting bodies, tossing them into the backs of the trucks.

Rémi turned the car around and followed one truck, keeping his distance, driving without headlights. David dozed off and on, unable to keep his eyes open. His dreams came in little clips. Guns, knives, red. He woke with a start, blinking to get his bearings. Rémi had stopped the car.

"Would ya look at that," he murmured. "Just like the rotten Nazis. Dumping them into the ground."

David leaned forward to gaze out the windshield. Far off he could make out the forms of men emptying their human cargo into wide holes.

They drove silently back to the Place. David stepped into the open air, which was thick, oppressive with the stench of death. The bodies had all been removed. Nothing but dark splotches of dried blood remained on the cobbled stones. For a long moment he walked as if in a trance around the square. Moustafa was gone. Murdered. And he had been powerless to stop it.

When they finally pulled up to Rémi's farmhouse in the wee hours of the morning, David could not bring himself to go inside. Somewhere in the house, his father lay asleep. Yet he felt more allegiance to Moustafa than to his father. He had no strength to work through that messy relationship. And the older man wasn't doing well anyway. Maybe David would go inside to find that Roger Hoffmann too was dead.

David turned and walked away from the farmhouse, out to the moonlit orange groves. He cursed this country, this war, this life. The tiny sprouts of faith that had barely broken through the soil in his heart were withering and dying within him. There was no God. It had been a hoax, a cruel joke, a fantasy. He ached at the core of his being, and he could find no comfort.

He tried praying, but his prayers were just angry accusations. "You can't be omnipotent! Or if You are, You are evil. You are a God who takes. You want my undying devotion while you strip me of all those I care for. Was it not enough to take Greta and Mama? Did you have to take Moustafa? And Gabby and Anne-Marie and Ophélie? Where is the hope?"

He cursed the tears that came to his eyes. The black sky would soon be bidden awake by the first touch of sun. "I hate You, God! Can You hear me? I hate You. Get out of my life! I was doing just fine without You."

David walked for a long time, coming up to the shell of a house he had known all those years ago. The Duchemins' place. He felt his pulse quicken, remembered his first encounter with the captain, stiffly shaking his hand with his other arm around Anne-Marie's shoulder. He remembered the proud allure of Captain Duchemin, and his determination to be equally proud and aloof.

He rammed the door with his foot, relieved to do something with his anger. The door swung inward. Windows were broken, leaving jagged glass edges. He ran his fingers over the dining-room table, tracing a deep gash drawn through the wood, perhaps by a knife. Fine layers of sand covered the few pieces of scattered furniture.

He walked into the kitchen. Broken china lay on the floor. Drawers hung open, empty. He went down the hallway and into Anne-Marie's bedroom. The sheets had been stripped off the bed and the mattress slashed. In the opposite corner sat an overturned crib with most of the slats broken. And everywhere, the sand, the fine whitish powder, blown in from the Sahara.

David walked back into the dining room and hit the table hard with his fist. Every bone in his body ached. His head wound began to bleed. He fell to his knees and sobbed. "I hate You, God. I hate You." Then, covering his face with his hands, he whispered, "But help me. If You leave me too, I'll have no one at all."

22

Henri Krugler put a paintbrush into a jar of turpentine. He dipped a rag into the potent liquid and rubbed at his blue-stained hands. He washed his hands thoroughly, dried them on a damp towel, and ran his fingers through his thick white hair. He removed his T-shirt and replaced it with a clean, starched button-down, which he tucked into his paint-splattered work pants.

He glanced at his wristwatch. Two fifteen. Locking the door behind him, Henri hurried through the streets of Lodève, nodding politely at those he passed on his way to the train station. Two days earlier a nun called Mother Griolet from an orphanage outside Montpellier had written to him. The handwriting was a bit shaky, but the tone of the letter was serious, businesslike. She had asked if she might come to see him, to discuss "urgent matters."

He had heard of Mother Griolet from Joseph Cohen and recalled the words Joseph had used to describe her: "The feistiest little nun you'll ever meet. As determined as she is compassionate."

The train from Montpellier pulled into the station and screeched to a halt. Several minutes later a small woman with wrinkled skin, dressed in a black nun's habit, emerged from the train. By her side, helping to steady her, was a striking young woman with long, curly red hair. The nun looked more feeble than feisty.

"Henri Krugler," he introduced himself, walking up and offering his hand. He felt suddenly big and awkward.

"*Enchantée, Monsieur Krugler.* I am Mother Griolet." She squeezed his hand firmly, then looked toward the girl. "And this is *Mademoiselle Madison*, a dear friend of mine."

The redhead smiled, though she looked at him suspiciously. He put out his hand, and she touched it briefly without meeting his eyes.

The old nun cleared her throat. "Thank you for agreeing to see us on such short notice."

"The pleasure is all mine. Joseph Cohen has spoken highly of you for many years. It's an honor to finally have the privilege of meeting you."

The young woman spoke. "Excuse me, M. Krugler. Mother Griolet has recently suffered a heart attack, although she would never tell you herself. Is there a place where we could sit down?"

Henri felt the blood rise in his cheeks as the girl regarded him with her bright, clear eyes. "Of course. *Mais bien sûr.*" He motioned to a bench nearby. "I'll go back and fetch my car. You just wait here."

Henri chided himself for not thinking of the car. He had been so wrapped up in his work that he had forgotten the time and then rushed off without considering that an elderly nun would need a ride back to the house. He felt equally embarrassed about his attire and for a moment considered changing his pants, then decided that would be even more awkward. Ever since Louise had died, his clothes were poorly matched. Ah well.

It took no more than fifteen minutes for Henri to return to the farmhouse, drive his gray Citroën to the train station, pick up the nun and the girl, and be back at the house-turned-centre aéré. Henri congratulated himself for at least having remembered to dust off the couch and chairs in the *salon*.

"Please have a seat, Mother Griolet. Mlle Madison. Can I get you anything to drink? A cup of coffee?

"A glass of water would be just fine," Mother Griolet responded.

"Yes, for me too," the young woman echoed.

Once the drinks were given and he had taken a seat, Henri felt much less nervous. "What exactly may I do for you, Mother Griolet?"

The nun smiled, and he saw that her eyes were a lively shade of green. Feisty. Yes, perhaps.

"I am interested in what you are doing in Lodève with the centre aéré. Your vision for the harki children. I would like to hear what is on your heart, and then I will tell you what is on mine."

"I'd be most happy to comply." He scooted forward in his chair, resting his hands on his knees. His fingernails were stained with blue paint. "I am Swiss-French. For many years I was a pastor in a small town north of Geneva.

"My ancestors were French Huguenots—part of the fourteen thousand refugees who fled to Switzerland. They arrived with nothing, half-starved and naked, and the people of Switzerland welcomed them with open arms. Geneva, which is where my family went, had only about sixteen thousand inhabitants at that time—yet every day they took in hundreds of refugees."

He stopped himself. "Forgive me. I'm sure you know your history lessons."

Mother Griolet said softly, "Please continue. It's always a blessing to hear of God's provision for His children."

"Amen," Henri said heartily. "Yes, well. After my wife died several years ago, I felt the call of these mountains where my ancestors had suffered for their faith. My dream is to reach another group of refugees, the Arabs. By establishing a centre aéré for the French and Arab children, I hope at the same time to offer them the opportunity to understand the truth. God's truth.

"Right now we have thirty children who come on Wednesdays when the schools are closed. Most of the children come after school on the other days for snacks and activities. And we have a group for the teenagers." He flashed a quick smile. "It is my belief that these different cultures must learn how to live side by side, to integrate, so that Arab children, who are really more French than Arab in their lifestyle, will feel at home, welcomed into this society. So they will have a future here."

The nun nodded her head in approval. "Very good, M. Krugler."

"And you, Mother Griolet. Tell me how I can be of help to you."

She massaged her temples and said, "I run an orphanage in a small village on the edge of Montpellier. Normally we house between twenty to twenty-five children. Their schooling is provided. But lately, due to extreme circumstances, we have accepted many more children at the orphanage. I forget the exact number."

"Fifty-eight. Fifty-eight children now," Mlle Madison broke in. "These new children have all arrived within the last six months, refugees from the war in Algeria. Pied-noir and harki children, escaped by the skin of their teeth. Mother Griolet has taken them in, and now the townspeople and the church are demanding they be sent away to refugee camps or the orphanage will be closed."

"Gabriella!" the nun reprimanded. "Dear, let me explain."

The girl blushed, bit her lip, and folded her hands in her lap. "I'm sorry."

Henri forced a chortle to stay in his throat. Quite feisty herself, this Mlle Madison!

"As Mlle Madison has said, we face a difficult time. We have fewer than thirty days now to solve this problem or be closed down. When Joseph Cohen wrote me about you, well, I thought it would be a good idea to meet you."

"Yes, it is so unfair!" the girl broke in again. "If you knew all that Mother Griolet has done for that town, for so many children. Why, during the Second World War she saved many Jewish children. Surely M. Cohen has mentioned it." The young woman stopped suddenly. "Excuse me, Mother Griolet. May I tell him some of your stories?"

They made quite a pair, the wise nun and the enthusiastic girl. Henri listened, spellbound, as they shared remarkable stories from both wars as well as from their present troubles. He thought of the families moving into the area. Would any of those Arabs, harki families, be willing to take in another child? It was possible. Anything was possible. He had seen much stranger things happen in his lifetime.

Hussein splattered a brushful of bright-green paint onto the mural in the classroom. He watched the thick blobs run down the paper. Just when several threatened to run off the edge, he gave a swish of his brush and stopped them.

"What are you making, Hussein?" Ophélie asked, coming to his side.

He shrugged. "I don't know. Nothing."

"Sister Isabelle says that you can even make mistakes into something pretty. She helped me—"

"It's not a mistake!" he answered gruffly. He wished Ophélie would leave him alone. He felt all tense inside. Worried and tense.

He wasn't alone. The tension vibrated throughout the orphanage. They were all trying desperately to busy themselves so they wouldn't have to think about it, but it wasn't working. Not for him, not for anyone.

When were they coming? Two full days had passed since independence. If Moustafa had gotten onto that harki ferry, as Mme Dramchini had explained, well, there should be some word soon.

Hussein saw the hurt expression on Ophélie's face. He reached out to touch her hand. "You're right. I'm sure I can make something out of this."

The child pushed her pigtails behind her and headed back to her spot on the wall. She picked up her paintbrush and then paused. "And don't worry about Papa and Moustafa, Hussein. They'll be here soon. You'll see."

She was the strangest little kid, Hussein thought. To think he had almost ... but Allah be praised, he had not followed through. When David and Moustafa returned, they could help him compose a letter to Ali. One that was believable.

"Hurry home," he whispered, and began painting the random spots of green, turning them into long, delicate leaves on a weeping willow tree.

The radio played continuously in the refectory kitchen. During the evening meal the women huddled around it, eager for news. The talk from Algeria was all of celebration, the new Algerian government, the exodus of the remaining pied-noirs.

Anne-Marie grabbed Gabriella's hands. "I can't stand the waiting any longer. There must be news!" She searched Gabriella's face. "I'm praying for it night and day. For protection for Moustafa and David." She pronounced the names cautiously, painfully.

"The crowds at the port must have been even worse than before. They may still be waiting, but it won't be long." Gabriella's voice did not sound optimistic.

The announcer reported on a group of harkis moving to a little village near Arles.

Anne-Marie leaned closer, motioning for silence. "Should I go there, Gabriella? Do you think Moustafa is there with Hacène?"

Mme Dramchini spoke in worried Arabic to Saiyda, and the young girl translated. "Mother thinks that the men are there. If not, she fears they have perhaps been forced to the refugee camps. She wants to go with you, Anne-Marie, to Arles."

"Should we wait one more day?" Gabriella suggested. "If they are there, David will know. Give them one more day." She squeezed Anne-Marie's hand.

"One more day then," Anne-Marie whispered.

On July 5, Rémi encouraged David to leave for the ferry with his father. "Go back to France. You heard what the doctor said. You both need medical attention. You'll be better off there."

David doubted it. Was there an orphanage still in Castelnau? He was overcome by fear and dread. But Moustafa had believed Ali was lying. Moustafa …

David had failed in every way. Moustafa was not coming back to Anne-Marie, and maybe there was no one to go back to. The thought made his head swim. The only choice was to take a ferry back to France and find out. And if it were true? Then there would be nothing but an awful gaping hole in his heart … and his father standing there to watch.

David slipped into the back bedroom to check on his father. He was sitting in bed, pillows propping him up. The gray stubble that had covered his face had now become a thick beard. He stared into the room with a vacant expression.

"Father. Are you ready to go?"

The older man nodded but made no effort to move.

"I'll be back in a sec for you."

Curse it all, David thought. His head throbbed. The wound was not healing properly. Blood and pus oozed onto the bandage. He unwrapped the gauze and changed the dressing again. Maybe he was simply losing his mind.

Rémi came into the house and stood beside him.

"Why don't you come now too, Rémi?"

"There are things to tie up. Tell Eliane it'll be a few weeks. After we finish with the oranges."

"It's dangerous to stay, Rémi."

"I know." He took another olive. "The pied-noirs were supposed to be able to stay in Algeria, you know. If the OAS hadn't committed so many unspeakable atrocities in these past months ... It's their fault we're leaving. The pied-noirs are afraid of what the FLN will do to get revenge, now that Algeria is free."

They did not speak of what they had seen. The mass graves, the bodies. The genocide in Philippeville had been complete, and they had stood by and watched. What had their feeble effort mattered? They had not rescued Moustafa or anyone else.

Rémi placed a hand on David's shoulder. "Don't live with guilt. You did what you could. Get on with life."

"Do you think it will be that easy?"

Rémi grimaced. "No. We'll wake up in the middle of the night, sweating and screaming. And only those who have lived through it will understand."

"And that isn't guilt?"

"Scarred. Scarred but healing," Rémi said. "Come on. We've got to get your father in the car. It'll be all right, David. You'll see."

They had waited twenty-eight hours before they found a place on a crowded ferry. It was now far out at sea, and David could not help thinking of his last crossing. He had stood alone, hopeful, confident in his new faith. Sure of his mission. Now he slumped over the railing, casting a glance behind him at his father, who slept with his back against a cabin door.

Rémi thought having charge of his father would help David get his mind off other things. But all David heard in his head was *Why are you here with me? Why must I care for you? Why didn't you die instead of Moustafa?* It filled him with an incredible sadness and guilt, but his anger was stronger. What blasted right did this man have to reappear now and ask forgiveness? What blasted right did he have? Was David supposed to smile a sick, sweet smile and say, "Sure, Dad. I understand. It's fine"?

It wasn't fine. Oh, he understood about the dreadful mistake and the concentration camp. His father himself had been detained in a camp, unable to help them. But how could he have left him, a six-year-old child, in charge? It was so David could harbor the guilt, the blame for their murders. The coward! How could he dare to think it would be all right?

I don't want to forgive you, and I certainly don't want to get to know you. So why must I drag you along in my pain? Why must you be here to complicate what is already too heavy to carry?

It actually crossed his mind to pick up his father while he slept and throw him into the sea. He held his head and moaned. "You're messed up, David."

He cursed the sea and then cursed God. It was His fault. Why was He showing Himself so helpless when David needed Him most? Why was He allowing this anger and hate, this blasphemy to well up within His child? David felt he would go mad with the questions.

His father called for him, and David knelt down beside the weakened man. That icy blue stare, softer now, met his son's gaze.

"David."

"Yes, Father?"

"We are on our way to France?"

"Yes."

"To your friends?"

"I hope."

His father closed his eyes, and David thought he had fallen back asleep. "Son, I'm sorry about Moustafa."

David cringed. What right did his father have to pronounce that name? To pretend to care? He was in the way. Out of place. "Yes. It's tragic."

"Thank you for bringing me along."

David gritted his teeth. He did not want to make conversation. *Leave me alone, old man.* He stood up quickly. "I'm going to walk about a little."

Walking was next to impossible. Every space was filled with the men who had stayed behind until now. Their large suitcases and bags stuffed with every imaginable possession gave evidence that the two-suitcase rule was being completely ignored. David pushed past a young man who held a rocking horse under his arm. The sight made him think of Ophélie. For the past few days he had almost forgotten that he had a daughter.

He tried to remember the good things that had happened before the harki massacre. He thought of Gabriella and relived every long conversation with her. Tomorrow he could hold her to his chest and let life start again. Surely there was a future out there.

But even as he imagined Gabriella coming to him, laughing, running, eyes dancing, he saw Anne-Marie behind her with a question in her dark, mournful eyes. *Where is Moustafa?*

And if there were no Gabriella or Anne-Marie or Ophélie? A chill ran through him. No response. Just darkness all around in the thick, balmy air. The colors faded into one another, the black-green of the sea and the white caps blending into the indigo sky, which was tinged with purple and the faintest shade of crimson.

He stood silently for another hour or maybe two, watching the wake the ferry made in the water. When he finally walked back to where his father sat, the older man was asleep.

23

The train from Marseille to Montpellier seemed painfully slow, and yet David was afraid it would arrive too fast. He had resisted the urge to call the orphanage from Marseille. What if Anne-Marie answered? What if no one answered at all? No, it was better to show up in person and face the questions head-on.

His father was in no shape to wait for a bus, so David signaled a taxi. It was a lazy summer day in Montpellier. People sipped cool drinks in sidewalk cafés, and old men played *pétanque* beneath the shade of the plane trees. The mood was calm. No bombed-out buildings or shells of cars littered the scenery as they drove by.

He could not calm his racing heart in those few minutes riding to Castelnau. He rolled down the window; the heat was blistering. Sweat ran down his face.

Suddenly the cobblestones of Castelnau were bumping under the taxi's tires, and St. Joseph's tall spire, and then the whole stone facade, came into view, sitting peacefully at the back of the square as it had done for hundreds of years. The same fountain sprayed forth water; the same shops offered fruits and wines and bread and cheeses, their doors flung open.

The taxi driver let them off in front of the church. For a brief moment David hesitated, one arm supporting his father. He set down his bags and knocked forcefully on the parsonage door. Blood pumped in his ears.

"*J'arrive*," came the sound of a jolly voice from within, and relief flooded through David. Ali had lied. All was well.

The door swung open, and Sister Rosaline stood wide-eyed before them. She looked from one man to the other, her expression changing from surprise to delight to confusion to worry.

"M. Hoffmann. God be praised! Come in, M. Hoffmann!"

David followed her into the hallway. "Sister Rosaline, this is my father, Roger Hoffmann. It's a long story."

"Well, he is welcome! Come in. Do come in." She led them into Mother Griolet's den; they sat on the faded brown couch while Sister Rosaline brought them each a glass of water. The nun, obviously flustered, said nothing but kept staring at the two men, shaking her head. Finally she spoke. "Let me go tell the others."

David touched her arm. Leaving his father on the couch, he walked with her into the hallway. "Sister Rosaline, I … I …" His voice caught. "I don't know how to say it, but … Moustafa did not come with us. He didn't make it." David broke into a sweat, caught the door, and felt his knees buckle under him.

"M. Hoffmann. M. Hoffmann!"

He pulled himself back into the den and collapsed into a chair.

Few things unnerved Sister Rosaline anymore, but she was obviously rattled as she hurried through the basement into the courtyard. It was David Hoffmann up there in the den. But so changed. He was unshaven, and his clothes were wrinkled and dirty. His black hair was long and unkempt, and a bandage covered the left side of his head above his ear. He looked thin and sad. Terribly sad.

Sister Rosaline wrung her hands. This was not the homecoming they had envisioned. An afflicted M. Hoffmann with an even weaker man in tow and no Moustafa at all. What was she to do? She had immediately understood what David Hoffmann could not say. Moustafa wasn't coming. Ever.

Everyone was eating dinner in the refectory. She reflected that it was a good thing she had been in the basement of the parsonage, or no one would have heard M. Hoffmann's knock. She entered the dining hall without making a fuss, thankful for the noise. Mother Griolet sat at a table with Gabriella and several children. Sister Rosaline fiddled with her headpiece, casually approaching the table.

"Mother Griolet," she said in her lightest voice. "Could I see you for a moment?" The others must not guess. Already they sat on pins and needles, desperate for news. But this was not the time to have it.

"Yes, Sister. Is there a problem?"

"Not at all, only I'm afraid I need a little advice." She helped the old nun up, wishing she did not have more distressing news to share.

As soon as they were in the courtyard, she whispered, "M. Hoffmann has just appeared looking *affreux*. And he brought with him his father of all things!" She lowered her voice to where it was barely audible. "But it's not who he brought with him that matters. It's who did not come." She met the nun's green eyes. "Moustafa … the man they call Moustafa is no more."

"Dear Lord," Mother Griolet said. "Dear Lord."

"They are in your den. I thought it not wise to announce it."

"No, of course not. You were right. Take me to see M. Hoffmann."

They hurried off, their black robes swishing together in the hallway.

Sister Rosaline had not minced words. David Hoffmann did look terrible. Mother Griolet shook his hand, wrinkling her brow, then took a seat next to him.

The other M. Hoffmann was sprawled out on her couch, his eyes closed. She remembered when he had stood before her so many years ago, a tall, distinguished-looking man.

"Let me call *les urgences*. Your father must get to a hospital at once. From the looks of it, you should see a doctor too."

"Yes, of course," David mumbled.

The young man was so obviously shaken, so completely exhausted. He hardly resembled the capable young teacher she had known.

"I am deeply grieved to learn of Moustafa. It is a terrible tragedy," Mother Griolet said.

"Yes. Terrible." David's face was ashen underneath his black stubble.

Sister Rosaline came back into the den. "An ambulance will be here shortly."

"Thank you." Mother Griolet smiled softly at the Sister, then turned to David. "Do you wish to see Gabriella alone?"

He held his head in his hands. "I don't know what to do."

Mother Griolet placed her hand on his head, praying silently. Then she gently said, "I'm so very sorry, David. Let me call Gabriella. The others will not have to know yet." She stood shakily, and David stood with her, offering his hand. "David," she said at last. "God does not waste our suffering. It always serves a purpose."

It was not at all the reunion Gabriella had expected. When Mother Griolet whispered for her to go to her apartment because David was there, she caught her breath. Then Mother Griolet cautioned, "He is not well, and his father is with him. An ambulance is coming to take them to the hospital. Go alone, just for a moment."

Gabriella tiptoed through the basement hall, her mind racing, asking herself a hundred questions. When she came to Mother Griolet's den, she stopped short. An older man, looking like a hobo, lay asleep on Mother Griolet's couch, his clothes torn. And David— yes, surely it was David—sat with his head in his hands, fresh blood seeping from a bandage around his head.

For a moment she could not bring herself to speak. She swallowed hard. "David?" she whispered.

He sat up quickly and looked at her. "Gabby," he said, and a weak smile came to his face.

She covered her mouth with her hand, but the gasp escaped. It was not so much the way he looked that shocked her. She had seen him badly injured before. It was the hopelessness in his dark eyes. She stood frozen, unsure of what he needed.

But then an emotion stronger than her uncertainty washed over her. She loved him. That much had not changed, whatever else had. She came to him and carefully cradled his head in her arms as he leaned against her breast. "David. You're here. It's going to be fine now."

"Dear Gabby." He took her hands and softly kissed them. Outside, the sound of a siren shrilled. "Come with me … please."

One look at Roger Hoffmann, and the young doctor on duty had sent him immediately to intensive care. Two hours later he was installed in a private room. "He will be here for a while," the doctor warned, motioning for David and Gabriella to follow him.

"*Et vous, Monsieur.* Let me take a look at you."

David stiffened as the doctor removed the bandages and inspected his head wound.

"You needed stitches," he stated. "When did this happen?"

"I don't know. About a week ago. Maybe a little longer."

"You should have come to the hospital immediately," the doctor reprimanded.

"I was in Algeria."

"Oh." There was silence. "It's a nasty wound. Infected."

David winced as the doctor cleaned it with antiseptic and covered the wound with a new bandage. "Thanks, doctor," he said gratefully. "Could you just check out the rib here? The doc in Algiers thinks it's cracked."

The X-rays revealed two cracked ribs.

"We'll need to bind you up. You'll have to undress."

"I'll-I'll wait in the hall," Gabriella stammered.

The intern shrugged. "As you wish, *mademoiselle*. But he only has to take off his shirt."

Gabriella's face turned bright red. In spite of the pain David could not suppress a throaty chuckle. *Dear Gabby*, he thought. *All innocence and imagination.* He was glad she still held a few illusions of propriety. His had all gone down the drain in Algeria. Every last one.

They had spoken only a few phrases during their afternoon at the hospital. Gabriella felt so far away from him, from his pain. She dared not touch him for fear of hurting him worse somewhere deep inside.

When they left the hospital and stepped out into the suffocating heat, he took her hand in his. "Let's go somewhere and get a drink. I can't go back there yet."

He called a taxi, and it amazed her how quickly David seemed to regain control. He was stiff, formal, rigid. Only his hand in hers gave a slight indication that he cared for her.

He took her to the Comédie, and they sat in the shade of the large, thick-leafed plane trees with their gray patchwork bark. The waiter came.

"A *pastis* and a *citron pressé*," David ordered without asking Gabriella, and for the first time she saw a sparkle in his eyes. "You see,

Gabby, I haven't forgotten your favorite drink." His dimple showed as he smiled wearily. "Does it bother you that everyone is staring at the unshaven wild man with the white turban who is seated beside you?"

"Not a bit," Gabriella whispered. "I hadn't even noticed."

They held hands across the table. He stared at her for a long, long time. She studied his face. The rough black of his beard covered his face and neck like a thin layer of pepper. The bandaged wound extended far up into his hairline. His coarse black hair curled over the gauze and at the back of his neck.

"I didn't know if I would ever see you again." He touched her hair, twirling the red strands around his finger. "I didn't think we'd ever make it back."

He fell silent again, letting go of her hands when the waiter brought the drinks. She forced the hundreds of questions she wanted to ask him back in her mind.

He watched the people milling on the Comédie, and it seemed to calm him. He was far, far away. Finally he looked at her, his eyes shining with tears, and said, "Moustafa is dead."

When they returned to St. Joseph, David stopped outside the chapel. "Can you bring Anne-Marie here, alone?"

Gabriella nodded and left him seated in the chapel's cool interior. She felt, as she had at other times in the past, like a child, expected to obey. She could not reach him, and she dared not question him.

The children were resting in the dorms. She found Anne-Marie stretched out on her bed, reading.

"Come in!" she said brightly, seeing Gabriella. "And where have you been?"

Immediately Gabriella knew she had betrayed it, simply meeting her friend's eyes. Anne-Marie sat up. "You have news?"

"Come with me." Gabriella could not say more. She could not pronounce the word *dead* to Anne-Marie. She held her hand and led her through the basement and out into the street, then stood beside the doors to the chapel. "David wants to talk to you alone," she whispered, swallowing hard. She caught Anne-Marie in her arms and hugged her tightly. She did not let go for a long time.

Then Anne-Marie stepped into the chapel. Gabriella did not wait, could not wait. She ran to Mme Leclerc's apartment, let herself in, and collapsed on her bed, sobbing.

David looked up to see Anne-Marie standing in the doorway, her dark eyes full of questions. He stood and watched her as he had done in Algiers three months ago. He studied the contour of her face, the high cheekbones, the olive skin that glowed from the incredible heat, the slight flush in her cheeks.

He held out his hand, and she took it. He did not have to speak. She understood him perfectly well. He squeezed her hand tightly, closing his eyes and silently cursing this moment. She did not cry, although her bottom lip quivered ever so slightly.

He pulled her to his chest, held her there, stroking her hair. "I'm so sorry." It was not his voice that spoke. It was as if someone else were forcing out the words through the tightness in his throat. "I'm so, so sorry."

David had decided that he would tell her whatever she wanted to know. He would not hide anything. He sat in the hard pew and held her as he spoke of Moustafa. Somehow the telling of it brought with it comfort.

He told her of the teenagers at the port who had attacked them, and of Moustafa's courage, and why he had made up his mind to stay. He spoke of Hussein and the trunk and Rémi and the *Capitaine*; of Moustafa's mother and the orphans. He explained the ambush in the night and finding his father and being imprisoned in the same dank basement where she had been months before. Then he told her of Ali's pronouncement of her death and the explosions at the orphanage.

"We didn't know. We could only wait and hope."

"Funny how we must do that, isn't it, David? Wait and hope."

Her voice was calm, and it amazed him.

Softly she asked, "And how did it end?"

He described the slaughter at Philippeville, reliving the moment in his mind, not looking at Anne-Marie. He did not realize that he was crying until she reached over and brushed away a few tears with the tips of her fingers. She had not yet shed a tear.

"He was a good, brave man, Anne-Marie. He loved you with everything within him. I can tell you that. He should be here now. It is not right!"

When he had nothing more in him, they sat in silence. He held her hands, clutching them as he repeated again and again, "Why? Why?"

The sun lowered itself in the sky and brought the chapel into shadows. She had not uttered another word but sat with a numb expression on her face. Perhaps not numb, he thought. Composed. Carefully he spoke. "I won't let anything happen to you, Anne-Marie. I'll care for you and Ophélie. I promise."

She cleared her throat. "There is so much that is unclear. Dear David, thank you. Thank you for being there with him, for trying, for telling me. I … I need to be alone now."

He left her sitting in the dark, staring at the small stained-glass window behind the altar. The sunlight blinded him. He felt disoriented, unsure of where to go. He wanted desperately to rest. He remembered Mme Pons's apartment and his room there.

It was a short walk through town. The sun beat down on him. Finding the key in his briefcase, he let himself into the apartment, fell into bed, and slept straight through the night.

Anne-Marie could not explain her reaction. She only knew that something was pulling her to the front of the chapel. She knelt on the hard stones, caressing the cross around her neck. She did not feel angry. She did not feel anything except a strange peacefulness, as if invisible arms were cradling her. She stayed kneeling, letting the quiet, the gentle breath of life wash over her. She was afraid to move, because with the slightest movement perhaps the blissful calm would pass.

In her mind she saw Moustafa smiling at her, his head covered up with curls. She could not cry for him, and she didn't know why, only that his memory came to her with joy. A slight breeze touched her hair; the door in the side of the chapel creaked. When she looked around, no one was there.

The bell in the tower chimed seven. Sometime later she realized that she had been praying, but she was sure the words were not her own. *Who shall separate us from the love of Christ? Shall tribulation or distress … or peril or sword …?*

She whispered it over and over again, took the cross to her lips and kissed it softly. Eventually she rose from her knees, feeling the stiffness, and brushed them off. For some reason she crossed herself as she had seen the nuns do. Then she said simply, "*Merci, Seigneur,*" and added, "I love you, Moustafa."

The Dramchini women moaned and wept through the night. Anne-Marie sat with them and spent her tears in their presence. She knew how Arab women mourned. She thought it tragic and beautiful. The weeping, the wailing, the tears, the swaying bodies, and the silence.

Later the women talked in quiet tones of Hacène and Moustafa, recalling many happy memories, remembering what their lives had meant to their family and friends. Once in the course of the night Mme Dramchini had cried out, "My sons! My sons!" in Arabic. Then she had taken Anne-Marie in her bosom and rocked her like an infant, sobbing.

"He loved you," she moaned in broken French. "You mourn with us. We sad together."

It seemed to Anne-Marie like a healthy, healing experience, the wailing and the questioning, the open display of grief. The women had asked to be left alone in the dining hall, and there they spent the night.

Tomorrow was a new day. The waiting was over. It was time to go forward. The peaceful feeling never left Anne-Marie, and when she lay down on her cot at three in the morning, she immediately fell asleep.

When David awoke, it was light, and he had no idea where he was. It could have been Rémi's farmhouse or the ferry. It took him a moment to register that he was in Mme Pons's apartment in his own room. He had no idea how long he had slept.

For the first time in days he looked in a mirror. A grisly, swollen face stared back. It seemed the most natural thing to do was to shower and shave. He was washing away months of fine Algerian sand that had seeped into his pores. If only he could wash away the pain.

The wound in his head had not seeped blood in the night, which seemed a positive sign. He found a pair of lightweight pants hanging in the closet where he had left them three and a half months ago, and put them on. He wrapped his torso with a thick white bandage. Carefully he pulled on a short-sleeved oxford shirt. The ribs still hurt when he moved too quickly.

The clay santon of the baker smiled at him from his desk. Poor Gabriella. What had he said to her yesterday? Had he said anything? And Anne-Marie … He intended to keep the promise he had spoken to her in the chapel. He did not yet know how, but he would keep it.

He remembered his father in the hospital and phoned to find out his condition. Stable, resting. Good. The old man needed complete rest, and that suited David fine.

He wanted more than anything to see Ophélie, and he finished dressing quickly. When he appeared in the kitchen, Mme Pons let out a scream, then cackled.

"*Ooh là là!* M. Hoffmann! You're back."

"*Bonjour, Madame Pons.*" He kissed her cheek. "Please excuse me for frightening you. Thoughtless of me."

"Let me fix you some breakfast. Poor M. Hoffmann. You are not well. *Oh là là.*" She bustled about her kitchen, whistling happily. "We were so worried, M. Hoffmann. And now you appear in my kitchen and frighten the wits out of me!" She chuckled. "I am very glad to have you back."

Thirty minutes later David left the apartment with his belly full. The pure banality of another summer's day with nothing much happening clashed with the memories of crowds of helpless refugees, of guns and knives. He forced Algeria out of his mind and waved at the women at the *marché* as they nodded and blushed.

He let himself into the parsonage, hurrying down the steps into the basement. The children were already in class. It surprised him to see Gabriella teaching. He walked into the classroom, which was crammed with desks and chairs and children and watched as Ophélie's eyes grew wide with astonishment. David strode to his daughter's desk, picked her up out of the chair, and hugged her tightly. Then he turned to Gabriella. "May I borrow my daughter for a little while?"

"Of course, M. Hoffmann," she stammered.

He saw that she did not know what to expect of him. Holding Ophélie's hand, he walked behind the desk, cupped Gabby's face in his other hand and, to the great delight of the whole class, kissed her forcefully on the lips. The children cheered, and a few chanted, "Encore! Encore!" Little Christophe shouted, "*Oh oh, les amoureux!*" and everyone clapped.

"See you after class," he whispered.

David and Ophélie sat on the warm grass in the shade of an olive tree in the courtyard and laughed for the longest time about nothing at all. Every few minutes Ophélie reached out and gently touched the bandage around David's head.

"Does it hurt very much, Papa?"

"No, sweetie, not now."

"You look funny, Papa," she said and giggled.

"Tell me. Tell me what I look like."

"Well ..." She furrowed her little brow and thought. Then she exclaimed gleefully, "I know! You look like a palm tree! You know how its trunk is wrapped around and around, and then at the very top, there are these big, wide leaves bursting out and draping down like your hair, Papa? It is so long and curly on the ends." She touched it with her fingers. David placed his hand over hers.

"I'm so glad to be with you, Ophélie. Papa has missed you so much."

"Will you ever go away again, Papa?"

"Not for a long time, *ma chérie*. Don't you worry."

Ophélie's face clouded. "But you couldn't bring Moustafa back for Mama, could you?"

"No, Ophélie. I tried. Very hard. And Moustafa wanted so much to come."

"But he won't be coming, will he?"

David shook his head and felt the tightness in his throat.

She contemplated this revelation for quite some time, looking very perplexed. "But I know I saw him coming, Papa. I know it."

He took her in his arms, and she cuddled in his lap. "There are things we can't understand," he said finally. "I'm sorry, Ophélie. So sorry."

"Oh, Papa. It's not your fault. It's just that Jesus has another way. That's all."

He stared in wonder at Ophélie. He did not understand her words, but he marveled at her faith. Perhaps healing would come to him through the faith of his small daughter. It made him smile to think so.

24

Ali watched the fury and debates among the political factions with little surprise. He backed Ben Bella, the man who had, after all, been named as the perpetrator of the War for Independence back in 1954. Soon after that, Bella had been arrested by the French and spent five long years in jail. Nonetheless his presence during the war had been keenly felt. Now was Ben Bella's chance, Ali felt sure.

And what of his own chances? He deserved a high place in this new government, whatever form it took. But would he have it? Would the others in the FLN recognize his shrewd leadership abilities? He had never questioned this before, but now he thought he read the slightest hint of pity in their eyes when they came to visit him. Surely not! He deserved a place in the new government, and he would have it!

The lack of news from Hussein irritated him. It would be easy enough to kill the boy's mother, but what if Hussein never knew of the threat? How to contact the boy? Fatima was eager to prove her worth, but it was much too dangerous to send her to France.

Ali paced in his cubicle, his walk now punctuated by a heavy limp from the bullet wound to his calf. It would heal. So would the wound that had come so near his heart. Rest, the doctor pleaded. But now was not the time to rest, not when the new republic was being birthed. It was time for fast, cunning action.

He spat his cigarette onto the floor and crushed it with his toe. As for Hussein, there was nothing to do but wait for news. The boy was a faithful follower. He had been trained well. He would not let Ali down.

Whatever Gabriella had expected when David got back, this was not it. She gathered her books for the children's class and spoke politely to Mme Leclerc over a *tartine* and cup of hot chocolate.

"So he has come back for you, Gabriella. *Ooh là là!* I knew he would."

Gabriella kissed her lightly on the cheeks, a forced smile on her face. "I'm off! I'm teaching the children this morning."

Perhaps Mme Leclerc was convinced of David's loyalty, but she wasn't. All she wanted to do was to listen to him, to care and understand, but he was avoiding her. After the kiss in front of the children two days ago, he had not come back to talk. Gabriella had the most awful feeling that he was trying to choose between her and Anne-Marie.

She felt sick inside. Sick about Moustafa. Angry that David would not explain his actions. Why had he kissed her in front of the children if he wasn't even sure of his feelings toward her? What was the matter with him?

She reprimanded herself. He had witnessed beastly acts, murders, the death of a friend. She must give him time.

She let herself into the classroom and spread the French grammar book out before her. Today she was teaching the children the difference between *et* and *est*. Pronounced the same way, but the meanings of the two words were completely different. It was simply a matter of memorizing a rule.

Why couldn't life be that simple? The rule said that David had written the words *I love you* in black and white. If he had written it, it should not change. That was the rule.

The worst part was that she could not confide in Anne-Marie. A sort of tension hung between them. They smiled at each other politely and talked of the children. But so much was lost. Gabriella had imagined them ecstatic upon the return of Moustafa and David, laughing, dreaming dreams. Two couples in love.

Instead there were two women for one man, and in spite of all that David had promised her in his letters, in spite of the fact that Anne-Marie had assured her that David was right for her, Gabriella doubted. She was not making it up in her head. It was happening. What she had hoped would be the happiest time at St. Joseph had turned into a time when she dreaded running into either of them.

When Hussein heard the news about Moustafa from Ophélie, it made him sick. He did not dare go to David Hoffmann and beg for help now. He was responsible for Moustafa's death. He felt a sharp pain, like a knife in his stomach, when he saw David striding over to him after class. He prepared himself to look indifferent.

"Hello, Hussein." David held out his hand. "Glad to see that you made it safely to St. Joseph."

Hussein took his hand without meeting his eyes.

"Let's take a little walk. Just the two of us."

With his hand heavy on Hussein's shoulder, David led him out into the streets of Castelnau. He walked him straight to an apartment. "This is my place. I thought we could talk better here."

Hussein felt a chill go down his spine. He half expected David to produce a knife.

"Tell me everything, Hussein." David's eyes were intense, penetrating. "I am not going to harm you, but I want the truth. You owe me that much."

Hussein bit his lip. Curse it all. He still had the explosives. Why not blow the whole place up, himself included? He said nothing.

"Hussein, it's not your fault about Moustafa. Ali didn't kill him. It is not your fault."

So the American was trying to soften him up. If only he knew.

"Hussein, listen." Now David took him by the shoulders and shook him forcefully. "I lived there. I saw what young boys were forced to do. It's not your fault."

The strength of David's hands on him somehow brought comfort. His mother's hands were strong like that. Before he could stop himself, he was clutching David and crying, "I'm sorry! I'm sorry about Moustafa. I'm sorry about the trunk."

David's voice was calm, soothing. "Can you tell me what happened?"

"He trained me for it. For months he trained me to be strong. I was afraid he would kill me. Kill Mama. Can't you see? I wanted to hate you. I wanted to hate you both so it wouldn't matter. But it did matter. I prayed every day to Allah that Ali would not kill you. And now …"

"He didn't, Hussein. It wasn't Ali. It was a massacre. Moustafa died in a massacre."

Perspiration formed on Hussein's forehead. He thought of little Ophélie. This man's daughter. How close he had been to pulling the trigger. He felt nauseated and dizzy.

"I'll do anything, M. Hoffmann. Anything. Only please don't send me back there. Please!"

"Do you have weapons?"

"In my drawer."

"Let's go get them."

"Anything, but please help me. I'm afraid."

M. Hoffmann looked very tired and weak. He patted Hussein's head. "We'll work it out, Hussein. It's going to be okay. Now let's go back to your dormitory."

David flashed Gabriella a smile as they waited for the dinner bell. He was sitting in the courtyard talking with a handful of the boys, showing them how to make paper airplanes. She could barely look at him, and when she did, her eyes filled up with tears. David regretted a hundred times that impromptu kiss in the classroom.

"How were classes today?" he asked flatly.

"The classes? They were fine." The conversation ended.

He did not know how to get around the awkwardness between them. Every time he thought of going to her, taking her on a long walk or to a café, he was overcome by a sense of guilt. Anne-Marie. He had not expected to feel so strongly about her. It was as if Moustafa's fierce loyalty to her had been transferred onto his shoulders. He could not leave her alone. He would not. So it was unfair to Gabby to suggest otherwise.

"M. Hoffmann, *regarde!* Watch how it flies!" Jérémie had folded a sheet of paper into the form of an airplane and let it sail through the air. It landed smoothly in a pile of mashed potatoes on Anne-Sophie's plate.

David shook his finger playfully. "None of that now. Not here. Come to my classroom tomorrow afternoon, and we'll make paper airplanes. All kinds."

"*Ouais!* Super!" Christophe and Jérémie shouted as one.

David turned back to Gabby and shrugged. "It doesn't take much to make them happy."

She only nodded. In her eyes he read a hundred questions and a deep desire just to talk with him. But he could not allow it.

He loved Gabby with abandon and hope and passion.

He loved Anne-Marie because she needed him, because Ophélie belonged to both of them, and it was right to be together.

It was too complicated. He stood up and took his tray to the kitchen with seven boys tagging behind. Momentarily forgetting his cracked ribs, David hefted André onto his back and rode him piggyback to the dorms. Immediately six other little boys begged for a ride. He watched the boys wrestle each other on the dormitory floor, bumping into cots and bunks. Sister Isabelle entered the room and raised her eyebrows disapprovingly but said nothing.

After the boys were tucked into bed and he had entertained them with stories of dinosaurs and dragons, David tiptoed into the girls' dorm and kissed Ophélie on the forehead. "Good night, sweetheart." Again he felt the disapproving eyes of Sister Isabelle. He went outside and stood in the courtyard, staring at the sky.

Anne-Marie appeared beside him. "Thank you for telling Ophélie good night. It means the world to her to have you here."

"I'm not sure Sister Isabelle feels the same way." He chuckled.

"Oh, no. It's not that. It's just that we try not to get the children too riled up before bed. And … and usually men are not allowed in the girls' dorm."

"Ah, of course. I wasn't thinking. Tomorrow night Ophélie shall have her kisses in the courtyard." He winked at Anne-Marie. "And I will have to postpone any more piggyback rides," he said, holding his side.

"David, could we talk?"

"Of course." He took her arm and began walking toward the dining hall.

At that moment Gabriella stepped out of the dormitory and practically bumped into them both. Her face went white, then red. "*Bonsoir*," she mumbled and left the courtyard, not looking back.

The dining hall was quiet and dark. They sat across from each other.

"David. I want to talk about us."

He was glad it was dark, for he could feel his face turning hot with embarrassment. "I meant what I said, Anne-Marie. I meant it."

"I know you did." Anne-Marie brushed her hair over her shoulders nervously. "David, you have done everything for me. But why? Why did you come here in the first place to help me? What is it that brought you here?"

"I've already told you that back in Algiers. I cared."

"Yes, you cared. I know that you care for me. But you do not love me. Not the way you love Gabriella. You are hers, and you are killing her with your silence. Can't you see it in her eyes?" She took his hand. "You feel a duty, a desire to do the right thing for me, and for Ophélie. But you are not obligated to me. You have paid me back a hundred times if you feel that you owed me something. I love you, David. I will love you till the day I die. But I will never be yours. I can't explain it. I just know."

He sighed. Why did life have to be so confusing? "Nothing is simple, Anne-Marie. I do love Gabby, but you're wrong. I'm not the one for her. She wants a husband who is strong and spiritual. Whatever faith I had died with Mou—" He slammed his fist on the table. "I'm sorry. Forgive me."

She kissed his hands. "We're all hurting very badly."

Her eyes were liquid. It was the first time he had seen her cry since his return.

"But listen to me, David. I was in love with Moustafa. Ready to give my life, everything for him. And I will be faithful to him until ..." A flicker of a smile appeared on her lips. "Until the heavens show me otherwise."

"What do you mean?"

"I have the strangest peace, David. As if Someone is carrying me. But it all goes away when I think of you giving up Gabriella for me. Please, David, listen to your heart. Share with her all you have lived. She deserves it; she wants it. If you only knew how she loves you." She took a tissue from her pocket and wiped her eyes. "What do you think we've been doing all these months but talking of the men we love? She's my friend. If I know anything at all, it is that you are meant to be with Gabriella."

So she was freeing him. She had read his heart.

"Yes, perhaps. Yes ... I will tell her tomorrow. Thank you, Anne-Marie." They stood up, and he held her for a long moment, kissing her forehead. "I do love you, and I will always be here for you."

"I know it. Now promise me only one thing."

"What is it?"

"That you won't wait till tomorrow. Don't make her spend another tortured night, David Hoffmann. Go now."

"Yes," he said, laughing. "Yes." He left her standing in the courtyard.

Anne-Marie sank onto the damp ground and cried and cried. She had done it, what she had somehow felt called to do, but it was breaking her heart. She had said it because it had to be said, because she knew what David was thinking. But how it hurt! It was truth she had spoken, and she had somehow had the strength to speak it.

"I'm alone," she whispered. "Alone with my daughter. What will we do when we have nowhere to go? When David and Gabriella are far away and this orphanage is closed up?"

She was kneeling on the ground, her eyes closed and her hands clutched together. Only a minute later did she realize that she had been praying. The peacefulness invaded her again. Such a friendly invasion! Absolutely nothing was certain, and yet she left the court-yard in peace. She could not explain why.

The light was on in Gabriella's room. David tossed a stone at the window. It missed, falling into the olive tree. The second stone hit the window with a pat and bounced off. When the third stone rang true, Gabriella came to the window and peered down. David motioned to her. She frowned and shook her head. He motioned again.

"Please, Gabby!" he shouted.

She put a finger to her lips.

"Come, please!"

She left the window, and the light went off in her room. She looked irritated when she joined him on the cobblestones. "What do you want?"

"You. I just want you."

"Don't give me that, David. I don't believe you anymore."

"Yes, I know. You're right. I'm a fool. I've been so confused."

"I've noticed."

"Can we talk?" he asked.

"How many young women will you make promises to tonight, David?" She whipped around and walked away.

"Gabby, please." He caught her arm, and she shook it free.

"Leave me alone!" she said as he grabbed both of her wrists. "You've done enough harm here. Don't cause a scene!"

"Gabby, please, wait!" He spoke quickly. "At least give me a chance to explain. You have every right to be angry and hurt. Please listen."

She pulled her hands away from his, crossed her arms across her chest, and walked in front of him to the little park outside the church walls. She sat down on a bench. The moon was full and the air balmy, scented with honeysuckle. "I'm listening."

David stood in front of her, leaning against the stone wall. He ran his hand through his hair, searching for the right words. "This isn't how the homecoming was supposed to be. Gabby, I've seen the most awful things, and God seemed so silent. I wanted to be a man of faith—for you.

"But when Moustafa ..." He lowered his voice and spoke with difficulty. "When the massacre occurred, rage overtook me. I hated your God. I blamed Him. I begged Him to leave. And I begged Him to stay." He shook his head. "I'm messed up, Gabby."

Almost unconsciously, he sat down beside her and took her hand. "All I want is to do the right thing, but it isn't as simple as that. Anne-Marie has no one now. My rational mind says I have a duty to her, to Ophélie. I care deeply for her, Gabby, but it isn't love ... love as I feel for you."

He squeezed her hand, but she continued sitting rigidly in her place.

"She asked to see me tonight, to talk. Anne-Marie knows my heart. She will not accept my charity. She knows I belong to you."

Gabriella leaned her head back, and her curly mane brushed the back of the bench. She sighed deeply. "How can you know? I thought I knew. I thought I was sure of you. And now a few miserable days have made me think it's impossible. I understand your sense of duty to Anne-Marie. I could understand if you loved her. She's an incredible woman—as well as a beautiful one...."

She stood and walked into the shadows. "I guess what I'm saying, David, is that you need time to make up your mind about a lot of things. It can't be decided in a convincing monologue."

There was a breeze, but the leaves were quiet, as if they dared not rustle. The moon was stark white with distant gray patches.

"I'm sorry for all you've been through, David. I have hurt and cried and prayed for you."

"So … what do you want me to do? About us?" He watched the moon so luminous, sitting high and white beside the steeple of St. Joseph.

She sighed again. "I don't know. How can I know? I only know this hurts very badly. Can that be right?"

"Love will hurt, Gabby. A lot. The hurting doesn't make it right or wrong. It's just so hard to know."

"Yes. So I guess we should just wait and see. Good night, David." She touched his cheek and walked back to Mme Leclerc's apartment.

Because it was expected of him, David went to see his father in the hospital each day. This morning Roger Hoffmann looked much better. He flirted with the nurse who took his temperature and cracked a joke with another who checked his pulse. He was clean shaven. The man looked again like his father, and David felt uncomfortable. He had not seized the opportunity to talk while his father was vulnerable. Perhaps it would not come again.

After exchanging a few banal words, he returned to St. Joseph. Haunted by Gabby's words, he hadn't slept much. Maybe they were all crazy. Maybe he just needed to get away from this place, go back to the States, let his mind clear.

The one thing he knew was that as long as he was still here, he was going to help Mother Griolet. He had asked to see her at eleven, and she was waiting when he knocked on her door. The old nun did not look well, but her eyes sparkled as she welcomed him into her office.

"There now, David. You look much better today. What a relief to have you back among us. And how is your father?"

"He is resting well. His condition has stabilized."

"You must have been surprised to see him in Algeria."

"To say the least."

"I hope you were able to settle your differences with him, David."

The way she spoke made him squirm the slightest bit in his chair. "Perhaps that will come one day. But I don't want to talk about my father. I've heard rumors that this place may close."

"Yes, we've had quite a time. First it was the exchange program. Then the overcrowding at the orphanage." She pointed to several neat stacks of papers on her desk. "Angry parents, angry superiors, angry townspeople. So much anger around here!"

"Dear Mother Griolet. I'm sorry I caused you such problems. Perhaps it was foolish for me to return to Algeria. In the end it has only made matters worse for everyone."

She shook her head. "No, David. Don't second-guess yourself. People just look for opportunities to complain and bicker. But we trust that God was leading you. We can't see the whole scheme of things as He does."

"I'm afraid I don't see much the way He does." David grimaced. "What I want to know is how I can help you."

"What are your plans, David?"

"I don't know." He shrugged. "I guess my real reason for being at St. Joseph is over. But I'm perfectly willing to help you with the children through the end of the summer. I never realized what fun it could be."

She breathed in deeply, then smiled. "Yes, that would be a great help." Sitting back in her chair, she continued, "After the heart attack, I realized I needed to slow down. Hand over the baton. I was planning to retire gradually. I was going to ask you to consider directing the exchange program." She cleared her throat. "But now, well, it seems that question is settled."

"I'm very sorry to hear it."

Mother Griolet closed her eyes. "I had it all worked out in my mind. You would direct the exchange program and Gabriella the orphanage. Such plans! But it seems the Lord has something else in store for us."

David sat forward in his chair. "Mother Griolet, you must get some rest. I'll teach the children as much as you need. It will be a refreshing change from the college students. There are many things yet to be decided, but you mustn't worry about the children. Between Gabby, Anne-Marie, the Sisters, and me, they will be in good hands. You must rest."

"We have only three weeks left, David. I'll be most obliged if you can stay on until then." She frowned. "It's not the way I wanted it to end, but God knows best."

David thought he saw a tear in the nun's eye.

She continued, "So often the things that seem like the worst mistakes in our lives turn out to be the stepping-stones to something much better, something that will bring God glory. Exceeding abundantly above all that we ask or think."

She closed her eyes, and David watched her wrinkled eyelids flutter.

"That's from one of my favorite verses. Third chapter of St. Paul's epistle to the Ephesians. God has proven it again and again. Don't give up on Him yet."

David listened intently to her words, feeling that he must keep them in mind to help him sometime later. He stood awkwardly. "I'll stay as you ask. You have nothing to worry about." He helped her stand and led her back to her bedroom. "You must rest, Mother Griolet. Everything will be fine."

He pulled the door closed, and as he did, the old nun whispered, "Don't give up on Gabriella, David. She needs you more than she will say."

David walked up the flight of steps and let himself into his classroom. From his window he watched the children playing in the courtyard. He counted them. Fifty-eight. Something had to change, and quickly. Perhaps it was best for the whole place to shut down. Mother Griolet certainly did not have the strength to continue.

He sat down at his desk, opened a drawer, and took out a thick stack of white paper. Slowly, deliberately, he began folding the paper, relishing the feel of it as he creased it carefully with his fingers. The bell rang for lunch. Satisfied, he left the room, looking back at seven paper airplanes, each a different model, sitting neatly on his desk, waiting for eager little hands to give them flight.

25

Eliane Cebrian went over and over the phone conversation in her mind. David Hoffmann, the man she had met at the port in Algiers, had called five days earlier to give her news. Rémi was still in Algiers. Amar and Abdul had helped in rescuing them from the Casbah, and Madira had tended to them as a nursemaid. Rémi would be there soon. But Moustafa was gone.

Dear, proud Rémi, staying until the end. She did not let the children see the worry lines on her face, but at night she cried into her pillow, terrified that Rémi would wait too long and he too would be lost. She tossed and turned in her bed. It seemed that her prayers were bumping against the ceiling and falling back upon her, hollow, unanswered.

The next morning as she hastened to nurse José before he woke up Samuel and Rachel with his crying, a thought struck her as if she had seen it painted on the dull-gray wall in front of her. *Weep with them that weep.* Anne-Marie was grieving a real loss. Anne-Marie was the one who needed help.

St. Joseph was merely thirty minutes away by bus. After breakfast she dressed the children and pulled them close around her. "Today we are going to bring sunshine."

Samuel wiped his brow. "It's hot enough, Mama. Why should we bring any more sun?"

Eliane laughed. "You'll see."

David sat in the back of the café-bar at "their table." He had taken a
great risk, slipping the note into Gabby's grammar book. All it had
said was *vendredi 13h00*, plus a reference to some lines from Byron. *A
long, long kiss, a kiss of youth, and love ...* What had he been thinking?
What if it just made her all the more angry? Would she even show up?

Then he saw her, and he stood as she approached, bowed slightly,
and pulled out a chair for her. "Thank you for coming," he said softly.

"How could I resist when you tempt me with stories of passionate kisses?"

She blushed, and David felt a spark of hope that the old ease and
playfulness they had shared might return. He leaned forward, raised
his eyebrows slowly, and said in a husky voice, "So, what are you
doing for the rest of your life?"

Gabriella laughed. "I have no idea. What about you?"

"Well," he said, narrowing his eyes, "I don't know, but I have
several ideas."

"Name one," she countered.

"A walk through the gardens of Versailles hand in hand with a
knockout redhead."

"Hmm ..."

"A long, passionate kiss in the gazebo leading to Marie
Antoinette's hamlet."

"Intriguing."

"An evening at the opera, maybe *La Flûte Enchantée*, and then a
late-night dinner at Maxim's."

"Very nice."

"And then ..." He reached across the table and took her hand. "Standing in the rain in front of Notre Dame, the young man whisks his lady into his arms and dashes down a flight of steps, where they find refuge in the galleys of the Métro as a lone violinist plays Vivaldi's "Spring." Wet and shivering, they walk back in the foggy night to their hotel ..." As he spoke, he lightly stroked her finger. "... where they spend a night of youthful bliss."

She stared at him, then caught her breath. "David! You're embarrassing me." She said it too loudly, and several men at the bar turned in their seats.

David took her hands again, then reached over and brushed a strand of her hair. "I was just trying out an idea, if ever ... if ever I needed to convince you of anything. What do you think? Pretty good, *n'est-ce pas?*"

"Pretty good. Although there are many more things in Paris to see, and you didn't describe the hotel at all."

"Good point," he reflected. "I guess that's because the hotel itself was of little significance, as long as there was a room and a bed."

"David! You're sounding like a modern-day Chaucer."

"I beg your pardon. In my tale it's all very moral. After all, they are married."

"Well, you didn't say anything about that part."

"No, I haven't quite imagined how it could happen."

"I see. Just a small detail."

He closed his eyes, concentrating, then opened them to look directly at her. "Someday, I promise—" He paused. "Someday I hope I'll have an answer to that." Suddenly he reached for her hand and stood, pulling her with him. "Let's get out of here. Can we go somewhere to talk, Gabby?"

"Talk?" She raised her eyebrows. "I've heard that line before."

"Silly girl. I have so much to tell you if you want to hear it. A hundred things to share and know before I can plan the future."

"Well … if it's talking you want to do, I know just the place."

They sat in the little stone alcove in the tiny street behind St. Joseph and told each other story after story of the months they were apart. Gabriella wept as David described the horror of the war. He held her close, wiping a tear off her cheek. She felt that her emotions were raw and exposed, but today she did not care. The David she knew was back, and he was going to be okay.

"David. I know you don't want to talk of it, but Moustafa … did he leave anything, say anything for Anne-Marie?"

"There was a letter, but it was in the trunk. The one Hussein came over in."

"That boy! He scares me."

"He's a terrified kid, another casualty of war. There's no reason to worry about him now."

She bit her lip, not wanting to broach the next subject. "What about Anne-Marie? I didn't want to hear anything you said the other night. I was so hurt and so angry."

"You had every right to be. I'm sorry. I wanted to explain, but I did it all wrong. Please hear me out, Gabby." He rose, massaged his temples, and offered Gabriella his hand. "Can we walk for a while?"

"Sure, if you don't mind the heat." She followed him through the tiny cobblestone street, pointing out the healthy geraniums that tumbled from their window pots.

This time she listened as David explained his feelings of responsibility toward Anne-Marie after Moustafa was killed and Anne-Marie's insistence that he belonged with Gabriella. They had come to a small park filled with chestnut trees, and he motioned to a bench in the shade of one tree's wide limbs. "And now," he said gently, "it's time to talk about us. What are your plans?"

"My parents and sisters are coming in three days. They'll stay with me at Mme Leclerc's while she goes away for the month of August. Then I guess I'll go back to the States with them, to college." She met his eyes. "But I'm afraid … afraid that I'll never see you again when I leave this little town."

She didn't give him a chance to reply. "Mother Griolet asked me to stay on and be her apprentice. Can you imagine? And I actually considered it before everything fell apart. I prayed and thought it out and made lists and came to the conclusion that God wanted me to stay here in Castelnau. It was the hardest decision I've ever had to make. And then it didn't matter after all."

"You would have done a terrific job." He shook his head, smiling. "Dear Mother Griolet had it all worked out. You with the orphans and I with the young ladies. I mean, heading up the exchange program."

"Would you have stayed, David?"

"Of course." He took her hand. "I would have stayed right here with you for a long, long time." Her head was bent, and David reached over and tenderly took her chin in his hand. "Look at me, please, Gabby."

Her eyes, bright blue, shining, dared to look.

"You have said we must trust. I've done a miserable job at times. But our God won't let me get away. I'm not sure I'm the man for you, with my raging and questions. But I catch on pretty quickly." He glanced at his watch. "Uh oh. It's past three. I've got a date with some pretty special guys back at the orphanage."

"So did we decide anything, David?"

"Yes," he said softly and drew her into his arms. "We decided to trust."

Sister Isabelle answered Eliane's knock at the parsonage door, a flustered look on her face. "*Bonjour, Madame Cebrian.* How very nice to see you."

She focused on the three children, and Eliane noticed the color draining from her face. "Don't worry, Sister Isabelle. We aren't staying. We've only come to fetch Anne-Marie and Ophélie."

The sister showed obvious relief. "Well, please come in. Is she expecting you?"

"No, not at all. I guess you could say I'm kidnapping her."

"What a lovely idea!" She reddened. "I mean, well, you know what I mean."

It didn't take much convincing to get Anne-Marie and Ophélie to leave St. Joseph for the afternoon. "I'm treating you to lunch," Eliane stated flatly.

"To lunch? With all the children?"

"Don't worry. It's all arranged."

They rode into Montpellier and got off the bus at place de la Comédie. Anne-Marie sighed with delight. "It's beautiful."

"You've never been to the Comédie?"

Lazy students sipped drinks in cafés, finding refuge from the heat under the brightly striped parasols that adorned every table.

"Look at the fountain!" Anne-Marie pointed to the statue of the Three Muses that stood several hundred feet away from the ornate opera house.

"Mama," Ophélie said, tugging on Anne-Marie's sleeve. "That's where Bribri and I met that awful man, Jean-Claude. Right over there."

"Oh, sweetheart," Anne-Marie said, hugging her close. "What an awful memory. I'm glad that's all over."

"*Ah, oui.* Let's not talk of bad things today," Eliane said. "Come this way; there's the most lovely park with a pond and ducks and swans and lots of swings and jungle gyms for the children. It's just over there, on the Esplanade."

The long tree-lined promenade with its splashing fountains opened before them. Again, Anne-Marie stopped and stared. "Just being here is like a taste of paradise. A city whose *vieille ville* is intact, where there are fountains and flowers and people enjoying the sunshine." She grabbed Eliane's hand. "Thank you for bringing us here!"

As they arrived at the park, a young Arab woman waved and came over to Eliane.

"Anne-Marie, this is Sarah. She lives beside our hotel, and she came with us on the train. She's going to watch the children while we have a bite to eat."

Before Anne-Marie could protest, Eliane led her back across the Esplanade where spacious, grassy rectangles were outlined with red and white impatiens that fluffed out into a round, brilliant hedge. On the other side of the Esplanade, they stopped at a little kiosk. The luncheon special for the day was written on a large blackboard that sat on a tripod. They studied it for a moment.

"What do think? A salad, *quiche*, and *sorbet* for only forty francs. With a *pichet de rosé* included."

"It looks divine, but can you afford it?"

"Yes, of course. Don't worry about that. This is our luncheon together." They chose a table and sat down.

"Eliane, you're so kind. It's beautiful here. But what about the children, their lunch?"

"I packed sandwiches and *petits suisses* and fruits and cookies and plenty of water. They'll be fine, and the park is in the shade. Sarah is very good with them. She's helped me several times when I thought I might just pull out my hair."

Anne-Marie looked surprised. "You feel that way too?"

"Are you kidding? With three little kids confined to a hotel room?" Eliane laughed.

Anne-Marie laughed too, and Eliane thought how lovely she was. For that brief moment she looked like a young, carefree woman, slim and stunning in her simple white silk blouse and floral skirt. Her hair was pulled back into a neat French braid.

"You look beautiful," Eliane remarked.

"Me? *Merci.* It's just the clothes." She blushed. "It was a gift from God—some rich woman donated a pile of clothes just my size to the orphanage."

"A gift from God, you said?"

Anne-Marie blinked, and she nodded slowly. "Yes. I don't know why I said that." She lowered her voice to only a whisper, so that Eliane had to lean forward and strain to hear. "Something strange has happened, Eliane. I haven't told anyone. It's been too ... difficult and confusing at St. Joseph lately, with David arriving and ... Moustafa ..." She frowned, her eyes filling up with tears. "Can you tell me what it feels like to believe?"

"To believe what?"

"In God, in the Christ. It's just so strange. When I learned about Moustafa, I couldn't cry at first. I was numb, but a sweet sort of numbness, as if someone were carrying me in his arms. It was like that beautiful psalm. I'm a scared lamb that the shepherd is gently leading by the still waters. Could that be so? Could it be God?"

Eliane wiped her eyes, moved by Anne-Marie's simple explanation. "Yes. I think so." She smiled. "It sounds a lot like Him."

"David talked to me. He ... he offered to take care of me. Of us."

Eliane nodded, not saying anything.

"I told him it would be wrong. That he belongs with Gabriella. I don't know why I said it. It would be so nice to have someone to take care of me. But the words just came." She took a sip of wine. "David cares for me, but he loves her. So here I am. The orphanage is closing, and I don't know what we will do. But I'm not worried." She gave a short laugh. "I try to worry, but I can't. It's that same feeling. Being carried."

"How can I help you, Anne-Marie?"

"You're helping me now. Taking me away for a moment to this beautiful place. I haven't forgotten what you said: We can start over.

A new chance." She folded her hands on the table as the waitress brought a salad drenched in vinaigrette. "So what do I do now? While God is holding me?"

Eliane placed a white starched napkin in her lap and said in her brightest voice, "You wait. Jesus calls it 'abiding.' 'Abide in Me,' He says. He'll show you what's next. And, Anne-Marie, I want you to know that we will always help you in any way we can. Anything."

"*Merci.*"

For a few minutes they ate in silence. The sky was a fervent blue without a cloud to be seen. The heat would have been unbearable if it were not for the faint breeze that rustled the trees on the Esplanade.

Then Eliane asked Anne-Marie about Ophélie, and for the next half hour the two women talked about their children. When they had finished their sorbet, as if on cue the children suddenly appeared, dashing across the Esplanade and squealing, Samuel chasing the girls and playfully pulling their pigtails. José wriggled in Sarah's arms.

"Shall we go for a stroll?" Eliane asked, paying the bill.

"Oh yes, let's. For just a little while. It is *une journée magnifique*. I don't want this day to end."

When the two women said good-bye a little later, kissing lightly on the cheeks before taking their separate buses toward their homes, Eliane felt happier than she had in all her time in France.

July 14. Bastille Day. A commemoration of that summer day in 1789 when French citizens stormed the prison in Paris and liberated the seven prisoners inside ... and started the French Revolution.

Hundreds of Montpellieriens were crammed together on the grassy slopes on either side of the Lez river to watch the fireworks. At nine thirty all they waited for was dark to touch the sky.

Ophélie snuggled between Gabriella and Anne-Marie, rubbing her eyes, eager for the spectacle to begin. Ten other girls from the orphanage crowded close to the two women. David had found a spot nearby and busily entertained fifteen boys, threatening that they would be forced to memorize all of *La Chanson de Roland* if they so much as strayed an arm's length from him. It amused Gabriella to see the respect these boys had for David. She bet they would've gladly jumped in the river and swum a mile upstream if he had asked it.

Mme Dramchini with Saiyda and Rachida kept watch on another bunch of children, and the Sisters had their hands full as well. Even M. Vidal was full of stories tonight, and children huddled close to him, listening intently. Seeing the growing crowds, Gabriella wondered if they had been foolish to bring all fifty-eight children into this mob. But when the first of the fireworks exploded in brilliant oranges and reds above the children's heads, she knew it had not been a mistake. They oohed and aahed, clapping enthusiastically with each burst of light.

At least we can give them this, she thought, *before we send them off to who knows where.* She was enjoying the display herself, but her mind wandered. There were only two weeks left for the orphanage. Mother Griolet had heard from Henri Krugler yesterday that he had found homes for several of the harki children in Lodève. That news had brought such a smile of relief to the nun's pale face that Gabriella almost wished she could fabricate a place for each child, just to keep her from worrying.

The plane touched down on the runway, and butterflies danced in Gabriella's stomach. Her family was really here. David and M. Vidal had both brought their cars to the airport so everyone would have plenty of room. Suddenly Gabriella was terrified at the thought of her family meeting David.

Jessica and Henrietta were the first through customs, waving and giggling shyly. They looked older, as if this year had matured them indeed beyond the adolescents they were when she had left. They were tanned, with their long, thick hair falling over their shoulders. Henrietta's was blond, Jessica's auburn.

"Gabriella!" they both exclaimed at once and rushed to embrace their sister.

"Oh, it's so good to see you," she answered, laughing. "You both look great."

"It sure feels good to be off that plane," Henrietta complained, scooping her hair up into one thick strand and holding it off her neck. "But it's like an oven in here."

"Wait till you go outside! Welcome to the Midi!"

"Ugh! I prefer the climate of Senegal."

Jessica lowered her voice. "Is that him over there?" She glanced in the direction of David, who stood a little ways off.

Gabriella could not suppress a smile. "Yes," she whispered. "But please don't stare!"

Jessica laughed, turning her back toward David and mouthing *Wow!* without making a sound. "I would never have expected it of you, Gab."

Gabriella rolled her eyes. "Thanks a lot."

Then her parents came through the doors, pushing a flat trolley filled with suitcases and duffel bags.

"Mother!"

Rebecca Madison looked ever the same—tall, poised, gracious—her long auburn hair pulled back in a thick braid that fell down her back.

"Gabriella," she said softly, her voice cracking the tiniest bit with emotion. She hugged her daughter to her breast.

Then Gabriella was in the arms of her father, tall and sturdy with his own curly shockingly red hair. He picked Gabriella off the ground with his hug. "Sweetheart! So good to see you!"

They talked about everything and nothing, until Gabriella motioned to David and M. Vidal to come over. "I want you to meet two friends of mine. They teach at the exchange program. This is Jean-Louis Vidal. He teaches European history."

The balding man pushed his glasses up on his nose, reddened, and extended his hand. *"Enchanté."*

"Yes, very good to meet you," Gabriella's father replied in French. "I'm William Madison. This is my wife, Rebecca."

"And this is David. David Hoffmann. He teaches the Visions of Man course I told you about."

David smiled stiffly and shook hands. "Pleased to meet you," he said. "I have greatly enjoyed having your daughter in my class. She's spoken often of you."

Gabriella sighed with relief. At least he was behaving in a charming, civil manner.

David then took the hand of Jessica and said, "Let's see, you must be Jessica."

Gabriella noted with amusement that Jessica's face went quite red.

"And Henrietta. Good to meet you both." Still in perfect control, David stood alongside the trolley. "Shall we get these bags to the cars?"

"I hope they'll all fit. Or perhaps we should call a taxi?" her father suggested.

"No, I think we'll be fine. We've brought two cars."

The ride back to Castelnau was a blur. Her father rode in the front seat with David. Jessica and Henrietta were in the backseat, hemmed in by luggage. Gabriella accompanied her mother and M. Vidal in his car. Her eyes never left the pale-blue *deux chevaux* in front of them. She wished with all her might that she could hear every word between her dad and David.

26

Late into the night Gabriella and her family sat around Mme Leclerc's dining-room table, talking. Her landlady had served a delicious meal and then discreetly disappeared.

Gabriella was beaming. There was something so right, so comfortable about being together, the five of them again. With all the events of the past months, she had not realized how much she had missed them. Jessica insisted Gabriella recap all of her adventures of the last nine months, and the others agreed.

Gabriella began with Mother Griolet and the classes and David. She told about the mysterious little child, Ophélie, and the cruel Jean-Claude and the operation David had started up to rescue children from Algeria. Her father's face grew grave, concerned. Her mother only nodded from time to time.

When Gabriella mentioned her flashback about Ericka, her mother reached across the table and gently took her hand. For a moment Gabriella could not continue, and she noticed that everyone's eyes were shining with tears.

She told about Anne-Marie's arrival, Mother Griolet's heart attack, and the threat to close the orphanage and exchange program.

"And then when David finally came back, he brought the terrible news of Moustafa's death." She sighed. "It has been the worst and the best of times, as Dickens says."

Mother broke in. "And what comes next for you, Gabriella?"

"I suppose I'll go with you all and finish my degree in the States, as we had originally planned. There is nothing to keep me here and … I'm … well, I'm just not sure what will happen between David and me. He needs time." She chuckled mournfully. "Trouble is, time is running out."

"So the two of you have made no definite plans?" her father reaffirmed.

She shook her head.

"Well," he said, and Gabriella thought he sounded relieved, "I look forward to getting to know this young man while I'm here."

The evening ended with the whole family holding hands as her father bowed his head and prayed for his eldest daughter.

The reunion between Mother Griolet and Rebecca Madison took place at the nun's bedside the next afternoon.

"God be praised," said Mother Griolet. "You are a bright light to me today. Please forgive me for not receiving you properly. For some silly reason this old body does not want to get out of bed today."

Rebecca's voice was firm and reassuring. "You must rest. These other women are doing a fine job handling the children. And I thoroughly enjoyed seeing M. Vidal again." She laughed. "He hasn't changed much in fifteen years."

"No, dear Jean-Louis is still the same. He's a big help to me." Her face clouded. "And I suppose you have met M. Hoffmann?"

"Yes, he was at the airport to meet us. Very striking and polite. I hope I'll get to know him better. I must confess I was relieved when Gabriella told us they haven't made any immediate plans."

"Yes, I can imagine. But, Rebecca, I want you to know he is a fine young man. I misjudged him for many months. He's finding his way. I believe that he would be a good man for Gabriella." She smiled. "I thought they should stay here and run the show, but *He*"—and she glanced heavenward—"obviously had other plans."

"Well, thank you for telling me, Mother Griolet. Your opinion means a lot." She patted the nun's hand. "And now I'm going to let you rest. I'm sure there is work that I can help with around here."

"Yes." Mother Griolet caught her hand. "Rebecca … did Gabriella mention about … about Ericka?"

Rebecca locked her hands together and bent her head. "Yes. We had written, of course. And last night all of us talked about it together. Thank you for being here for her, as you were for me all those years ago." She took a long breath. "I'm sorry you had to be the one who got the brunt of Gabriella's anger. I suppose it should have been me."

"No, Rebecca. I'm glad I was here."

"The hurt never seems to lessen, losing a child. But God has filled up the emptiness in other ways. For that I am grateful. *Merci.*"

Rebecca bent over and kissed Mother Griolet's forehead, then left the nun sitting in her bed and quietly slipped out the door.

When Mother Griolet did not show up for breakfast the next morning, Sister Rosaline excused herself from kitchen duty and went through the courtyard into the parsonage. She walked in her typically brisk manner, reaching the nun's quarters out of breath. As she opened the door to the apartment, an eerie silence greeted her.

"*Coucou*, Mother Griolet?" she called out, trying to sound cheery. The walk down the hall took a few seconds, but to Sister Rosaline it seemed like hours. She came to the nun's bedroom. There she lay, with a peaceful smile on her face and her worn Bible lying in one arm.

She's still sleeping, Sister Rosaline told herself as she felt for a pulse, but Mother Griolet's hand felt cool to the touch. Sister Rosaline recoiled, drawing her hand to her mouth. "*Oh, non!*"

Was there no breath, no hope? Mother Griolet looked so serene lying there. Sister Rosaline knew that this body no longer housed the nun's soul. She bit her lip, crossed herself, then sank to her knees with a low groan. Tenderly she took Mother Griolet's white hand and kissed it.

"I loved you like my own mother. I would have done anything for you. Your faith gave me faith in the worst of times." She sniffed and wiped her round cheeks with the back of her hand.

Sister Rosaline thought for a moment that she had heard a sound, and she glanced up. Outside it was beginning to rain, and the drops hit the window in sharp pellet-like strokes.

"Are You weeping, Lord?" she asked. "Not for Yourself, not for her, for she is with You now. But for us. Oh, what shall we do now, Lord Jesus? What shall we do?"

The rain fell harder, and Sister Rosaline knelt by the bed and watched it for a long time. "You took her, Father. It would have killed her to leave St. Joseph. You took her before she was forced away. You took her peacefully."

She waited for a while longer, watching from the bedroom window as Gabriella and Sister Isabelle dashed across the courtyard and retrieved a handful of umbrellas from the dorm. Then, in single file, Gabriella led the children into the basement of the parsonage. Soon Sister Rosaline could hear their sweet voices chattering excitedly about the rain in the classroom below.

"Show me how to tell them, Father." She stood up slowly, her joints aching. She stood for another moment staring at the nun, bowed slightly, crossed herself again, and left the room.

Gabriella looked up quizzically at David's entrance to the classroom. He gave her a sad little smile and said, "May I have the pleasure of teaching these children the conjugations of the verbs *aller*, *être*, and *avoir*?" Then, drawing closer, he whispered, "Sister Rosaline needs to see you."

Gabriella found Sister Rosaline and Sister Isabelle crying in the dining hall. Amid hugs and tears, Sister Rosaline pronounced the words, "She is gone."

The three women sat in stunned silence and watched the downpour, listening to its drowning repetition. It seemed appropriate for it to rain, particularly this type of driving, persistent rain, as if the storm itself were delivering the final, deliberate blow to St. Joseph.

The thirty days would soon be up and the orphanage closed. It did not seem to matter, now that Mother Griolet was gone. Gabriella swallowed, but the lump in her throat wouldn't go away. She thought about Henri Krugler working hard to find families to take in the children. She thought about the children who had already found homes in Lodève.

And then she thought about Mother Griolet lying, as Sister Rosaline had described, serene and still, her ash-white hands folded over her abdomen.

Gabriella had no desire to fight anymore. Let the authorities come and pronounce their sentence. She watched the windowpane fill up with drops of rain.

Presently Sister Rosaline sighed and stood up. "I'm going to call M. Cohen. He'll help us let people know." She wiped her brow. "And I need to inform her superiors. There's a certain protocol for that." Her voice caught, and she turned quickly and left the room.

"*Alors, moi*," said Sister Isabelle, wiping her eyes. "I'm going to tell Pierre. He'll see to it that the whole town knows quickly." She tiptoed out of the room without looking back, an umbrella tucked under her arm.

In that short moment Gabriella saw her future more clearly. Soon she was really going to leave St. Joseph with her parents and start a new life in the States. Her soul ached. Her mouth went dry. "But, Lord, I don't want to leave," she whispered.

She buried her head in her hands. She knew what Mother Griolet would say: don't give up until the Lord Himself directs otherwise.

She was doing no good just sitting there. A hundred details needed attending to. It was not the time to give in to the numbing power of the rain. But before she did anything else, Gabriella had an appointment to keep. She left the room and walked outside, letting hundreds of wet drops fall on her face before she found refuge in the parsonage.

It did indeed look as if the nun were merely asleep, she thought as she calmly entered the room. It was as if Mother Griolet had known what was happening, and awareness had brought a faint smile to her lips.

"At home with the Lord," Gabriella said softly. She touched the nun's cool hand. "I know you're not here," she said, "but I had to come see you again. I had to tell you that you are the godliest woman I have ever known." She dropped to her knees, resting her head against the bed. "I'm not ready for you to be gone, Mother Griolet. It was so much easier to trust when you were here. I could have stayed here, just observing you work, for many years."

Slowly she stood up. "You said God turns tragedy to triumph, but I don't see it. There's only a whole lot of hurt around here right now." She cupped the gold Huguenot cross hanging around her neck, then bent forward and kissed Mother Griolet's cold cheeks. "I haven't forgotten that He is in control. I won't forget."

As she stood back up, the cross spun slowly around on its chain. Outside the rain continued to fall.

David's initial response to the news of Mother Griolet's death was to take charge. It helped him to be busy, because the crazy, angry questions did not come as quickly to mind. He spent the morning with the orphans, working on verbs. When he felt composed enough, he gently broke the news to the children.

They stared at him, speechless. Finally little Christophe blurted out, "Where is she? Is she still up there? In her room?"

When David nodded, several girls squealed and hid their faces. Most of the boys remained silent, their young faces stoic. Ophélie ran to the front of the room and hugged her father. "It can't be, Papa! It just can't be!"

"Shh." David cuddled her and cleared his throat. "I am very, very sorry to have to tell you this. We all loved Mother Griolet very much."

He could not think of what else to say. Their sad eyes were pleading for comfort, but he had none to give.

"What will happen to us now?" Anne-Sophie asked. "Will they send us away?"

"No, children. Don't worry. It will be all right. It's okay to be sad and to cry, but remember, as Mother Griolet has told you …" He faltered for a moment. "God is in control." Saying those words, whether he truly believed them or not, somehow helped David regain his composure.

"Shall we pray?" he suggested, and the children nodded. He watched them, their heads bowed, eyes closed, small hands folded neatly on top of the desks. They trusted him completely in that moment. But no words came to his mind.

Ophélie, who was sitting on his desk, whispered, "Do you want me to pray, Papa?"

He nodded.

"Oh, dear Lord," she prayed in a strong, sorrowful voice. "Thank You for Mother Griolet. Thank You that she took good care of us. Thank You that she has gone to heaven now, and I'm sure she must be very happy." She began to cry again. "Please take care of us, Jesus. Please, oh please, take care of us. We don't want to leave. Amen."

For several minutes afterward the children sat in silence. Then Anne-Sophie started to sing a simple chorus, and the others gradually joined in.

"God is watching over me,
No matter how small I may be.
He is listening to my prayers.
How good to know that my God cares.
God is watching over me."

It seemed to calm them; it also calmed David's heart.

Sister Isabelle came into the classroom, red eyed and sniffling. "Thank you, M. Hoffmann, for your help. Children, you have thirty minutes of rest time in the dorms before lunch. We'll take you by threes under the umbrellas."

David left the classroom, promising Sister Isabelle that he would let M. Vidal know about the news. She smiled gratefully at him as the children lined up three by three at the door.

He had never been to the old history teacher's house, but he knew where it was located: down the hill and back on a tiny side street of the village. The rain was coming with such force that, in spite of his umbrella, by the time he reached the small stone house, his shoes and pant legs were sopping wet. He knocked forcefully on the door.

After what seemed an eternity, the older man opened it, blinking behind his glasses. "David! *Quelle* surprise! Look at you. Please, come in."

David felt vulnerable, unprepared, and unworthy to speak to the older man, as he stood before him, dripping on the tile floor.

"What brings you here today?" Jean-Louis asked brightly. Then he saw David's face. "What's happened?"

Jean-Louis hurried him into the kitchen, where a single chair sat in front of the small, narrow table. A half-full bottle of red wine was the only thing on the table. Jean-Louis retrieved another chair from the salon, and they sat down. He cleared the wine bottle off the table and wiped his bloodshot eyes.

"It's Jeanette, *n'est-ce pas?*"

David nodded. "I'm sorry to be the one to bring you this news." He shivered, although the air was heavy and warm. "Sister Rosaline found her this morning. It appears she died peacefully in her sleep."

"I see." Jean-Louis thoughtfully stroked his chin. "Yes, I see."

He turned away, and David felt like an intruder in the other man's grief. "Would you like me to leave?" he asked finally.

"No," Jean-Louis said quickly, almost desperately. "Could you stay for a moment?" Jean-Louis went into his salon again and returned with a bottle of pastis. "Will you have a drink with me, David? I think I need a drink."

"Yes, of course."

For the next hour they sat in strained silence and slowly sipped their tall glasses of pastis. Jean-Louis seemed completely lost in thought, perhaps anesthetized by the constant sound of the pouring rain. At length he said, "She was my dearest friend." Then he looked down at his empty glass, his face bright red, and mumbled, "I loved that woman. I did." After another long silence he asked, "She is still … she is still in her room?"

"Yes. I need to call the authorities to report the death, but I thought you might …"

"Yes, I shall go and see her. Would you please wait for me to get my coat?"

"Of course."

They left the little stone house five minutes later and walked with their umbrellas pushed in front of them to keep the driving rain away.

Word of Mother Griolet's death spread quickly throughout the town of Castelnau. In their voices over the phone, Pierre Cabrol could hear it as he announced the news. In the eyes of those who came into the bakery, he could see it. Sorrow and shame.

They wonder if their obstinate complaining had anything to do with it, Pierre thought. Well, let them wonder. Even his wife, Denise, had shed quite a few tears.

A hundred different scenarios flashed through Pierre's mind as he rolled out his dough and baked it in the large ovens in the back of his shop. He remembered when Mother Griolet had first come to Castelnau. He had been a boy of sixteen and enchanted by the young nun with the dancing eyes and rippling laughter. The black habit she had worn had never been able to hide her beauty.

He remembered Sebastien Vidal, who had stolen her heart while she was still in training. That had been the talk of the town! Would the pretty young novice give up her calling for the fleshly desire of marriage? And then he remembered, with sorrow, the news of Sebastien's death on the battlefield so far away. Pierre had helped Jean-Louis install the stone plaque on a column in the chapel all those years ago, in remembrance of those lost during the First World War.

He thought of the really terrifying times during the Second War when the three of them, Jeanette, Jean-Louis, and he, had taken their part in the Resistance. Terrifying and extremely rewarding.

Denise had always watched Mother Griolet jealously when she had business to do with Pierre. More than once Pierre had felt a pang of guilt. He cared for this nun. It had long ago stopped being the foolish crush of his youth. Over the years his feelings had mellowed into great respect for this woman who had a wonderful ability to joke and trust in God's surprises.

He brushed his flour-coated hand across his face to wipe a tear, leaving a patch of dough over his right eye. *I'm going to miss you, Jeanette.* And he knew he wasn't the only one. Not by a long shot.

After the orphans were snuggled on their beds for nap time, Anne-Marie quietly made her way to the parsonage and up to Mother Griolet's apartment, which Sister Isabelle had assured her was unlocked. The rain had stopped, and from time to time a ray of sun peeped out from behind thick gray clouds.

Anne-Marie did not turn on any lights but made her way to the bedroom. The corpse looked very white in the room's shadows. Anne-Marie stood transfixed in the doorway. She did not feel worthy to go in.

"I came to tell you good-bye," she whispered. "I wish I could have known you better. But anyway, I thought you would want to know that ... that I believe. In spite of Moustafa, in spite of the war and this place closing and David going and now you ... I still believe. I can't tell you why. I think you must know that better than I. But wherever you are now"—she looked upward—"for I know you are with Him if ever anyone is, well, I just wanted you to know. Thank you." She took her gold chain with its strange cross in her hands, tracing its outline with her fingers, and whispered again, "I believe."

27

The Place at the port in Philippeville was busy with activity. In the heat of midday, the Arab woman quickly bought her pears and peaches, a head of lettuce, carrots, potatoes. The mood was happy today, but every time she came into the square, she remembered the massacre that had taken place over two weeks ago.

Algeria was free. A shaky freedom. But oh, the price!

The vendor weighed the fruits and vegetables and handed them to her. "Allah be praised. It's a good day!" he sang out in robust Arabic.

She merely nodded and placed the items carefully in her straw basket. She was neither old nor young, a soft, timid woman who had never married and who spent her days caring for her elderly father. The people of Philippeville called her Selma, which meant "peaceful one," although her real name was Fatiah.

She was respected as a wise woman and a healer. Day and night hurting people appeared at her door. Without a sound she moved her hands slowly, thoughtfully over their bodies or prepared strange herbal dressings. Those who were healed did not leave money. They left chickens and vegetables and olives.

Selma pulled her white scarf around her neck as she climbed the stairs to her apartment. She knocked four times, pausing in between each rap. It was their code.

Her father opened the door, relief in his eyes. "You were not followed?"

"No, Father. All is well. How is he?"

The old man smiled. "Better. You will see. He's opened his eyes."

Selma set down her basket in the tiny kitchen and hurried into the darkened room at the back of the apartment. A young man lay perfectly still on the bed, his olive skin glistening with perspiration. She bent over him, and his eyes flickered open. They were soft brown in color, kind eyes, fearful.

"It's okay. Don't be afraid," she whispered as she gently brushed his thick black curls away from his face. She held a glass of water to his lips, and he drank. "You're going to be fine."

The young man opened his mouth, trying to speak, but his words were garbled.

"Don't worry. You'll speak in time. Rest now. You're safe here."

She left the room, closing the door behind her. "It is good, Father. He's awake. We'll have to move him soon."

But where? It had been their question for these seventeen excruciatingly long days. Where could they hide a harki man? She stood out on the tiny balcony with its wrought-iron railing, staring into the square. Seventeen days ago she had stood there with tears streaming down her face, watching the bodies and the terrible stillness before the Algerian army men had carried the dead away to nameless graves. Then out by the sea, she had seen it. A movement amid the stillness.

With quivering legs she had walked out into the terrible heat of the afternoon, the stench of death overpowering her. She had covered her entire face with her white veil, stepping over bodies, trying not to look at the faces with their wide eyes filled with their last feeling: terror. There, by the water, a young man lay bleeding, pulling himself slowly toward the water.

Now he lay in her bed.

She forced herself to think about preparing lunch and not about the backbreaking struggle to bring the man, nearly dead, here. Not the agonizing fear that had gripped her every moment, that the madmen would come back and kill her as well.

The young man had lived. It was a miracle that even she could not explain. He had lived, and now he had opened his eyes. Allah be praised.

Later in the afternoon Selma tiptoed back into the bedroom where the young man lay. His head was turned toward the door, his eyes open. She lowered her eyes and sat down in the chair by his bed. She reached down to retrieve a cool rag that lay in a small bucket by the bed. Day and night she had sponged cool water over his body, trying to bring the fever down.

As she touched his forehead with the cool rag, the young man opened his mouth. "Thank you," he said with difficulty.

She glanced at him, smiled, then again lowered her eyes. She felt almost embarrassed to be with him now that he was awake. For days she had cleaned his wounds and sponged his body while he slept. But now he knew what she was doing.

She gave him a drink of water, which he sipped quickly. Before, it had been almost impossible to get him to drink liquids, and they had feared he would die of dehydration. At times he had come into a sort of semiconsciousness, where he would drink. But always his eyes had remained closed.

He made another sound. She leaned closer. "What is it?"

"Bro ... brother?"

Selma shook her head. "I do not know. You were the only one."

His eyes were intense. "Tell me."

She had no desire to recount it again. "I found you by the dock at the edge of the water, crawling out from under two other slain men. You had been stabbed twice."

"When was this?"

"You've been here over two weeks."

Pain registered on his face. "Where am I?"

"In Philippeville. In my apartment. It looks over the square where it happened. That's how I found you."

"Take me—Algiers," he choked.

"I have no car, nor does my father. Do you have someone in Algiers?" She felt a terrible pity for him. Surely anyone from his family would have long since been killed.

"Friends. Pied-noirs. Help me, please." He closed his eyes and seemed exhausted with his effort to speak.

Selma wiped his brow again. "If I find a car, do you know somewhere to go? It is so extremely dangerous for you now."

"Yes," he mumbled with his eyes still closed, and Selma was not sure what he meant.

The last bag was packed, and Rémi Cebrian put it into the old car. He had salvaged every possible item that he could transport from the farmhouse. There were two suitcases, a large duffel bag, a cardboard box, and the trunk. He was determined not to lose this one. Rémi ran his fingers over the little openings he had installed in the front and back of this trunk, just like the other. But no one would be hiding in this one.

Abdul and Amar followed him back into the farmhouse, where Madira was preparing their last meal together. The scent of the couscous greeted them in the den.

"El Amin! Quick. Help me get the food on the table!" Madira called to her son, and the young boy went into the kitchen.

They all sat down, and Rémi bowed his head; the others did so too. "God our Protector and Provider, thank You for this food. Be with my friends." He paused and sniffed. "Have mercy upon them, protect them. Grant me safe passage. Amen." There was a stinging in his chest at the thought of really leaving. He wanted to get it over with now.

"Remember, Abdul. This house is yours, for your family. You keep it. The fields, the groves, it is yours as we have spoken. You have all the papers."

"Yes, M. Rémi. We'll see what happens. We'll do our best to keep the house."

"Will Samuel ever come back to play with me?" El Amin blurted out.

Madira regarded her son sadly.

"I cannot say what will happen," Rémi said to the child. "I know he misses you."

The sound of a car pulling up to the house startled them all. Rémi's eyes darted to Madira, who immediately took the boy to the back of the house. The men stood up, quickly positioning themselves by the windows, where the rifles lay. Rémi shook his head, disgusted. So close, and now was the FLN coming to his door?

They watched as a veiled Arab woman stepped out of the car
and waited. Perhaps it was a trap. She glanced back at the car, then
tentatively walked toward the house. When she came to the door, she
spoke slowly and distinctly.

"M. Rémi Cebrian. I have come from Philippeville to bring you
a friend whom you thought dead. Moustafa Dramchini is in the car.
Please help us bring him to the house."

Rémi's mind whirled. Moustafa! Impossible. Had Ali somehow
cooked up another scheme? "Who are you?"

"My name is Fatiah; people call me Selma."

Rémi peered through the window, trying to see the car. An old
man sat in the passenger's seat. "Show me Moustafa," Rémi called.

The veiled woman bowed and returned to the car. She opened
the door to the backseat and bent over. A few minutes later, with the
woman supporting him, a young man sat up.

Rémi's eyes grew wide, and without hesitation he raced out the
door. He stood beside the car, calling softly, "Moustafa? Moustafa!"

Moustafa laughed weakly. "Rémi. You are still here."

"Yes." He felt his eyes well up with tears. In another hour he
would have already left for the docks.

Carefully Abdul, Amar, and Rémi lifted Moustafa from the car
and carried him to the worn couch in the den. When Rémi turned
around to thank the woman, she was gone. The car was disappearing
from sight in a stream of dust.

Rémi did not leave for France that day. Instead he called the same
doctor who had helped him three weeks ago. When the doctor saw

Moustafa, he cursed lightly. "You again? My son, what has happened now? Weren't two bullets enough for you?"

Removing the bandages, he examined the wounds and gave a low whistle. "You're mighty lucky, lad. It's a wonder you did not bleed to death. And how they kept the infection out … amazing."

The doctor went to speak with Rémi. "He was sliced up in the chest and the side. How long has he been here?"

"Just an hour. A woman brought him here. We thought he was murdered at Philippeville with the rest of the harkis."

"*Bon sang.* He's worse than a cat with nine lives. What will you do with him?"

"I'll take him with me."

"Rémi, are you mad? No one will let him on a boat. You know that. They'll get him for sure, and I guarantee you he won't survive another wound."

"But if I had a way, doctor. If I did, could he travel? Could he sit up?"

"What are you thinking?"

Rémi nodded to the car. "There's a trunk in the car. It has already worked once. We smuggled a boy over to France. Moustafa would fit."

The doctor rubbed his chin thoughtfully, looking skeptical. "It's quite a risk. He is so weak. If you could wait a few more days … feed him well. Get a little strength into him. Then perhaps."

"Thanks, Doc."

"*De rien.* You take care of yourself, Rémi."

"I will. And you? You're still determined to stay?"

"As long as I have work to do, I'm staying right here in Algiers. Good-bye."

Rémi watched the doctor go. Then he called to Amar, and they took the heavy trunk from the car. Setting it in the den, Rémi smiled at Moustafa. "Looks like I'm not through packing after all."

Gabriella and the Sisters painstakingly went through every drawer and every file in Mother Griolet's office, finding names and addresses, trying to contact those who would want to know about the funeral.

Sister Isabelle stood in front of a bookcase, touching the brittle spines of Mother Griolet's treasured volumes. "Ah, here she is. The santon." She carefully picked up the clay figurine, studying the face of the old woman who was hunched over under her bundle of sticks. "I've always loved this little lady," she commented. "Do you remember the children who brought her to Mother Griolet?"

Sister Rosaline came to Sister Isabelle's side. "Christine and Yves. I could never forget them," she said softly. "Those pitiful children begging to be hidden, imploring Mother Griolet to take them in. And offering her this old santon, their only treasure." She bit her lip. "Their parents' names eventually appeared on the list of those who were lost in the camps."

"Have they been contacted?" Sister Isabelle asked. "They would certainly want to know."

Sister Rosaline picked up a manila folder stuffed with papers. "I think I saw them on the list of names M. Cohen said he had contacted."

"I just love the santons," Gabriella said, standing in front of the old clay woman and thinking of the clay baker she had given David for Christmas. "'Little saints,' bringing their humble treasures to lay at the feet of the Christ child." She touched the fine pieces of real wood on the old woman's back. "You are bringing your burden to the Christ child. He will carry it for you now." When she looked around, the two nuns' faces were shining with tears.

It took quite a few phone calls to Washington for David's father to update his colleagues on the extraordinary circumstances he had encountered in Algeria and to reassure them that he was now safe in France. It took only one more call to convince them that he needed an extended vacation there. So at Monique Pons's insistence, he moved into the widow's apartment.

"Of course he must stay with you, M. Hoffmann!" she told David. "It is no trouble, and you will have the place to yourselves. I'll be leaving on vacation with Yvette Leclerc after the funeral." She blew her nose loudly into a plaid handkerchief. "It is too sad."

That evening she prepared them a *taboulé* and a plate of cold cuts, saying, "Eat whenever you want. I must go out for a while."

So David found himself alone with his father in the dining room. "You look much better, Father."

"Feel much better too, Son. I'm certainly glad to be out of that hospital." He helped himself to the taboulé, then passed it across the oblong table. "Looks good. Very nice woman, this Mme Pons. You say you've been here two years?"

"Two years this month."

His father put down his fork. "Can you tell me what it was, really, that brought you over here, David?"

"I've told you before." David's voice was crisp. "I came to help Anne-Marie."

His father took a sip of wine. "You haven't told me everything, David. I learned quite a bit from the wild man, Ali. A fascinating story. 'Operation Hugo' I believe he called it."

"Yes, well, I'm sorry you had to get involved. The guy is a lunatic. Dragged you into something that had nothing to do with you."

"I'm proud of you, David." He said it stiffly, formally, a stern expression on his face.

David did not want to talk, did not want his father's accolades. He started to say something sharp, but he hesitated and instead simply replied, "Thank you."

"I've been a wretched father, David," the older man said at length. "I don't blame you for whatever you feel toward me." He dabbed the white cloth napkin over his mouth. "Could we ... I ... I'd like to catch up with you, David. Before I go back to Washington. Could we try?"

"Maybe," David said unenthusiastically. Then something pierced him like a sharp knife. This was his chance. He had missed it on the boat. "Sure, Father. Would you like to go for a drive?"

The evening air was cooler, and they drove out into the country as the sun left the sky. His father seemed to want to talk, and David forced himself to listen, consciously pushing the anger away for this one night.

"I've always thought this part of France was one of the loveliest spots on earth. It brought back hope to me all those years ago. When I got out of the camp, I looked for you and your mother and sister for a long, long time. Eventually I learned of the fate of Annette and Greta, but I still held a tiny hope for you. St. Joseph was the twenty-fifth institution I visited, looking for you."

"Mother Griolet said you cried when you found me."

"Of course I did." His father stared out the car window into the darkness. "You know I'm not very good at saying I'm sorry. But I want you to know I mean it. Can you forgive me, Son, for keeping my distance from you? I've wasted so much time."

David could see the strain on his father's face. Every word was an effort to pronounce, an admission of his failure.

"Do you think we could start over, Son?"

David kept his eyes on the road. "I suppose anything is possible."

The silence between them pounded in his ears as he thought about his father's question. It was his chance and his choice. He could cut the proud man down with one simple word. Or he could find his father after all these years. Another minute and the opportunity would be gone. David blinked his eyes and heard himself say quietly, "I forgive you, Father."

He said it without emotion, but as soon as the words were out of his mouth, he felt a weight lift from his shoulders. A smile flickered on his lips. With one hand on the steering wheel, he held the other out to his father, who took it warmly in his. "I forgive you."

Bedtime was the hardest for the children. They plagued Gabriella, Anne-Marie, and the Sisters with questions about the future. The orphans who had been at St. Joseph for a good while cried into their pillows, calling out for Mother Griolet. The Arab children simply cried out in fear, feeling the tension and the overwhelming sadness all around them.

Ophélie clung to Anne-Marie, begging to sleep in her bed with her. "Why hasn't Papa come to tell me good night? Where is he?"

"He's with his father, sweetheart. He'll see you in the morning. Tomorrow you'll meet your grandfather."

"I don't want my grandfather. I want my papa now."

Anne-Marie's face clouded. "*Ma petite*, you must calm down."

"No, I won't! I won't." She sat up in bed, clutching her mother. "Mother Griolet is dead, and Moustafa is dead. Are you going to die too, Mama?"

"No, Ophélie. We're together. We're safe. Mama will never leave you again. I promise."

But Ophélie would not be comforted. She sniffled and wiped her nose and then burst into tears again. Finally Anne-Marie led her out of the dormitory. She knelt down beside her daughter in the bathroom, wiping the child's eyes with a tissue.

"Darling, I'm so sorry about Mother Griolet and Moustafa. But it's going to be all right. I just know it is, because … because I believe. I believe in this strange, kind Savior, and He has given me His peace." She took Ophélie in her arms and held her tightly.

"Oh, Mama," the child said, sobbing. "You believe! I knew you would someday. And you have told me on the day I needed it most."

Anne-Marie cupped Ophélie's face in her hands. "You see so much, my child. Sometimes I think this God has given you a different type of eyes, eyes that see the heart." She kissed Ophélie on the forehead. "Shall I pray?"

The little girl nodded.

"Dear God …" Anne-Marie's voice was shaky. "We are very sad, God." She bit her lips and brushed her hand across her face. "We miss Moustafa and Mother Griolet very much. I think You understand, because You lost someone very dear to You once. Please help us, as we are sad. And please, God, don't stop holding us in Your arms. We need You. Amen."

She carried her daughter back to her bed, pulled the sheet over her, and kissed her cheek. "I love you, Ophélie, very much."

Ophélie was already asleep.

A heavy depression took hold of Hussein when he heard of Mother Griolet's death. If Allah had permitted that Moustafa and the good nun should die, why should he allow Hussein to live?

David Hoffmann had tried to help him, but his words had fallen flat. Staring at the top of the bed above him, Hussein frowned. The American had taken all the explosives, but he didn't know that Hussein also had a gun. He kept it hidden under his mattress, the pistol that he had almost used on Ophélie. He did not plan to use it

on any of these people at St. Joseph. There was already enough grief
for them. But he would use it. He had already composed the letter
to Ali.

> *Master Ali,*
>
> *Allah be praised. Algeria is free, and my work here
> is accomplished. The old nun is dead, and everyone is
> gone. There is no more St. Joseph, no more orphanage.
> Moustafa never made it from Algeria, slaughtered at
> the docks.*
>
> *I have completed my task, and you may celebrate.
> By the time you read of this note, I will be no more. My
> final task will be accomplished. A death with honor
> for Allah.*
>
> *Farewell, Ali.*
>
> *Your humble servant, Hussein*

It pleased Hussein in a twisted sort of way that he had not lied
to Ali in the letter. Everything he had written was perfectly true. The
orphanage would soon be closed, and everyone gone.

He would wait until after the funeral tomorrow, then he would
simply disappear. He turned the cold revolver over in his hands.
With one bullet from this pistol, he could end his misery. When
someone finally discovered his body—and he intended to make that
hard—there would be no one left at St. Joseph to remember him
anyway.

28

When Saturday arrived, bright and sunny, there was almost a feeling of joy in the air that neither the Sisters nor Gabriella could explain. They busied themselves in the dining hall, preparing food to be offered after the funeral. Sister Rosaline took pride in creating the centerpiece, a hollowed-out watermelon filled with Mother Griolet's favorite summer fruits.

Pierre Cabrol appeared at the parsonage door early in the morning, carrying an elaborate *pièce montée*, layers of pastry puffs that had been stuffed with cream and stacked up to form a tall pyramid. His wife followed, carrying every imaginable type of bread. Jean-Louis came next, with two large trays full of pizza.

"Pierre, you've prepared a feast!" Sister Isabelle gasped.

Pierre's eyes twinkled. "It is the least I could do for Mother Griolet. A farewell party for a dear friend."

Mme Leclerc and Mme Pons came to St. Joseph together, slipping into the dining hall with large platters of sliced pork garnished with red potatoes, parsley, and tomatoes. "We expect there will be a big crowd," Mme Leclerc whispered to Sister Rosaline. "Is there anything else we can do to help?"

As they were speaking, Roger Hoffmann, looking stronger and refreshed, carried in a wooden carton filled with bottles of wine. "It's a small contribution. I hope it will help." He flashed Monique Pons a smile, and she reddened.

In spite of themselves, the women giggled happily when he left the room.

"Oh, forgive me," said Sister Isabelle. "I'm not showing proper respect for Mother Griolet."

"Don't be silly," chirped Sister Rosaline, pulling the wine bottles out of the carton and setting one on each table. "Can't you just see Mother Griolet laughing? The last thing she would want is a bunch of long, distraught faces at her funeral."

Mme Dramchini and her daughters brought in three large bowls full of steaming *tagine*.

"If you please," Mme Dramchini said awkwardly. "You can use this?" She motioned to Saiyda and Rachida, who presented the bowls to Sister Rosaline.

Mme Pons, Mme Cabrol, and Mme Leclerc eyed the Arab women suspiciously.

Sister Rosaline took the bowls of food at once. "It looks delicious. How thoughtful of you." She kissed the Arab women on the cheeks, and the tension in the room seemed to melt.

Soon the French women were gathered around the Arab women, inspecting the bowls of thick stew and asking for the recipe.

"I'm sure my girls would love this dish," Mme Leclerc clucked. She reflected for a moment, then added under her breath, "If I have any more girls."

Mme Pons brushed away her friend's comment. "Oh yes, I've always heard that this Algerian stew is superb."

Mme Dramchini beamed.

Gabriella left the dining hall, shaking her head in amazement. French and Arab women laughing together as they prepared for a funeral! She went through the parsonage to the chapel.

Stepping into the interior, she gasped at the display of bright colors in the normally somber room. Her mother was setting up bouquet after bouquet of flowers at the front of the chapel, and the sweet scent permeated the room. "They're gorgeous," Gabriella exclaimed.

"Oh, and, Mother, look at these! Aren't they beautiful?" Gabriella bent over and inhaled the sweet aroma from a bunch of bright-white daisies. "It's such a touching testimony of her life. There's a stack of letters on her desk that we haven't even had time to open." She sat down in a pew and closed her eyes. "I can't explain it, but it's as if my heart were lighter today. Isn't that strange, Mother?"

Her mother smiled. "Not so strange, my dear. After all, this is a celebration. Mother Griolet is with the Lord. She is perfectly happy."

"Yes, I see what you mean. It's not nearly so sad as with Ericka." Her eyes met her mother's and held them in a steady gaze.

"No, it's quite different. Mother Griolet lived a full, productive life. She served God and touched lives. But one thing is the same for Ericka and Mother Griolet. They are both happy now."

A celebration. Perhaps Mother was right. Whatever the reason, Gabriella found herself humming a hymn later that morning as she checked on the children, helping to tie a bow or straighten a sock. She had instructed them to wear their darkest clothes as proper etiquette for a funeral.

As she left the dormitories, David came to her and held her hands. "How are you doing, Gabby?"

"I'm doing well. I can't explain it exactly. It warms me deep inside to see what one life can mean to so many. I want to be like her, David. Oh, how I want to be like her."

He held her in his arms and stroked her hair. "Yes, quite an awe-inspiring woman." He reached into his pocket and pulled out a folded sheet of paper. "I've written something … a eulogy of sorts. I wondered if you'd take a look at it and tell me if you think it would be appropriate to read at the funeral."

"Why, David," Gabriella said as her eyes quickly scanned the page. "It's beautiful. Yes, you must read it."

"You don't think it would be too radical, for someone to just get up and read something at a funeral? I don't want to horrify anyone."

"I don't know of anyone who was more radical than Mother Griolet. It's perfect."

In the late morning Joseph and Emeline Cohen had driven to St. Joseph from their hotel in Montpellier, having arrived from Switzerland the day before.

A moment later Henri Krugler came into the dining hall.

"Pleased to meet you, M. Krugler." Sister Rosaline bowed slightly. "M. Cohen was just telling us that you wish to say a few words during the funeral service."

"If I may, yes."

"Well, I suppose that would be fine. M. Madison will be speaking as well. And the *curé*, Père Thomas, will officiate. He should be here any minute." She shrugged. "It will not be a typical funeral, but somehow I'm sure Mother Griolet would approve."

"I think that's so." Joseph handed Sister Rosaline a letter. "She left these instructions with me when we reworked her will. She wants no pomp and circumstance. She named some Bible verses she would like to have read and even suggested that the children could repeat them by heart."

Sister Rosaline chuckled as she read the letter. "Yes, it will certainly be different. She wants rejoicing at her funeral. Short and simple, she says. And pointing to the Lord."

The funeral was scheduled for two o'clock, but by one thirty, cars were parked up and down the side streets of Castelnau. Inside the chapel every inch of space was filling up. At the front of the nave, just before the altar rail, sat the casket.

Gabriella waited near the doors, helping the Sisters find empty seats for those who were arriving. David and his father, along with several of the older boys from the orphanage, had gone into the parsonage to bring in extra chairs from the dining hall. The other children sat fidgeting on the first three rows of pews. Anne-Marie, Mme Dramchini, and her daughters were dispersed among them, intent on keeping them quiet.

Eliane Cebrian came down the aisle with her three children, and Anne-Marie scooted closer to the orphans, making room for them. M. Krugler took a seat directly behind the children in the same row as the Madison family.

Pierre and Denise sat with Yvette and Monique, both of whom wore hats with veils and dabbed their eyes now and then with handkerchiefs. Jean-Louis shuffled into the chapel, dressed in a neatly pressed dark-brown suit with a white carnation in the lapel. He looked around the chapel, walked to the front, crossed himself, and sat down.

The chapel was full, and still the townspeople poured in, nodding to one another in solemn silence, wiping the perspiration from their faces, closing their eyes to say silent prayers.

Joseph Cohen stood near the back, shaking hands with many young people who were not from the village.

"Some of the Jewish children who were here during the war," Sister Isabelle whispered to Gabriella. "M. Cohen contacted them. They've come quite a ways to pay their respects to Mother Griolet."

Gabriella thought for sure that the crowds would thin out, but when she peeped out the side door to the chapel, she saw that there was still a long line waiting to come in. Inside, some arrivals were moving to the left, where there were no pews, and standing tightly together. Meanwhile, David and his father placed folding chairs on either side of the pews, so that the center aisle became a narrow path.

Gabriella greeted the goldsmith from Montpellier, Edouard Auguste, at the door, then kissed Madeleine de Saléon from Aix-en-Provence lightly on the cheeks before she slipped into a chair that David had just set up.

Three men, staunch and solemn in their black robes, processed to the front of the chapel, lifting their eyebrows in surprise when they saw the crowded conditions.

"Père Thomas and two of Mother Griolet's superiors from the church," Sister Isabelle whispered to Gabriella when the men were out of earshot.

Sister Rosaline directed them to the front pew where three seats had been reserved for the clergy.

"Oh dear, what are we going to do? There's no more room and still so many people outside," Sister Isabelle worried.

"I've got an idea," Gabriella said. She made her way to the front three pews where the children sat. "This is our last chance to help Mother Griolet. Would you like to do that?"

They nodded, surprised.

"So many people have come to the funeral that there is no more room to sit. Would you mind moving to the side and sitting on the floor?"

The children's faces lit up with glee.

"But you must behave. Sit absolutely still until it is your turn. Understand?"

Again they nodded. Quietly they left the pews and took seats on the cool stone floor.

Gabriella, sitting on the floor beside the children, counted silently to herself. Over three hundred fifty people were crowded into the chapel. The air was muggy and pungent with the smell of flowers.

Père Thomas watched, perplexed, as the line of people continued to file in. He mopped his brow and caught Joseph Cohen's eye. Joseph shook his head as if to say that the funeral could not yet start.

It was stuffy and hot, but no one spoke. Gabriella felt it again. A velvety softness, a hushed anticipation. At long last, Père Thomas stood and walked to the simple wooden pulpit.

"*Messieurs, dames*, we are here today to honor the life of Jeanette Griolet, a faithful servant of our Lord Jesus for well over fifty years."

His voice droned on, and it struck Gabriella as completely inappropriate to have this man who barely knew Mother Griolet preside at her funeral. But he spoke for no more than five minutes before relinquishing his place to Henri Krugler.

Henri smiled out at the people of Castelnau. "You do not know me," he said in his booming voice, "and I do not know you. But for years I have heard of a feisty little nun in Castelnau who ran an orphanage. Recently I had the privilege of meeting this rare woman. You, like me, have been blessed by this woman's life. You, like me, have come to pay your respects to her.

"Some of you have only walked through the town to be here today. Others have traveled from the farthest parts of France. There are people from Switzerland, Senegal, America, Algeria. We represent many different countries; we are Catholic and Protestant, Jew and Muslim, French and Algerian. But we are gathered together to honor a woman who honored her God."

Henri spoke for a few more minutes, then took his seat.

William Madison then went to the pulpit. "You do not know me either, but some of you have come to know my daughter, Gabriella Madison. Fifteen years ago, when the war had just ended, my wife and daughters spent three months in Montpellier. The circumstances of those months drew my wife, a Protestant missionary, and Mother Griolet, a Catholic nun, close. Mother Griolet had a remarkable impact on our family during the hardest time in our lives."

Gabriella listened to her father's words as beads of perspiration dripped down her back. Mother Griolet had brought people together. The funeral was the testimony.

From somewhere in the crowded chapel, a low, strong voice rang out. "I would like to say a few words," David began. "Rarely in this life do we meet such a woman as Mother Griolet. A woman of goodness and humility. A woman who refuses to judge and embraces love. A woman with courage enough to stand up to prejudice and hatred, and yet humility to trust a Higher Power for direction...." David's voice cracked. He paused and wiped his eyes, then continued, "She had the gift of knowing how to make God real."

He imparted the same confidence as if he were standing in front of his class, and yet by his words he drew attention not to himself, but to the woman they had come to honor. And ultimately he called the congregation to consider the God the courageous nun had served.

David's eyes met Gabriella's as he spoke. "It has been my privilege to know this woman. And to examine and embrace the faith she had, a faith that says that in the midst of the worst in life there is a hope for tomorrow—because there is a God who sees past our differences and calls us to Himself."

The people in the chapel had never seen anything like it. One by one, townspeople from Castelnau as well as guests who had come from far away stood and gave brief testimony to what Mother Griolet meant to them.

At last Anne-Marie rose stiffly. "I know Mother Griolet's decision to keep the pied-noir and harki children here has not been a popular one. But I bless her for it. Here my daughter's life was spared. And many others' as well. Here I was reunited with Ophélie. It used to bother me that everyone at St. Joseph quoted Mother Griolet, but now I see why. It was because she received her words from the Master."

Then Sister Rosaline came over to where the children sat, squeezing her buxom body in between the people. She whispered encouragement, and one by one the orphans recited verses of Scripture, pronouncing the words with conviction.

Then, at a cue from Gabriella, all the orphans stood where they were and broke forth into song. *"My Jesus, I love Thee, I know Thou art mine ... I'll love Thee in life, I will love Thee in death ..."*

Almost joyfully they lifted their voices louder, higher, to sing the last verse:

In mansions of glory and endless delight,
I'll ever adore Thee in heaven so bright;
I'll sing with the glittering crown on my brow;
If ever I loved Thee, my Jesus, 'tis now.

The simple hymn echoed in the church and out into the streets of Castelnau through the sweet voices of the children.

Suddenly Denise Cabrol rose and stared about the room. "I-I was perhaps wrong in my judgment of the orphanage," she choked out. She pursed her lips and looked toward the front of the chapel. "Forgive me. Can you ever forgive me?" She covered her face with her hands and wept.

Roger Hoffmann's six-foot-four frame commanded the audience's attention when he rose to speak. He looked around the chapel for several moments, until his eyes met David's. He fumbled with his tie. "Thanks to this orphanage and to that dear woman, I have found my son twice." He spoke briefly of his experience during the Second World War, then told of his present situation. "On both occasions, I thought he was lost forever. I have been doubly blessed to find him this time."

Jean-Louis Vidal coughed dryly two or three times. He removed his wire-rimmed glasses, rubbed his eyes and nose. "It has been said that to love another person is to see the face of God. I have seen His face in my dear Jeanette."

When Sister Isabelle rose to speak, Gabriella doubted she could get a word out. But the shy nun surprised her.

"I have served under Mother Griolet for twenty-seven years. She did not simply talk of faith—she lived it, in the midst of all of life's questions and hurts.

"She called life a tapestry that we see from the wrong side, full of knots and tangled threads. But God is weaving it, each life, each circumstance, to make something beautiful for Him. The tapestry of Mother Griolet's life is represented here today by you. Can't you see it? A magnificent work. There are faults, but even so, remember what she used to say? 'God specializes in turning tragedy into triumph.' Perhaps, by her death, God has done that again for us today."

The eight pallbearers came and carefully lifted the casket from the stone floor and stoically carried it into the town square, where the hearse waited. The long black car crawled over the cobblestones, and the people walked behind it in a solemn procession, through the town to the small cemetery that was enclosed by a low stone wall in the fields beyond Castelnau.

Henri Krugler drew Joseph Cohen aside. "Who is that woman there? Do you know her?" He pointed to a black-haired young woman walking in front of them, holding the hand of a little girl.

"No, I don't. I'm sure one of the Sisters could tell you."

In the dining hall later, as the mourners ate and talked in soft, respectful tones, Henri drew Gabriella aside. "Mlle Madison," he said. "I'm happy to see you again, even under these circumstances."

Gabriella smiled sympathetically. "It has been a remarkable day, hasn't it, M. Krugler?"

"Yes, indeed. The Lord has met us here." He coughed uncomfortably. "Could I ask you, could you tell me the name of the young woman who said she had found her daughter at St. Joseph?"

"You mean Anne-Marie?"

He lifted his eyebrows. "Yes, is that her name? Anne-Marie? And her last name? Do you know it?"

"Why, of course. She's Anne-Marie Duchemin."

For a moment the color drained from Henri Krugler's face.

"Is something the matter, M. Krugler?"

"The matter? No, no, not at all. Thank you, Mlle Madison. Thank you very much."

It was not the time for further questions. Henri mingled among the people and silently thanked God for this day. "A day of miracles," he said to himself. His work with the orphanage at St. Joseph was far from over.

29

In the marshlands outside the city of Arles, an hour's drive from Montpellier, mile after mile of flat farmland stretched out until eventually, at the back door of the immense Rhône River, there sat a tiny community called Mas-Thibert. The village had been there for centuries, housing a handful of families who had tried to tame the swampy plains, making them bear fruit.

Now Saïd Boualam, a wealthy Algerian landowner who had sided with the French throughout the war, had another idea for Mas-Thibert. With his own money he decided to make it into a village for his people, the harki refugees. And so some harki families came to live there, among the already existing French population. Here, there was hope of integration.

But in other parts of France, the housing offered to the refugees looked shockingly similar to the barracks in the death camps of another war. These refugee camps were set up away from the French people. In this way, the leaders of the country reasoned, "these people" could live together, secluded and safe with their own traditions.

The French government boasted of this humanitarian step to provide for their loyal brothers. But it seemed that the whole country breathed a sigh of relief that these Arabs, these strange misfits, were hidden away from the rest of the nation. France had its hands more than full with the pied-noirs.

In other pockets of France, especially the southern part, groups of harkis gathered in the low-rent housing they found available within the cities and hid themselves from the angry glances of the French. There was no way to tell, after all, if these Arabs were the enemy that had claimed so many young French lives or those who had fought for France. Most of the French citizens didn't give it a thought. These immigrants were different and beneath the French standard. Even more than the bothersome pied-noirs, these harkis were completely unwanted.

In the middle of the humid Algerian night, as the stars twinkled in the black sky, Rémi shook Moustafa awake. The curly-haired Arab managed a smile and blinked a few times. There was a gleam of excitement in his brown eyes.

"So this is it. This time, by God's grace, we'll make it, Moustafa."

Moustafa regarded the strong farmer. "You're a good man, Rémi." He stood, resting his arm on Rémi's shoulders.

Another chance to leave. Another chance to find Anne-Marie, his mother, his sisters, Ophélie. A letter had arrived from Eliane just yesterday confirming that all was well at the orphanage. David and his father had arrived safely a few days earlier. Eliane expressed her extreme sorrow over Moustafa.

They are mourning for me, he realized. It made him long to be there even more quickly, to end their pain.

The car was packed, except for the rounded-top wooden trunk.

"I'll wake Amar," Rémi said.

"Could we pray first, Rémi?" It was an urgent request that Moustafa made without really knowing why.

"Of course."

Moustafa sat on the dust-covered couch and bent over, resting his elbows on his knees. "You know the first time I prayed? I mean really prayed, my own prayer?"

"When?"

"When I woke up in this very same house after we escaped from the Casbah. It seems like a hundred years ago. I've died a hundred deaths since then."

"You have lived, Moustafa. God has His hand on you."

Moustafa shrugged, his long curls almost touching his shoulders. "I hope so, Rémi. I hope so."

Silently they bent their heads, and Rémi spoke quietly. "Holy God. You have brought us this far. Protect us now. We're afraid. Give Moustafa strength. Take us to France. Our lives are in Your hands."

The men whispered "Amen" together. Then Rémi opened the lid of the trunk. "Are you ready?"

In answer, Moustafa climbed into the trunk and sat down, his knees hugged tightly against him. Rémi placed two canteens filled with water in Moustafa's lap. Then he shut the lid. "Can you manage a drink?"

Cramped inside the trunk, with his head touching his knees, Moustafa fumbled with the top of the canteen, unscrewed it, and brought the bottle to his mouth. "Yes, it's okay."

His voice was calm, but he felt himself shaking. Perhaps he would panic and cry out at the port, begging to be released. He had not realized how tightly he fit in the trunk. Hussein was much smaller. His clothes were drenched with sweat even before Abdul, Amar, and Rémi carried him to the car.

The trunk was placed on the backseat, and Rémi took off for the port with Amar. Inside the stuffy compartment, Moustafa repeated over and over to himself something he had read in David's New Testament, the comforting words of the Christ: *And lo, I am with you always, even unto the end of the world.* They were the words that had swum through his mind as he lay in a coma in the Arab woman's apartment in Philippeville. Somehow they had brought him peace. And tonight, when again he felt he had no more strength, he said them again and again to himself. In the end he fell asleep.

Moustafa awoke with a start as the trunk tilted and was lifted from the car. The horn of a ferry sounded loudly beside them. A chill ran through his body.

"We've been waiting in the car for the ferry. It's here now," Rémi whispered through the small opening in the trunk. "There are no crowds. We'll be getting on very soon."

Peering through the small hole, Moustafa could make out a few suitcases in the predawn light. There were shouts and commands. Fear struck him like a cold knife. He could almost feel it slicing through him as the soldier's knife had done in Philippeville. Blood pumped in his ears. His body rebelled, every joint tingling with sleep. Now he was swaying slightly, now the trunk bumped against a railing, now it was lifted at a steep angle. The gangplank! Would he make it?

A French officer cursed Amar. "Who is he?"

Moustafa listened for Rémi's calm reply. "A worker. Helping me with my things. He's not leaving on the ferry."

At long last the trunk was placed on the ground. The odor of gas made Moustafa's head swim. *Take me home*, he thought. *Oh please, someone, take me home.*

Sometime later, Rémi spoke again. "I can't get you out just yet. You'd be spotted. Can you hold on?"

Moustafa groaned back his response. Sharp, terrible pain from his wounds and his cramped position shot through him. He longed to sit up straight for only a minute. He struggled to take a drink of the water. The fumes from the boat rushed upon him again. His head felt so light, so very dizzy ... then everything went black.

Several times during the ferry ride, Rémi came and lifted the lid of the trunk and helped Moustafa step out and stretch his limbs. He walked him cautiously to the bathroom, which was nearby. But Moustafa saw that Rémi was afraid of trouble, even in the middle of the sea. He did not stay out for long.

Each time he climbed back into his cage, he dreaded the claustrophobic feeling when the lid was shut. He rested his head against his knees and thought of what was on the other side of the sea. His stomach churned with every rise and swell of the waves. He longed to cry out. Instead he repeated that same verse in his mind. Eventually he dozed off.

Hours later he felt a wet splash on his face and opened his eyes to see Rémi's concerned face peering down at him.

"Moustafa! Moustafa!" Rémi cried, and tears came into his eyes. "We made it. You're alive, and we're here! France. Marseille!"

Rémi put both hands under Moustafa's armpits, slowly lifting him to his feet. Again Moustafa was overcome with dizziness. He fell against Rémi's shoulder.

"Hold on," Rémi said. "Sit down a sec." He lowered him back into the trunk.

Rémi placed the canteen to Moustafa's lips, and he drank in several long gulps. He rubbed his temples.

"Ready to try again?"

This time he was able to stand, and, leaning heavily on Rémi, he stepped with one leg, then the other, out of the trunk. Immediately his legs buckled, and he collapsed in Rémi's arms.

They sat down together with a bump and burst into laughter. Every joint in his body burned with pain, but still Moustafa laughed, an uncontrollable laugh, until tears ran down the faces of the two men, and they held each other in their arms.

"Is it true? We made it?" Moustafa took in his surroundings. They were in a secluded area of the port, just off the docks. The ferry floated peacefully five hundred yards in front of them. "How did you manage to get me over here?"

"A few friendly sailors. Listen, I've got us a hotel room. I'm taking you there. I'll get you something to eat, wash you up. You can rest while I look for the other trunk. Do you mind terribly? I promised Eliane."

"No, of course not. Will you call her? Will you tell them we're here?"

"Don't worry, Moustafa. I'll take care of everything."

They laughed again, until their sides ached and their faces were stained with tears.

"People will think we're drunk!" Moustafa said.

"But we are," said Rémi. "We're drunk with life!"

It took a while for Rémi to get Moustafa to the hotel, although it was only a block away. The old building was located in a seamy, foul-smelling part of town, and the room backed up on a putrid alley. But the room had a bed and a sink. After changing Moustafa's bandages and coaxing him to eat a small quiche purchased at the boulangerie around the corner, Rémi left him to sleep.

He looked at his watch. He had only an hour to get to the warehouse where the lost baggage was stored before it closed for the day. He called a taxi and directed the driver to the side street the sailors had indicated, then paid the cabbie with his newly changed French francs, leaving a sizable tip. "I'll make it worth it to you if you can be back here in an hour to pick me up."

The cabbie nodded, grinned, and mumbled, "*Bonne chance.*"

The warehouse was immense and, on first glance, completely disorganized. The soldier in charge was a young man, barely more than a boy. He slid the heavy wooden doors open and gestured for Rémi to go inside.

"A bunch of junk I tell you," the soldier muttered. "What are you looking for anyway? And when was it lost? We arrange things by month."

Rémi lifted his eyebrows. It didn't look as though they arranged things at all. "A big wooden trunk with black metal casing." He thought for a moment, counting backward in his head. "It would've gotten here around the twentieth of May or thereabouts. Yes, a good two months ago."

The young soldier scratched the stubble on his chin, eyeing Rémi with distrust. "An old trunk you say?"

"Yes, about this high. It had little openings built in the front and the back. If you'll just show me where to start looking, I won't bother you anymore."

The boy frowned, kicked the floor, and pointed in a vague direction. "Over there, I think. This isn't my normal job. I'm just filling in." He followed Rémi, peering over his shoulder.

Rémi shuffled through the piles: two torn duffel bags with clothes strewn on the floor, a yellow leather suitcase tied around the middle with a piece of string, several children's toys. He spent twenty minutes sifting through the lost items in this part of the warehouse.

"You're sure this is all you have from the month of May? Is it possible it could've been put elsewhere?"

The soldier shrugged. "Have a look if you like." He let his arm circle the whole room, a slight smirk on his face.

Rémi felt irritated. "Surely it's still here. I must find it."

"What kinda stuff have you got inside?"

"Nothing of much interest to anyone else. Photo albums, china, a few books. Family papers."

The soldier scratched his head. "And the trunk, is it valuable?"

"No, it's not the trunk I want. It's the contents."

The boy narrowed his eyes. "I'll make you a deal. You leave me the trunk if we find it, and you can have all the stuff inside."

Rémi's head was throbbing. In frustration he grabbed the boy by the shirt collar. "Look here, do you know where that trunk is?"

Grudgingly the soldier led him to the other end of the warehouse. He disappeared behind row upon row of suitcases; eventually he lifted away some smaller boxes to reveal the trunk.

A smile broke out on Rémi's face. He hugged the soldier, who recoiled and cursed. Rémi paid no attention. "You found it!"

The boy reddened. "Yeah, I saw it here a month ago. I was planning to take the trunk for my mom's birthday. You know, to store quilts in."

"You can have the trunk, my boy. Take it! But first help me get it out of here and find me something else to put my things in."

They heaved and pushed aside suitcases and finally managed to dislodge the trunk. For a moment Rémi dared not open the top. What if everything was gone?

The lid fell open, and Rémi laughed again. Papers scattered inside. One broken teacup. But it was all there! The family Bible, the pictures of the children. He found himself brushing away the tears that stung his eyes.

The young soldier came back with several cardboard boxes. "Will these do?"

"Absolutely." Carefully, delicately, Rémi placed his wife's treasures in the boxes, and for the first time in many weeks, he let himself imagine what it would be like to hold her again. To kiss her soft lips while the children grabbed on to his legs, squealing, "Papa!"

At the bottom of the trunk in the open center space where the boy had sat, a letter marked "Anne-Marie" lay amid the fallen papers. He recognized Moustafa's handwriting. The documents for the Duchemin will were there too, with the sealed letter from Anne-Marie's father.

By the time the taxi drove up to the old warehouse, Rémi had carried three full cardboard boxes out to the curb. He placed the boxes in the taxi, a simple smile answering the puzzled expression on the cabbie's face. As they drove off, Rémi waved to the young soldier, who was sitting contentedly on top of his empty treasure chest.

It was with trembling fingers that Rémi dialed the number and let it ring. The receptionist answered and explained that Mme Cebrian had left for the afternoon, gone to an orphanage just out of town.

Rémi woke Moustafa. "Do you feel up to a train ride to Montpellier?"

Moustafa grinned. "I've been waiting for this day for a long time."

"And I found this." Rémi handed Moustafa the letter. "Thought you might know what to do with it."

"Do I ever." He made a feeble effort to comb his hair, staring in the cracked mirror above the sink. "I wonder if she'll know me. I look like some wild man escaped from the jungle."

"Escaped. That's the important word."

A taxi took them to the train station, where a porter helped Rémi with the trunk, duffel bags, and boxes. Moustafa waited on a bench, and it struck Rémi as odd and sad that Moustafa had nothing to bring with him. No clothes, no bags. He had escaped with his life.

As Rémi helped him onto the train, the Arab grinned a very tired grin, clutching the letter for Anne-Marie in his hands. "It's all I've got for her. All I have in the world." He collapsed into the seat on the train. "Somehow I think it will be enough."

Fortunately there was so much work to be done at St. Joseph that Anne-Marie could not let herself analyze her thoughts. After the inexplicable beauty and peace of the last two weeks, reality had suddenly hit her full in the face. The orphanage was closing, and she had nowhere to go, and no one to go to.

She felt the hollowness as she entered the cool chapel. It was solemn and still once again, empty of the throngs of people who had come on Saturday. On this Monday afternoon only the scent of the flowers rising to greet her bore testimony to the moving funeral forty-eight hours earlier. Sister Rosaline had asked her to bring a few of the bouquets downstairs to add a little color to the dining hall. Anne-Marie chose a bouquet of roses and Gerbera daisies and another of blue, pink, and white carnations. She found herself praying in her head. *Strength for today, God. Just for today.*

Immediately a verse came into her mind, the verse Mother Griolet had shown her only a few days before her death. She had patted Anne-Marie's hands and said with quiet confidence, "This is what I have held on to in the times of deep pain, my child. He will get us through one day at a time. It is enough. He says so."

Anne-Marie had memorized that verse, and now she repeated it to herself: *But seek first the kingdom of God and His righteousness, and all these things shall be added unto you. Take therefore no thought of the morrow; for the morrow shall take thought for the things of itself. Sufficient unto the day is the evil thereof.*

A soft rap on the chapel door interrupted her, and she walked to the back of the chapel. "Yes?" she said, squinting into the bright sun.

A stocky, ruggedly handsome young man in his thirties stood there with his hands in his pockets, looking quite lost.

"May I help you?" she asked. Then before he could answer, she narrowed her eyes. "Rémi? Rémi Cebrian, is it you?"

"Anne-Marie?" They shook hands forcefully, then embraced, laughing.

"Thank God you're here! You made it! Did you know that Eliane is here? Let me go fetch her."

Rémi caught her hand. He had the strangest look on his face. "No, don't bother, Anne-Marie. I'll go find her. But over there, in the taxi. I've brought our things and—"

"Of course, let me help you. But don't you want to take them to your hotel room?"

She followed him across the square as he explained, "I wasn't quite sure where to find the orphanage, so I just asked the taxi driver to wait over there."

"Yes, of course. Oh, how wonderful to see you again. It is just what we needed today." She wondered why Rémi didn't hurry to his wife.

"There's something here for you, Anne-Marie," he said.

"For me?" She looked perplexed. Then she said, "Oh, you must have found the trunk."

"Yes, I did. Go ahead." He pushed her along to the taxi, then turned back to the orphanage. She looked back over her shoulder with a question in her eyes.

"Go on," Rémi said. There was an urgency in his voice that made her feel funny inside. She broke into a run, crossing the cobblestone road to where the taxi sat in the shade. The cabbie stood on the other side of the car, leaning against the driver's door. She saw that someone else was there, a man with his head resting on the back of the seat. A young man with long, curly hair.

Anne-Marie was beside the car now and peered in the window. She gave a cry and grabbed the handle. Pulling the door open, she burst into tears. "Moustafa?" She could barely get out the word.

He laughed and weakly held out both hands toward her. Anne-Marie climbed into the car, ignoring the thick, suffocating heat.

"Moustafa … how can it be?" She reached out to touch his face, run her fingers through his hair. "You are real. You're alive! But how?"

"Shh," he cooed softly. He put his arms around her and held her there in the unbearable heat. She could hear his heart beating rapidly in his chest.

"I love you, Anne-Marie," he murmured.

She kissed him softly on the lips, afraid that even a gentle kiss might harm him.

The cabbie poked his head into the car, a broad smile on his face. "M. Cebrian said I was to take him to the hospital in Montpellier just as soon as a lovely young woman came."

"Yes, yes, of course. Only let me tell his mother."

Moustafa squeezed her hand. "Rémi is taking care of all of that. Come with me now, Anne-Marie. Just you and me right now."

Anne-Marie felt that strange peace welling up inside of her again. She leaned very lightly on Moustafa's shoulder, touching his face and hair every so often to be sure that he was real. He looked so thin and weak. "Are you hurt very badly?"

"I'll be all right now, my love."

"I thought you were—"

"Shh. A miracle. I'm back."

She took the canteen lying on the seat and gently dabbed water on his face. "Rest, Moustafa. It will be okay."

"I brought you this," he said, handing her a sealed envelope. "You should have had it months ago."

She carefully unsealed the envelope and took out two folded pages. The letter was dated May 20.

> *My habibti Anne-Marie,*
>
> *Surely I will be with you soon, if we can only wait just a little longer. Surely there is something bigger than the terror that surrounds us here. Knowing that you are there spurs me on. Remember that you are beautiful to me, that all I have ever wanted from the first days of our childhood is to spend every day with you. To grow old together. And even if it must be in another country, far away from all we have known, I*

am sure we will be happy together, with little Ophélie.

To pass the time, David and I are looking at the Koran and the New Testament. It is quite fascinating. I am convinced of neither so far. David says there is a God, although he questions His silence amidst the atrocities of this war. I like this man. He is very real. We speak often of the women we love, and I dream of you at night. Someday very soon, we will be together.

Hug Ophélie for me very tight. Tell her that Moustafa will be coming very soon.

With all my love, je t'embrasse avec tout mon coeur.

Moustafa

Rémi Cebrian went back into the chapel and gathered up an armful of flowers. There must have been a funeral, but he didn't think anyone would mind his taking some flowers away now. He found his way to the parsonage door and knocked loudly.

It opened a moment later, and Roger Hoffmann stood in the doorway, tall, distinguished, healthy.

"Rémi! Rémi Cebrian! You've made it, my boy. Come in! Your wife is just down in the courtyard."

The older man, looking like a complete gentleman, led Rémi down the steps and through the basement.

"It's nothing like I imagined," Rémi confided. "And who has died?"

"Mother Griolet, the nun in charge. It's been a most exhausting weekend. I'm afraid this place is a bit in chaos, but we're trying to set things in order."

Many children were running everywhere in the courtyard, so that it took Rémi a moment to spot his own. When he did, he dropped the flowers on the ground and yelled out, "Samuel! Rachel!"

The children wheeled around and, seeing their father, squealed with delight, tackling him in a bear hug.

Eliane came out of the dining hall with José on her hip, her face shining. "Rémi! Rémi, you've come." She hugged him fiercely with her free arm and kissed him while the children clung to his legs. "How on earth did you find me here?"

"I called from Marseille, and the receptionist knew where you were. We got in around noon, and I was looking for the trunk."

"We? Who do you mean? Did you bring others with you?"

"Yes! Yes, Eliane. Come, we must tell the others. David, the Dramchini women."

There was a bustling from the dining hall, and soon Roger Hoffmann emerged with David, two nuns, and a striking redhead.

David embraced Rémi. "It's so good to see you! Have you seen Anne-Marie?"

"Yes," he said, beaming. "She's gone to the hospital with all of our things."

The small group stared at him, puzzled.

Rémi spoke slowly, a broad smile on his face. "She's gone to take Moustafa to the hospital."

David's face went white. "Moustafa?"

"I know it's impossible, but it's true. He survived, and an Arab woman nursed him back from the grave. She brought him to my door four days ago."

David erupted into a loud "Whoop!" as he hugged Gabriella, then ran to tell Moustafa's mother and sisters, who were changing sheets in the dormitories.

"Moustafa!" he yelled. "Moustafa is here. He's alive."

Within the next few minutes, David had loaded Mme Dramchini and her daughters and Ophélie into his deux chevaux.

"Send the cabbie back here," Rémi called. "He's got all our things!"

He turned back to his wife. "After all, there was a reason for my waiting, Eliane. Moustafa appeared at the door an hour before I was planning to leave Algeria. Can you believe it? The incredible timing of the thing? I didn't know what I was waiting for, but God did."

Eliane kissed his lips very softly. "Who can explain it? All I know is that He is in control. Every moment of our lives is in His hands."

30

When the dorm lights were turned out and the other boys were quiet, Hussein took the pistol from under his mattress, tucked it into his pajamas, and went to the bathroom. He stepped onto the toilet, climbed up to the window, and peered down into the courtyard. Dusk had fallen, but it was not yet completely dark. He could hear voices coming from the girls' dorm, but the courtyard was empty. Quickly he slid through the window and ran into the shadows. He climbed onto the stone wall and let himself over it, holding on to the jagged stones as he let himself down fifteen feet into the small park below.

He did not know where to go, but he had all night to get there and complete his task before anyone at St. Joseph noticed he was gone. There was only one thing left to do. He held the letter he had written for Ali in his hand; it was addressed and even the stamp was in place. No one had questioned his need for a stamp amid the activities of the last few days.

Tonight there had been much excitement, with people coming and going. But Hussein had stayed to himself. He did not want to let anything deter him from his task. He kept repeating to himself, "There is no God but Allah, and Mohammed is his prophet," but the words sounded empty and dull.

He came to the little square with the fountain and cursed. There were too many people milling about for him to post the letter unnoticed. He should have done it earlier in the day.

He went back to the deserted park and waited in the shadows. He had all night. Nothing would spoil his plan.

Ophélie could not settle down. Moustafa was alive! She chattered excitedly with Mme Dramchini, who had tucked her into bed since Anne-Marie was still at the hospital.

"Mme Dramchini, we must tell Hussein. He has to hear the news!"

"No news tonight," Mme Dramchini scolded her playfully, tucking the covers around her.

Ophélie pouted. "Please!" she begged. For some reason it seemed urgent to see Hussein, now that she had seen Moustafa. She thought of another tactic. "I didn't get to tell Papa good night," she complained. "Please let me see him."

Mme Dramchini pursed her lips and frowned, shaking her finger at the child. "You tease me." But she left the dorm room and came back a moment later. "Papa leaves. You must hurry."

Ophélie sprang from bed and fell into David's arms in the hallway. He looked at her with a hint of disapproval in his eyes. "Ophélie, I've already told you good night."

She grabbed his shirt and pulled him close to her. "Papa, does Hussein know about Moustafa? He has to know!"

"I have to go now; you know I'm going out to dinner with Grandpapa and Gabriella's family. If Hussein hasn't heard tonight, he'll hear in the morning."

"But that will be too late," she blurted, without really knowing why.

"Too late?" He sounded irritated. "What do you mean?"

Ophélie started crying, real, worried tears. "I don't know, Papa. I don't know. Please tell him tonight. Please."

David sighed. "All right. You win. Now run back to bed. I'll tell him, even if it does make us late to dinner."

She watched him carefully, until she was sure he had gone into the boys' dormitory, then turned on her heels and dashed to her bed. She snuggled under the covers, feeling content. Everyone had made it home safely. Even Mother Griolet. And now Hussein would know that everything was okay.

❖

It struck David as strange that Ophélie would insist so. In the past months he had learned not to question his daughter's intuition, though she was only a child. So he peeked into the boys' dorm.

"Have you seen Hussein?" he questioned Sister Isabelle, coming back into the hallway. "He's not in his bed."

"Well, I'm sure he was there fifteen minutes ago when we turned the lights out. Perhaps he got up to use the bathroom."

David checked the bathroom. Then he stepped into the courtyard, where Gabriella met him.

"What's up, David? We're going to be late."

"Ophélie wanted me to tell Hussein about Moustafa. She was quite insistent. But I can't find the boy. He's not in his bed or the bathroom."

"Oh great. Do we have to go looking for him?" Gabriella said crossly. "He's a strange kid. Maybe he wanted a little night air."

"Gabby." He grabbed her arm. "I know this evening is important to you. It is to me too. But I think there's something the matter. I think Hussein has run away."

Gabriella sighed, exasperated. "Well, if he has, he can't have gone too far. I know I saw him a little while ago."

"Will you help me look? It won't take long."

"Oh all right. But Mme Leclerc and Mme Pons are waiting to tell us all good-bye. They're leaving early tomorrow morning, you know. And the dinner reservations were for eight thirty."

He took her by the hand and kissed it. "I promise I'll make it up to you, Gabby. This will be a night you won't forget."

She rolled her eyes and laughed. "Right."

It took only five minutes to inspect the dining hall and the parsonage. No Hussein.

"Now what?" Gabriella asked. "We could just shout out for him."

"Good idea." David cupped his hands around his mouth and called out loudly, "Hussein. Hey, Hussein! Wherever you're hiding, come here. I've got some great news." He paused. Nothing. "Hey, Hussein. Moustafa is alive! He's here in Montpellier. I saw him tonight. He wants to see you too."

They waited a few more minutes. Then they looked at each other and shrugged.

Ophélie still could not sleep. She heard her father's faint voice calling out to Hussein. She stared at the top of the bunk bed, chewed on her hair, and wondered what to do. Tiptoeing into the hall, she went into the bathroom. She could never make it up into the window without help. She came back into the hallway.

Sister Isabelle poked her head out of her room. "Ophélie! What are you doing?"

"Didn't you hear Papa calling out? Hussein is missing."

Sister Isabelle looked very tired. "Sweetheart, he'll come back. You go on to bed."

"Please, let me just check. If he's sad, he might listen to me."

"Oh all right."

Ophélie ran out into the courtyard. Her father was no longer there.

"Hussein!" she called. "Hussein, where are you? I know you're around here. Please come back." She looked around and tried the doors. The dining room and parsonage were both locked. She went over to the stone wall and stood on her tiptoes. "Hussein! Are you down there? Please come back. Moustafa is alive. I saw him!"

Sister Isabelle patted her head. "I'm afraid it will have to wait until tomorrow, dear."

Ophélie swung around. "If another child was missing, you would be worried. Why don't you care about Hussein?"

Sister Isabelle knelt down beside Ophélie. "Of course I care about Hussein, dear. I love all of the children. It's just that I am so tired tonight. So much has happened. But you're right; we must find him. Wait for me here. I'll get my robe."

A stone hit the wall. Then another came over the wall from the park below and landed near Ophélie's feet. She peered over. "Hussein? Is it you?"

A voice called up to her. "Shh. Yes. Is it true? About Moustafa?"

"Yes! Yes! Mama's staying with him at the hospital tonight. Isn't it wonderful? Now come back here. What are you doing anyway? If you were going to run away, you could have at least told me. I thought we were friends." She leaned far over the wall, trying to see him.

"Hey, what are you doing, Ophélie? You're going to fall!"

She laughed. "I'm staying right here until you come back up, that's what I'm doing."

"You little brat," he muttered, but she could tell he was smiling. "You promise he's alive?"

"Yes, you big bully. I promise. And if you get up here and go to bed, we can both go see him in the morning."

"All right, but I don't know if I can climb back up."

"Well, don't then. Go all the way around. I'll fetch Sister Isabelle, and we'll meet you at the front door to the parsonage."

"*D'accord.*"

"You're coming, aren't you? You promise?"

"I'm coming."

For the second time in his life Hussein felt as if something outside of himself was controlling his destiny. The first time had been when he had not shot the little girl. And now here she was, begging him to come back. It was very, very strange.

He walked around the exterior of the church, and as he came into the street, he almost bumped into David and Gabriella.

"Hussein! There you are! Whatever are you doing?"

He regarded David sullenly.

"You go on, Gabby. I'll be there in a minute."

David put his arm around Hussein's shoulder and walked him back toward the parsonage. "What's the matter? Did you hear the good news?"

"Yeah, I heard you."

David stopped him and took hold of his arms. "What's the matter, Hussein?"

Hussein turned away, and David saw the revolver protruding from under the boy's pajamas. He reached for it. "Where in the world did you get this? What were you going to do, Hussein?"

Hussein stared at the ground. "What do you think? Anyway, it's none of your business."

David shook him hard. "What do you mean?"

Hussein looked up. "I wasn't going to use it on anyone else." He turned his eyes down again. "Just on myself. That's all."

"Oh, Hussein! Son, people here care about you! What good will it do you to blow your brains out?"

"What do you know? I've screwed it all up. Everything." He began to cry, and he hated himself for it.

"You're only a child, Hussein. A child caught up in a terrible grown-up war. It's going to be okay. Somehow, I promise, it's going to be okay."

Hussein sobbed into David's shirt. "You can say that. Your mother isn't weeping for you. You aren't worried that any day Ali will go into her house and shoot her because he hasn't heard from me." He handed David the envelope. "Will you mail this for me? You can read it if you want."

"Yes, Hussein. We'll take care of this tomorrow. I'll help you. Now go back to bed."

They were at the parsonage door, where Ophélie and Sister Isabelle waited.

"You don't have any more little toys like this, do you?" David asked, turning the gun over in his hands.

Hussein shook his head.

"Go on then. We'll work it out tomorrow."

Hussein suddenly felt a great wave of relief. Impulsively he gave David a hug. As he walked into the parsonage, Ophélie took his hand.

He heard David whisper to Sister Isabelle, "Keep an eye on him tonight, will you? He's having a rough time. When I get back, I'll sleep in the dorm. We won't be too late."

Maybe they do care, Hussein thought. *Maybe they care about me after all.*

David had chosen a restaurant overlooking the Lez river, which ran between Montpellier and Castelnau. It took two trips in his deux chevaux to get all seven of them to the restaurant. The maître d'

frowned a bit, explaining that it had been impossible to hold their reservation for an hour, but eventually they were seated at a round table outside under the parasols. The river reflected the images of the buildings around it through a light on the sidewalk. A large fountain spewed water high into the sky, and some of the sprinkles drifted in the slight breeze to their table.

"This must be a really expensive place," Jessica whispered.

"Shh," Gabriella warned. "David's dad is paying."

David gave her a nod as she chatted happily with her sisters and mother, content to let David pursue a conversation with their fathers.

When the main course arrived, each plate was covered with a silver dome. Three waiters surrounded the table and, all at once, lifted the domes to reveal the beautifully arranged food on the plates.

"Well, if it tastes as good as it looks, we're in for a treat," Roger noted, thanking the waiters and picking up his fork to taste his *tournedos au poivre*.

Rebecca Madison addressed David politely. "Do you have any plans for the future now that the exchange program has been discontinued?"

David dabbed his mouth, a tiny grin playing there as he watched Gabriella squirm. "Actually I have several possibilities, but nothing definite. I'm afraid I haven't had the time to think of much beyond the moment."

"Of course not. Do you think you will stay in France?"

"I know I want to be close to my daughter, to see her as often as possible." He felt a little tension at the table. "But of course I plan to keep in close touch with your daughter also." He touched Gabriella's hand, and she blushed. "That is, if you don't mind."

This he said to Gabriella's father, who scratched his brow nervously and chewed for a moment before replying. "Well, no. I'm sure that's a good idea, however it can be arranged. If nothing else, letters are a great way to get to know each other better."

"I for one have had quite enough of letters for a while," David stated, winking at Gabriella. There was a moment of awkwardness, and David pressed on, feeling the beads of sweat forming on his brow. "What I mean is ..." He looked around the table, then turned to Gabriella and took her hand in his. Staring only at her, he started again. "What I mean is that I would like to keep her very close to me for a while. For a long, long while."

No one spoke. Gabriella looked at him, horrified, as if to say, *You are ruining the evening. Please don't shock them.*

Gabriella's mother cleared her throat, and Jessica giggled.

"What I'm trying to say, Mr. and Mrs. Madison, is that I would like to marry your daughter." Then he added, almost sheepishly, "If-if that is all right with you."

Gabriella burst into tears, a waiter rushed to the table looking terribly flustered, and Mrs. Madison stood up and hugged her. Roger looked at his son sternly with a hint of amusement in his eyes. Gabriella's sisters just sat there, wide-eyed, and William Madison, speechless, held his fork in midair, sauce dripping from it onto the plate.

Then, regaining his composure, Mr. Madison set down his fork and looked at his daughter. "I think you had better ask her first.... And if she says yes, well, I have nothing to say to the contrary."

David's father stood up, wine glass in hand. "Dear Gabriella, what do you say?"

Eyes shining, she stammered, "I-I-I say yes. Yes, of course, yes." She glanced at David, her eyes filled with questions.

"Very good then," Roger continued. "I propose a toast to the newly engaged couple, Gabriella and David."

Wine glasses and water goblets clinked together; everyone began talking at once. There was cheek kissing and handshaking and laughter. The waiters raised their eyebrows and shrugged and left the happy party alone.

"This is just right," Roger continued. "In France when a young couple becomes engaged, the two families plan a meal together to discuss the happy event. It's called the *fiançailles*. Bravo, David. Well done."

When the meal was over, David gave his father the keys to the car to drive the Madisons home. "We'll be back later," he said. "It's a pleasant walk down by the river."

The others nodded and smiled and waved them good night.

When the deux chevaux was out of sight, David cocked his head and motioned for Gabriella to follow. She obeyed, saying nothing. "Are you angry with me?" he asked.

She shook her head.

"Are you terribly disappointed?"

She shrugged.

"I know it was a shock. It was unplanned. I wanted to ask you first, when the moon was full and we were alone by the smooth flowing river with the smell of hyacinth and honeysuckle in the air." He took her in his arms, and she grinned slightly but did not look up at him.

"But all of a sudden it seemed like it was my best chance to show them, to let them know that even though I don't know what is next, I do know I want you to share it with me."

She still didn't reply.

"Talk to me, Gabby. Please, say something. Did you mean it when you said yes?"

She looked up at him coyly. "Did you mean it when you asked?"

"Yes, a thousand times, yes."

"Are you sure?" She narrowed her eyes, teasing. "It wasn't the most convincing proposal in the world, you know. I think you could've done better."

A hurt expression registered on his face, like a rebuked puppy, as he watched her and the outline of the river behind her. "Yes, I know. I had it all planned. Honest, I did."

"Really?"

"Yes. I was going to take you on a walk tonight, by this very river. And just when we were out of sight of everyone, with only those splendid tall plane trees looking down on us, I was going to fall to my knees, like this, and kiss your hands, like this, and say, 'It is my lady; O! it is my love. O! that she knew she were.'

"Then I would swear by my life, my love unto no other, as I do now. And then I would say, 'How do I love thee? Let me count the ways. I love thee to the depth and breadth and height my soul can reach.' And I would name your beauty, Gabby, your bright-blue eyes that light up your whole face when you smile. I would say that your hair is like Rapunzel's, if you would only let it down for me to admire.

"Then I would speak as the lover speaks in the Song of Songs: 'How fair is thy love, my sister, my spouse! How much better is thy love than wine and smell of thine ointments than all spices!'

"All this, Gabby, is but the beginning, because if I were to describe your soul, if I were to try …" And his voice grew soft, tender. "I would only say that I have never met a soul mate like you, and I am quite sure that if I travel for a hundred years and launch a thousand ships, I will come back again and again to you."

She was on her knees beside him, holding him, unable to speak or move. He watched her soak in the magic of the moment, letting his words wash over her like a gentle refreshing stream on the hottest of nights. She opened her mouth to speak, but he placed his finger over her mouth, and she kissed it softly.

In a whisper he continued, "That is what I was going to tell you, Gabby. Then I was going to beg you to say yes, to marry me, to come with me wherever this strange God leads us together, reminding you of Solomon's words that 'two are better than one, for if they fall, the one will lift up his fellow … and again if two lie together, then they have heat.' And then I would lay you gently on your back, like this, and kiss you softly on your lips, like this, and stare into those eyes and say, what is your answer, my precious Gabby?" He kissed her again.

Holding his face in her hands, she looked deep into his black eyes. "I would say, that's more like it! Of course I'll marry you!"

They broke into giddy laughter.

"Then this is for you." David handed her a small envelope with a single sheet inside. It was a poem penned in his hand.

"Read it for me, David. Read it to me."

"Gladly," he consented, kissing her cheek, her forehead, her neck.

E L I Z A B E T H   M U S S E R

Sonnet for the Wife of My Youth

I asked one balmy night to take your hand
And make it mine, your lips, your love, your soul.
Then tied your heartstrings with one strong, smooth
  strand
Unending love, you, better half, my whole.
Bestowed a golden band to hold my heart
Forever in the sweetness of your charm,
To braid together what was once apart
And promise peace from anger and alarm.

And springing from our "yes" of equal love,
Unequaled by desire to give and serve,
To want to please and, pleased, to want above
To plan, protect, provide for and preserve,
A three-strand cord, entwined to wait and trust
One will divine, eternity with us.

"I love you, Gabby. Will you marry me?"

She gave a little gasp. "You really *were* planning to ask me tonight."

He nodded.

"You really did write this for me."

He nodded again.

"It's beautiful. Read it again, David." And after he did, she leaned over and kissed him. "Is this real?"

"Oui, mademoiselle."

She furrowed her brow. "There's just one thing I don't quite understand. This bit about 'Bestowed a golden band to hold my heart.' I suppose that's merely symbolic?"

"Well, now that you ask, there was something else to do with that line." He fished in the pocket of his suit coat. "Ah, yes. Here it is." With a confident smile, he handed her a tiny square box.

Gabriella opened the box, and there inside was a simple gold band embedded with tiny diamonds and sapphires. She started crying, sniffed, wiped her nose, and cried again. "However did you have time to find this? It's gorgeous. How did you know I wanted sapphires? I never even thought …"

He slipped the ring onto her finger. "A fellow has to find a way to surprise a girl, doesn't he? It would be a pity for her to refuse to marry him simply because he bungled the proposal."

Gabriella tilted her head. "When did you know?"

"Know what?"

"That you wanted to marry me?"

"I think it must have been that first day in class when you knew Pope's poem … or maybe it was when you reminded me of that field of poppies. Ah, no, now I remember. It was when you were hanging off the cliff in Les Baux, holding to my hand for dear life, that it hit me. I didn't ever want to let you go."

"Quit teasing, David. I mean it. You've never even said the word before tonight."

They stood up and continued walking. "It was when your God convinced me that even if I could never be good enough for you, I was still the right one."

"I'm so glad He did. It makes all the waiting worth it."

"I love you, Gabby." There was the faintest breeze, and the leaves rustled slightly, as if the limbs of the trees were waving their approval. "I love you with every part of me." He grinned down at her. "And I look forward to learning to love you even more, day by day."

They reached St. Joseph when the clock in the bell tower was striking one. It was so comfortable to be together in the stark stillness of the night, when the rest of the town and all its ensuing problems lay dormant around them. They walked interlaced, arm in arm, never quite close enough and yet as naturally as if they had been walking like this for years. Gabriella was surprised by the sudden, easy intimacy. Now they were walking toward a point of time when they would be one, and it was right to hold each other closer as they neared that moment.

They were standing in front of Mme Leclerc's apartment.

"I must leave you for a few hours, my love," David said with a sigh. He brushed her lips with his. "Did you really say yes?"

"Yes, my love. And I will say it a hundred more times if you wish."

31

Gabriella lifted her hair off her neck and glanced around at the other people seated at the long tables in the dining room. Joseph Cohen had convened them for the reading of Mother Griolet's will, but she could tell that no one's mind was on it. Instead they talked among themselves about the closing of St. Joseph, only four days away. The end of an era. The thought of it caused a large knot to form in her throat.

She turned her attention to Anne-Marie, who sat between Sister Rosaline and Sister Isabelle, telling them about Moustafa, who was still in the hospital but recovering quickly.

"He has a lot of motivation to get well now," Sister Rosaline broke in. "His family is waiting for him, and a beautiful woman as well."

Anne-Marie ran her fingers through her black hair, pushing it away from her face, which glistened with perspiration. "I believe summer in the Midi is worse even than in Algiers. But it doesn't matter one bit. What matters is that we are all here together."

David, Roger, Jean-Louis, and Pierre the boulanger talked in low tones with Rémi and Eliane. Joseph and Emeline Cohen made polite conversation with Gabriella's mother and father.

Henri Krugler came through the door, breathing heavily, his white hair wet with sweat. "Excuse me for being late. At the last moment we had a problem with one of the kids."

Joseph welcomed him warmly, introducing him to those who had not already met him at the funeral. When he met Anne-Marie,

Henri smiled faintly and held her hand for a long, awkward moment. "I'm very glad to meet you, *Mademoiselle Duchemin*," he said finally. "A real pleasure."

After a few more moments Père Thomas, the curé from the church, arrived. "Please forgive me for being late," the priest apologized. "I hope I haven't inconvenienced anyone." The door to ·the dining hall opened once again, and Edouard Auguste, the goldsmith from Montpellier, came in, equally apologetic.

Joseph invited Père Thomas and M. Auguste to sit on either side of him. Then he wiped his brow and shuffled through a pile of official-looking documents. He glanced at Sister Rosaline. "Everyone is present now. May we begin? The children are cared for?"

"Heavens, yes!" the Sister assured him. "Between Saiyda and Rachida and the Madison girls, the orphans are being thoroughly entertained." She addressed Anne-Marie. "Mme Dramchini is not here?"

"No, she's with Moustafa."

"Well then, M. Cohen, everyone is accounted for. You may begin."

Joseph looked at his watch and rubbed his chin. "We are here today, as all of you know, to read the last will and testament of Jeanette Griolet. I have summoned each of you here for a purpose, and I appreciate your willingness to attend. Mother Griolet was a woman of few earthly possessions, but she was very specific about who was to receive what.

"As we are all aware, St. Joseph faces closure in the imminent future. Père Thomas is here as a representative of the church, and he will explain the procedures after the will has been read."

Several heads nodded, their expressions grim.

"A few months ago Mother Griolet spent two weeks with Emeline and me at our chalet in Switzerland. At that time, she asked me to help her update her will. As you will see, the good woman guessed that death was near. As executor of her will, I have tried as far as possible to honor her wishes. In the course of the past week there have been a few, shall we say, complications that have taken me several days to work through."

He paused and mopped his brow. "I shall now read the will."

I, Jeanette Griolet, on this, the 3rd day of May, 1962, do hereby write my last will and testament.

To Jean-Louis Vidal I leave my personal possessions included in this dossier. You have been my oldest and most faithful friend, and it is my desire that you continue to be employed by the school as professor of European history for as long as the school shall run.

To Sister Rosaline I leave all of the items in my personal kitchen with prayers that you can use them to bring glory to our Lord as you prepare meals for the children. This includes my recipe books, my old rolling pin, and the apron you gave me for Christmas one year.

"This is also for you, Sister Rosaline." Joseph held up a small envelope.

To Sister Isabelle, I leave you my family Bible. My dear friend and student of God's Word, may it bless you as it has me. I know you will care for it as a daughter would.

To both of the Sisters I leave my many photographs that line the walls of the office. Keep those that please you, distribute the other pictures to those with whom you may have kept in contact.

To Pierre Cabrol, who has worked with me in many a dangerous mission, I leave all the documents of those days gone by, some long past and others more recent, when we worked clandestinely to provide for children in hiding. It is my wish that you, Pierre, shall continue to provide bread for St. Joseph as long as you are able to do so.

To Rebecca Madison I leave a small folder of pictures that I have kept near to me all these years.

To David Hoffmann I leave my worn volumes of French and English literature, with prayers that you will find great pleasure in perusing them from time to time. I ask that you make sure that any other books that perhaps do not interest you find a proper home.

I also wish to state that, should my death precede the opening of a new school year at St. Joseph, it is my wish to name M. David Hoffmann as the future director of the Franco-American exchange program, and hereby entrust to him the school's records of all the past years as well as the lists of benefactors to the program.

To Gabriella Madison I leave my old santon, knowing how she has admired it. And with this, should I not be around, I symbolically pass on to her the directorship of the orphanage of St. Joseph. It is my hope that she will have already completed an apprenticeship with me. I am confident in her complete capability, seconded by Sister Rosaline and Sister Isabelle, to continue the work.

Joseph wiped his brow and looked up. "We all realize, of course, that Mother Griolet was merely expressing her desire for the continuation of the programs at St. Joseph. Since the time of the writing of the will, many things have transpired, as you are all aware. This we will discuss momentarily." He resumed reading.

To Joseph and Emeline Cohen, friends from far back, I leave these documents of the days when the Jewish children were among us. May they always remind you of the power of our God.

Joseph Cohen, obviously moved, set the papers down in front of him, pushed his glasses up on his nose, and picked up a piece of white stationery. "Finally, Mother Griolet left a letter for all of us gathered here. Sister Rosaline, would you read it aloud?"

"Why, of course," Sister Rosaline said, and took it from him. "*You have been my true friends, whether I have known you for months or years,*" she began.

Tears ran down several faces as the nun read the simple message.

"*Carry on*," the letter concluded, "*and may the Lord Jesus, our gentle Shepherd, be with you always.*"

Joseph rose. "Thank you for your patience. This concludes the reading of the will. But I would like to share with you some most surprising news. Following the funeral of Mother Griolet, we have received an abundance of donations for St. Joseph." He picked up a letter. "From the Jewish children hidden during the war, we have received a check for fifty thousand francs. The enclosed note reads, 'It is our deep desire that this money be used in any way necessary to provide for the orphanage of St. Joseph so that it may remain open and ready to welcome children like us and so many others, who found shelter and hope there.'"

There was a soft murmur as the men and women turned their heads and raised their eyebrows.

"How did they know about the problems at St. Joseph?" Sister Isabelle asked naively.

Joseph pursed his lips, repressing a grin. "I felt it was my duty to inform those who asked about the orphanage of its particular plight. But I was not responsible for the rest. Several of the young people organized everything."

He chose another letter. "From the townspeople of Castelnau, sixty thousand francs. This letter specifies, and I quote, 'We the people of Castelnau, in appreciation for the faithful work of Mother Jeanette Griolet and in desire to see St. Joseph continue in its important service to children and to its community, do hereby give the said amount and revoke our previously given petition.'"

"It's a miracle," Sister Isabelle exclaimed.

"Well, I'll be," Jean-Louis said with a whistle.

Gabriella embraced David, and he kissed her on the lips. Eliane reached across the table and squeezed Anne-Marie's hand.

But Joseph Cohen had not finished. "We have received many more donations as well, from orphans who were housed at St. Joseph over the years and from others who appreciate what this place has done. To put it simply …" Joseph grinned, unable to hide his extreme pleasure. "By my calculations, based on the records from previous years, the money St. Joseph has received in memory of Mother Griolet will allow the orphanage to function, on its own with no aid from anyone, for two and a half years."

The small group stared at each other, mouths opened, then burst into laughter, hugging and kissing and backslapping and handshaking.

"It truly is a miracle," Gabriella whispered to David.

Joseph spoke again. "Before I invite Père Thomas to give us his opinion on this matter, I have one other story to recount. At Mother Griolet's funeral were a brother and sister, Yves and Christine Millot. Seventeen years ago they arrived at St. Joseph half-starved and in rags, Jewish orphans. They presented Mother Griolet with the aforementioned santon." He picked up the clay statue of the bent-over old woman. "While at the funeral this weekend, the young woman, Christine, spotted the santon. She was surprised to see it among Mother Griolet's possessions and asked me why no one had broken it. I looked at her quite stupidly and assured her I had no idea why anyone would want to do such a thing.

"She replied that when they had given the santon to Mother Griolet, she had repeated the words her mother had told her to say to whoever agreed to take care of her children. The words were these: 'Break this old woman whenever you find yourself in desperate need.'"

Joseph Cohen motioned to Gabriella. "Since this santon is yours now, I will ask you to do the honors."

Gabriella looked baffled. "But I don't want to break her. I will treasure her forever!"

Joseph called Edouard Auguste to come to his aid. M. Auguste produced a small tool, like a delicate, finely sharpened knife. "I believe this will do the trick."

Worried, Gabriella approached the two men. "Why in the world would you want to break her?"

"If you will allow me to show you, Gabriella, I believe this will be of great importance to all of us." Carefully the goldsmith removed the floral material of the old woman's skirts as if he were undressing a doll. With tiny scissors he snipped away at the underclothes until a plain red clay figurine was exposed. "Just as I thought," he said, pointing to the center of the clay woman. "She has been broken before, just here. See?"

Gabriella leaned forward to inspect an uneven crack that ran around the santon's middle.

"I'm afraid I will need to break her again," M. Auguste said, almost apologetically. He inserted a small knife in the crack and tapped it with a tiny hammer. The santon broke in two.

As the santon broke, Gabriella saw concealed inside the lower torso a piece of wrinkled newsprint. She touched it, pulling it carefully out with two fingers. It was bunched together, and the withered paper practically disintegrated as she held it. Carefully opening the newsprint, she saw inside what appeared to be a cluster of diamonds, rubies, emeralds, pearls, and sapphires.

"Jewels!" Gabriella exclaimed. The others crowded around for a look.

Joseph was shaking his head in wonder. "So Christine Millot was right. On Saturday she told me that her parents, living in Lyon, feared the worst for their children. As more and more Jews were deported to concentration camps, the family, well-known jewelers, began hiding their possessions. Christine remembers watching her father break this santon, hollow out the interior, and stuff it with the most precious of his stones. She even helped him glue the statue back together and put the clothes back on. 'This will adequately provide for those who care for you,' her father told her.

"Obviously Mother Griolet never broke the santon, although she surely had been told to do so. When Christine revealed to me what was inside, she had no idea of its real worth, but she felt it was extremely valuable. I offered the santon to her, at least what was inside, but she refused, stating vehemently that whatever was inside belonged to Mother Griolet alone." He took a deep breath. "Christine Millot begged me to make sure that whatever was found in this santon would go toward helping with the upkeep of the orphanage. And so I have invited M. Auguste here, assuming that there would indeed be jewels for him to inspect."

M. Auguste wrinkled his brow and said, "I must admit to you that I find this hard to believe. These jewels are worth a small fortune. Of course I will have to inspect them more closely, but I believe that if you sold these stones today, you could keep this place running for a long, long time."

There was a moment of shocked silence; then all eyes turned to Joseph.

"Yes, you see there have been quite a few surprises this week. After hearing Christine's story and counting all the other contributions, I took it upon myself to call Père Thomas and discuss matters with him."

The aged priest now spoke. "St. Joseph has always been for us in the church a bit of an enigma. With little funding from the church it managed to stay open and thrive. Mother Griolet was a genius at stretching the centimes. And she believed in a God of miracles. I would say that He has granted her, by her death, the miracle St. Joseph needed. I have come to report that St. Joseph will remain open—"

Sister Rosaline and Sister Isabelle gave out a loud "*Ouais!*" and hugged each other.

"There will be several revisions that the church will wish to make. Precisely, in accordance with Mother Griolet's wishes, I am ready to name M. Hoffmann as the new director of St. Joseph's exchange program." He grinned in spite of himself. "And the church is willing to allow Mlle Madison to assume the role as director of the orphanage, with a few stipulations."

He addressed Gabriella. "If you agree, the church wishes for you to take classes at the Faculté des Lettres in Montpellier to complete your teaching degree. The church will send someone, probably myself, every three to six months to inspect the orphanage and its school program." He turned to David. "M. Hoffmann will have ultimate control over the functioning of the orphanage until Mlle Madison has completed her degree."

Gabriella turned to David. Her face went white, then red. Little pools of tears formed in her eyes.

After a long pause, Sister Rosaline asked, "Well, what do you say?"

"Oh, isn't it just perfect?" cooed Sister Isabelle. "They got engaged two days ago, and today they get their marching orders. How wonderful."

Gabriella looked at David, who grinned back at her. He took Gabriella's hand and said, "It seems events have been turning and turning for a good while now, so that I'm not sure any of us know which end is up anymore. So please give us a few days to reflect and pray on this together. I am deeply honored. And in keeping with my desire to start our life together on the right foot, I will let Gabriella speak for herself."

Gabriella stood, still holding the bottom half of the broken santon, and stammered, "David is right. Too much has happened at once. I don't know what to say, except that I am very, very happy, and I only wish Mother Griolet could be here to see us now."

"Don't you worry about that, Gabriella," said Sister Rosaline. "I'm sure she knows."

Joseph added, "I know we have had quite enough surprises for today. Sister Isabelle has provided some drinks, if you would like to take a pause. There is, however, another matter of business to be discussed, which is why we have asked the Cebrians, Mlle Duchemin, and M. Krugler to join us." He addressed them personally. "If you would meet back here in ten minutes, please. And the rest of you are welcome to stay if you wish."

The small group stretched and rose.

David squeezed Gabriella around the waist. "We have so much to talk about, you and I."

"I can't believe it. It's like a dream." She picked up the other piece of the santon, walked out into the courtyard, and stared down at the statue. She recalled something Mother Griolet had said to her once … *We must be broken before we are useful to the Lord. Broken of our selfishness, broken of ourselves. In that brokenness, we have so much more to offer him.*

Gabriella hugged the statue to herself and cried.

✠

Anne-Marie didn't like the way the man called Henri Krugler looked at her. She had not completely understood why this big, white-haired man from Lodève had shown up at Mother Griolet's funeral. She understood even less why he was here today.

Joseph Cohen motioned to the group to once again take their seats. A butterfly danced in Anne-Marie's stomach as she anticipated the letter from her father. She was almost afraid to read it. She had set her hopes on a few simple words—as important to her as a fistful of jewels.

"As you all know," Joseph began, "Rémi has recovered the contents of his lost trunk in a warehouse in Marseille. Within the trunk was the will of Captain Maxime Duchemin. Eliane, I will let you explain the rest."

"Thank you, M. Cohen. I was the executor of this testament." She held up a thick envelope. "But when I studied the will four years ago now, I realized that there was nothing left. The Duchemin home neighboring ours in Algiers was looted." She turned to Anne-Marie. "As I have told you before, there is nothing to be recovered from the house or the banks in Algiers. However, there was also this letter for Anne-Marie, to be given to you in case of his death." Eliane produced a folded piece of parchment sealed with a gold medallion that had not been broken. "I'm very happy for you to have it at long last."

Anne-Marie took the letter, stared at it, and ran her fingers over the seal. On the back in her father's penmanship were written the words *To be opened in the presence of a notary public.* Then she looked up questioningly. "Am I supposed to open it now?"

"I think that would be best, if you don't mind. You will understand, I believe, afterward," Joseph said softly. Then he added, "And yes, I am a businessman but also a notary."

She tore the gold seal with her fingernail. Inside was a one-page letter written in her father's hand. Anne-Marie's deep-brown eyes soaked in the words, and suddenly she was transported back to Algiers, in the large farmhouse, with her father singing lullabies to Ophélie.

November 15, 1957

My dearest Anne-Marie,

If you are reading this letter, it is because my fears have become a reality. I will not see you again on this earth. You must know how much I love you, how much I have always loved you, even though my proud, disciplined manner might have at times suggested otherwise.

Anne-Marie, all that we had in Algeria is worthless now, as you have doubtless understood from the will. You must leave Algeria at once. Flee to France. I know it will be hard, but I have provided for you there. This past summer, when I went to France for talks, I took some of our money and put it in an account in Switzerland. And I bought a house in a small town in the Cévennes mountains called Lodève. It is not too far from the city of Montpellier. My good friend Henri Krugler has the property rights for the house. It has been paid for in full, and he has agreed on the upkeep until you have need of it.

Henri is a Swiss pastor, a Huguenot descendant, a great man of faith. You would not remember him, but he was in Algeria years ago, and it was through his preaching that I began to see things differently. He is a man of God. He will help you, Anne-Marie, should anything befall me. Please contact him. In this way, I have made provision for you and Ophélie.

It is my fervent wish that we all be reunited at this little place in Lodève, in the foothills of the Cévennes mountains. But if you hold this letter, I fear that this wish shall not be granted. Therefore, I pray night and day that we will be reunited in another place where the God of the Bible promises no more crying or death. Until

then, remember always that I have loved you—
never have I stopped and never will I. You have
brought me great delight, and now, with Ophélie,
I am overwhelmed.

> *Je t'aime, ma fille,*
> *Papa*

Anne-Marie let the letter drop onto the table. She bit her lip, sniffed, and brushed her hand across her eyes, which were filling with tears. It seemed too incredibly impossible, and she was afraid to meet Henri Krugler's eyes for confirmation.

Eventually she looked up at him. "I see now," she said simply. "That is why you have been looking at me so intently. Papa says that he bought a house in the city of Lodève and that you, M. Krugler, have been keeping it up for me. Can it possibly be true?"

The white-haired man's face broke into a gentle smile. "Yes, it's true, Anne-Marie. I had given up hope, but you see, our God is full of surprises. When I saw you at the funeral, I was almost certain." He produced a small photo of Anne-Marie holding Ophélie when she was an infant. "I went home and found this picture that your father had given me, and then I contacted Joseph. He suggested that I come this afternoon because, well, because my story is a bit wrapped up in St. Joseph as well."

He stroked his goatee. "I'm afraid that the house is being used as a centre aéré at the present time. It is a rather complicated story. But don't worry." He flashed another smile. "The house is yours, all yours. I have the deed here in your name." He handed her an envelope. "You'll find also the number of your Swiss account.

Everything is quite in order. I'm delighted that this has worked out so well for you, *Mademoiselle Duchemin*."

"And what about the centre aéré?" Gabriella blurted out. She addressed Anne-Marie. "It's a beautiful place. I've been there with Mother Griolet. It's all been redone. There is land, and the mountains for a backyard."

"Don't worry about the centre aéré," Henri Krugler stated. "The Lord has always provided just what I needed. If I could have a little time to warn the parents that the center will be closing ..."

"But you've only just opened!" Gabriella protested.

Anne-Marie repressed a chuckle at her friend's obvious distress.

Gabriella turned to her. "I'm sorry, Anne-Marie. You know I'm thrilled for you, but it is only that I know of M. Krugler's story. He came to reach out to the Arabs, the harkis, and he has only recently opened the center. Didn't you say, M. Krugler, that you had looked for other buildings?"

"Dear Mlle Madison. Thank you for your vote of confidence, but the house is by no means mine. As I said, I had given up hope and decided to put the place to good use."

"Is it a large house?" Anne-Marie asked.

"Yes, actually it is. Very spacious. What they call an old *mas*. We have fixed it up a bit from when your father bought it."

Anne-Marie felt sorry for this gentle man with the rich, soothing voice and the blazing eyes. "Oh, M. Krugler. I'm sure something can be worked out. Ophélie and I are quite used to living with other people, you see." She smiled at Gabriella and the Sisters. "Don't close the center."

Henri shook his head. "The house is yours, Mlle Duchemin. You must come see it. Then you can decide."

"Yes, yes. That is right. Of course." She felt suddenly so light-headed, the room was spinning around her. "I don't know what to say. It is like a dream that I never even thought to dream."

"*Ooh là*, my child! Look how pale you are!" Sister Rosaline rushed to the kitchen and fetched a glass of water. "Drink this up now. Such a shock for you, and in this terrible heat."

Anne-Marie closed her eyes and rested her head in her hands. She thought for a moment she saw Ophélie running in an open field with the mountains as a backdrop, and behind her daughter, Moustafa coming in from the fields, smiling and covered in sweat. It was a delicious vision. Today she had come to know another facet of her God. She had met the Christ first as a comforter; now she saw Him as a provider. She was sure that it would take her whole life, if she lived a very long time, to be fully introduced to this Person. It baffled her to think of it.

Gabriella felt chilled, and she could not imagine why. Perhaps she was coming down with the flu. Why else would she be shivering when the hot summer sun was setting records in the Midi?

She hoped David had understood that she had to be alone. Completely alone for one hour. She tried to think back on the past few days and weeks, but they were a blur. Everything in her ached. She felt as though for months someone had been tossing her emotions to and fro until she was sore and exhausted. It was all good. Good?

Wonderful, extravagantly wonderful. Better than anything she could have possibly dreamed up.

Then why did she feel so absolutely drained?

She twirled the engagement ring on her finger. She needed time to think. Think! But there was no time. They needed an answer soon. If St. Joseph was to remain open, the answer must be given. The thirty days were almost up.

Only yesterday she had dreamed of a final year in school in the States with weekend trips to visit David and months to plan every detail of their wedding with her mother. A few days before that she had been sure a wedding would never happen at all. And if she thought further back, she had been wrestling through the same question that was before her now: whether to take on a job that was nothing by the world's standards yet would require every ounce of her energy.

In her mind's eye she saw Mother Griolet—the serene smile, the lively green eyes, the tiny frame that she held erect as she walked through the halls of St. Joseph. *Why did you have to leave when I need you most?*

The question tumbled back toward her. It was by Mother Griolet's death that all of this had come to pass.

Gabriella sat down in a field of dried grass. A few yellow dandelions offered the only color to the countryside. She lay on her back, shading her eyes from the sun with one hand, then rolled over onto her stomach and picked a dandelion. She needed an answer, and she needed it now.

On that day in May when the nun had offered Gabriella the job, what had she said? *Trust, Gabriella. God is perfectly trustworthy ... perfectly capable of convincing you of His will, if you listen.*

Yes, of course. That same little word. Trust. She had made her decision two months ago. Now it was coming back to welcome her. The only thing that was left for her to do was to walk into it with outstretched arms and a heart ready to serve.

32

When Anne-Marie walked into the restored farmhouse in Lodève, she had the sudden feeling that she had been there before. The couch in the spacious living room was the same tan leather one that had been in her parents' home in Algiers for years. Two mahogany chairs, which her father had refinished, sat on the other side of a large stuccoed fireplace. Several paintings, her mother's favorites, hung on the walls.

"Your father brought them over when he purchased the house," Henri said, watching her look around. "He knew trouble was coming."

Yes. Father had hinted at it, but she had been too preoccupied with baby Ophélie and her own concerns to let it register. And now these furnishings reached out to surprise and welcome her to her new home. She could barely take it in.

Opening behind the living room was an eating room that expanded the whole length of the house. It was crowded with five long metal tables, much like the ones in the refectory at St. Joseph. This room adjoined a well-equipped kitchen, clean, orderly, the appliances new.

"We had to enlarge a bit to meet the regulations for the center," Henri explained as Anne-Marie stared wide-eyed into the shining facility. She touched the counters, the cabinets, the white gas stove. Then Henri led her through a long hallway that smelled of fresh paint and was lined with photographs. There was even one of M. Krugler with her father in his army uniform.

Leading to the second floor was an old, tiled, winding staircase that emptied into a vast hall with doorways running off it in every direction. "How many bedrooms are there?" she questioned, stunned.

"Seven, Mlle Duchemin, and two bathrooms."

"Seven bedrooms? Why, it's practically a castle!"

Henri chuckled. "It's big all right."

Anne-Marie felt distressed. "I can't take this place from you. You've spent your own money fixing it up. It wouldn't be right." She began opening doors and peering into the rooms, each one expansive and recently redecorated. At the end of the hall, one door led into an apartment.

"This was the servants' quarters long ago and was later joined to the house," Henri explained.

"Is this where you live?"

Henri shook his head. "No, I have a little place in town. It's quite nearby."

Anne-Marie pushed open the doors. "Servants' quarters! Why, it's a perfect place for us! And look! There's even a fireplace and bathroom." She turned her radiant face to Henri. "May I go in?"

"Of course," he said kindly, and she thought she heard a strange catch in his voice.

In the corner of the room sat an old oak rocking chair with a crocheted baby quilt hanging over one arm. She ran to it, fell on her knees, and buried her face in the pink and green needlework. She looked around at Henri Krugler as if he were her closest friend. "The quilt Mama crocheted for Ophélie when she was born ... and the chair I rocked her in."

She clutched the quilt, pulling it close to her, and then gasped. "And look! Ophélie's baby book!" A narrow bookshelf stood on the opposite wall, filled with scrapbooks and worn volumes. "It's all from home. All of it!" Anne-Marie sat down in the chair and began to rock back and forth, back and forth. It was as if someone had come ahead to prepare this place for her, a home just to her liking. Someone who knew all about her.

"It's like this room has been just waiting for me," she said in wonder.

"Indeed it has, Mlle Duchemin. For the longest time."

Overwhelmed, Anne-Marie reached out and clasped Henri's big, rough hand. "M. Krugler, keep your center open. We will help you run it. Ophélie and I will live here, in these rooms. Where we belong." For just a brief second she looked longingly at the sturdy double bed and thought of Moustafa.

"Mlle Duchemin, give yourself time. We will talk of details later. If you desire it, I'm sure something can be arranged. I cannot tell you how much it means to me."

Anne-Marie, still holding his hand, rocked back and forth gently. "Nor I. Thank you, M. Krugler. You're a very good man."

On July 31, the official end of the church's thirty-day period, Gabriella and David met with Père Thomas at his office in the old part of Montpellier to sign the papers concerning St. Joseph. To Gabriella, it seemed she was signing away her life. Her hand trembled, and her simple ring caught the rays of the sun and glittered. What might have been was swallowed up in what was actually happening.

"Excuse me for asking, Père Thomas," she said after penning her signature. "But I am so curious. What made the church change its mind? Just the money? Even with the funds, you could have decided to send another nun to take over the place. Why did you choose us?"

Père Thomas chuckled, scratching his white head. "My child, do you know the verse in the Holy Scriptures that says God's ways are far above ours?"

"Yes, Père."

"Then that is my answer. God made hard hearts soft. How else can you explain a French Catholic priest listening to a Swiss Jewish businessman who wanted him to hire two American Protestant young people to run an orphanage filled with French, pied-noir, and Arab children?"

Gabriella laughed out loud. "Yes, I see what you mean. Are you telling me not to try to understand?"

The old priest smiled, and the wrinkles by his eyes spread across his temples. "I am merely saying that I myself am confounded. Confounded and delighted. As for your question about the church's backing, you must also realize that Mother Griolet did not come to us very often for help."

Gabriella blushed. "Yes, I am not surprised."

"And by this new contract, we will keep St. Joseph under the church's standing, with minimal aid," David clarified.

"Yes. As M. Cohen has told you, the donations given at the time of the funeral will assure that the orphanage functions smoothly for several years. In that time, the church will decide upon its funding. And of course you have the jewels. I suppose M. Cohen is working on that end with the goldsmith?"

"Yes," David replied. "And then there is the question of the exchange program. It will have to borrow funds from the orphanage at first, until we can find other benefactors. But I'm not worried. My father has several ideas." He grinned at Gabriella. "Old friends from Princeton whose kids are college-age now and just itching for a year abroad."

"Oh, yes, very good of you to mention that, M. Hoffmann," Père Thomas added. "This letter came a few days ago. I opened it only to realize that it would be best for you now, considering the circumstances."

Père Thomas shuffled through a stack of papers, retrieved a letter, and handed it to David. Then he stood and shook hands with Gabriella and David. "God be with you, children. You are taking on quite a task, but I believe Mother Griolet knew what she was doing when she picked you. Don't hesitate to call if you need anything."

As they left his office, David skimmed the letter. "Hey, listen to this, Gabby. It's from Caroline Harland's father, sending his condolences for Mother Griolet's death. He says that he has contacted his friends and that, under the circumstances, they are willing to continue their support if the right director is found."

"And you think they'll approve of you, after all the heartache you've caused Caroline?" Gabriella teased.

"Of course! All is forgiven," David countered. "He even says Caroline will be coming back for another year."

Gabriella's face went white. "No ..."

David picked her up in his arms and kissed her hard on the mouth. "Just kidding!"

She flashed her eyes. "Honestly, David. You are always looking for a reaction! And you usually get one!"

He took her hands and led her beside the fountain of the Three Graces on the place de la Comédie. "Gabby," he said, "now that the question of our jobs is settled, is there any reason we shouldn't get married soon? Right in Castelnau, while our families and friends are here with us?"

"Are you serious? We couldn't possibly be ready!"

He raised his eyebrows, pulled her close to him, and murmured, "I've been ready for a long time."

David and Gabriella were still discussing the idea of an impromptu wedding two hours later, as they stepped off the bus in Castelnau.

"David, I feel like my head will explode with decisions. How can I know? It seems that for the year I've known you we've only jumped from one crisis to the next, one wild adventure to another. I wish I had some time just to get to know you, the way normal people do. I think it's called dating."

"You're right, of course. But as long as we're doing everything else backward, couldn't we start being normal *after* we're married? We'll be legal and can do whatever we jolly well please. I'll even take you on a two-week honeymoon to Paris and Switzerland."

"You will? How? We've got our jobs to do."

He flashed her a smile. "Leave it to me. There are many willing souls around here right now. I'll bet your family could be persuaded to stick around a few more weeks to help out while we go away. And my dad is having a blast here, obviously. He keeps prolonging his leave of absence. Plus Moustafa's mom and sisters. Piece of cake."

"It sounds so nice." She sighed. "David, I'm just so very, very tired. You do what you want; just let me rest for a few days."

"Good idea!" he said and scooped her up in his arms. He carried her across the cobblestones, as she settled comfortably against him. She handed him her keys, and he let them into Mme Leclerc's apartment, where he laid her gently on her bed. Bending down, he kissed her softly. "To bed with you, my dear. Sweet dreams. I'll work it out. And I don't want to see you until breakfast tomorrow, understand?"

She smiled up at him dreamily as she kicked off her shoes and snuggled beneath the sheets. She hardly remembered him leaving the room. She was already dreaming of a long white dress.

It was the first time David had seen Moustafa alone since their planned escape in Algiers had failed. The two men regarded each other with a mixture of compassion and awe.

"I never expected to see you again."

"No." Moustafa smiled wryly. "I imagine not."

"How on earth did you get away? I was there. I saw the horror."

"There was no getting away. I saw Hacène pushed off the boat, and then an Arab soldier found me lying there and stabbed me, twice. He would have slit my throat, only right then, from out in the harbor, I heard my name. I swear it; someone shouted my name.

"The soldier heard it too. It distracted him, and he went to the water's edge and fired into the harbor. In that brief time, I managed to pull myself under the dead bodies of two other harkis, and that was my shelter from the massacre. It was a blessing that my wounds were cruel and deep. I fainted from loss of blood, and I guess the soldiers thought I was dead." Moustafa paused.

"Much later I woke up to a terrible silence. Bodies everywhere. My compatriots, my brother." He closed his eyes and wiped his hand over his face. "I began crawling back to the water, petrified that the soldiers would return and see me. But as it turns out, only a poor Arab woman with kind eyes saw me. And she came into the bloody square. Can you imagine the courage it took? The courage and iron will to walk past the slaughter and drag me to the safety of her apartment?

"I must have lain there for two weeks, coming in and out of consciousness. Until one day I opened my eyes and asked her to take me to Rémi's house."

David whistled softly. "What a remarkable story."

"I still wonder about the voice calling my name, distracting the soldier. It was like a messenger from heaven."

David looked at him. "It was my voice," he said.

Moustafa's eyes grew wide, and David shrugged.

"We swam, Rémi and I, toward the dock, the boat. I couldn't see you, but I screamed your name, twice. Then when the soldiers came to the water's edge, we knew we had to leave."

Moustafa shook his head and grinned. "I should have known. You promised you would get me out, and you did. You're a pretty rough-looking angel, I might add."

They clasped hands and held the grip, neither saying a word.

Finally Moustafa asked, "Why? Why did I survive? What do you call it? Luck?"

"I call it an answer to prayer."

Moustafa leaned back in the bed, his eyes closed. "An answer to prayer. Yes, I believe you're right."

David stood. "When are they going to let you out of here anyway?"

"In a week, they say."

"Good. Then you'll be able to make it to my wedding."

"Your wedding? So soon?"

"I figure we might as well do it while we have all the family and friends in one spot. Who knows when that will happen again."

"And your Gabriella? What does she think?"

David laughed. "Poor Gabby. She panicked at first, declaring that we weren't ready, that it couldn't be done. But I promised her a two-week honeymoon, complete with Paris and Switzerland. She has reconsidered."

Moustafa laughed heartily. "You're a strange man, David Hoffmann. I have yet to meet this Gabriella, you know. Imagine! A wedding! So soon. Well, just tell me the date, and I will be there."

"And what about you? And Anne-Marie?"

"I don't know. At first I thought it was too soon to speak of marriage. I didn't want to impose." He made a tight fist. "I think I'm afraid that, now that she has the farmhouse, she won't want me. In Algeria the bridegroom presents his bride with a lot of gold jewelry. Many men work for years to be able to have this dowry. I have nothing to give her."

David thumped his friend's head playfully. "You're crazy! Anne-Marie would do anything to be with you. And she is pied-noir. She's not bound to Algerian customs." His voice grew serious. "She's a very loyal woman. And she loves you with the right kind of love."

"Yes, I know. I know."

"I'll be going now." David turned in the doorway. "Don't wait too long, Moustafa. She needs to know."

He had said the phrase almost glibly to Moustafa. An answer to prayer. But as David walked out of the hospital toward his car, he did not feel glib. How did this God work? It was too far above and beyond him to be understood. In his rage and folly and help-lessness, he had jumped into a polluted harbor and screamed out foolishly for Moustafa. It had been a weak and desperate attempt. Yet God had used it, supported it with His own divine design, to save Moustafa's life.

❈

When Anne-Marie saw Moustafa at the hospital that day, she was bubbling over with news about the farmhouse in Lodève.

"The harkis are moving to the city. M. Krugler is already work-ing among them. Can you imagine, Moustafa? We can all move there, you and your family, Ophélie and me. We can help him with his work."

Moustafa, who was sitting up in bed, pulled her close to him. "I don't want you to think I am taking advantage of a good situation," he joked, "but, Anne-Marie ... I want you to marry me. I want us to be together forever. Will you?"

"I thought you would never ask."

"Is that a yes?"

"It is a yes, my love." She pushed the curls from his face and kissed him softly.

"I didn't believe this moment would actually arrive. I am so very thankful." He furrowed his brow. "But I have nothing to give you, my *habibti*."

"Hush now, Moustafa. You have given me yourself, forever. It's far better than I had hoped. It's a miracle." She kissed his lips, his forehead, his hands. "Rest, my love. Get well. I will be waiting for you. Now we have a place to call our own."

Gabriella slept straight through the night and late into the next morning. It was an exhausted, deep sleep without dream or movement. When she woke, her mother was sitting in a chair by her bedside, reading.

"Sleeping Beauty awakes." Mother laid down the book and brushed a few hairs from Gabriella's face. "How do you feel, sweetheart?"

"Groggy." Gabriella sat up in bed, stretched, and yawned. "But better. Much better. And I'm starving." She hopped out of bed, her feet touching the cool tiles, and went toward the large oak armoire. Opening the heavy doors, she asked, "What have I missed, Mother, while I've been sleeping?"

She heard her mother laugh, and at the same moment, she gave
a gasp. Hanging in the armoire was an exquisite white wedding dress.
She felt the smooth, cool silk. "What is this?"

"Well, my dear, it seems that while you have slept, your charming fiancé has planned a wedding. Would you like to know the
date?"

Gabriella gulped. "I don't know. What do you think?"

Her mother smiled and crossed the room to give her a hug. "It's
planned for August 25. Everyone insisted we must wait for Mme
Pons and Mme Leclerc to return from their *vacances*. That will give
you time for a honeymoon before David needs to be back for orien-
tation in the exchange program."

As she spoke, her mother took the dress from the armoire and
draped it across the bed. "It will coincide nicely with our plans too.
We can stay to help with the children while you and David are away
and still get back to America by September 15 when Jessica and
Henrietta's school begins."

As if in a trance Gabriella undressed and lifted her arms as her
mother slipped the dress over her head.

"Oh my, there are a hundred buttons in the back," her mother
commented. She led Gabriella to the mirror over the porcelain sink.
"But at least you can get an idea." She pulled the dress closed in the
back and fastened a few buttons.

"Mother," Gabriella said in wonder, "it's the most gorgeous dress
I've ever seen. Where did it come from?" She turned to the side,
admiring the snug bodice and the modestly sloping neckline. "Am I
dreaming? You tell me my wedding has been planned while I slept,
and now my dress has appeared magically in my armoire."

"It came from St. Joseph. You should have seen Sister Isabelle's face last night when David announced that the wedding would be taking place in Castelnau. I thought she might pop with excitement. She raced out of the room and reappeared with this dress, which was apparently given to St. Joseph years ago by a wealthy woman in Castelnau. Even though the Sisters saw no need for it, they couldn't bear to give it away. It's been waiting all these years for you." She examined Gabriella, walking around her. "Just a few small alterations, and it will be perfect."

She caught Gabriella in her arms and hugged her fiercely. "Oh, dear child. I know this is all so wild and new. And of course, we are only half-serious. David is waiting to know what you think." Her voice faltered for a moment.

"Mother, what do *you* think? Am I crazy to marry him so soon?"

"Gabriella, when I was twenty-one, I had been married two years and you were on the way. We moved to Africa only weeks after our wedding. It was so hard to be far away from everyone. We struggled. But God drew us close because we only had each other and Him."

"Thank you, Mother." Gabriella twirled around again, sneaking another peek in the mirror. Then she put her hand to her mouth. "There's no time to waste. I've got to find David! We have so many plans to make!"

Ophélie stepped into the room and studied Moustafa. He looked very peaceful, asleep in his hospital bed. She tiptoed to the side of the bed, bent over, and kissed his tangled hair. Its smooth, tight texture had always fascinated her.

His eyes flickered open. She had always liked his eyes too. They were a delicious-looking chocolate brown, warm, inviting.

"Ophélie," he murmured. "Dear child, how good it is to see you."

She grasped his hands. "Oh, Moustafa! I knew you would come back! I knew you were not dead. You were the very last pony to come, but you made it."

He wrinkled his brow. "Pony?"

Ophélie produced her colored picture. "See," she said, pointing to the brown pony running behind a group of others. "See, that's you. You caught up after all."

"I remember now, Ophélie. You drew it for your papa. Yes, he showed it to me in Algeria."

Ophélie threw her arms around Moustafa's neck, burying her head in his curls. "I knew you would come back. I prayed to God every day. And now everyone is here. No one is lost. Even Mother Griolet, see here?" She pointed to the gray pony. "She has just gone ahead of us, to Jesus. I wish you could have known her."

"Me too, little one."

She touched his cheek. It was wet. "Did I make you cry?"

Moustafa shook his head and swallowed. "Happy tears, Ophélie. Do you know what I mean?"

"Oh yes! I know what happy tears are!"

Moustafa scooted up in bed, took Ophélie's hands, and asked, "Has your mama told you the good news?"

"About the farmhouse?" she said eagerly.

"Yes, the farmhouse, but … has she told you that we are all going to live there together? You and Mama and me."

She furrowed her brow. "No, she didn't say it."

"I'm going to marry your mama, Ophélie. Is that all right with you?"

Ophélie clapped her hands together. "Oh yes. Oh yes! Now I see. It will all work out. Papa will marry Bribri, and you will marry Mama. Then it will be like I have two mamas and two papas." She laughed, then grew serious. "I guess it wouldn't work for you to marry Gabriella and Papa to marry Mama?"

Moustafa laughed. "No, dear, I don't think so."

She contemplated the idea. "Then this will be fine. I'm a very lucky girl." Then she said, "Your mama is outside with someone else who wants to see you, Moustafa. Hussein. Please don't be mad at him. He's been so worried."

Ophélie left the room, and Moustafa closed his eyes, exhausted from his visits. He heard the door open again but did not look up at once. He had no desire to see the boy.

"Moustafa …" said Hussein.

"Hello, Hussein," Moustafa said. Suddenly he felt the room draw round him, close and confining. Almost suffocating. He felt a stab of hatred, remembered helping the boy, remembered learning of his betrayal. He couldn't bear to look at him.

There was no sound, and at length Moustafa opened his eyes.

Hussein stood in the middle of the room, shoulders slumped, looking very small and very vulnerable, like a frightened puppy.

"Come sit down, Hussein," he said, but the words were dry in his mouth, like cotton.

Mechanically the boy obeyed. He stared blankly around the room and sniffed twice.

"How are you, Hussein?"

"Fine."

"Doing okay in France?"

He nodded.

"I'm glad you got out of Algeria."

Suddenly the boy burst into tears, leaned forward, and grabbed Moustafa by the shoulders. "I'm so sorry. It was all my fault. I don't know how you got here, Moustafa, but seeing you here means that maybe, maybe I can go on." He sobbed for a moment, out of control, then composed himself. "I know what I did was wrong, but I didn't know what else to do. I was so afraid. Can you forgive me?"

Moustafa closed his hand softly around the back of the boy's neck. These words were not rehearsed. They rang true, coming up from the deepest part of his soul.

"It's okay, Hussein. Everything is okay."

Pronouncing the words, Moustafa looked away, out the window. At fourteen he had run through the orange groves with Anne-Marie. He had dreamed of an impossibility and followed it all his life. And today his stubborn hope had paid off. He had a feeling it was not at all his hope so much as that little phrase that both David and Ophélie had used. An answer to prayer.

Compassion welled up within and warmed him, like a gulp of hot mint tea going down his throat. Maybe this boy deserved a chance too. He had hardly had time to dream in his short lifetime.

"I forgive you, Hussein."

The letter from Hussein could not have arrived at a better time. On this, the fourth of August, Ben Bella took his position as head of state in Algeria. He immediately began in his charismatic way to put into place the socialist government he had planned for the newly independent state. Ali's hopes for his own future seemed secure. And today he also had news from Hussein.

Ali ripped open the envelope and perused the letter, nodding with satisfaction. "Ha, it is no more, this orphanage! No more."

He frowned to read of Hussein's planned suicide. Why would the boy choose that? He had other plans for him. A moment of doubt registered on Ali's face. Where were the newspaper articles attesting to the explosions, the deaths? Why had Hussein neglected to send proof?

It frustrated him that his satisfaction could not be certain and therefore complete. The urge for power and the need for revenge were in conflict now, and Ali had to choose. To push forward or to remain in the past. To trust the letter of an adolescent boy and put it out of his mind or to find someone else to carry out his anger and revenge. He wondered why he could never find the blessed peace that came from being totally satisfied.

The craving for power gnawed at him. Perhaps if he climbed high enough, became truly important to the new Algeria, perhaps then he would fill the shoes that his father had left empty so abruptly. Nothing could be sure in this life, he reasoned. He tore the letter into small pieces.

"Father, you are avenged. Quiet now, my soul." He held the torn pieces in his clutched fists as tears ran down his cheeks. "You are avenged, Father!" He spoke loudly now, almost shouting. "Avenged!"

He limped pitifully to a trash can, deposited the letter, and threw in a match.

"Good-bye, Father. Good-bye, Hussein."

He watched the paper curl and turn red and then black. Still the pain gnawed at him. Still he cried. He fell back into his chair, grasping his head in his hands.

"Is there no peace?" he cried out. "Is there no peace?"

Algeria was free, but a war still raged inside Ali. He swore to himself that he would spend the rest of his life trying to find peace.

33

It seemed perfectly appropriate that their wedding have a mixture of European and American flair. The simple ceremony was to take place in the chapel of St. Joseph at four o'clock; later that evening, in true French fashion, the reception would be a seven-course meal in the refectory that lasted all night. Gabriella insisted on bridesmaids, an American tradition, choosing her sisters and Anne-Marie, with Ophélie as flower girl. But she also insisted that David's deux chevaux be covered, not with tin cans and toilet paper, but with carnations as she had seen so often in wedding processions in France.

"You're a bundle of nerves, Gab." Jessica laughed as she helped her sister with the buttons on the back of her wedding gown.

Gabriella bit her lip. "I know it. I can't believe I'm marrying David today!"

Mme Leclerc's apartment had been transformed into a bride's parlor with Henrietta, Jessica, Anne-Marie, and Ophélie busily putting on the pastel Provençal print dresses that Gabriella's mother had made. They crowded around the one small mirror over the sink in Gabriella's room until Mme Leclerc came in and saw them pinching their cheeks and trying to apply makeup.

"For goodness' sakes, girls! Come back to my room. I have a proper mirror, the whole length of the armoire."

Gabriella and her mother were left in the room alone, as Mother plaited a small strand of Gabriella's hair, interlacing it with baby's breath. The wedding gown fit Gabriella like a glove.

"You're glowing!" her mother attested.

Gabriella hugged her tightly. "Oh, Mother! Do I really look all right?"

"Perfect, sweetheart. Perfect."

Gabriella took a deep breath. "Well, then, I guess I'm ready!"

Yvette watched the women leave for the chapel. "*Ooh là là! Ma fille!*" she exclaimed, kissing Gabriella's cheek. "There's never been a prettier bride."

When the apartment was empty, she scurried around, putting on her fanciest dress and pinning her hat with the lace veil in place. She grabbed her purse and hurried into the street toward Monique's apartment.

The two friends had returned from their vacation three days ago to find the town abuzz with news. The orphanage was staying open, the exchange program would continue also, the Madisons were still in Castelnau, and best of all, Gabriella and David were getting married. Imagine! Two Americans getting married right here in Castelnau. And she and Monique were invited to the meal after the ceremony. She hummed to herself. Such excitement!

"Do you think they'll want to stay here with me?" she had asked her friend. "I mean, they will need a place to live, the young couple."

"With you, Yvette! Nonsense. M. Hoffmann has already arranged everything. While they're gone on their honeymoon, the fathers of the young couple are going to give Mother Griolet's apartment a fresh coat of paint. Mrs. Madison will make curtains and the like. Oh, they're turning it into a little love nest. No, don't you worry! At least they'll have a little bit of privacy." Monique rolled her eyes, then continued.

"And M. Hoffmann assures me that enrollment for the new year is not down. We'll both have new boarders. He says, that sly M. Hoffmann, that he expects the enrollment to double once the young ladies hear that a wedding took place after a couple met at St. Joseph!"

They laughed merrily, then took turns pinning a corsage on each other's dress. "For the groom's beloved landlady," Yvette said, giggling.

"And for the bride's adoring *proprietaire*," Monique cooed. "Just as we predicted. Now we really are practically related!"

The bride was indeed radiant as she walked down the aisle beside her father. She nodded to the small group of family and friends gathered in the chapel as she slowly walked past them: Pierre and Denise Cabrol, Madeleine de Saléon, Henri Krugler, Edouard Auguste, Joseph and Emeline Cohen, Moustafa's mother and sisters, Mme Leclerc and Mme Pons, Eliane and Rémi with their three children, Sister Rosaline and Sister Isabelle and all the orphans. Her mother sat in the front row.

At the altar stood her bridesmaids, Jessica, Henrietta, and Anne-Marie, beaming back at her. Ophélie clutched a small woven basket filled with real rose petals from the bushes in the courtyard. From Mme Pons's old phonograph played Purcell's "Trumpet Tune."

And mostly, there was David, tall and erect, smiling at her with that vulnerable look on his face, a look of awe and fascination and love. He wore a black pin-striped suit that matched his eyes. Beside him stood his father, Jean-Louis, and Moustafa.

Gabriella's father presided over the ceremony. Having walked her down the aisle, he placed her hand in David's and turned to face the congregation. "Marriage is a solemn ceremony and a joyful celebration. It is the first sacrament prescribed by God in the Bible. 'Therefore shall a man leave his father and mother and shall cleave unto his wife, and they shall be one flesh.'" He paused to clear his throat.

Gabriella looked up at David. He seemed so serious, stiff, staring intently at her father. She squeezed his hand, and his eyes met hers. She raised one eyebrow to remind him that it was she he should be focusing on. He squeezed her hand back, and throughout the rest of the ceremony, his shining black eyes never left hers.

When at last Gabriella's father pronounced the happy couple husband and wife, David lifted Gabriella's veil and kissed her a long moment. She was almost sure she heard little Christophe whispering "Yuck" from the first row, and then the whole audience broke into applause as the couple walked down the aisle and out into the bright August sun.

Each course in the meal was followed by a dance or some type of light entertainment. David and Gabriella were amazed at the silly skits and poems their friends and family came up with during the evening. The refectory had been transformed into a celebration hall, all the tables adorned with flowers and candles.

Halfway through the meal, at ten o'clock, the Dramchini women hurried the children off to bed to dream of the beautiful bride and her dashing groom. As they left, the boys sent a vast array of paper airplanes floating toward David's plate. The girls came and sprinkled rose petals onto Gabriella's white dress. Then Ophélie climbed into David's lap.

"I'm so happy for you, Papa. And you too, Bribri." She hugged them tightly and whispered, "This is even better than I imagined!"

David held his daughter closely. He looked to Gabriella so tender and mature, so kind. The cocky allure was no longer evident. He had changed so much in this short year. She ached inside, watching him with Ophélie. Could it truly be that he was her husband? It took her breath away.

It was four in the morning when the meal was finished and the good-byes said. Her mother caught Gabriella in a long embrace. "God be with you, my dear. And have a wonderful time!"

She wondered in that moment if her mother had been afraid when she had married her father. It was not exactly fear. It was anticipation.

David's father drove the young couple to a secluded inn amid the vineyards in a small village outside of Montpellier.

"Have a delightful honeymoon," he said. "Congratulations! You've made an excellent choice, Son, if I do say so myself!" He kissed Gabriella on the cheek, got back in the car, and drove off.

Gabriella's eyes were shining as David registered with the night clerk, who led them to a gracious suite overlooking the swimming pool. The door was barely closed when they fell, laughing, into each other's arms.

"Mrs. Hoffmann," David said with a whistle. "My, but you look exquisite!" He twirled her around him, admiring her. "But don't you want to get into something a little more comfortable?"

"Yes," she agreed, blushing. "But you'll have to help me." She lifted her hair off her neck and turned her back, with its long row of silk-covered buttons, toward her husband.

There was a brief pause, and then he said, "This will take me the rest of the night to get undone."

Gabriella laughed. "No need to hurry, my love. We have all the time in the world."

✤

Henri liked the wiry young Arab the first time he laid eyes on him. The young man made no apologies for his pained movements or slowness but worked beside Henri without complaint, painting, hammering, fixing up. Moustafa was a good match for Anne-Marie, Henri concluded. And this old mas was going to suit them well. There were bedrooms enough for Mme Dramchini and Saiyda and Rachida each to have her own. The little apartment at the end of the hall would give Moustafa and Anne-Marie their privacy, with a small adjoining room for Ophélie.

As they worked up on the roof in the blazing heat of the end of August, Moustafa asked Henri questions, and the gentle pastor delighted in answering.

"You see what I mean?" he said. "One God, three distinct personalities. Father, Son, and Holy Spirit." Henri breathed heavily in the sun and patted Moustafa on the back. "Keep up your questions. God is not afraid of them."

"M. Krugler. Pastor. I have wanted to ask you … Anne-Marie and I would consider it a great privilege if you would marry us, right here in your church in Lodève." He spoke quickly, as if he were afraid of being reprimanded. "We have spoken of our love for so long. It seems impossible, the cultures that separate us. But we are in love, and we have been through so much. We are not afraid. Will you help us, M. Krugler?"

Henri was too touched to speak. Would he help them!

Moustafa frowned as Henri remained silent. "If it is too awkward, we do not have to be married in a church."

"Too awkward? No, my son! There is nothing I would enjoy more. Nothing."

They shook hands on the top of the roof. An impossible love, Henri thought. But nothing was impossible with God.

After numerous phone calls between Joseph in Geneva and Henri in Lodève, they were most pleased with the progress they had made. Many pied-noirs and harkis throughout France had heard through word of mouth about the rescued children at St. Joseph's. Some adoptions were pending. Other families gladly agreed to take in foster children. Amazingly a few Algerian parents who had escaped to France found their children in Castelnau.

And throughout France those who had come to Mother Griolet's funeral or had heard the news of her death began to respond to the overcrowded situation. Orphans who had found a home at St. Joseph, later had been adopted, and had now married and had children of their own wrote to say they were interested in adopting a child. By the end of 1962, they hoped, the orphanage would once again house under thirty children.

Henri was truly worried for only one child. Hussein. No harki family wanted to take in an Arab child. They looked the same, these harkis and Arabs, but the war had made them enemies. The boy did not really fit in anywhere. He would probably end up staying at St. Joseph with the French children, Henri reflected. Well, at least he was safe.

"Mmm, this is heaven," Gabriella murmured, stretching and staring at the Swiss mountains outside the picture window. She cuddled up against David and was surprised again at how natural, how right, that simple movement felt. Husband and wife.

The week at Joseph and Emeline Cohen's chalet in Switzerland had been the ideal way to start their married life. They had taken long walks through the mountains past the cows jiggling their lazy heads, tasted the strong Swiss cheeses and eaten fondue as the nights cooled ever so slightly. And mostly they just had time together. Time to know each other and begin to learn how to love.

On their last afternoon there, Gabriella insisted on leaving the chalet, as she had at least once every day. "Otherwise, people will ask us what we did all the time, and what will we say?"

David picked her up, squeezing her hard. "I love you, Gabby. My angel! What will we say?" He grabbed her, and they toppled on the bed together, laughing. "We'll say, 'What do you think a young couple would do on their honeymoon! I bet you can't even guess.'"

Anne-Marie grew impatient during the two weeks Gabriella and David were away. She had such wonderful news! Moustafa wanted for them to get married as soon as the mas was ready. Day after day he worked alongside Henri Krugler, making the place into their home. Henri talked of hiring Moustafa as his assistant at the centre aéré. This plus the funds from her father would be adequate money to start with. It seemed to both of them a small fortune. They had lived so long on nothing.

Anne-Marie and Ophélie spent the afternoons at the farmhouse rearranging furniture, cleaning spots where paint had been spilled, giving the place a feminine touch. Often Anne-Marie found herself standing beside the couch, caressing it lovingly with her fingers, remembering the time when it sat in the farmhouse in Algiers. She could almost hear her father's stern voice growing soft as he held baby Ophélie.

When she shook herself back to the present, she was smiling. Her father had loved her, cared immensely for Ophélie. He had provided for them. She had been loved by him, and now she was loved by Moustafa. They had a lifetime in front of them, and nothing, not prejudice or difficulties, could change that. They had survived. God be praised. Yes, this God really did seem to be in control, not only of the universe, but also of her life. He was trustworthy, and He was in charge.

Anne-Marie wondered at all the people who had showed up in her life in the past year. It was like Mother Griolet's tapestry, the many-colored threads inching themselves through her life, weaving their pattern of hope and faith. She told herself then that the waiting, the impossible months of waiting and wondering, had been worth it. If things had gone more smoothly, perhaps she would have never taken the time to seek and to understand.

She did not know. All she knew was that when Eliane came that afternoon to take her shopping for a wedding dress, she was going to buy white. She felt clean, pure, and yes, forgiven. She was no longer condemned. This God accepted her as she was. And so did Moustafa. She had gotten her new chance after all.

Eliane and Anne-Marie came back from shopping, their faces glowing. "We've found the perfect dress for the wedding," Eliane confided to Rémi and Moustafa. "But that's all we'll tell you for now."

The two couples sipped tisane in the farmhouse den, talking excitedly. "I want to hear about you," Anne-Marie insisted. "I've been rattling on and on, and we haven't even heard. What have you found?"

"An apartment on the west side of Montpellier. Many pied-noirs are moving into the complex," Eliane said.

"Oh, so you won't have a yard?"

"No, not yet, but after three months in a hotel room, this apartment looks pretty good." She sounded, as always, cheery and optimistic. "And Rémi has several leads for work. It will all be fine." She leaned back against Rémi. They seemed so happy just to be together. They shared a cozy familiarity, an easy intimacy that came, Anne-Marie suspected, from years of living together, sharing dreams, hurts, practicalities. She hoped she and Moustafa would grow into that same kind of love.

"Oh, I almost forgot! We brought your wedding gift," Eliane exclaimed. She motioned to Rémi, who slipped outside and came back a few minutes later carrying the old trunk that had brought Moustafa to France.

"You can't give this away!" Anne-Marie cried. "It's an heirloom."

Eliane shook her head. "No. It held my heirlooms. But this trunk is for you two." She suddenly looked at Rémi, unsure. "If you want it, that is."

"Of course we do. What a lovely idea." Anne-Marie kissed Eliane softly on the cheeks. "You do like it, don't you, Moustafa?"

The young man grinned. "Let's just say I'm glad I can observe it from the outside."

"Well then, open it up!" Rémi said.

Moustafa lifted the lid and laughed. Anne-Marie came alongside and peered into the trunk. It was filled with towels and sheets.

"A young couple's got to have something to start out with," Rémi explained.

"Oh, Eliane, Rémi. You shouldn't have. You're having to start over yourselves. It's too much." Anne-Marie was genuinely concerned.

"Our pleasure," Eliane reassured her. "Don't forget, these two trunks did eventually bring me my things from Algeria." She reached inside the trunk. "Oh, and there's something else." Lifting the towels and sheets, Eliane brought out a thick black leather Bible with *Moustafa and Anne-Marie* engraved on the front in gold.

The young couple took the book and reverently leafed through its gold-lined pages. "It's beautiful. Really."

"We thought you might as well start out with one together."

Anne-Marie touched Moustafa's hand. "Yes, we have so much to learn ... together."

When Gabriella and David returned from their honeymoon, everyone insisted that David carry her over the threshold into their new apartment.

Gabriella looked around her and gasped. "Thank you! Thank you, everyone. I don't know what else to say."

She had wondered what it would feel like to live in Mother Griolet's apartment, but it was so transformed that it seemed to have taken on a life of its own. The walls were lighter, the windows outlined by curtains in bright, bold prints. The worn furniture in the den had been replaced with more modern pieces.

She walked into their bedroom. A double bed was there, covered with a thick yellow comforter and half a dozen pillows. "Mother! It looks like something from a designer's magazine! It's beautiful!"

David murmured in her ear, "Beautiful, sure, but don't expect it to stay like that for long." He politely shooed the happy group of spectators out of the apartment, caught Gabriella in his arms, and whispered, "Welcome home."

34

During the fall of 1962, routine murders took place throughout Algeria as the FLN attempted to rid the country of every last harki and his family. For the most part they were successful. Selma and her father never talked about the harki they had housed in their apartment. It was a badge they wore on their hearts, along with many other secrets.

They prayed to Allah for the new Algeria. The country was in ruins, and many cities resembled deserted battlegrounds. Selma could not look out in the square without remembering the day of bloodshed. From the carnage one life had been spared. She wondered about the young Arab man. Had he reached France? Had he indeed been saved?

She wondered too what the future held for the pied-noirs whose empty stores testified, like sealed tombs, to their flight from this world. Their world. Algeria. Had they found peace in France, among their own?

The questions had no answers. Selma's young, independent country was struggling, struggling. The birth had been so long and painful. Would the new child survive? She did not know. She only knew that she loved this land. She prayed five times a day to Allah that their costly freedom would bring them peace at last.

Throughout France, in pockets of cities, the pied-noirs settled among themselves. Perhaps it was their pride in their origins; perhaps it was their distrust of the French. More likely it was their complete indifference, but early on the lines seemed drawn. The pied-noirs were not truly French.

Many struggled to find jobs and rebuild their lives. They were grateful for the government loans, yet a bitterness settled in their souls against all that came from President de Gaulle. That traitor. They would never be able to make the French understand how he had betrayed them. The war was over, and that was all that seemed to matter to France.

Eliane and Rémi saw that the rift was inevitable. But at least their one small family would try to go forward, to forgive and be forgiven. As Eliane put on her fanciest dress, she called out to Rémi, "The excitement of the weddings has certainly brought a bright spot to the situation, *n'est-ce pas?*"

"Quite remarkable, the way it has all turned out, Eliane." He came and wrapped his arms around her. "Remarkable, like you."

She pushed him playfully out of the room, retrieved her hat and purse, and picked up baby José, who was chewing on a soggy cookie. "Oh, look at you, child. *Tant pis.* I don't have time to change you now. We can't be late for Anne-Marie and Moustafa's wedding!"

One week after Gabriella and David returned from their honeymoon, Anne-Marie and Moustafa were married in the chapel of le Temple

Protestant in Lodève. They wanted the simplest of ceremonies, with no reception. Only let them be married!

From beneath the lace veil of her cream-colored hat, Anne-Marie glanced at Gabriella, who winked back. Eliane was smiling from ear to ear. Ophélie sat beside David, with Mme Dramchini on the other side. The little girl bounced in the pew, whispering, "My mama is so beautiful!" loudly enough for everyone to hear.

Anne-Marie had never been happier. She had family, she had friends, and now, God be praised, she had her impossible love. They had agreed on a Christian ceremony, and this thought brought tears to Anne-Marie's eyes. Apart for all these months, she and Moustafa had each come to believe in the Christ.

M. Krugler performed the ceremony and afterward said to them, "Remember, I am here for you, my children."

He was a mixture of father and guardian angel, Anne-Marie speculated. Why did he care for them so, desiring to help and protect a pied-noir bride and her harki husband? She wondered if it had been planned long ago that M. Krugler's life would be woven into theirs. Tapestry! Perhaps it was back when he had preached in Algeria and her father had believed. She thought it went even further back than that, to the heart of a perfect God who had chosen to die for His people.

There was plenty of work to keep both Henri and Moustafa busy all day and often well into the evenings. For Moustafa, it was a gift that was being offered to him: the ability to work and work hard. Then at night he sat at one of the long tables, surrounded by women. *His* women, he thought often to himself, playfully. Sometimes he stared so long and intently at Anne-Marie that the others started teasing and whistling. But he couldn't help it. She still seemed like a mirage, and yet he was holding her hand.

The farmhouse suited them well. It was big enough to give Moustafa and his bride the privacy they needed but still give his mother and sisters a feeling of belonging there. He appreciated how quickly and fully they accepted Anne-Marie into the family with kindness, letting her fill some of the void left by his father and Hacène.

Impossible love. He considered the words and then smiled. At least for them, for Anne-Marie and him, it had worked. They had gotten their impossible love.

Every other week, on Saturday afternoons, Moustafa joined Henri Krugler with a group of Arab teenagers. Each time they met, the number grew as they played sports and board games and talked of their fears and frustrations. These harki teens liked the white-haired pastor, and they immediately trusted Moustafa. It was as if his wounds, his struggle, represented a part of each of their lives. When Moustafa spoke of his life, timidly at first, he was surprised that the youths listened intently.

Henri called this informal meeting Oasis. That had made Moustafa smile, with a stinging in his eyes. Of course. An oasis. The kids weren't the only ones searching. He too had looked and longed for something strong and intangible. He had not understood at first. But now he knew. He had stumbled onto it, like a famished traveler in the desert. It swept over him, cool and refreshing, full of hope. An oasis for his soul.

Henri Krugler looked out at his small congregation, smiling at the elderly French who wrinkled their brows as his booming voice announced the first hymn. On the other side of the chapel, much farther back, sat a row of Arab kids, huddled together, casting suspicious glances around them.

Moustafa and Anne-Marie entered the chapel with Ophélie. They hesitated, then looked at Henri, who waved them in. It was the young couple's first time at the Sunday service. Moustafa rumpled the hair of one of the Arab youths as he walked by, then motioned for the whole group to follow him to the front of the chapel.

Slowly, one by one, the Arabs got out of their seats and moved forward, trailing behind the young couple and the little girl. An elderly French man rose and extended his hand, first to Moustafa and Anne-Marie, then to one of the teenagers. "*Bienvenue*," he said softly. "Welcome."

It was a humble beginning, Henri mused. But it was a beginning. The first Arabs to attend a service! He stared out at the strange little flock. He swallowed twice, but he couldn't dislodge the lump in his throat.

"May we all rise," he managed to say.

The organ warmed up with a whine, and the dear old organist pressed her fingers onto the keys to form the first chord. It resounded in the chapel. Blended. Harmony.

Their faces buried in the hymnbooks, the small congregation began to sing, as soft as a whisper at first. By the third verse, Henri raised his voice to sing more loudly, and they followed. He even saw them smiling at one another. He felt very close to God.

Later, as Henri preached about Jesus' visit with a woman at a well, he pointed out that this woman had no right to Jesus. She was not Jewish, His chosen race. She was from a despised minority, she was only a woman, and she was an adulteress. But Jesus offered her living water.

He wondered if they would understand. Maybe, with time …

He concluded the service and walked briskly to the back of the church, standing at the door to greet his people as they left. *I wish you could be here to see it, Maxime Duchemin,* he thought. *You would be mighty surprised at what God has done.*

David woke and glanced quickly at the clock by the bed. Six forty-five. He turned to Gabriella and gently shook her awake. "Sweetheart, it's time to get up."

She stretched and yawned as she always did, looking to David like a beautiful red Persian cat. It fascinated him to watch her wake up. She rubbed her eyes, yawned again, and fell against him.

"Do we have to get up already?"

"Honey, yes," he said, with a tinge of impatience in his voice. He climbed out of bed. "Classes start today, remember?"

"You're nervous," Gabriella teased.

"Yes, I think I am."

"You will be wonderful. Only …" She pouted a bit. "Only don't charm them too much, please. Remember, you're taken now."

He grabbed her and laughed. "Am I ever!" Then, "Gabby? Could you come to the chapel with me this morning? I want the girls to meet you."

"Well, I wish you would have asked earlier. I could have gotten Sister Isabelle to take the children's class for me."

"Could you ask at breakfast? No, never mind. I'll ask her. She won't dare tell me no."

"David!"

He kissed her forehead. "Don't worry. She likes me more than you think!"

They dressed quietly, and then, as had become their habit in the first weeks of marriage, they sat cuddled together in the den and read from the Bible. Then David took Gabriella's hands and offered up a prayer for those they loved, for the orphanage, and for this day.

"Dear God," he concluded. "You see how much has happened since last year at this time. When I think that … that only a year ago I first laid eyes on Gabby. Well, You understand the emotion." He held her tightly. "Give us Your grace for today. Amen."

Snuggled in her bed, Ophélie watched the morning sky come awake with pinks and blues. She thought of the orphanage at St. Joseph; she missed her friends there.

She tiptoed into the adjoining bedroom, where her mother and Moustafa were still sleeping.

"Mama," she whispered, "can we go visit Papa this weekend?"

Her mother shook herself awake. "This weekend? You were just there last week, honey."

"I know, but I miss him. I miss everyone."

Ophélie wished she had the courage to say it, the idea that had been floating around in her head for a while now. Perhaps they would think she was crazy. But she had this feeling ...

"Mama?"

"Hmm, sweetheart?"

She liked to see her mother leaning comfortably against Moustafa. She looked so relaxed, without a worry in the world. Ophélie certainly didn't want to make her mama frown.

"Have you ever thought about having another child?"

Her mother sat up suddenly and laughed. "Why, Ophélie! We've only been married a month. Give us a little time!"

Ophélie smiled. "I didn't mean a baby. I was thinking about if you adopted someone."

Moustafa and Anne-Marie exchanged glances. She saw the question in their eyes.

"What do you mean, Ophélie?"

"It's ... it's Hussein. He is so alone. He is so afraid. He needs a family. I think we are the ones he needs."

Gabriella still did not feel right sitting on the other side of Mother Griolet's desk, looking through her files and papers and school notes. She wished her elderly friend were with her. But things were going well. The children were laughing in the courtyard, and the women were learning from David. Last year at this time ... A lot had happened in a year.

The office walls were still filled with old photos of Mother Griolet and the orphans. But where several pictures had been taken down and given away, Gabriella had hung a wedding picture of herself and David, another wedding shot of Anne-Marie and Moustafa, a photo of Ophélie and David and her. And one of Jean-Louis, the Sisters, Mme Pons, and Mme Leclerc smiling happily at the reception. They were each holding a glass of champagne, and Sister Isabelle's eyes were wide with mischief.

Gabriella felt cozy in her little office. At times the weight of responsibility she had taken onto her shoulders would frighten her, and a tear for Mother Griolet would come to her eye. That dear nun had imparted much wisdom to her within these office walls.

David's santon, the white baker, stood on a shelf in front of the volumes that Mother Griolet had left him. Beside the baker, the old woman santon, with the bundle of sticks on her back, had returned to her original place. David had glued her back together. Gabriella liked to look at the two santons together and remember their secrets.

David came into the office at the end of his class and planted a kiss on her lips.

"How did it go?"

"Very well," he said. "Fewer distractions than last year when that angel sat in my class."

She stuck her tongue out playfully, then nodded to the santons. "Look, sweetie. There we are, growing old together."

He picked her up out of her chair, kissed her, and said, "I can't think of anything I'd rather do."

Hussein stood in the doorway of the farmhouse and looked around with wide eyes. It seemed impossible. He was going to live with Anne-Marie and Moustafa, as their ward. Ophélie's brother. He could only shake his head. He didn't know if he could ever get used to this new land. He thought of his mother, alone in Algeria with all her questions. If only he could know she was safe. If only he could bring her to France.

But that was not possible right now. Moustafa had promised that Hussein could write to her later, when things were calmer in Algeria. Perhaps someday he would be with her again. For now he was taking a very big step. It scared him to death.

Why would Anne-Marie and Moustafa want him? He was so different from them. And they were already different enough from each other. He thought about it for a long, long time. What was it that broke through walls of hatred and prejudice?

Maybe it was the love that pastor, M. Krugler, talked about in his meetings with the young people. Maybe he would be able to fit in there. He didn't know. They were harki kids, and he was just plain Arab. The enemy.

He wondered again if he were making a big mistake. What would he become, tied to these people? There were no bloodlines. The hatred that had brewed and exploded in Algeria was not swept away with the end of the war. But what could he do?

Start over. Trust.

"Come on in, Hussein," Ophélie encouraged him. He stepped through the doorway and let Anne-Marie and Moustafa take him in their arms. It felt good.

That night he lounged in the den with his new family, watching the embers of the fire change from blue to orange to red. The old trunk with its black casing sat in front of the couch. It intrigued him more than ever. He could not look at it without thinking of the other trunk, the one that had brought him to France—it had first been a prison and then a way of escape. Freedom, confining freedom. Maybe that was how life was supposed to be.

�֎

When mid-October came to Castelnau, the first pansies went on sale. Gabriella bought three trays from the florist in the village. She planted some in the courtyard, one tray by the dormitory, and another by the dining room. Then on a windy afternoon, with the mistral beginning to blow and the leaves on the vines a bright red, she walked alone through the town of Castelnau, past the fountain in the square and the olive tree outside Mme Leclerc's apartment.

She came to the old cemetery where Mother Griolet was buried. It was filled with thick, massive tombstones that stood high and wide, engraved with names and dates. Occasionally a photo of a loved one had been placed on the tomb. A little farther out she knelt by the grave of Mother Griolet. In sharp contrast to the larger tombstones, her simple headstone read *For to me, to live is Christ and to die is gain.*

Gabriella removed a small trowel from her pocket and dug in the soft earth. She planted a row of bright-yellow pansies in front of the stone. Satisfied, she stood, brushed the dirt from her dress, and watched the flowers bob their heads.

She peered at them closely. She thought indeed that she saw a face in each flower. The faces of those she loved: her family, Ophélie and Anne-Marie and Moustafa, the two Sisters, Jean-Louis, Mme Leclerc and Mme Pons, the children. And David. And then the twinkling eyes of Mother Griolet came into her mind.

Now unto Him that is able to do exceeding abundantly above all that we ask or think ...

She could almost hear the old nun's voice floating out to her, full of hope and faith, carried in the wind.

... a little more ...

When a delightful concert comes to an end,

the orchestra might offer an encore.

When a fine meal comes to an end,

it's always nice to savor a bit of dessert.

When a great story comes to an end,

we think you may want to linger.

And so, we offer ...

AfterWords—just a little something more after you

have finished a David C Cook novel.

We invite you to stay awhile in the story.

Thanks for reading!

Turn the page for ...

- **A Historical Note**
- **The Opening Scenes from *Two Destinies*, the Conclusion
to the Secrets of the Cross Trilogy, Coming September 2012**
- **About the Author**

A Historical Note

In France, the integration of pied-noirs into French society has been slow and painful, and many to this day do not feel welcome, harboring bitter memories of all they left in Algeria in 1962. Most of these families have never returned to Algeria, even for a visit. Among those who have, some have found in their homes, now inhabited by Algerians, the exact same furniture and other household goods that they had left in their flight to France.

Many years after the war, when the truth came out about the mass murders of the harkis who were abandoned in Algeria, France felt great sorrow and great shame. The harkis, with their children and grandchildren, remain an enigma and embarrassment for the country. Many of those living in France still feel like outcasts, comfortable neither with the millions of Algerians in France nor with the French, although their children and grandchildren are French citizens.

With the end of the Algerian War for Independence in July 1962, different factions within Algeria struggled to gain control of the new republic. Finally it was Ben Bella who triumphed and began a revolutionary socialist government. Three years later Houari Boumediène took over as chief of state through a *coup d'état*. For fifteen years Algeria prospered under his leadership, as profits from its natural resource of oil allowed Boumediène to move the country forward in agriculture and industrialization, becoming an example for the whole Third World. However, Boumediène enforced a single-party, military-backed socialist government with which many were dissatisfied. This ended in 1988 when a new constitution was voted in by referendum, separating the socialist party from the state and allowing a multiparty system to emerge.

It was in this context that a political movement of fundamentalist Islam swept across the nation. In 1984 a law was passed that severely restricted women's rights. Mosques in every village and hamlet became the forum from which the ideology of fanatical Islam was spread to an unwary populace. The government was trapped within the religious and cultural aspects of Algeria, undermining its economic progress.

In 1992 civil war broke out. An extremist militant Muslim faction, the Islamic Salvation Front (FIS), was on the brink of winning national elections when the vote was canceled and the military installed a president. In the ensuing years more than fifty thousand people lost their lives in Algeria, many of them civilians murdered by the FIS, who wished to make Algeria an Islamic state. Missionaries and Algerian believers were forced into hiding, worshipping in secret, often traveling long distances to find other believers.

The story of these events as they affected the lives of the Duchemins, the Hoffmanns, the Cebrians, and a host of other colorful characters will be told in the third and final book in the Secrets of the Cross Trilogy, *Two Destinies*, coming in September 2012.

Opening Scenes from Two Destinies

Montpellier, France
November 1994

Rislène Namani stepped off the bus in front of the parc de Peyrou at the highest point of Montpellier's *centre ville*. She glanced to her left, where dozens of people mingled leisurely in the wide square that was flanked on either side by two rows of naked plane trees with their dappled bark. The air was brisk but the sun high on this bright Sunday afternoon in late November. She took in a deep breath and let a smile erase the frown she'd been wearing.

She glanced around her, then crossed the wide avenue, walking away from the park and through the thick Roman arches that had earned this monument the name of le petit Arc de Triomphe. She thought it as beautiful as the one in Paris.

She turned down a side street that meandered around and opened into a small square. It too was crowded with students sitting on benches and children playing in the dirt around an ancient fountain that sprayed out water from little mermaids' mouths. Again Rislène looked behind her, heart thumping in her chest.

She was practically jogging now, pushing her thick black hair off her neck, feeling a pulsing in her head, a tingling in every part of her body. Almost there!

She glanced once more over her shoulder as she stepped into the little Café de la Paix, around the corner from the bustling little place.

"Bonjour, mademoiselle," the barkeeper crooned.

Rislène kept her head down, her multicolored scarf twirled carelessly around her neck, and hurried to the back of the little café.

He was there!

"Eric," she whispered and let the tall boy with the coarsely cropped red hair draw her into an embrace.

"Rislène! You made it!" Then his freckled face wrinkled at the brow. "No problems? No one following you?"

"No. Nazira went out with her friends for the afternoon. She glared at me the whole morning as if she knew a big secret, but she didn't try to follow me."

Now they were sitting at a little round table, holding hands, staring into each other's eyes. Eric's were a bright green. How she loved his eyes! How she loved him! She was out of breath with the thought.

They ordered two cups of coffee, and when the waiter set them on the table, the couple held each other's gaze with the steam from the coffee rising between them.

"Don't worry, Eric. We're safe. No one knows."

A faint smile spread across his thin face, and he breathed a sigh of relief. "So many months of hiding our love ... But soon, Rislène. Someday soon, I'll tell my sister. Ophélie will surely understand—why, she writes plays that are filled with impossible love stories. She'll be thrilled, and she'll help us."

"Yes, I hope she will. I know she likes me—as a student in her class, that is. I don't think she looks at me and thinks, *She'd make a good girlfriend for my little brother!*" Rislène's smile vanished, and her voice dropped to a whisper. "I'm scared about Father. He grows more fanatical each day. And Nazira is even worse. It's not the peaceful Islam I grew up with." She fumbled with a paper napkin, turning it over in her hands.

"Shhh. Please. Let's just enjoy this time together." Eric grabbed both of her hands tightly.

She looked at his pale, thin fingers entwined with her dark-olive-skinned ones. She loved this young man with a head filled with dreams and a heart of courage and conviction. But how complicated he made her life. Why, she wondered for the thousandth time, had she allowed herself to fall in love with a Christian, the son of two American-born French citizens?

She hadn't meant to. It had happened gradually, over the course of the past year … when she had become a Christian too.

�֎

Eric Hoffmann watched as Rislène left the café, then followed her out, putting a distance between them. How hard to hide his love for her from the rest of the world!

The Algerian beauty had stolen his heart the first night they'd met, over a year ago now. He thought of the young people gathered on the beach, the end of the summer's heat warm on their shoulders as the sun set and the lazy Mediterranean lapped at their feet.

"Meet my friend Rislène," Oumel had said, smiling broadly. "She wanted to tag along tonight and see what in the world I've been talking about."

He had hardly taken his eyes off her the whole evening, while he strummed his guitar and the young people munched on *chipolata* and Merguez sausages cooked over a makeshift grill. He'd felt his face turn red each time she glanced his way. She was so delicate, her *café au lait* skin so smooth, her eyes dark ovals that flashed pleasure and maybe even mischief, her black hair, soft and thick and full, tumbling past her shoulders …

"Rislène!"

Eric watched her board the bus near the Arc de Triomphe. She turned and looked his way, eyes full of love. The doors closed behind her, and as the bus pulled away from the curb, he let out a sigh of relief.

Rislène felt the tension the moment she stepped back into her family's apartment. Her mother regarded her suspiciously as Rislène hurried back to the bedroom she shared with her sister. Nazira was standing there, a wicked gleam in her eyes, holding up a small leather book.

"You're a traitor, Rislène."

Rislène's legs buckled under her, and she collapsed on her bed. "Nazira, let me explain."

"Explain!" her sister shrilled. "Yes, explain it to me, Rislène! Why are you hiding a Bible under your mattress? Explain that!"

This wasn't the way Rislène had imagined sharing her new-found faith with her sister, but it seemed the moment had been decided for her. Nazira didn't want to listen, though, and her face grew red with rage.

"We'll see what Father has to say about such beliefs!"

"Please, Nazira, don't tell him!"

Nazira gave a cold laugh. "I would never keep news like this from Father!"

With a groan, Rislène watched Nazira leave their bedroom, calling out, "Father! Father! Come quick!"

When he stepped into the room, Rislène shrank from her father's harsh gaze. Usually his deep brown eyes held a fierce pride in them for his oldest daughter. But not today.

"What is this, Rislène? What have you done?"

Rislène stood and reached for him. "It's nothing against the family, Father. Please let me try to explain what I've discovered … in this book."

His hand was swift and strong across her face, sending her reeling backward so that she fell across her bed with a sharp cry. She hid her face in her hands and whimpered, "Please, try to understand."

But she knew he would never understand. As he left the room, with Nazira behind, Rislène knew that she had just lost the innocence of her youth to the angry hand of her father.

At seven forty-five Monday morning, traffic was moving slowly along the broad avenue on the east side of Montpellier. Ophélie Duchemin frowned as the light turned red, and she pulled to a stop.

A man tapped on her window, a cardboard sign in his hand. She read the sign and shook her head, not meeting the man's eyes. These homeless people! They were forever begging for handouts at every major intersection in Montpellier. She felt a stab of guilt. Sometimes she handed them a few francs, but today she didn't have time to rummage through her purse. Anyway, how could she be sure this man would take the francs and buy bread instead of a cheap bottle of red wine? She couldn't help everyone on a high school teacher's salary.

Still, she wished she could offer the man something. She stared straight ahead, willing the light to turn green so she could get past this pitiful man and get to school. If he looked at her, if she met his eyes, she knew that feelings of sorrow would overtake her. The light changed. Ophélie sighed and inched the car forward as the homeless man stepped back onto the curb and waited for the next group of victims trapped by a traffic light.

Ophélie smiled at the young people who hurried into the classroom, talking among themselves. She stood and welcomed the teenagers to her French class as she did every day, challenging their intellects with an obscure quote from a favorite French author.

"Je te frapperai sans colère. Et sans haine, comme un boucher ..."

The students contemplated the quote, some leafing quickly through their literature books from which, Ophélie promised them, all the quotes came.

Finally a girl in the front row called out, "Baudelaire, *Les Fleurs du Mal.*"

Ophélie nodded her approval, gave the class a half grin, and started her lecture. She was tall for a French woman, five foot seven, and slim, with long shining hair that fell past her shoulders, brown and thick. For years she had been kidded that she looked like one of the students, with her jeans and T-shirts. Even now, at thirty-eight, she could pass for a university student.

She had already begun her lecture when the door opened and a young woman of Algerian descent slipped into the classroom, her face turned down, her notebooks gathered tightly to her chest. Rislène Namani—the girl who had converted to Christianity last year, was attending Oasis meetings for teenage Muslim converts and had even started coming to church services. As she found her seat, Ophélie followed her with her eyes.

After class Rislène waited until the other students had left before approaching Ophélie's desk. "Mlle Duchemin, could I … could I talk with you?"

Ophélie gasped slightly, seeing the girl's bruised face. "Rislène, what happened?"

Normally Rislène's smile was infectious. But today the girl was obviously terrified.

"My father found out I've been reading the Bible."

"Oh, Rislène!" Ophélie stood and took the shaking young woman into her arms. "I'm so sorry."

"My sister betrayed me," Rislène continued. "She found my Bible hidden under my mattress." She wiped a tear and covered her mouth. "I'm afraid to go back tonight. I don't know what he might do."

Ophélie closed her eyes to think. It was a very shaky time for Algerians. The civil war in their country was threatening to spread to

France. Fear could be tasted. And Rislène's story resembled that of so many others. As a young North African woman who had grown up in France, she was French in every way. Yet in the past few years, a sudden reemphasis on Islam was encouraging North African fathers to demand that their daughters wear the *hijab* and attend the newly built mosques popping up throughout France.

Rislène's danger was greater, however. She had converted to Christianity, and her father saw that as an unpardonable sin. A black eye might just be the beginning.

Ophélie held Rislène's hands and looked her in the eye. "You'll come to my apartment, then, until we can think of what to do." She touched the girl's face. The ugly bruise covered her left eye and cheek. "Come back after classes, at five. Don't worry. It'll be okay."

About the Author

Elizabeth Goldsmith Musser, an Atlanta native and the best-selling author of *The Swan House*, is a novelist who writes what she calls "entertainment with a soul." For over twenty years, Elizabeth and her husband, Paul, have been involved in missions work with International Teams. They presently live near Lyon, France. The Mussers have two sons and a daughter-in-law. To learn more about Elizabeth and her books, and to find discussion questions as well as photos of sites mentioned in the stories, please visit www.elizabethmusser.com.

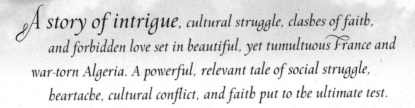